S0-AJI-628

There were four major tribes of Wagon Peoples, living off their herds of constantly moving bosk, riding their savage, fighting kaiila, the women secured in the Wagons they called Home. Fierce, proud and intensely suspicious, the Wagon Peoples had a nasty habit of killing strangers on sight. In fact, their word for stranger was synonymous with enemy. When they couldn't find strangers, they fought among themselves. Thus, all sensible folk avoided them except at certain times of the year when trading took place. For despite their simple way of life, this piratical people was rich—rich with stolen goods, jewels, slaves taken in raids.

On the Plain of Turia where Tarl finally found them, all creatures, all men, fled before the thundering herds of the Wagon People.

Except Tarl Cabot.

He alone stood, and waited.

And finally began to move toward the clouds of oncoming dust that might hold his death.

By John Norman

THE GOREAN CYCLE

TARNSMAN OF GOR

OUTLAW OF GOR

PRIEST-KINGS OF GOR

NOMADS OF GOR

ASSASSIN OF GOR

RAIDERS OF GOR

Available from Ballantine Books

This is an original publication—not a reprint.

JOHN NORMAN
NOMADS OF GOR

BALLANTINE BOOKS • NEW YORK

Copyright © 1969 by John Norman

All rights reserved.

SBN 345-02488-5-095

First Printing: November, 1969
Second Printing: December, 1971

Cover Painting: Bob Foster

Printed in the United States of America

BALLANTINE BOOKS, INC.
101 Fifth Avenue, New York, New York 10003
An Intext Publisher

Contents

NOMADS
OF GOR

I

The Plains of Turia

"Run!" cried the woman. "Flee for your life!"

I saw her eyes wild with fear for a moment above the rep-cloth veil and she had sped past me.

She was peasant, barefoot, her garment little more than coarse sacking. She had been carrying a wicker basket containing vulos, domesticated pigeons raised for eggs and meat.

Her man, carrying a mattock, was not far behind. Over his left shoulder hung a bulging sack filled with what must have been the paraphernalia of his hut.

He circled me, widely. "Beware," he said, "I carry a Home Stone."

I stood back and made no move to draw my weapon. Though I was of the caste of warriors and he of peasants, and I armed and he carrying naught but a crude tool, I would not dispute his passage. One does not lightly dispute the passage of one who carries his Home Stone.

Seeing that I meant him no harm, he paused and lifted an arm, like a stick in a torn sleeve, and pointed backward. "They're coming," he said. "Run, you fool! Run for the gates of Turia!"

Turia the high-walled, the nine-gated, was the Gorean city lying in the midst of the huge prairies claimed by the Wagon Peoples.

Never had it fallen.

Awkwardly, carrying his sack, the peasant turned and stumbled on, casting occasional terrified glances over his shoulder.

1

I watched him and his woman disappear over the brown wintry grass.

In the distance, to one side and the other, I could see other human beings, running, carrying burdens, driving animals with sticks, fleeing.

Even past me there thundered a lumbering herd of startled, short-trunked kailiauk, a stocky, awkward ruminant of the plains, tawny, wild, heavy, their haunches marked in red and brown bars, their wide heads bristling with a trident of horns; they had not stood and formed their circle, shes and young within the circle of tridents; they, too, had fled; farther to one side I saw a pair of prairie sleen, smaller than the forest sleen but quite as unpredictable and vicious, each about seven feet in length, furred, six-legged, mammalian, moving in their undulating gait with their viper's heads moving from side to side, continually testing the wind; beyond them I saw one of the tumits, a large, flightless bird whose hooked beak, as long as my forearm, attested only too clearly to its gustatory habits; I lifted my shield and grasped the long spear, but it did not turn in my direction; it passed, unaware; beyond the bird, to my surprise, I saw even a black larl, a huge catlike predator more commonly found in mountainous regions; it was stalking away, retreating unhurried like a king; before what, I asked myself, would even the black larl flee; and I asked myself how far it had been driven; perhaps even from the mountains of Ta-Thassa, that loomed in this hemisphere, Gor's southern, at the shore of Thassa, the sea, said to be in the myths without a farther shore.

The Wagon Peoples claimed the southern prairies of Gor, from the gleaming Thassa and the mountains of Ta-Thassa to the southern foothills of the Voltai Range itself, that reared in the crust of Gor like the backbone of a planet. On the north they claimed lands even to the rush-grown banks of the Cartius, a broad, swift flowing tributary feeding into the incomparable Vosk. The land between the Cartius and the Vosk had once been within the borders of the claimed empire of Ar, but not even Marlenus, Ubar of Ubars, when master of luxurious, glorious Ar, had flown his tarnsmen south of the Cartius.

In the past months I had made my way, afoot, overland, across the equator, living by hunting and occasional service in the caravans of merchants, from the northern to the southern hemisphere of Gor. I had left the vicinity of the Sardar Range in the month of Se'Var, which in the northern hemisphere is a winter month, and had journeyed south for months; and had now come to what some call the Plains of Turia, others the Land of the Wagon Peoples, in the autumn of this hemisphere; there is, due apparently to the balance of land and water mass on Gor, no particular moderation of seasonal variations either in the northern or southern hemisphere; nothing much, so to speak, to choose between them; on the other hand, Gor's temperatures, on the whole, tend to be somewhat fiercer than those of Earth, perhaps largely due to the fact of the wind-swept expanses of her gigantic land masses; indeed, though Gor is smaller than Earth, with consequent gravitational reduction, her actual land areas may be, for all I know, more extensive than those of my native planet; the areas of Gor which are mapped are large, but only a small fraction of the surface of the planet; much of Gor remains to her inhabitants simply *terra incognita.**

---

*For purposes of convenience I am recounting directions in English terms, thinking it would be considerably difficult for the reader to follow references to the Gorean compass. Briefly, for those it might interest, all directions on the planet are calculated from the Sardar Mountains, which for the purposes of calculating direction play a role analogous to our north pole; the two main directions, so to speak, in the Gorean way of thinking are Ta-Sardar-Var and Ta-Sardar-Ki-Var, or as one would normally say, Var and Ki-Var; 'Var' means a turning and 'Ki' signifies negation; thus, rather literally, one might speak of 'turning to the Sardar' and 'not turning to the Sardar', something like either facing north or not facing north; on the other hand, more helpfully, the Gorean compass is divided into eight, as opposed to our four, main quadrants, or better said, divisions, and each of these itself is of course subdivided. There is also a system of latitude and longitude figured on the basis of the Gorean day, calculated in Ahn, twenty of which constitute a Gorean day, and Ehn and Ihn, which are subdivisions of the Ahn, or Gorean hour. Ta-Sardar-Var is a direction which appears on all Gorean maps; Ta-Sardar-Ki-Var, of course, never appears on a map, since it would be any direction which is not Ta-Sardar-Var. Accordingly, the main divisions of the map are Ta-Sardar-Var, and the other seven; taking the Sardar as our "north pole" the other directions, clockwise as Earth clocks move (Gorean clock hands move in the opposite direction) would be, first, Ta-Sardar-Var, then, in order, Ror, Rim, Tun, Vask (sometimes spoken of as Verus Var, or the true turning away), Cart, Klim, and Kail, and then again, of course, Ta-Sardar-Var. The Cartius River incidentally, mentioned earlier, was named for the direction it lies from the city of Ar. From the Sardar I had gone largely Cart, sometimes Vask, then Cart again until I had come to the Plains of Turia, or the Land of the Wagon Peoples. I crossed the Cartius on a barge, one of several hired by the merchant of the caravan with which I was then serving. These barges, constructed of layered timbers of Ka-la-na wood, are towed by teams of river tharlarion, domesticated, vast, herbivo-

For some minutes I stood silently observing the animals and the men who pressed toward Turia, invisible over the brown horizon. I found it hard to understand their terror. Even the autumn grass itself bent and shook in brown tides toward Turia, shimmering in the sun like a tawny surf beneath the fleeing clouds above; it was as though the unseen wind itself, frantic volumes and motions of simple air, too desired its sanctuary behind the high walls of the far city.

Overhead a wild Gorean kite, shrilling, beat its lonely way from this place, seemingly no different from a thousand other places on these broad grasslands of the south.

I looked into the distance, from which these fleeing multitudes, frightened men and stampeding animals, had come. There, some pasangs distant, I saw columns of smoke rising in the cold air, where fields were burning. Yet the prairie itself was not afire, only the fields of peasants, the fields of men who had cultivated the soil; the prairie grass, such that it might graze the ponderous bosk, had been spared.

Too in the distance I saw dust, rising like black, raging dawn, raised by the hoofs of innumerable animals, not those that fled, but undoubtedly by the bosk herds of the Wagon Peoples.

The Wagon Peoples grow no food, nor do they have manufacturing as we know it. They are herders and it is said, killers. They eat nothing that has touched the dirt. They live on the meat and milk of the bosk. They are among the proudest of the peoples of Gor, regarding the dwellers of the cities of Gor as vermin in holes, cowards who must fly behind walls, wretches who fear to live beneath the broad sky, who dare not dispute with them the open, windswept plains of their world.

The bosk, without which the Wagon Peoples could not live, is an oxlike creature. It is a huge, shambling animal, with a thick, humped neck and long, shaggy hair. It has a

---

rous, web-footed lizards raised and driven by the Cartius bargemen, fathers and sons, interrelated clans, claiming the status of a caste for themselves. Even with the harnessed might of several huge tharlarion drawing toward the opposite shore the crossing took us several pasangs downriver. The caravan, of course, was bound for Turia. No caravans, to my knowledge, make their way to the Wagon Peoples, who are largely isolated and have their own way of life. I left the caravan before it reached Turia. My business was with the Wagon Peoples, not the Turians, said to be indolent and luxury-loving; but I wonder at this charge, for Turia has stood for generations on the plains claimed by the fierce Wagon Peoples.

wide head and tiny red eyes, a temper to match that of a sleen, and two long, wicked horns that reach out from its head and suddenly curve forward to terminate in fearful points. Some of these horns, on the larger animals, measured from tip to tip, exceed the length of two spears.

Not only does the flesh of the bosk and the milk of its cows furnish the Wagon Peoples with food and drink, but its hides cover the domelike wagons in which they dwell; its tanned and sewn skins cover their bodies; the leather of its hump is used for their shields; its sinews forms their thread; its bones and horns are split and tooled into implements of a hundred sorts, from awls, punches and spoons to drinking flagons and weapon tips; its hoofs are used for glues; its oils are used to grease their bodies against the cold. Even the dung of the bosk finds its uses on the treeless prairies, being dried and used for fuel. The bosk is said to be the Mother of the Wagon Peoples, and they reverence it as such. The man who kills one foolishly is strangled in thongs or suffocated in the hide of the animal he slew; if, for any reason, the man should kill a bosk cow with unborn young he is staked out, alive, in the path of the herd, and the march of the Wagon Peoples takes its way over him.

Now there seemed to be fewer men and animals rushing past, scattered over the prairie; only the wind remained; and the fires in the distance, and the swelling, nearing roll of dust that drifted into the stained sky. Then I began to feel, through the soles of my sandals, the trembling of the earth. The hair on the back of my neck seemed to leap up and I felt the hair on my forearms stiffen. The earth itself was shaking from the hoofs of the bosk herds of the Wagon Peoples.

They were approaching.

Their outriders would soon be in sight.

I hung my helmet over my left shoulder with the sheathed short sword; on my left arm I bore my shield; in my right hand I carried the Gorean war spear.

I began to walk toward the dust in the distance, across the trembling ground.

2

I Make the Acquaintance of the Wagon Peoples

As I walked I asked myself why I did so—why I, Tarl Cabot—once of Earth, later a warrior of the Gorean city of Ko-ro-ba, the Towers of the Morning, had come here.

In the long years that had passed since first I had come to the Counter-Earth I had seen many things, and had known loves, and had found adventures and perils and wonders, but I asked myself if anything I had done was as unreasoning, as foolish as this, as strange.

Some years before, perhaps between two and five years before, as the culmination of an intrigue enduring centuries, two men, humans from the walled cities of Gor, had, for the sake of Priest-Kings, undertaken a long, secret journey, carrying an object to the Wagon Peoples, an object bestowed on them by Priest-Kings, to be given to that people that was, to the Goreans' knowledge, the most free, among the fiercest, among the most isolated on the planet—an object that would be given to them for safekeeping.

The two men who had carried this object, keeping well its secret as demanded by Priest-Kings, had braved many perils and had been as brothers. But later, shortly after the completion of their journey, in a war between their cities, each had in battle slain the other, and thus among men, save perhaps for some among the Wagon Peoples, the secret had been lost. It was only in the Sardar Mountains that I had learned the nature of their mission, and what it was that they had carried. Now I supposed that I alone, of humans on Gor, with the possible exception of some among the Wagon

Peoples, knew the nature of the mysterious object which once these two brave men had brought in secrecy to the plains of Turia—and, to be truthful, I did not know that even I—should I see it—would know it for what I sought.

Could I—Tarl Cabot, a human and mortal, find this object and, as Priest-Kings now wished, return it to the Sardar—return it to the hidden courts of Priest-Kings that it might there fulfill its unique and irreplaceable role in the destiny of this barbaric world—Gor, our Counter-Earth?

I did not know.

What is this object?

One might speak of it as many things, the subject of secret, violent intrigues; the source of vast strifes beneath the Sardar, strifes unknown to the men of Gor; the concealed, precious, hidden hope of an incredible and ancient race; a simple germ; a bit of living tissue; the dormant potentiality of a people's rebirth, the seed of gods—an egg—the last and only egg of Priest-Kings.

But why was it I who came?

Why not Priest-Kings in their ships and power, with their fierce weapons and fantastic devices?

Priest-Kings cannot stand the sun.

They are not as men and men, seeing them, would fear them.

Men would not believe they were Priest-Kings. Men conceive Priest-Kings as they conceive themselves.

The object—the egg—might be destroyed before it could be delivered to them.

It might already have been destroyed.

Only that the egg was the egg of Priest-Kings gave me occasion to suspect, to hope, that somehow within that mysterious, presumably ovoid sphere, if it still existed, quiescent but latent, there might be life.

And if I should find the object—why should I not myself destroy it, and destroy thereby the race of Priest-Kings, giving this world to my own kind, to men, to do with as they pleased, unrestricted by the laws and decrees of Priest-Kings that so limited their development, their technology? Once I had spoken to a Priest-King of these things. He had said to me, "Man is a larl to man; if we permitted him, he would be so to Priest-Kings as well."

"But man must be free," I had said.

"Freedom without reason is suicide," had said the Priest-King, adding, "Man is not yet rational."

But I would not destroy the egg—not only because it contained life—but because it was important to my friend, whose name was Misk and is elsewhere spoken of; much of the life of that brave creature was devoted to the dream of a new life for Priest-Kings, a new stock, a new beginning; a readiness to relinquish his place in an old world to prepare a mansion for the new; to have and love a child, so to speak, for Misk, who is a Priest-King, neither male nor female, yet can love.

I recalled a windy night in the shadow of the Sardar when we had spoken of strange things, and I had left him and come down the hill, and had asked the leader of those with whom I had traveled the way to the Land of the Wagon Peoples.

I had found it.

The dust rolled nearer, the ground seemed more to move than ever.

I pressed on.

Perhaps if I were successful I might save my race, by preserving the Priest-Kings that might shelter them from the annihilation that might otherwise be achieved if uncontrolled technological development were too soon permitted them; perhaps in time man would grow rational, and reason and love and tolerance would wax in him and he and Priest-Kings might together turn their senses to the stars.

But I knew that more than anything I was doing this for Misk—who was my friend.

The consequences of my act, if I were successful, were too complex and fearful to calculate, the factors involved being so numerous and obscure.

If it turned out badly, what I did, I would have no defense other than that I did what I did for my friend—for him— and for his brave kind, once hated enemies, whom I had learned to know and respect.

There is no loss of honor in failing to achieve such a task, I told myself. It is worthy of a warrior of the caste of Warriors, a swordsman of the high city of Ko-ro-ba, the Towers of the Morning.

Tal, I might say, in greeting, I am Tarl Cabot of Ko-ro-ba; I bring no credentials, no proofs; I come from the Priest-Kings; I would like to have the object which was brought to you from them; they would now like it back; thank you; farewell.

I laughed.

I would say little or nothing.

The object might not even be with the Wagon Peoples any longer.

And there were four Wagon Peoples, the Paravaci, the Kataii, the Kassars, and the dreaded Tuchuks.

Who knew with which people the object might have been placed?

Perhaps it had been hidden away and forgotten?

Perhaps it was now a sacred object, little understood, but revered—and it would be sacrilege to think of it, blasphemy to speak its name, a cruel and slow death even to cast one's eyes upon it.

And if I should manage to seize it, how could I carry it away?

I had no tarn, one of Gor's fierce saddlebirds; I had not even the monstrous high tharlarion, used as the mounts of shock cavalry by the warriors of some cities.

I was afoot, on the treeless southern plains of Gor, on the Plains of Turia, in the Land of the Wagon Peoples.

The Wagon Peoples, it is said, slay strangers.

The words for stranger and enemy in Gorean are the same.

I would advance openly.

If I were found on the plains near the camps or the bosk herds I knew I would be scented out and slain by the domesticated, nocturnal herd sleen, used as shepherds and sentinels by the Wagon Peoples, released from their cages with the falling of darkness.

These animals, trained prairie sleen, move rapidly and silently, attacking upon no other provocation than trespass on what they have decided is their territory. They respond only to the voice of their master, and when he is killed or dies, his animals are slain and eaten.

There would be no question of night spying on the Wagon Peoples.

I knew they spoke a dialect of Gorean, and I hoped I would be able to understand them.

If I could not I must die as befitted a swordsman of Ko-ro-ba.

I hoped that I would be granted death in battle, if death it must be. The Wagon Peoples, of all those on Gor that I know, are the only ones that have a clan of torturers, trained as carefully as scribes or physicians, in the arts of detaining life.

Some of these men have achieved fortune and fame in various Gorean cities, for their services to Initiates and Ubars, and others with an interest in the arts of detection and persuasion. For some reason they have all worn hoods. It is said they remove the hood only when the sentence is death, so that it is only condemned men who have seen whatever it is that lies beneath the hood.

I was surprised at the distance I had been from the herds, for though I had seen the rolling dust clearly, and had felt and did feel the shaking of the earth, betraying the passage of those monstrous herds, I had not yet come to them.

But now I could hear, carried on the wind blowing toward distant Turia, the bellowing of the bosks. The dust was now heavy like nightfall in the air. The grass and the earth seemed to quake beneath my tread.

I passed fields that were burning, and burning huts of peasants, the smoking shells of Sa-Tarna granaries, the shattered, slatted coops for vulos, the broken walls of keeps for the small, long-haired domestic verr, less belligerent and sizeable than the wild verr of the Voltai Ranges.

Then for the first time, against the horizon, a jagged line, humped and rolling like thundering waters, seemed to rise alive from the prairie, vast, extensive, a huge arc, churning and pounding from one corner of the sky to the other, the herds of the Wagon Peoples, encircling, raising dust into the sky like fire, like hoofed glaciers of fur and horn moving in shaggy floods across the grass, toward me.

And then I saw the first of the outriders, moving toward me, swiftly yet not seeming to hurry. I saw the slender line of his light lance against the sky, strapped across his back.

I could see he carried a small, round, leather shield, glossy, black, lacquered; he wore a conical, fur-rimmed iron helmet, a net of colored chains depending from the helmet protecting his face, leaving only holes for the eyes. He wore a quilted jacket and under this a leather jerkin; the jacket was trimmed with fur and had a fur collar; his boots were made of hide and also trimmed with fur; he had a wide, five-buckled belt. I could not see his face because of the net of chain that hung before it. I also noted, about his throat, now lowered, there was a soft leather wind scarf which might, when the helmet veil was lifted, be drawn over the mouth and nose, against the wind and dust of his ride.

He was very erect in the saddle. His lance remained on his back, but he carried in his right hand the small, powerful horn bow of the Wagon Peoples and attached to his saddle was a lacquered, narrow, rectangular quiver containing as many as forty arrows. On the saddle there also hung, on one side, a coiled rope of braided boskhide and, on the other, a long, three-weighted bola of the sort used in hunting tumits and men; in the saddle itself, on the right side, indicating the rider must be right-handed, were the seven sheaths for the almost legendary quivas, the balanced saddleknives of the prairie. It was said a youth of the Wagon Peoples was taught the bow, the quiva and the lance before their parents would consent to give him a name, for names are precious among the Wagon Peoples, as among Goreans in general, and they are not to be wasted on someone who is likely to die, one who cannot well handle the weapons of the hunt and war. Until the youth has mastered the bow, the quiva and the lance he is simply known as the first, or the second, and so on, son of such and such a father.

The Wagon Peoples war among themselves, but once in every two hands of years, there is a time of gathering of the peoples, and this, I had learned, was that time. In the thinking of the Wagon Peoples it is called the Omen Year, though the Omen Year is actually a season, rather than a year, which occupies a part of two of their regular years, for the Wagon Peoples calculate the year from the Season of Snows to the Season of Snows; Turians, incidentally, figure the year from summer solstice to summer solstice; Goreans generally, on the other hand, figure the year from vernal equinox to vernal equinox, their new year beginning, like nature's, with the spring; the Omen Year, or season, lasts several months, and consists of three phases, called the Passing of Turia, which takes place in the fall; the Wintering, which takes place north of Turia and commonly south of the Cartius, the equator of course lying to the north in this hemisphere; and the Return to Turia, in the spring, or, as the Wagon Peoples say, in the Season of Little Grass. It is near Turia, in the spring, that the Omen Year is completed, when the omens are taken, usually over several days by hundreds of haruspexes, mostly readers of bosk blood and verr livers, to determine if they are favorable for a choosing of a Ubar San, a One Ubar, a Ubar who would be High Ubar, a Ubar of all the Wagons, a Ubar of all the Peoples, one who could lead them as one people.*

The omens, I understood, had not been favorable in more than a hundred years. I suspected that this might be due to the hostilities and bickerings of the peoples among themselves; where people did not wish to unite, where they relished their autonomy, where they nursed old grievances and sang the glories of vengeance raids, where they considered all others, even those of the other Peoples, as beneath themselves, there would not be likely to exist the conditions for serious confederation, a joining together of the wagons, as

---

*A consequence of the chronological conventions of the Wagon Peoples, of course, is that their years tend to vary in length, but this fact, which might bother us, does not bother them, any more than the fact that some men and some animals live longer than others; the women of the Wagon Peoples, incidentally, keep a calendar based on the phases of Gor's largest moon, but this is a calendar of fifteen moons, named for the fifteen varieties of bosk, and functions independently of the tallying of years by snows; for example, the Moon of the Brown Bosk may at one time occur in the winter, at another time, years later, in the summer; this calendar is kept by a set of colored pegs set in the sides of some wagons, on one of which, depending on the moon, a round, wooden plate bearing the image of a bosk is fixed. The years, incidentally, are not numbered by the Wagon Peoples, but given names, toward their end, based on something or other which has occurred to distinguish the year. The year names are kept in living memory by the Year Keepers, some of whom can recall the names of several thousand consecutive years. The Wagon Peoples do not trust important matters, such as year names, to paper or parchment, subject to theft, insect and rodent damage, deterioration, etc. Most of those of the Wagon Peoples have excellent memories, trained from birth. Few can read, though some can, perhaps having acquired the skill far from the wagons, perhaps from merchants or tradesmen. The Wagon Peoples, as might be expected, have a large and complex oral literature. This is kept by and occasionally, in parts, recited by the Camp Singers. They do not have castes, as Goreans tend to think of them. For example, every male of the Wagon Peoples is expected to be a warrior, to be able to ride, to be able to hunt, to care for the bosk, and so on. When I speak of Year Keepers and Singers it must be understood that these are not, for the Wagon Peoples, castes, but more like roles, subsidiary to their main functions, which are those of the war, herding and the hunt. They do have, however, certain clans, not castes, which specialize in certain matters, for example, the clan of healers, leather workers, salt hunters, and so on. I have already mentioned the clan of torturers. The members of these clans, however, like the Year Keepers and Singers, are all expected, first and foremost, to be, as it is said, of the wagons—namely to follow, tend and protect the bosk, to be superb in the saddle, and to be skilled with the weapons of both the hunt and war.

the saying is; under such conditions it was not surprising that the "omens tended to be unfavorable"; indeed, what more inauspicious omens could there be? The haruspexes, the readers of bosk blood and verr livers, surely would not be unaware of these, let us say, larger, graver omens. It would not, of course, be to the benefit of Turia, or the farther cities, or indeed, any of the free cities of even northern Gor, if the isolated fierce peoples of the south were to join behind a single standard and turn their herds northward—away from their dry plains to the lusher reaches of the valleys of the eastern Cartius, perhaps even beyond them to those of the Vosk. Little would be safe if the Wagon Peoples should march.

A thousand years ago it was said they had carried devastation as far as the walls of Ar and Ko-ro-ba.

The rider had clearly seen me and was moving his mount steadily toward me.

I could now see as well, though separated by hundreds of yards, three other riders approaching. One was circling to approach from the rear.

The mount of the Wagon Peoples, unknown in the northern hemisphere of Gor, is the terrifying but beautiful kaiila. It is a silken, carnivorous, lofty creature, graceful, long-necked, smooth-gaited. It is viviparous and undoubtedly mammalian, though there is no suckling of the young. The young are born vicious and by instinct, as soon as they can struggle to their feet, they hunt. It is an instinct of the mother, sensing the birth, to deliver the young animal in the vicinity of game. I supposed, with the domesticated kaiila, a bound verr or a prisoner might be cast to the newborn animal. The kaiila, once it eats its fill, does not touch food for several days.

The kaiila is extremely agile, and can easily outmaneuver the slower, more ponderous high tharlarion. It requires less food, of course, than the tarn. A kaiila, which normally stands about twenty to twenty-two hands at the shoulder, can cover as much as six hundred pasangs in a single day's riding.*

The head of the kaiila bears two large eyes, one on each side, but these eyes are triply lidded, probably an adaptation to the environment which occasionally is wracked by severe

---

*The pasang, a common unit of Gorean land measurement, is approximately seven-tenths of a mile.

storms of wind and dust; the adaptation, actually a transparent third lid, permits the animal to move as it wishes under conditions that force other prairie animals to back into the wind or, like the sleen, to burrow into the ground. The kaiila is most dangerous under such conditions, and, as if it knew this, often uses such times for its hunt.

Now the rider had reined in the kaiila.

He held his ground, waiting for the others.

I could hear the soft thud of a kaiila's paws in the grass, to my right.

The second rider had halted there. He was dressed much as the first man, except that no chain depended from his helmet, but his wind scarf was wrapped about his face. His shield was lacquered yellow, and his bow was yellow. Over his shoulder he, too, carried one of the slender lances. He was a black. Kataii, I said to myself.

The third rider placed himself, reining in suddenly, pulling the mount to its hind legs, and it reared snarling against the bit, and then stood still, its neck straining toward me. I could see the long, triangular tongue in the animal's head, behind the four rows of fangs. The rider, too, wore a wind scarf. His shield was red. The Blood People, the Kassars.

I turned and was not surprised to see the fourth rider, motionless on his animal, already in position. The kaiila moves with great rapidity. The fourth rider was dressed in a hood and cape of white fur. He wore a flopping cap of white fur, which did not conceal the conical outlines of the steel beneath it. The leather of his jerkin was black. The buckles on his belt of gold. His lance had a rider hook under the point, with which he might dismount opponents.

The kaiila of these men were as tawny as the brown grass of the prairie, save for that of the man who faced me, whose mount was a silken, sable black, as black as the lacquer of the shield.

About the neck of the fourth rider there was a broad belt of jewels, as wide as my hand. I gathered that this was ostentation. Actually I was later to learn that the jeweled belt is worn to incite envy and accrue enemies; its purpose is to encourage attack, that the owner may try the skill of his weapons, that he need not tire himself seeking for foes. I knew, though, from the belt, though I first misread its purpose, that the owner was of the Paravaci, the Rich People, richest of the wagon dwellers.

"Tal!" I called, lifting my hand, palm inward, in Gorean greeting.

As one man the four riders unstrapped their lances.

"I am Tarl Cabot," I called. "I come in peace!"

I saw the kaiila tense, almost like larls, their flanks quivering, their large eyes intent upon me. I saw one of the long, triangular tongues dart out and back. Their long ears were laid back against the fierce, silken heads.

"Do you speak Gorean?" I called.

As one, the lances were lowered. The lances of the Wagon Peoples are not couched. They are carried in the right fist, easily, and are flexible and light, used for thrusting, not the battering-ram effect of the heavy lances of Europe's High Middle Ages. Needless to say, they can be almost as swift and delicate in their address as a saber. The lances are black, cut from the poles of young tem trees. They may be bent almost double, like finely tempered steel, before they break. A loose loop of boskhide, wound twice about the right fist, helps to retain the weapon in hand-to-hand combat. It is seldom thrown.

"I come in peace!" I shouted to them.

The man behind me called out, speaking Gorean with a harsh accent. "I am Tolnus of the Paravaci." Then he shook away his hood, letting his long hair stream behind him over the white fur of the collar. I stood stock still, seeing the face.

From my left came a cry. "I am Conrad, he of the Kassars." He threw the chain mask from his face, back over the helmet and laughed. Were they of Earth stock, I asked myself. Were they men?

From my right there came a great laugh. "I am Hakimba of the Kataii," he roared. He pulled aside the wind scarf with one hand, and his face, though black, bore the same marks as the others.

Now the rider in front of me lifted the colored chains from his helmet, that I might see his face. It was a white face, but heavy, greased; the epicanthic fold of his eyes bespoke a mixed origin.

I was looking on the faces of four men, warriors of the Wagon Peoples.

On the face of each there were, almost like corded chevrons, brightly colored scars. The vivid coloring and intensity of these scars, their prominence, reminded me of the hideous markings on the faces of mandrills; but these disfigurements, as I soon recognized, were cultural, not congenital, and

bespoke not the natural innocence of the work of genes but
the glories and status, the arrogance and prides, of their
bearers. The scars had been worked into the faces, with
needles and knives and pigments and the dung of bosks over
a period of days and nights. Men had died in the fixing of
such scars. Most of the scars were set in pairs, moving
diagonally down from the side of the head toward the nose
and chin. The man facing me had seven such scars ceremo-
nially worked into the tissue of his countenance, the highest
being red, the next yellow, the next blue, the fourth black,
then two yellow, then black again. The faces of the men I
saw were all scarred differently, but each was scarred. The
effect of the scars, ugly, startling, terrible, perhaps in part
calculated to terrify enemies, had even prompted me, for a
wild moment, to conjecture that what I faced on the Plains
of Turia were not men, but perhaps aliens of some sort,
brought to Gor long ago from remote worlds to serve some
now discharged or forgotten purpose of Priest-Kings; but
now I knew better; now I could see them as men; and now,
more significantly, I recalled what I had heard whispered of
once before, in a tavern in Ar, the terrible Scar Codes of the
Wagon Peoples, for each of the hideous marks on the face of
these men had a meaning, a significance that could be read
by the Paravaci, the Kassars, the Kataii, the Tuchuks as
clearly as you or I might read a sign in a window or a
sentence in a book. At that time I could read only the top
scar, the red, bright, fierce cordlike scar that was the Courage Scar. It is always the highest scar on the face. Indeed,
without that scar, no other scar can be granted. The Wagon
Peoples value courage above all else. Each of the men facing
me wore that scar.

Now the man facing me lifted his small, lacquered shield
and his slender, black lance.

"Hear my name," cried he, "I am Kamchak of the
Tuchuks!"

As suddenly as he had finished, as soon as the men had
named themselves, as if a signal had been given, the four
kaiila bounded forward, squealing with rage, each rider bent
low on his mount, lance gripped in his right hand, straining to
be the first to reach me.

3

The Spear Gambling

One, the Tuchuk, I might have slain with a cast of the heavy Gorean war spear; the others would have had free play with their lances. I might have thrown myself to the ground as the larl hunters from Ar, once their weapon is cast, covering myself with the shield; but then I would have been beneath the clawed paws of four squealing, snorting kaiila, while the riders jabbed at me with lances, off my feet, helpless.

So gambling all on the respect of the Wagon Peoples for the courage of men, I made no move to defend myself but, heart pounding, blood racing, yet no sign visible of agitation on my face, without a quiver of a muscle or tendon betraying me, I stood calmly erect.

On my face there was only disdain.

At the last instant, the lances of four riders but a hand's breadth from my body, the enraged, thundering kaiila, hissing and squealing, at a touch of the control straps, arrested their fierce charge, stopping themselves, tearing into the deep turf with suddenly emergent claws. Not a rider was thrown or seemed for an instant off balance. The children of the Wagon Peoples are taught the saddle of the kaiila before they can walk.

"Aieee!" cried the warrior of the Kataii.

He and the others turned their mounts and backed away a handful of yards, regarding me.

I had not moved.

"My name is Tarl Cabot," I said. "I come in peace.

The four riders exchanged glances and then, at a sign from the heavy Tuchuk, rode a bit away from me.

I could not make out what they were saying, but an argument of some sort was in progress.

I leaned on my spear and yawned, looking away toward the bosk herds.

My blood was racing. I knew that had I moved, or shown fear, or attempted to flee, I would now be dead. I could have fought. I might perhaps then have been victorious but the probabilities were extremely slim. Even had I slain two of them the others might have withdrawn and with their arrows or bolas brought me to the ground. More importantly, I did not wish to introduce myself to these people as an enemy. I wished, as I had said, to come in peace.

At last the Tuchuk detached himself from the other three warriors and pranced his kaiila to within a dozen yards of me.

"You are a stranger," he said.

"I come in peace to the Wagon Peoples," I said.

"You wear no insignia on your shield," he said. "You are outlaw."

I did not respond. I was entitled to wear the marks of the city of Ko-ro-ba, the Towers of the Morning, but I had not done so. Once, long, long ago, Ko-ro-ba and Ar had turned the invasion of the united Wagon Peoples from the north, and the memories of these things, stinging still in the honest songs of camp skalds, would rankle in the craws of such fierce, proud peoples. I did not wish to present myself to them as an enemy.

"What was your city?" he demanded.

But to such a question, as a warrior of Ko-ro-ba, I could not but respond.

"I am of Ko-ro-ba," I said. "You have heard of her."

The Tuchuk's face tightened. Then he grinned. "I have heard sing of Ko-ro-ba," he said.

I did not reply to him.

He turned to his fellows. "A Koroban!" he cried.

The men moved on their mounts, restlessly, eagerly said something to one another.

"We turned you back," I said.

"What is your business with the Wagon Peoples?" demanded the Tuchuk.

Here I paused. What could I tell him? Surely here, in this matter, I must bide my time.

"You see there is no insignia on my shield or tunic," I said.

He nodded. "You are a fool," he said, "to flee to the Wagon Peoples."

I had now led him to believe that I was indeed an outlaw, a fugitive.

He threw back his head and laughed. He slapped his thigh. "A Koroban! And he flies to the Wagon Peoples!" Tears of mirth ran from the sides of his eyes. "You are a fool!" he said.

"Let us fight," I suggested.

Angrily the Tuchuk pulled back on the reins of the kaiila, causing it to rear, snarling, pawing at the sky. "And willingly would I do so, Koroban sleen," he spit out. "Pray thou to Priest-Kings that the lance does not fall to me!"

I did not understand this.

He turned his kaiila and in a bound or two swung it about in the midst of his fellows.

Then the Kassar approached me.

"Koroban," said he, "did you not fear our lances?"

"I did," I said.

"But you did not show your fear," said he.

I shrugged.

"Yet," said he, "you tell me you feared." There was wonder on his face.

I looked away.

"That," said the rider, "speaks to me of courage."

We studied each other for a moment, sizing one another up. Then he said, "Though you are a dweller of cities—a vermin of the walls—I think you are not unworthy—and thus I pray the lance will fall to me."

He turned his mount back to his fellows.

They conferred again for a moment and then the warrior of the Kataii approached, a lithe, strong proud man, one in whose eyes I could read that he had never lost his saddle, nor turned from a foe.

His hand was light on the yellow bow, strung taut. But no arrow was set to the string.

"Where are your men?" he asked.

"I am alone," I said.

The warrior stood in the stirrups, shading his eyes.

"Why have you come to spy?" he asked.

"I am not a spy," I said.

"You are hired by the Turians," he said.

"No," I responded.

"You are a stranger," he said.

"I come in peace," I said.

"Have you heard," he asked, "that the Wagon Peoples slay strangers?"

"Yes," I said, "I have heard that."

"It is true," he said, and turned his mount back to his fellows.

Last to approach me was the warrior of the Paravaci, with his hood and cape of white fur, and the glistening broad necklace of precious stones encircling his throat.

He pointed to the necklace. "It is beautiful, is it not?" he asked.

"Yes," I said.

"It will buy ten bosks," said he, "twenty wagons covered with golden cloth, a hundred she-slaves from Turia."

I looked away.

"Do you not covet the stones," he prodded, "these riches?"

"No," I said.

Anger crossed his face. "You may have them," he said.

"What must I do?" I asked.

"Slay me!" he laughed.

I looked at him steadily. "They are probably false stones," I said, "amber droplets, the pearls of the Vosk sorp, the polished shell of the Tamber clam, glass colored and cut in Ar for trade with ignorant southern peoples."

The face of the Paravaci, rich with its terrible furrowed scars, contorted with rage.

He tore the necklace from his throat and flung it to my feet.

"Regard the worth of those stones!" he cried.

I fished the necklace from the dust with the point of my spear and regarded it in the sun. It hung like a belt of light, sparkling with a spectrum of riches beyond the dreams of a hundred merchants.

"Excellent," I admitted, handing it back to him on the tip of the spear.

Angrily he wound it about the pommel of the saddle.

"But I am of the Caste of Warriors," I said, "of a high city and we do not stain our spears for the stones of men—not even such stones as these."

The Paravaci was speechless.

"You dare to tempt me," I said, feigning anger, "as if I

were of the Caste of Assassins or a common thief with his dagger in the night." I frowned at him. "Beware," I warned, "lest I take your words as insult."

The Paravaci, in his cape and hood of white fur, with the priceless necklace wrapped about the pommel of his saddle, sat stiff, not moving, utterly enraged. Then, furiously, the scars wild in his face, he sprang up in the stirrups and lifted both hands to the sky. "Spirit of the Sky," he cried, "let the lance fall to me—to me!" Then abruptly, furious, he wheeled the kaiila and joined the others, whence he turned to regard me.

As I watched, the Tuchuk took his long, slender lance and thrust it into the ground, point upward. Then, slowly, the four riders began to walk their mounts about the lance, watching it, right hands free to seize it should it begin to fall.

The wind seemed to rise.

In their way I knew they were honoring me, that they had respected my stand in the matter of the charging lances, that now they were gambling to see who would win me, to whose weapons my blood must flow, beneath the paws of whose kaiila I must fall bloodied to the earth.

I watched the lance tremble in the shaking earth, and saw the intentness of the riders as they watched its slightest movement. It would soon fall.

I could now see the herds quite clearly, making out individual animals, the shaggy humps moving through the dust, see the sun of the late afternoon glinting off thousands of horns. Here and there I saw riders, darting about, all mounted on the swift, graceful kaiila. The sun reflected from the horns in the veil of dust that hung over the herds was quite beautiful.

The lance had not yet fallen.

Soon the animals would be turned in on themselves, to mill together in knots, until they were stopped by the shaggy walls of their own kind, to stand and graze until the morning. The wagons would, of course, follow the herds. The herd forms both vanguard and rampart for the advance of the wagons. The wagons are said to be countless, the animals without number. Both of these claims are, of course, mistaken, and the Ubars of the Wagon Peoples know well each wagon and the number of branded beasts in the various herds; each herd is, incidentally, composed of several smaller herds, each watched over by its own riders. The bellowing seemed now to come from the sky itself, like thunder, or from the horizon,

like the breaking of an ocean into surf on the rocks of the
shore. It was like a sea or a vast natural phenomenon slowly
approaching. Such indeed, I suppose, it was. Now, also, for
the first time, I could clearly smell the herd, a rich, vast,
fresh, musky, pervasive odor, compounded of trampled grass
and torn earth, of the dung, urine and sweat of perhaps more
than a million beasts. The magnificent vitality of that smell,
so offensive to some, astonished and thrilled me; it spoke to
me of the insurgence and the swell of life itself, ebullient,
raw, overflowing, unconquerable, primitive, shuffling, smell-
ing, basic, animal, stamping, snorting, moving, an avalanche
of tissue and blood and splendor, a glorious, insistent, invinci-
ble cataract of breathing and walking and seeing and feeling
on the sweet, flowing, windswept mothering earth. And it was
in that instant that I sensed what the bosk might mean to the
Wagon Peoples.

"Ho!" I heard, and spun to see the black lance fall and
scarcely had it moved but it was seized in the fist of the
scarred Tuchuk warrior.

4

The Outcome of Spear Gambling

The Tuchuk warrior lifted the lance in triumph, in the same instant slipping his fist into the retention knot and kicking the roweled heels of his boots into the silken flanks of his mount, the animal springing towards me and the rider in the same movement, as if one with the beast, leaning down from from the saddle, lance slightly lowered, charging.

The slender, flexible wand of the lance tore at the seven-layered Gorean shield, striking a spark from the brass rim binding it, as the man had lunged at my head.

I had not cast the spear.

I had no wish to kill the Tuchuk.

The charge of the Tuchuk, in spite of its rapidity and momentum, carried him no more than four paces beyond me. It seemed scarcely had he passed than the kaiila had wheeled and charged again, this time given free rein, that it might tear at me with its fangs.

I thrust with the spear, trying to force back the snapping jaws of the screaming animal. The kaiila struck, and then withdrew, and then struck again. All the time the Tuchuk thrust at me with his lance. Four times the point struck me drawing blood, but he did not have the weight of the leaping animal behind his thrust; he thrust at arm's length, the point scarcely reaching me. Then the animal seized my shield in its teeth and reared lifting it and myself, by the shield straps, from the ground. I fell from some dozen feet to the grass and saw the animal snarling and biting on the shield, then it shook it and hurled it far and away behind it.

I shook myself.

The helmet which I had slung over my shoulder was gone. I retained my sword. I grasped the Gorean spear.

I stood at bay on the grass, breathing hard, bloody.

The Tuchuk laughed, throwing his head back.

I readied the spear for its cast.

Warily now the animal began to circle, in an almost human fashion, watching the spear. It shifted delicately, feinting, and then withdrawing, trying to draw the cast.

I was later to learn that kaiila are trained to avoid the thrown spear. It is a training which begins with blunt staves and progresses through headed weapons. Until the kaiila is suitably proficient in this art it is not allowed to breed. Those who cannot learn it die under the spear. Yet, at a close range, I had no doubt that I could slay the beast. As swift as may be the kaiila I had no doubt that I was swifter. Gorean warriors hunt men and larls with this weapon. But I did not wish to slay the animal, nor its rider.

To the astonishment of the Tuchuk and the others who observed, I threw away the weapon.

The Tuchuk sat still on his mount, as did the others. Then he took his lance and smote it on the small, glossy shield, acknowledging my act. Then so too did the others, even the white-caped man of the Paravaci.

Then the Tuchuk drove his own lance into the dirt and hung on the lance his glossy shield.

I saw him draw one of the quivas from a saddle sheath, loosen the long, triple-weighted bola from his side.

Slowly, singing in a gutteral chant, a Tuchuk warrior song, he began to swing the bola. It consists of three long straps of leather, each about five feet long, each terminating in a leather sack which contains, sewn inside, a heavy, round, metal weight. It was probably developed for hunting the tumit, a huge, flightless carnivorous bird of the plains, but the Wagon Peoples use it also, and well, as a weapon of war. Thrown low the long straps, with their approximate ten-foot sweep, almost impossible to evade, strike the victim and the weighted balls, as soon as resistance is met, whip about the victim, tangling and tightening the straps. Sometimes legs are broken. It is often difficult to release the straps, so snarled do they become. Thrown high the Gorean bola can lock a man's arms to his sides; thrown to the throat it can strangle him; thrown to the head, a difficult cast, the whipping weights can crush a skull. One entagles the victim with the bola, leaps from one's mount and with the quiva cuts his throat.

I had never encountered such a weapon and I had little notion as to how it might be met.

The Tuchuk handled it well. The three weights at the end of the straps were now almost blurring in the air and he, his song ended, the reins in his left hand, quiva blade now clenched between his teeth, bola in his swinging, uplifted right arm, suddenly cried out and kicked the kaiila into its charge.

He wants a kill, I told myself. He is under the eyes of warriors of the other peoples. It would be safest to throw low. It would be a finer cast, however, to try for the throat or head. How vain is he? How skillful is he?

He would be both skillful and vain; he was Tuchuk.

To the head came the flashing bola moving in its hideous, swift revolution almost invisible in the air and I, instead of lowering my head or throwing myself to the ground, met instead the flying weighted leather with the blade of a Koroban short sword, with the edge that would divide silk dropped upon it and the taut straps, two of them, flew from the blade and the other strap and the three weights looped off into the grass, and the Tuchuk at the same time, scarcely realizing what had occurred, leaped from the kaiila, quiva in hand, to find himself unexpectedly facing a braced warrior of Ko-ro-ba, sword drawn.

The quiva reversed itself in his hand, an action so swift I was only aware of it as his arm flew back, his hand on the blade, to hurl the weapon.

It sped toward me with incredible velocity over the handful of feet that separated us. It could not be evaded, but only countered, and countered it was by the Koroban steel in my hand, a sudden ringing, sliding flash of steel and the knife was deflected from my breast.

The Tuchuk stood struck with awe, in the grass, on the trembling plains in the dusty air.

I could hear the other three men of the Wagon Peoples, the Kataii, the Kassar, the Paravaci, striking their shields with their lances. "Well done," said the Kassar.

The Tuchuk removed his helmet and threw it to the grass. He jerked open the jacket he wore and the leather jerkin beneath, revealing his chest.

He looked about him, at the distant bosk herds, lifted his head to see the sky once more.

His kaiila stood some yards away, shifting a bit, puzzled, reins loose on its neck.

The Tuchuk now looked at me swiftly. He grinned. He did not expect nor would he receive aid from his fellows. I studied his heavy face, the fierce scarring that somehow ennobled it, the black eyes with the epicanthic fold. He grinned at me. "Yes," he said, "well done."

I went to him and set the point of the Gorean short sword at his heart.

He did not flinch.

"I am Tarl Cabot," I said. "I come in peace."

I thrust the blade back in the scabbard.

For a moment the Tuchuk seemed stunned. He stared at me, disbelievingly, and then, suddenly, he threw back his head and laughed until tears streamed down his face. He doubled over and pounded on his knees with his fist. Then he straightened up and wiped his face with the back of his hand.

I shrugged.

Suddenly the Tuchuk bent to the soil and picked up a handful of dirt and grass, the land on which the bosk graze, the land which is the land of the Tuchuks, and this dirt and this grass he thrust in my hands and I held it.

The warrior grinned and put his hands over mine so that our hands together held the dirt and the grass, and were together clasped on it.

"Yes," said the warrior, "come in peace to the Land of the Wagon Peoples."

5

The Prisoner

I followed the warrior Kamchak into the encampment of Tuchuks.

Nearly were we run down by six riders on thundering kaiila who, riding for sport, raced past us wildly among the crowded, clustered wagons. I heard the lowing of milk bosk from among the wagons. Here and there children ran between the wheels, playing with a cork ball and quiva, the object of the game being to strike the thrown ball. Tuchuk women, unveiled, in their long leather dresses, long hair bound in braids, tended cooking pots hung on tem-wood tripods over dung fires. These women were unscarred, but like the bosk themselves, each wore a nose ring. That of the animals is heavy and of gold, that of the women also of gold but tiny and fine, not unlike the wedding rings of my old world. I heard a haruspex singing between the wagons; for a piece of meat he would read the wind and the grass; for a cup of wine the stars and the flight of birds; for a fat-bellied dinner the liver of a sleen or slave.

The Wagon Peoples are fascinated with the future and its signs and though, to hear them speak, they put no store in such matters, yet they do in practice give them great consideration. I was told by Kamchak that once an army of a thousand wagons turned aside because a swarm of rennels, poisonous, crablike desert insects, did not defend its broken nest, crushed by the wheel of the lead wagon. Another time, over a hundred years ago, a wagon Ubar lost the spur from

27

his right boot and turned for this reason back from the gates of mighty Ar itself.

By one fire I could see a squat Tuchuk, hands on hips, dancing and stamping about by himself, drunk on fermented milk curds, dancing, according to Kamchak, to please the sky.

The Tuchuks and the other Wagon Peoples reverence Priest-Kings, but unlike the Goreans of the cities, with their castes of Initiates, they do not extend to them the dignities of worship. I suppose the Tuchuks worship nothing, in the common sense of that word, but it is true they hold many things holy, among them the bosk and the skills of arms, but chief of the things before which the proud Tuchuk stands ready to remove his helmet is the sky, the simple, vast beautiful sky, from which falls the rain that, in his myths, formed the earth, and the bosks, and the Tuchuks. It is to the sky that the Tuchuks pray when they pray, demanding victory and luck for themselves, defeat and misery for their enemies. The Tuchuk, incidentally, like others of the Wagon Peoples, prays only when mounted, only when in the saddle and with weapons at hand; he prays to the sky not as a slave to a master, nor a servant to a god, but as warrior to a Ubar; the women of the Wagon Peoples, it might be mentioned, are not permitted to pray; many of them, however, do patronize the haruspexes, who, besides foretelling the future with a greater or lesser degree of accuracy for generally reasonable fees, provide an incredible assemblage of amulets, talismans, trinkets, philters, potions, spell papers, wonder-working sleen teeth, marvelous powdered kailiauk horns, and colored, magic strings that, depending on the purpose, may be knotted in various ways and worn about the neck.

As we passed among the wagons I leaped back as a tawny prairie sleen hurled itself against the bars of a sleen cage, reaching out for me with its six-clawed paw. There were four other prairie sleen in the cage, a small cage, and they were curling and moving about one another, restlessly, like angry snakes. They would be released with the fall of darkness to run the periphery of the herds, acting, as I have mentioned, as shepherds and sentinels. They are also used if a slave escapes, for the sleen is an efficient, tireless, savage, almost infallible hunter, capable of pursuing a scent, days old, for hundreds of pasangs until, perhaps a month later, it finds its victim and tears it to pieces.

I was startled by the sound of slave bells and saw a girl,

stripped save for bells and collar, carrying a burden among the wagons.

Kamchak saw that I had noticed the girl and chuckled, sensing that I might find it strange, seeing a slave so among the wagons.

She wore bells locked on both wrists, and on both ankles, thick cuffs and anklets, each with a double line of bells, fastened by steel and key. She wore the Turian collar, rather than the common slave collar. The Turian collar lies loosely on the girl, a round ring; it fits so loosely that, when grasped in a man's fist, the girl can turn within it; the common Gorean collar, on the other hand, is a flat, snugly fitting steel band. Both collars lock in the back, behind the girl's neck. The Turian collar is more difficult to engrave, but it, like the flat collar, will bear some legend assuring that the girl, if found, will be promptly returned to her master. Bells had also been affixed to her collar.

"She is Turian?" I asked.

"Of course," said Kamchak.

"In the cities," I said, "only Pleasure Slaves are so belled, and then customarily for the dance."

"Her master," said Kamchak, "does not trust her."

In his simple statement I then understood the meaning of her condition. She would be allowed no garments, that she might not be able to conceal a weapon; the bells would mark each of her movements.

"At night," said Kamchak, "she is chained under the wagon."

The girl had now disappeared.

"Turian girls are proud," said Kamchak. "Thus, they make excellent slaves."

What he said did not surprise me. The Gorean master, commonly, likes a spirited girl, one who fights the whip and collar, resisting until at last, perhaps months later, she is overwhelmed and must acknowledge herself his, utterly and without reservation, then fearing only that he might tire of her and sell her to another.

"In time," said Kamchak, "she will beg for the rag of a slave."

I supposed it was true. A girl could take only so much, and then she would kneel to her master, her head to his boots, and beg for a bit of clothing, even though it be only to be clad Kajir.

Kajira is perhaps the most common expression for a female slave. Another frequently heard expression is Sa-Fora, a compound word, meaning, rather literally, Chain Daughter, or Daughter of the Chain. Among the Wagon Peoples, to be clad Kajir means, for a girl, to wear four articles, two red, two black; a red cord, the Curla, is tied about the waist; the Chatka, or long, narrow strip of black leather, fits over this cord in the front, passes under, and then again, from the inside, passes over the cord in the back; the Chatka is drawn tight; the Kalmak is then donned; it is a short, open, sleeveless vest of black leather; lastly the Koora, a strip of red cloth, matching the Curla, is wound about the head, to hold the hair back, for slave women, among the Wagon Peoples, are not permitted to braid, or otherwise dress their hair; it must be, save for the Koora, worn loose. For a male slave, or Kajirus, of the Wagon Peoples, and there are few, save for the work chains, to be clad Kajir means to wear the Kes, a short, sleeveless work tunic of black leather. As Kamchak and I walked to his wagon, I saw several girls, here and there, clad Kajir; they were magnificent; they walked with the true brazen insolence of the slave girl, the wench who knows that she is owned, whom men have found beautiful enough, and exciting enough, to collar. The dour women of the Wagon Peoples, I saw, looked on these girls with envy and hatred, sometimes striking them with sticks if they should approach too closely the cooking pots and attempt to steal a piece of meat.

"I will tell your master!" screamed one.

The girl laughed at her and with a toss of her auburn hair, bound in the Koora, ran off between the wagons.

Kamchak and I laughed.

I gathered that the beauty had little to fear from her master, saving perhaps that she might cease to please him.

The wagons of the Wagon Peoples are, in their hundreds and thousands, in their brilliant, variegated colors, a glorious sight. Surprisingly the wagons are almost square, each the size of a large room. Each is drawn by a double team of bosk, four in a team, with each team linked to its wagon tongue, the tongues being joined by tem-wood crossbars. The two axles of the wagon are also of tem-wood, which perhaps, because of its flexibility, joined with the general flatness of the southern Gorean plains, permits the width of the wagon.

The wagon box, which stands almost six feet from the ground, is formed of black, lacquered planks of tem-wood. Inside the wagon box, which is square, there is fixed a rounded, tentlike frame, covered with the taut, painted, varnished hides of bosks. These hides are richly colored, and often worked with fantastic designs, each wagon competing with its neighbor to be the boldest and most exciting. The rounded frame is fixed somewhat within the square of the wagon box, so that a walkway, almost like a ship's bridge, surrounds the frame. The sides of the wagon box, incidentally, are, here and there, perforated for arrow ports, for the small horn bow of the Wagon Peoples can be used to advantage not only from the back of a kaiila but, like the crossbow, from such cramped quarters. One of the most striking features of these wagons is the wheels, which are huge, the back wheels having a diameter of about ten feet; the front wheels are, like those of the Conestoga wagon, slightly smaller, in this case, about eight feet in diameter; the larger rear wheels are more difficult to mire; the smaller front wheels, nearer the pulling power of the bosk, permit a somewhat easier turning of the wagon. These wheels are carved wood and, like the wagon hides, are richly painted. Thick strips of boskhide form the wheel rims, which are replaced three to four times a year. The wagon is guided by a series of eight straps, two each for the four lead animals. Normally, however, the wagons are tied in tandem fashion, in numerous long columns, and only the lead wagons are guided, the others simply following, thongs running from the rear of one wagon to the nose rings of the bosk following, sometimes as much as thirty yards behind, with the next wagon; also, too, a wagon is often guided by a woman or boy who walks beside the lead animals with a sharp stick.

The interiors of the wagons, lashed shut, protected from the dust of the march, are often rich, marvelously carpeted and hung, filled with chests and silks, and booty from looted caravans, lit by hanging tharlarion oil lamps, the golden light of which falls on the silken cushions, the ankle-deep, intricatly wrought carpets. In the center of the wagon there is a small, shallow fire bowl, formed of copper, with a raised brass grating. Some cooking is done here, though the bowl is largely to furnish heat. The smoke escapes by a smoke hole at the dome of the tentlike frame, a hole which is shut when the wagons move.

There was the sudden thud of a kaiila's paws on the grass between the wagons and a wild snorting squeal.

I jumped back avoiding the paws of the enraged, rearing animal.

"Stand aside, you fool!" cried a girl's voice, and to my astonishment, astride the saddle of the monster I espied a girl, young, astonishingly beautiful, vital, angry, pulling at the control straps of the animal.

She was not as the other women of the Wagon Peoples I had seen, the dour, thin women with braided hair, bending over the cooking pots.

She wore a brief leather skirt, slit on the right side to allow her the saddle of the kaiila; her leather blouse was sleeveless; attached to her shoulders was a crimson cape; and her wild black hair was bound back by a band of scarlet cloth. Like the other women of the Wagons she wore no veil and, like them, fixed in her nose was the tiny, fine ring that proclaimed her people.

Her skin was a light brown and her eyes a charged, sparkling black.

"What fool is this!" she demanded of Kamchak.

"No fool," said Kamchak, "but Tarl Cabot, a warrior, one who has held in his hands with me grass and earth."

"He is a stranger," she said. "He should be slain!"

Kamchak grinned up at her. "He has held with me grass and earth," he said.

The girl gave a snort of contempt and kicked her small, spurred heels into the flanks of the kaiila and bounded away.

Kamchak laughed. "She is Hereena, a wench of the First Wagon," he said.

"Tell me of her," I said.

"What is there to tell?" asked Kamchak.

"What does it mean to be of the First Wagon?" I asked.

Kamchak laughed. "You know little of the Wagon Peoples," he said.

"That is true," I admitted.

"To be of the First Wagon," said Kamchak, "is to be of the household of Kutaituchik."

I repeated the name slowly, trying to sound it out. It is pronounced in four syllables, divided thus: Ku-tai-tu-chik.

"He then is the Ubar of the Tuchuks?" I said.

"His wagon," smiled Kamchak, "is the First Wagon—and it is Kutaituchik who sits upon the gray robe."

"The gray robe?" I asked.

"That robe," said Kamchak, "which is the throne of the Ubars of the Tuchuks."

It was thus I first learned the name of the man whom I understood to be Ubar of this fierce people.

"You will sometime be taken into the presence of Kutai-tuchik," said Kamchak. "I myself," he said, "must often go to the wagon of the Ubar."

I gathered from this remark that Kamchak was a man of no little importance among the Tuchuks.

"There are a hundred wagons in the personal household of Kutaituchik," said Kamchak. "To be of any of these wagons is to be of the First Wagon."

"I see," I said. "And the girl—she on the kaiila—is perhaps the daughter of Kutaituchik, Ubar of the Tuchuks?"

"No," said Kamchak. "She is unrelated to him, as are most in the First Wagon."

"She seemed much different than the other Tuchuk women," I said.

Kamchak laughed, the colored scars wrinkling on his broad face. "Of course," said Kamchak, "she has been raised to be fit prize in the games of Love War."

"I do not understand," I said.

"Did you not see the Plains of a Thousand Stakes?" asked Kamchak.

"No," I said. "I did not."

I was about to press Kamchak on this matter when we heard a sudden shout and the squealing of kaiila from among the wagons. I heard then the shouts of men and the cries of women and children. Kamchak lifted his head intently, listening. Then we heard the pounding of a small drum and two blasts on the horn of a bosk.

Kamchak read the message of the drum and horn.

"A prisoner has been brought to the camp," he said.

6

To the Wagon of Kutaituchik

Kamchak strode among the wagons, toward the sound, and I followed him closely. Many others, too, rushed to the sound, and we were jostled by armed warriors, scarred and fierce; by boys with unscarred faces, carrying the pointed sticks used often for goading the wagon bosk; by leather-clad women hurrying from the cooking pots; by wild, half-clothed children; even by enslaved Kajir-clad beauties of Turia; even the girl was there who wore but bells and collar, struggling under her burden, long dried strips of bosk meat, as wide as beams, she too hurrying to see what might be the meaning of the drum and horn, of the shouting Tuchuks.

We suddenly emerged into the center of what seemed to be a wide, grassy street among the wagons, a wide lane, open and level, an avenue in that city of Harigga, or Bosk Wagons.

The street was lined by throngs of Tuchuks and slaves. Among them, too, were soothsayers and haruspexes, and singers and musicians, and, here and there, small peddlers and merchants, of various cities, for such are occasionally permitted by the Tuchuks, who crave their wares, to approach the wagons. Each of these, I was later to learn, wore on his forearm a tiny brand, in the form of spreading bosk horns, which guaranteed his passage, at certain seasons, across the plains of the Wagon Peoples. The difficulty, of course is in first obtaining the brand. If, in the case of a singer, the song is rejected, or in the case of a merchant, his merchandise is rejected, he is slain out of hand. This acceptance brand, of course, carries with it a certain stain of ignominy, suggesting that those who approach the wagons do so as slaves.

Now I could see down the wide, grassy lane, loping towards us, two kaiila and riders. A lance was fastened between them, fixed to the stirrups of their saddles. The lance cleared the ground, given the height of the kaiila, by about five feet. Between the two animals, stumbling desperately, her throat bound by leather thongs to the lance behind her neck, ran a girl, her wrists tied behind her back.

I was astonished, for this girl was dressed not as a Gorean, not as a girl of any of the cities of the Counter-Earth, not as a peasant of the Sa-Tarna fields or the vineyards where the Ta grapes are raised, not even as a girl of the fierce Wagon Peoples.

Kamchak stepped to the center of the grassy lane, lifting his hand, and the two riders, with their prize, reined in their mounts.

I was dumbfounded.

The girl stood gasping for breath, her body shaking and quivering, her knees slightly bent. She would have fallen except for the lance that kept her in place. She pulled weakly at the thongs that bound her wrists. Her eyes seemed glazed. She scarcely could look about her. Her clothing was stained with dust and her hair hung loose and tangled. Her body was covered with a sparkling sheen of sweat. Her shoes had been removed and had been fastened about her neck. Her feet were bleeding. The shreds of yellow nylon stockings hung about her angles. Her brief dress was torn by being dragged through brush.

Kamchak, too, seemed surprised at the sight of the girl, for never had he seen one so peculiarly attired. He assumed, of course, from the brevity of her skirt, that she was slave. He was perhaps puzzled by the absence of a metal collar about her throat. There was, however, literally sewn about her neck, a thick, high leather collar.

Kamchak went to her and took her head in his hands. She lifted her head and seeing the wild, fearsome scarred face that stared into hers, she suddenly screamed hysterically, and tried to jerk and tear herself away, but the lance held her in place. She kept shaking her head and whimpering. It was clear she could not believe her eyes, that she understood nothing, that she did not comprehend her surroundings, that she thought herself mad.

I noted that she had dark hair and dark eyes, brown.

The thought crossed my mind that this might lower her price somewhat.

She wore a simple yellow shift, with narrow orange stripes, of what must once have been crisp oxford cloth. It had long sleeves, with cuffs, and a button down collar, not unlike a man's shirt.

It was now, of course, torn and soiled.

Yet she was not an unpleasing wench to look on, slim, well-ankled, lithe. On the Gorean block she would bring a good price.

She gave a little cry as Kamchak jerked the shoes from about her neck.

He threw them to me.

They were orange, of finely tooled leather, with a buckle. They had heels, a bit more than an inch high. There was also lettering in the shoe, but the script and words would have been unfamiliar to Goreans. It was English.

The girl was trying to speak. "My name is Elizabeth Cardwell," she said. "I'm an American citizen. My home is in New York City."

Kamchak looked in puzzlement at the riders, and they at him. In Gorean, one of the riders said, "She is a barbarian. She cannot speak Gorean."

My role, as I conceived it, was to remain silent.

"You are all mad!" screamed the girl, pulling at the straps that bound her, struggling in the bonds. "Mad!"

The Tuchuks and the others looked at one another, puzzled.

I did not speak.

I was thunderstruck that a girl, apparently of Earth, who spoke English, should be brought to the Tuchuks at this time—at the time that I was among them, hoping to discover and return to Priest-Kings what I supposed to be a golden spheroid, the egg, the last hope of their race. Had the girl been brought to this world by Priest-Kings? Was she the recent victim of one of the Voyages of Acquisition? But I understood them to have been curtailed in the recent subterranean War of Priest-Kings. Had they been resumed? Surely this girl had not been long on Gor, perhaps no more than hours. But if the Voyages of Acquisition had been resumed, why had they been resumed? Or was it actually the case that she had been brought to Gor by Priest-Kings? Were there perhaps—others—somehow others? Was this woman sent to the Tuchuks at this time—perhaps released to wander on the plains—inevitably to be picked up by outriders—for a purpose—and if so, to what end—for whose purpose or purposes? Or was there somehow some fantastic accident or coincidence involved in the event of her arrival? Somehow I knew the latter was not likely to be the case.

Suddenly the girl threw back her head and cried out hysterically. "I'm mad! I have gone mad! I have gone mad!"

I could stand it no longer. She was too piteous. Against my better judgment I spoke to her. "No," I said, "you are sane."

The girl's eyes looked at me, she scarcely believing the words she had heard.

The Tuchuks and others, as one man, faced me.

I turned to Kamchak. Speaking in Gorean, I said to him, "I can understand her."

One of the riders pointed to me, crying out to the crowd, excitedly. "He speaks her tongue!"

A ripple of pleasure coursed through the throng.

It then occurred to me that it might have been for just this purpose that she had been sent to the Tuchuks, to single out the one man from among all the thousands with the wagons who could understand her and speak with her, thus identifying and marking him.

"Excellent," said Kamchak, grinning at me.

"Please," cried the girl to me. "Help me!"

Kamchak said to me. "Tell her to be silent."

I did so, and the girl looked at me, dumbfounded, but remained silent.

I discovered that I was now an interpreter.

Kamchak was now, curiously, fingering her yellow garment. Then, swiftly, he tore it from her.

She cried out.

"Be silent," I said to her.

I knew what must now pass, and it was what would have passed in any city or on any road or trail or path in Gor. She was a captive female, and must, naturally, submit to her assessment as prize; she must also be, incidentally, examined for weapons; a dagger or poisoned needle is often concealed in the clothing of free women.

There were interested murmurs from the crowd when, to the Gorean's thinking, the unusual garments underlying her yellow shift were revealed.

"Please," she wept, turning to me.

"Be silent," I cautioned her.

Kamchak then removed her remaining garments, even the

shreds of nylon stockings that had hung about her ankles.

There was a murmur of approval from the crowd; even some of the enslaved Turian beauties, in spite of themselves, cried out in admiration.

Elizabeth Cardwell, I decided, would indeed bring a high price.

She stood held in place by the lance, her throat bound to it with the wood behind her neck, her wrists thonged behind her back. Other than her bonds she now wore only the thick leather collar which had been sewn about her neck.

Kamchak picked up the clothing which lay near her on the grass. He also took the shoes. He wadded it all up together in a soiled bundle. He threw it to a nearby woman. "Burn it," said Kamchak.

The bound girl watched helplessly as the woman carried her clothing, all that she had of her old world, to a cooking fire some yards away, near the edge of the wagons.

The crowd had opened a passage for the woman and the girl saw the clothing cast on the open fire.

"No, no!" she screamed. "No!"

Then she tried once more to free herself.

"Tell her," said Kamchak, "that she must learn Gorean quickly—that she will be slain if she does not."

I translated this for the girl.

She shook her head wildly. "Tell them my name is Elizabeth Cardwell," she said. "I don't know where I am—or how I got here—I want to get back to America—I'm an American citizen—my home is in New York City—take me back there—I will pay you—anything!"

"Tell her," repeated Kamchak, "that she must learn Gorean quickly—and that if she does not she will be slain."

I translated this once more for the girl.

"I will pay you anything," she pleaded. "Anything!"

"You have nothing," I informed her, and she blushed. "Further," I said, "we do not have the means of returning you to your home."

"Why not!" she demanded.

"Have you not," I pressed, "noted the difference in the gravitational field of this place—have you not noted the slight difference in the appearance of the sun?"

"It's not true!" she screamed.

"This is not Earth," I told her. "This is Gor—another earth perhaps—but not yours." I looked at her fixedly. She must understand. "You are on another planet."

She closed her eyes and moaned.

"I know," she said. "I know—I know—but how—how—how?"

"I do not know the answer to your question," I said. I did not tell her that I was, incidentally, keenly interested—for my own reasons—in learning the answer to her question.

Kamchak seemed impatient.

"What does she say?" he asked.

"She is naturally disturbed," I said. "She wishes to return to her city."

"What is her city?" asked Kamchak.

"It is called New York," I said.

"I have never heard of it," said Kamchak.

"It is far away," I said.

"How is it that you speak her language?" he asked.

"I once lived in lands where her language is spoken," I said.

"Is there grass for the bosk in her lands?" asked Kamchak.

"Yes," I said, "but they are far away."

"Farther even than Thentis?" asked Kamchak.

"Yes," I said.

"Farther even than the islands of Cos and Tyros?" he asked.

"Yes," I said.

Kamchak whistled. "That is far," he said.

I smiled. "It is too far to take the bosk," I said.

Kamchak grinned at me.

One of the warriors on the kaiila spoke. "She was with no one," he said. "We searched. She was with no one."

Kamchak nodded at me, and then at the girl.

"Were you alone?" I asked.

The girl nodded weakly.

"She says she was alone," I told Kamchak.

"How came she here?" asked Kamchak.

I translated his question, and the girl looked at me, and then closed her eyes and shook her head. "I don't know," she said.

"She says she does not know," I told Kamchak.

"It is strange," said Kamchak. "But we will question her further later."

He signaled to a boy who carried a skin of Ka-la-na wine over his shoulder. He took the skin of wine from the boy and bit out the horn plug; he then, with the wineskin on his shoulder, held back the head of Elizabeth Cardwell with one hand and with the other shoved the bone nozzle of the skin between her teeth; he tipped the skin and the girl, half choking, swallowed wine; some of the red fluid ran from her mouth and over her body.

When Kamchak thought she had drunk enough he pulled the nozzle from her mouth, pushed back the plug and returned the skin to the boy.

Dazed, exhausted, covered with sweat, dust on her face and legs, wine on her body, Elizabeth Cardwell, her wrists thonged behind her and her throat bound to a lance, stood captive before Kamchak of the Tuchuks.

He must be merciful. He must be kind.

"She must learn Gorean," said Kamchak to me. "Teach her 'La Kajira'."

"You must learn Gorean," I told the girl.

She tried to protest, but I would not permit it.

"Say 'La Kajira'," I told her.

She looked at me, helplessly. Then she repeated, "La Kajira."

"Again," I commanded.

"La Kajira," said the girl clearly, "La Kajira."

Elizabeth Cardwell had learned her first Gorean.

"What does it mean?" she asked.

"It means," I told her, "I am a slave girl."

"No!" she screamed. "No, no, no!"

Kamchak nodded to the two riders mounted on kaiila. "Take her to the wagon of Kutaituchik."

The two riders turned their kaiila and in a moment, moving rapidly, the girl running between them, had turned from the grassy lane and disappeared between the wagons.

Kamchak and I regarded one another.

"Did you note the collar she wore?" I asked.

He had not seemed to show much interest in the high, thick leather collar that the girl had had sewn about her neck.

"Of course," he said.

"I myself," I said, "have never seen such a collar."

"It is a message collar," said Kamchak. "Inside the leather, sewn within, will be a message."

My look of amazement must have amused him, for he laughed. "Come," he said, "let us go to the wagon of Kutaituchik."

7

La Kajira

The wagon of Kutaituchik, called Ubar of the Tuchuks, was drawn up on a large, flat-topped grassy hill, the highest land in the camp.

Beside the wagon, on a great pole fixed in the earth, stood the Tuchuk standard of the four bosk horns.

The hundred, rather than eight, bosk that drew his wagon had been unyoked; they were huge, red bosk; their horns had been polished and their coats glistened from the comb and oils; their golden nose rings were set with jewels; necklaces of precious stones hung from the polished horns.

The wagon itself was the largest in the camp, and the largest wagon I had conceived possible; actually it was a vast platform, set on numerous wheeled frames; though at the edges of the platform, on each side, there were a dozen of the large wheels such as are found on the much smaller wagons; these latter wheels turned as the wagon moved and supported weight, but could not of themselves have supported the entire weight of that fantastic, wheeled palace of hide.

The hides that formed the dome were of a thousand colors, and the smoke hole at the top must have stood more than a hundred feet from the flooring of that vast platform. I could well conjecture the riches, the loot and the furnishings that would dazzle the interior of such a magnificent dwelling.

But I did not enter the wagon, for Kutaituchik held his court outside the wagon, in the open air, on the flat-topped grassy hill. A large dais had been built, vast and spreading, but standing no more than a foot from the earth. This dais was covered with dozens of thick rugs, sometimes four and five deep.

There were many Tuchuks, and some others, crowded about the dais, and, standing upon it, about Kutaituchik, there were several men who, from their position on the dais and their trappings, I judged to be of great importance.

Among these men, sitting cross-legged, was Kutaituchik, called Ubar of the Tuchuks.

About Kutaituchik there were piled various goods, mostly vessels of precious metal and strings and piles of jewels; there was silk there from Tyros; silver from Thentis and Tharna; tapestries from the mills of Ar; wines from Cos; dates from the city of Tor. There were also, among the other goods, two girls, blonde and blue-eyed, unclothed, chained; they had perhaps been a gift to Kutaituchik; or had been the daughters of enemies; they might have been from any city; both were beautiful; one was sitting with her knees tucked under her chin, her hands clasping her ankles, absently staring at the jewels about her feet; the other lay indolently on her side, incuriously regarding us, her weight on one elbow; there was a yellow stain about her mouth where she had been fed some fruit; both girls wore the Sirik, a light chain favored for female slaves by many Gorean masters; it consists of a Turian-type collar, a loose, rounded circle of steel, to which a light, gleaming chain is attached; should the girl stand, the chain, dangling from her collar, falls to the floor; it is about ten or twelve inches longer than is required to reach from her collar to her ankles; to this chain, at the natural fall of her wrists, is attached a pair of slave bracelets; at the end of the chain there is attached another device, a set of linked ankle rings, which, when closed about her ankles, lifts a portion of the slack chain from the floor; the Sirik is an incredibly graceful thing and designed to enhance the beauty of its wearer; perhaps it should only be added that the slave bracelets and the ankle rings may be removed from the chain and used separately; this also, of course, permits the Sirik to function as a slave leash.

At the edge of the dais Kamchak and I had stopped, where our sandals were removed and our feet washed by Turian slaves, men in the Kes, who might once have been officers of the city.

We mounted the dais and approached the seemingly somnolent figure seated upon it.

Although the dais was resplendent, and the rugs upon it

even more resplendent, I saw that beneath Kutaituchik, over these rugs, had been spread a simple, worn, tattered robe of gray boskhide. It was upon this simple robe that he sat. It was undoubtedly that of which Kamchak had spoken, the robe upon which sits the Ubar of the Tuchuks, that simple robe which is his throne.

Kutaituchik lifted his head and regarded us; his eyes seemed sleepy; he was bald, save for a black knot of hair that emerged from the back of his shaven skull; he was a broad-backed man, with small legs; his eyes bore the epican-thic fold; his skin was a tinged, yellowish brown; though he was stripped to the waist, there was about his shoulders a rich, ornamented robe of the red bosk, bordered with jewels; about his neck, on a chain decorated with sleen teeth, there hung a golden medallion, bearing the sign of the four bosk horns; he wore furred boots, wide leather trousers, and a red sash, in which was thrust a quiva. Beside him, coiled, perhaps as a symbol of power, lay a bosk whip. Kutaituchik absently reached into a small golden box near his right knee and drew out a string of rolled kanda leaf.

The roots of the kanda plant, which grows largely in desert regions on Gor, are extremely toxic, but, surprisingly, the rolled leaves of this plant, which are relatively innocuous, are formed into strings and, chewed or sucked, are much favored by many Goreans, particularly in the southern hemisphere, where the leaf is more abundant.

Kutaituchik, not taking his eyes off us, thrust one end of the green kanda string in the left side of his mouth and, very slowly, began to chew it. He said nothing, nor did Kamchak. We simply sat near him, cross-legged. I was conscious that only we three on that dais were sitting. I was pleased that there were no prostrations or grovelings involved in ap-proaching the august presence of the exalted Kutaituchik. I gathered that once, in his earlier years, he might have been a rider of the kaiila, that he might have been skilled with the bow and lance, and the quiva; such a man would not need ceremony; I sensed that once this man might have ridden six hundred pasangs in a day, living on a mouthful of water and a handful of bosk meat kept soft and warm between his saddle and the back of the kaiila; that there might have been few as swift with the quiva, as delicate with the lance, as he; that he had known the wars and the winters of the prairie; that he had met animals and men, as enemies, and had lived; such a man did not need ceremony; such a man, I sensed, was Kutaituchik, called Ubar of the Tuchuks.

And yet was I sad as I looked upon him, for I sensed that for this man there could no longer be the saddle of the kaiila, the whirling of the rope and bola, the hunt and the war. Now, from the right side of his mouth, thin, black and wet, there emerged the chewed string of kanda, a quarter of an inch at a time, slowly. The drooping eyes, glazed, regarded us. For him there could no longer be the swift races across the frozen prairie; the meetings in arms; even the dancing to the sky about a fire of bosk dung.

Kamchak and I waited until the string had been chewed.

When Kamchak had finished he held out his right hand and a man, not a Tuchuk, who wore the green robes of the Caste of Pysicians, thrust in his hand a goblet of bosk horn; it contained some yellow fluid. Angrily, not concealing his distaste, Kutaituchik drained the goblet and then hurled it from him.

He then shook himself and regarded Kamchak.

He grinned a Tuchuk grin. "How are the bosk?" he asked.

"As well as may be expected," said Kamchak.

"Are the quivas sharp?"

"One tries to keep them so," said Kamchak.

"It is important to keep the axles of the wagons greased," observed Kutaituchik.

"Yes," said Kamchak, "I believe so."

Kutaituchik suddenly reached out and he and Kamchak, laughing, clasped hands.

Then Kutaituchik sat back and clapped his hands together sharply twice. "Bring the she-slave," he said.

I turned to see a stout man-at-arms step to the dais, carrying in his arms, folded in the furs of the scarlet larl, a girl.

I heard the small sound of a chain.

The man-at-arms placed Elizabeth Cardwell before us, and Kutaituchik, and drew away the pelt of the scarlet larl.

Elizabeth Cardwell had been cleaned and her hair combed. She was slim, lovely.

The man-at-arms arranged her before us.

The thick leather collar, I noted, was still sewn about her throat.

Elizabeth Cardwell, though she did not know it, knelt before us in the position of the Pleasure Slave.

She looked wildly about her and then dropped her head.

Aside from the collar on her throat she, like the other girls on the platform, wore only the Sirik.

Kamchak gestured to me.

"Speak," I said to her.

She lifted her head and then said, almost inaudibly, trembling in the restraint of the Sirik. "La Kajira." Then she dropped her head.

Kutaituchik seemed satisfied.

"It is the only Gorean she knows," Kamchak informed him.

"For the time," said Kutaituchik, "it is enough." He then looked at the man-at-arms. "Have you fed her?" he asked.

The man nodded.

"Good," said Kutaituchik, "the she-slave will need her strength."

The interrogation of Elizabeth Cardwell took hours. Needless to say, I served as translator.

The interrogation, to my surprise, was conducted largely by Kamchak, rather than Kutaituchik, called Ubar of the Tuchuks. Kamchak's questions were detailed, numerous, complex. He returned to certain questions at various times, in various ways, connecting subtly her responses to one with those of another; he wove a sophisticated net of inquiry about the girl, delicate and fine; I marveled at his skill; had there been the least inconsistency or even hesitation, as though the girl were attempting to recollect or reconcile the details of a fabrication, it would have been instantly detected.

During all this time, and torches had been brought, the hours of the night being burned away, Elizabeth Cardwell was not permitted to move, but must needs retain the position of of the Pleasure Slave, knees properly placed, back straight, head high, the gleaming chain of the Sirik dangling from the Turian collar, falling to the pelt of the red larl on which she knelt.

The translation, as you might expect, was a difficult task, but I attempted to convey as much as I could of what the girl, piteously, the words tumbling out, attempted to tell me.

Although there were risks involved I tried to translate as exactly as I could, letting Miss Cardwell speak as she would, though her words must often have sounded fantastic to the Tuchuks, for it was largely of a world alien to them that she spoke—a world not of autonomous cities but of huge nations; not of castes and crafts but of global, interlocking industrial complexes; not of bartar and tarn disks but of fantastic systems of exchange and credit; a world not of tarns and the tharlarion but of aircraft and motor buses and trucks; a world in which one's words need not be carried by a lone rider on the swift kaiila but could be sped from one corner of the earth to another by leaping through an artificial moon.

Kutaituchik and Kamchak, to my pleasure, tended to restrain judgment on these matters; to my gratification they did not seem to regard the girl as mad; I had been afraid, from time to time, that they might, losing patience with what must seem to them to be the most utter nonsense, order her beaten or impaled.

I did not know then, but Kutaituchik and Kamchak had some reason for supposing that the girl might be speaking the truth.

What they were most interested in, of course, and what I was most interested in, namely, how and why the girl came to be wandering on the Plains of Turia—in the Lands of the Wagon Peoples—they, and I, did not learn.

We were all, at last, satisfied that even the girl herself did not know.

At last Kamchak had finished, and Kutaituchik, too, and they leaned back, looking at the girl.

"Move no muscle," I said to her.

She did not. She was very beautiful.

Kamchak gestured with his head.

"You may lower your head," I said to the girl.

Piteously, with a rustle of chain, the girl's head and shoulders fell forward, and though she still knelt, her head touched the pelt of the larl, her shoulders and back shaking, trembling.

It seemed to me, from what I had learned, that there was no particular reason why Elizabeth Cardwell, and not one of Earth's countless others, had been selected to wear the message collar. As yet the collar had not been removed and examined. It was perhaps only that she was convenient, and, of course, that she was lovely, thus a fitting bearer of the collar, herself a gift with the message to please the Tuchuks, and perhaps better dispose them toward its contents.

Miss Cardwell was little different from thousands of lovely working girls in the great cities of Earth, perhaps more intelligent than many, perhaps prettier than most, but essentially the same, girls living alone or together in apartments, working in offices and studios and shops, struggling to earn a living in a glamorous city, whose goods and pleasures they could ill afford to purchase. What had happened to her might, I gathered, have happened to any of them.

She remembered arising and washing and dressing, eating a hurried breakfast, taking the elevator downstairs from her apartment, the subway, arriving at work, the routines of the morning as a junior secretary in one of the larger advertising agencies on Madison Avenue, her excitement at being invited to interview for the position of assistant secretary to the head of the art department, her last-minute concern with her lipstick, the hem of her yellow shift, then steno pad in hand, entering his office.

With him had been a tall, strange man, broad of shoulder with large hands, a grayish face, eyes almost like glass. He had frightened her. He wore a dark suit of expensive cloth and tailoring, and yet somehow it seemed not that he wore it as one accustomed to such garments. He spoke to her, rather than the man she knew, the head of the department, whom she had seen often. He did not permit her to take the seat by the desk.

Rather he told her to stand and straighten herself. He seemed to scorn her posture. Angry, she nevertheless did so until, embarrassed, she stood insolently erect before him. His eyes regarded her ankles with care, and then her calves and she was acutely aware, blushing, that standing as she did, so straight before him, the simple yellow, oxford-cloth shift ill concealed her thighs, the flatness of her belly, the loveliness of her figure. "Lift your head," he said, and she did, her chin high, the lovely, angry head set proudly on her aristocratic delicate neck.

He then backed away from her.

She turned to face him, eyes flashing.

"Do not speak," he said.

Her fingers went white with anger, clutching the steno pad and pencil.

He gestured to the far side of the room. "Walk there," he said, "and return."

"I will not," she said.

"Now," said the man.

Elizabeth had looked, tears almost in her eyes, at the department head, but he seemed suddenly to her soft, pudgy, distant, sweating, nothing. He nodded hastily, "Please, Miss Cardwell, do as he says."

Elizabeth faced the tall, strange man. She was breathing rapidly now. She felt the pencil clutched in her sweating hand. Then it broke.

"Now," said the man.

Looking at him she suddenly had the feeling, a strange one, that this man, in some circumstances and for some purpose or another, had assessed and judged many women.

This infuriated her.

It seemed to her a challenge that she would accept. She would show him a woman indeed—allowing herself for the instant to be insolently and fully female—showing him in her walk her contempt and scorn for him.

She would then leave and go directly to the personnel office, tendering her resignation.

She threw back her head. "Very well," she said. And Elizabeth Cardwell walked proudly, angrily, to the far side of the room, wheeled there, faced the man, and approached him, eyes taunting, a smile of contempt playing about her lips. She heard the department head quickly suck in his breath. She did not take her eyes from the tall, strange man.

"Are you satisfied," she asked, quietly, acidly.

"Yes," he had said.

She remembered then only turning and starting for the door, and a sudden, peculiar odor, penetrating, that seemed to close about her face and head.

She had regained consciousness on the Plains of Gor. She had been dressed precisely as she had been the morning she had gone to work save that about her throat she had found sewn a high, thick leather collar. She had cried out, she had wandered. Then, after some hours stumbling confused, terrified, hungry through the high, brown grass, she had seen two riders, mounted on swift, strange beasts. They had seen her. She called to them. They approached her cautiously, in a large circle, as though examining the grass for enemies, or others.

"I'm Elizabeth Cardwell," she had cried. "My home is in New York City. What place is this? Where am I?" And then she has seen the faces, and had screamed.

"Position," said Kamchak.

I spoke sharply to the girl. "Be as you were before."

Terrified the girl straightened herself and again, knees placed, back straight and head high, knelt before us in the position of the Pleasure Slave.

"The collar," said Kamchak, "is Turian."

Kutaituchik nodded.

This was news to me, and I welcomed it, for it meant that probably, somehow, the answer to at least a part of the mystery which confronted me lay in the city of Turia.

But how was it that Elizabeth Cardwell, of Earth, wore a Turian message collar?

Kamchak drew the quiva from his belt and approached the girl. She looked at him wildly, drawing back.

"Do not move," I told her.

Kamchak set the blade of the quiva between the girl's throat and the collar and moved it, the leather collar seeming to fall from the blade.

The girl's neck, where the collar had been sewn, was red and sweaty, broken out.

Kamchak returned to his place where he again sat down cross-legged, putting the cut collar on the rug in front of him.

I and Kutaituchik watched as he carefully spread open the collar, pressing back two edges. Then, from within the collar, he drew forth a thin, folded piece of paper, rence paper made from the fibers of the rence plant, a tall, long-stalked leafy plant which grows predominantly in the delta of the Vosk. I suppose, in itself, this meant nothing, but I naturally thought of Port Kar, malignant, squalid Port Kar, which claims suzerainty over the delta, exacting cruel tributes from the rence growers, great stocks of rence paper for trade, sons for oarsmen in cargo galleys, daughters for Pleasure Slaves in the taverns of the city. I would have expected the message to have been written either on stout, glossy-surfaced linen paper, of the sort milled in Ar, or perhaps on vellum and parchment, prepared in many cities and used commonly in scrolls, the process involving among other things the washing and liming of skins, their scraping and stretching, dusting them with sifted chalk, rubbing them down with pumice.

Kamchak handed the paper to Kutaituchik and he took it but looked at it, I thought, blankly. Saying nothing he handed it back to Kamchak, who seemed to study it with great care, and then, to my amazement, turned it sideways and then upside down. At last he grunted and handed it to me.

I was suddenly amused, for it occurred to me that neither of the Tuchuks could read.

"Read," said Kutaituchik.

I smiled and took the piece of rence paper. I glanced at it and then I smiled no longer. I could read it, of course. It was in Gorean script, moving from left to right, and then from right to left on alternate lines. The writing was quite legible. It was written in black ink, probably with a reed pen. This again suggested the delta of the Vosk.

"What does it say?" asked Kutaituchik.

The message was simple, consisting of only three lines. I read them aloud.

Find the man to whom this girl can speak.
He is Tarl Cabot.
Slay him.

"And who has signed this message?" asked Kutaituchik.

I hesitated to read the signature.

"Well?" asked Kutaituchik.

"It is signed," I said, "—Priest-Kings of Gor."

Kutaituchik smiled. "You read Gorean well," he said.

I understood then that both men could read, though perhaps many of the Tuchuks could not. It had been a test.

Kamchak grinned at Kutaituchik, the scarring on his face wrinkling with pleasure. "He has held grass and earth with me," he said.

"Ah!" said Kutaituchik. "I did not know."

My mind was whirling. Now I understood, as I had only suspected before, why an English-speaking girl was necessary to bear the collar, that she might be the device whereby I would be singled out from the hundreds and thousands among the wagons, and so be marked for death.

But I could not understand why Priest-Kings should wish me slain. Was I not engaged, in a sense, in their work? Had I not come to the Wagon Peoples on their behalf, to search for the doubtless golden sphere that was the last egg of Priest-Kings, the final hope of their race?

Now they wished me to die.

It did not seem possible.

I prepared to fight for my life, selling it as dearly as possible on the dais of Kutaituchik, called Ubar of the Tuchuks, for what Gorean would dare reject the command of Priest-Kings? I stood up, unsheathing my sword.

One or two of the men-at-arms immediately drew the quiva.

A small smile touched the broad face of Kutiatuchik.

"Put your sword away and sit down," said Kamchak.

Dumbfounded, I did so.

"It is," said Kamchak, "obviously not a message of Priest-Kings."

"Now do you know?" I asked.

The scarred face wrinkled again and Kamchak rocked back and slapped his knees. He laughed, "Do you think Priest-Kings, if they wished you dead, would ask others to do this for them?" He pointed at the opened collar lying before him on the rug. "Do you think Priest-Kings would use a Turian message collar?" He pointed his broad finger at Elizabeth Cardwell. "Do you think Priest-Kings would need a girl to find you?" Kamchak threw back his head and laughed loudly, and even Kutaituchik smiled. "No," said Kamchak, slapping his knee, "Priest-Kings do not need Tuchuks to do their killing!"

What Kamchak had said then seemed to make a great deal of sense to me. Yet it seemed strange that anyone, no matter whom, would dare to use the name of Priest-Kings falsely. Who, or what, could dare such a thing? Besides, how did I know that the message was not from Priest-Kings? I knew, as Kamchak and Kutaituchik did not, of the recent Nest War beneath the Sardar, and of the disruption in the technological complexes of the Nest—who knew to what primitive devices Priest-Kings might now find themselves reduced? Yet, on the whole, I tended to agree with Kamchak, that it was not likely the message came from Priest-Kings. It had been, after all, months since the Nest War and surely, by now, to some extent, Priest-Kings would have managed to restore significant portions of the equipment, devices of surveillance and control, by means of which they had, for such long millenia, managed to maintain their mastery of this barbarian sphere. Besides this, as far as I knew, Misk, who was my friend and between whom and myself there was Nest Trust, was still the highest born of the living Priest-Kings and the final authority in matters of importance in the Nest; I knew that Misk, if no other, would not have wished my death. And finally, I reminded myself again, was I not now engaged in their work? Was I not now attempting to be of service to them? Was I not now among the Wagon Peoples, in peril perhaps, on their behalf?

But, I asked myself, if this message was not from Priest-Kings, from whom could it be? Who would dare this? And who but Priest-Kings would know that I was among the Wagon Peoples? But yet I told myself—someone, or something—must know—others, not Priest-Kings. There must be others—others, who did not wish me to succeed in my work, who wished Priest-Kings, the race, to die, others who were capable even of bringing humans from Earth for their purposes—technologically advanced—others who were, perhaps, cautiously, invisibly, at war with Priest-Kings—who perhaps wished as prize this world, or perhaps this world and Earth as well, our sun and its planets—others, who perhaps stood on the margins of our system, waiting perhaps for the demise of the power of Priest-Kings, perhaps the shield which unknown to men, had protected them—perhaps from the time of the first grasping of stones, from the time even before an intelligent, prehensile animal could build fires in the mouth of its lair.

But these speculations were too fantastic, and I dismissed them.

There was remaining, however, a mystery, and I was determined to resolve it.

The answer possibly lay in Turia.

In the meantime I would, of course, continue my work. I would try, for Misk, to find the egg, and return it to the Sardar. I suspected, truly as it turned out, that the mystery and my mission were not utterly unconnected.

"What," I asked Kamchak, "would you do if you thought the message were truly from Priest-Kings?"

"Nothing," said Kamchak, gravely.

"You would risk," I asked, "the herds—the wagons—the peoples?" Both Kamchak and I knew that Priest-Kings were not lightly to be disobeyed. Their vengeance could extend to the total and complete annihilation of cities. Indeed their power, as I knew, was sufficient to destroy planets.

"Yes," said Kamchak.

"Why?" I asked.

He looked at me and smiled. "Because," said he, "we have together held grass and earth."

Kutaituchik, Kamchak and I then regarded Elizabeth Cardwell.

I knew that, as far as the interrogation was concerned, she had served her purpose. There was nothing more to be learned from her. She, too, must have sensed this, for she seemed, though she did not move, terribly frightened. Her fear could be read in her eyes, in the slight, tremulous movement of her lower lip. In the affairs of state she was now without value. Then uncontrollably, piteously, suddenly, trembling in the Sirik, she put her head down to the pelt of the larl. "Please," she said, "do not kill me."

I translated for Kamchak and Kutaituchik.

Kutaituchik addressed the question to her.

"Are you zealous to please the fancy of Tuchuks?"

I translated.

With horror Elizabeth Cardwell lifted her head from the pelt and regarded her captors. She shook her head, wildly, "No, please no!"

"Impale her," said Kutaituchik.

Two warriors rushed forward and seized the girl under the arms, lifting her from the pelt.

"What are they going to do?" she cried.

"They intend to impale you," I told her.

She began to scream. "Please, please, please!"

My hand was on the hilt of my sword, but Kamchak's hand rested on mine.

Kamchak turned to Kutaituchik. "She seems zealous," he said.

Once again Kutaituchik addressed his question to her, and I translated it.

"Are you zealous to please the fancy of Tuchuks?"

The men who held the girl allowed her to fall to her knees between them. "Yes," she said, piteously, "yes!"

Kutaituchik, Kamchak and I regarded her.

"Yes," she wept, her head to the rug, "I am zealous to please the fancy of Tuchuks."

I translated for Kutaituchik and Kamchak.

"Ask," demanded Kutaituchik, "if she begs to be a slave girl."

I translated the question.

"Yes," wept Elizabeth Cardwell, "yes—I beg to be a slave girl."

Perhaps in that moment Elizabeth Cardwell recalled the strange man, so fearsome, gray of face with eyes like glass, who had so examined her on Earth, before whom she had stood as though on a block, unknowingly being examined for her fitness to bear the message collar of Turia. How she had challenged him, how she had walked, how insolent she had been! Perhaps in that moment she thought how amused the man might be could he see her now, that proud girl, now in the Sirik, her head to the pelt of a larl, kneeling to barbarians, begging to be a slave girl; and if she thought of these things how she must have then cried out in her heart, for she would have then recognized that the man would have known full well what lay in store for her; how he must have laughed within himself at her petty show of female pride, her vanity, knowing it was this for which the lovely brown-haired girl in the yellow shift was destined.

"I grant her wish," said Kutaituchik. Then to a warrior nearby, he said, "Bring meat."

The warrior leapt from the dais and, in a few moments, returned with a handful of roasted bosk meat.

Kutaituchik gestured for the girl, trembling, to be brought forward, and the two warriors brought her to him, placing her directly before him.

He took the meat in his hand and gave it to Kamchak, who bit into it, a bit of juice running at the side of his mouth; Kamchak then held the meat to the girl.

"Eat," I told her.

Elizabeth Cardwell took the meat in her two hands, confined before her by slave bracelets and the chain of the Sirik, and, bending her head, the hair falling forward, ate it.

She, a slave, had accepted meat from the hand of Kamchak of the Tuchuks.

She belonged to him now.

"La Kajira," she said, putting her head down, then covering her face with her manacled hands, weeping. "La Kajira. La Kajira!"

8

The Wintering

If I had hoped for an easy answer to the riddles which concerned me, or a swift end to my search for the egg of Priest-Kings, I was disappointed, for I learned nothing of either for months.

I had hoped to go to Turia, there to seek the answer to the mystery of the message collar, but it was not to be, at least until the spring.

"It is the Omen Year," had said Kamchak of the Tuchuks.

The herds would circle Turia, for this was the portion of the Omen Year called the Passing of Turia, in which the Wagon Peoples gather and begin to move toward their winter pastures; the second portion of the Omen Year is the Wintering, which takes place far north of Turia, the equator being approached in this hemisphere, of course, from the south; the third and final portion of the Omen Year is the Return to Turia, which takes place in the spring, or as the Wagon Peoples have it, in the Season of Little Grass. It is in the spring that the omens are taken, regarding the possible election of the Ubar San, the One Ubar, he who would be Ubar of all the Wagons, of all the Peoples.

I did manage, however, from the back of the kaiila, which I learned to ride, to catch a glimpse of distant, high-walled, nine-gated Turia.

It seemed a lofty, fine city, white and shimmering, rising from the plains.

"Be patient, Tarl Cabot," said Kamchak, beside me on his

kaiila. "In the spring there will be the games of Love War and I will go to Turia, and you may then, if you wish, accompany me."

"Good," I said.

I would wait. It seemed, upon reflection, the best thing to do. The mystery of the message collar, intriguing as it might be, was of secondary importance. For the time I put it from my mind. My main interests, my primary objective, surely lay not in distant Turia, but with the wagons.

I wondered on what Kamchak had called the games of Love War, said to take place on the Plains of a Thousand Stakes. I supposed, in time, that I would learn of this.

"After the games of Love War," said Kamchak, "the omens will be taken."

I nodded, and we rode back to the herds.

There had not been, I knew, a Ubar San in more than a hundred years. It did not seem likely, either, that one would be elected in the spring. Even in the time I had been with the wagons I had gathered that it was only the implicit truce of the Omen Year which kept these four fierce, warring peoples from lunging at one another's throats, or more exactly put, at one another's bosk. Naturally, as a Koroban, and one with a certain affection for the cities of Gor, particularly those of the north, particularly Ko-ro-ba, Ar, Thentis and Tharna, I was not disappointed at the likelihood that a Ubar San would not be elected. Indeed, I found few who wished a Ubar San to be chosen. The Tuchuks, like the other Wagon Peoples, are intensely independent. Yet, each ten years, the omens are taken. I originally regarded the Omen Year as a rather pointless institution, but I came to see later that there is much to be said for it: it brings the Wagon Peoples together from time to time, and in this time, aside from the simple values of being together, there is much bosk trading and some exchange of women, free as well as slave; the bosk trading genetically freshens the herds and I expect much the same thing, from the point of view of biology, can be said of the exchange of the women; more importantly, perhaps, for one can always steal women and bosk, the Omen Year provides an institutionalized possibility for the uniting of the Wagon Peoples in a time of crisis, should they be divided and threatened. I think that those of the Wagons who instituted the Omen Year, more than a thousand years ago, were wise men.

How was it, I wondered, that Kamchak was going to Turia in the spring?

I sensed him to be a man of importance with the wagons.

There were perhaps negotiations to be conducted, perhaps having to do with what were called the games of Love War, or perhaps having to do with trade.

I had learned, to my surprise, that trade did occasionally take place with Turia. Indeed, when I had learned this, it had fired my hopes that I might be able to approach the city in the near future, hopes which, as it turned out, were disappointed, though perhaps well so.

The Wagon Peoples, though enemies of Turia, needed and wanted her goods, in particular materials of metal and cloth, which are highly prized among the Wagons. Indeed, even the chains and collars of slave girls, worn often by captive Turian girls themselves, are of Turian origin. The Turians, on the other hand, take in trade for their goods—obtained by manufacture or trade with other cities—principally the horn and hide of the bosk, which naturally the Wagon Peoples, who live on the bosk, have in plenty. The Turians also, I note, receive other goods from the Wagon Peoples, who tend to be fond of the raid, goods looted from caravans perhaps a thousand pasangs from the herds, indeed some of them even on the way to and from Turia itself. From these raids the Wagon Peoples obtain a miscellany of goods which they are willing to barter to the Turians, jewels, precious metals, spices, colored table salts, harnesses and saddles for the ponderous tharlarion, furs of small river animals, tools for the field, scholarly scrolls, inks and papers, root vegetables, dried fish, powdered medicines, ointments, perfume and women, customarily plainer ones they do not wish to keep for themselves; prettier wenches, to their dismay, are usually kept with the wagons; some of the plainer women are sold for as little as a brass cup; a really beautiful girl, particularly if of free birth and high caste, might bring as much as forty pieces of gold; such are, however, seldom sold; the Wagon Peoples enjoy being served by civilized slaves of great beauty and high station; during the day, in the heat and dust, such girls will care for the wagon bosk and gather fuel for the dung fires; at night they will please their masters. The Wagon Peoples sometimes are also willing to barter silks to the Turians, but commonly they keep these for their own slave girls, who wear them in the secrecy of the wagons; free women, incidentally, among the Wagon Peoples are not permitted to wear silk; it is claimed by those of the Wagons, delightfully I think, that any woman who loves the feel of silk on her body is, in the secrecy of her heart and blood, a slave girl, whether or not some master has yet forced her to don the collar. It might be added that there are two items which the Wagon Peoples will not sell or trade to Turia, one is a living bosk and the other is a girl from the city itself, though the latter are sometimes, for the sport of the young men, allowed, as it is said, to run for the city. They are then hunted from the back of the kaiila with bola and thongs.

The winter came fiercely down on the herds some days before expected, with its fierce snows and the long winds that sometimes have swept twenty-five hundred pasangs across the prairies; snow covered the grass, brittle and brown already, and the herds were split into a thousand fragments, each with its own riders, spreading out over the prairie, pawing through the snow, snuffing about, pulling up and chewing at the grass, mostly worthless and frozen. The animals began to die and the keening of women, crying as though the wagons were burning and the Turians upon them, carried over the prairies. Thousands of the Wagon Peoples, free and slave, dug in the snow to find a handful of grass to feed their animals. Wagons had to be abandoned on the prairie, as there was no time to train new bosk to the harness, and the herds must needs keep moving.

At last, seventeen days after the first snows, the edges of the herds began to reach their winter pastures far north of Turia, approaching the equator from the south. Here the snow was little more than a frost that melted in the afternoon sun, and the grass was live and nourishing. Still farther north, another hundred pasangs, there was no snow and the peoples began to sing and once more dance about their fires of bosk dung.

"The bosk are safe," Kamchak had said. I had seen strong men leap from the back of the kaiila and, on their knees, tears in their eyes, kiss the green, living grass. "The bosk are safe," they had cried, and the cry had been taken up by the women and carried from wagon to wagon, "The bosk are safe!"

This year, perhaps because it was the Omen Year, the Wagon Peoples did not advance farther north than was necessary to ensure the welfare of the herds. They did not, in fact, even cross the western Cartius, far from cities, which they often do, swimming the bosk and kaiila, floating the wagons, the men often crossing on the backs of the swimming bosk. It was the Omen Year, and not a year, apparently, in which to risk war with far peoples, particularly not those of cities like Ar, whose warriors had mastered the tarn and might, from the air, have wrought great destruction on the herds and wagons.

The Wintering was not unpleasant, although, even so far north, the days and nights were often quite chilly; the Wagon Peoples and their slaves as well, wore boskhide and furs during this time; both male and female, slave or free, wore furred boots and trousers, coats and the flopping, ear-flapped caps that tied under the chin; in this time there was often no way to mark the distinction between the free woman and the slave girl, save that the hair of the latter must needs be unbound; in some cases, of course, the Turian collar was visible, if worn on the outside of the coat, usually under the furred collar; the men, too, free and slave, were dressed similarly, save that the Kajiri, or he-slaves, wore shackles, usually with a run of about a foot of chain.

On the back of the kaiila, the black lance in hand, bending down in the saddle, I raced past a wooden wand fixed in the earth, on the top of which was placed a dried tospit, a small, wrinkled, yellowish-white peachlike fruit, about the size of a plum, which grows on the tospit bush, patches of which are indigenous to the drier valleys of the western Cartius. They are bitter but edible.

"Well done!" cried Kamchak as he saw the tospit, unsplit, impaled halfway down the shaft of the lance, stopped only by my fist and the retaining strap.

Such a thrust was worth two points for us.

I heard Elizabeth Cardwell's cry of joy as she leaped into the air, clumsy in the furs, clapping her hands. She carried, on a strap around her neck, a sack of tospits. I looked at her and smiled. Her face was vital and flushed with excitement.

"Tospit!" called Conrad of the Kassars, the Blood People, and the girl hastened to set another fruit on the wand.

There was a thunder of kaiila paws on the worn turf and Conrad, with his red lance, nipped the tospit neatly from the tip of the wand, the lance point barely passing into it, he having drawn back at the last instant.

"Well done!" I called to him. My own thrust had been full thrust, accurate enough but rather heavily done; in war, such a thrust might have lost me the lance, leaving it in the body of an enemy. His thrust was clearly, I acknowledged, worth three points.

Kamchak then rode, and he, like Conrad of the Kassars, deftly took the fruit from the wand; indeed, his lance entering the fruit perhaps a fraction of an inch less than had Conrad's. It was, however, also a three-point thrust.

The warrior who then rode with Conrad thundered down the lane in the turf.

There was a cry of disappointment, as the lance tip sheared the fruit, not retaining it, knocking it from the wand. It was only a one-point thrust.

Elizabeth cried out again, with pleasure, for she was of the wagon of Kamchak and Tarl Cabot.

The rider who had made the unsatisfactory thrust suddenly whirled the kaiila toward the girl, and she fell to her knees, realizing she should not have revealed her pleasure at his failure, putting her head to the grass. I tensed, but Kamchak laughed, and held me back. The rider's kaiila was now rearing over the girl, and he brought the beast to rest. With the tip of his lance, stained with the tospit fruit, he cut the strap that held the cap on her head, and then brushed the cap off; then, delicately, with its tip, he lifted her chin that she might look at him.

"Forgive me, Master," said Elizabeth Cardwell.

Slave girls, on Gor, address all free men as master, though, of course, only one such would be her true master.

I was pleased with how well, in the past months, Elizabeth had done with the language. Of course, Kamchak had rented three Turian girls, slaves, to train her; they had done so, binding her wrists and leading her about the wagons, teaching her the words for things, beating her with switches when she made mistakes; Elizabeth had learned quickly. She was an intelligent girl.

It had been hard for Elizabeth Cardwell, particularly the first weeks. It is not an easy transition to make, that from a bright, lovely young secretary in a pleasant, fluorescently lit, air-conditioned office on Madison Avenue in New York City— to a slave girl in the wagon of Tuchuk warrior.

When her interrogation had been completed, and she had collapsed on the dais of Kutaituchik, crying out in misery, "La Kajira. La Kajira!" Kamchak had folded her, still weeping, clad in the Sirik, in the richness of the pelt of the red larl in which she had originally been placed before us.

As I had followed him from the dais I had seen Kutaituchik, the interview ended, absently reaching into the small golden box of kanda strings, his eyes slowly beginning to close.

Kamchak, that night, chained Elizabeth Cardwell in his wagon, rather than beneath it to the wheel, running a short length of chain from a slave ring set in the floor of the wagon box to the collar of her Sirik. He had then carefully wrapped her, shivering and weeping, in the pelt of the red larl.

She lay there, trembling and moaning, surely on the verge of hysteria. I was afraid the next phase of her condition would be one of numbness, shock, perhaps of refusal to believe what had befallen her, madness.

Kamchak had looked at me. He was genuinely puzzled by what he regarded as her unusual emotional reactions. He was, of course, aware that no girl, Gorean or otherwise, could be expected to take lightly a sudden reduction to an abject and complete slavery, particularly considering what that would mean among the wagons.

He did, however, regard Miss Cardwell's responses as rather peculiar, and somewhat reprehensible. Once he got up and kicked her with his furred boot, telling her to be quiet. She did not, of course, understand Gorean, but his intention and his impatience were sufficiently clear to preclude the necessity of a translation. She stopped moaning, but she continued to shiver, and sometimes she sobbed. I saw him take a slave whip from the wall and approach her, and then turn back and replace it on the wall. I was surprised that he had not used it, and wondered why. I was pleased that he had not beaten her, for I might have interfered. I tried to talk to Kamchak and help him to understand the shock that the girl had undergone, the total alteration of her life and circumstances, unexplained—finding herself alone on the prairie, the Tuchuks, the capture, the return to the Wagons, her examination in the grassy avenue, the Sirik, the interrogation, the threat of execution, then the fact, difficult for her to grasp, of being literally an owned slave girl. I tried to explain to Kamchak that her old world had not prepared her for these things, for the slaveries of her old world are of a different kind, more subtle and invisible, thought by some not even to exist.

Kamchak said nothing, but then he got up and from a chest in the wagon he took forth a goblet and filled it with an amber fluid, into which he shook a dark, bluish powder. He

then took Elizabeth Cardwell in his left arm and with his
right hand gave her the drink. Her eyes were frightened, but
she drank. In a few moments she was asleep.

Once or twice that night, to Kamchak's annoyance and my
own loss of sleep, she screamed, jerking at the chain, but we
discovered that she had not awakened.

I supposed that on the morrow Kamchak would call for
the Tuchuk Iron Master, to brand what he called his little
barbarian; the brand of the Tuchuk slave, incidentally, is not
the same as that generally used in the cities, which, for girls,
is the first letter of the expression Kajira in cursive script, but
the sign of the four bosk horns, that of the Tuchuk standard;
the brand of the four bosk horns, set in such a manner as to
somewhat resemble the letter "H," is only about an inch
high; the common Gorean brand, on the other hand, is
usually an inch and a half to two inches high; the brand of the
four bosk horns, of course, is also used to mark the bosk of
the Tuchuks, but there, of course, it is much larger, forming
roughly a six-inch square; following the branding, I supposed
that Kamchak would have one of the tiny nose rings affixed;
all Tuchuk females, slave or free, wear such rings; after these
things there would only remain, of course, an engraved
Turian collar and the clothing of Elizabeth Cardwell Kajir.

In the morning I awakened to find Elizabeth sitting, red-
eyed, at the side of the wagon, leaning back against one of
the poles that supported the wagon hides, wrapped in the pelt
of the red larl.

She looked at me. "I'm hungry," she said.

My heart leaped. The girl was stronger than I had
thought. I was very pleased. On the dais of Kutaituchik I had
feared that she might not be able to survive, that she was too
weak for the world of Gor. I had been troubled that the
shock of her radical transposition between worlds, coupled
with her reduction to servitude, might disarrange her mind,
might shatter her and make her worthless to the Tuchuks,
who might then have simply cast her to the kaiila and herd
sleen. I saw now, however, that Elizabeth Cardwell was
strong, that she would not go mad, that she was determined
to live.

"Kamchak of the Tuchuks is your master," I said. "He will
eat first. Afterward, if he chooses, you will be fed."

She leaned back against the wagon pole. "All right," she
said.

When Kamchak rolled out of his furs Elizabeth, involuntarily, shrank back, until the pole would permit her to withdraw no further.

Kamchak looked at me. "How is the little barbarian this morning?" he asked.

"Hungry," I said.

"Excellent," he said.

He looked at her, her back tight against the wagon pole, clutching the pelt of the larl about her with her braceleted hands.

She was, of course, different from anything he had ever owned. She was his first barbarian. He did not know exactly what to make of her. He was used to girls whose culture had prepared them for the very real possibility of slavery, though perhaps not a slavery as abject as that of being a wench of Tuchuks. The Gorean girl is, even if free, accustomed to slavery; she will perhaps own one or more slaves herself; she knows that she is weaker than men and what this can mean; she knows that cities fall and caravans are plundered; she knows she might even, by a sufficiently bold warrior, be captured in her own quarters and, bound and hooded, be carried on tarnback over the walls of her own city. Moreover, even if she is never enslaved, she is familiar with the duties of slaves and what is expected of them; if she should be enslaved she will know, on the whole, what is expected of her, what is permitted her and what is not; moreover, the Gorean girl is literally educated, fortunately or not, to the notion that it is of great importance to know how to please men; accordingly, even girls who will be free companions, and never slaves, learn the preparation and serving of exotic dishes, the arts of walking, and standing and being beautiful, the care of a man's equipment, the love dances of their city, and so on. Elizabeth Cardwell, of course, knew nothing of these things. I was forced to admit that she was, on almost all counts, pretty much what Kamchak thought—a little barbarian. But, to be sure, a very pretty little barbarian.

Kamchak snapped his fingers and pointed to the rug, Elizabeth then knelt to him, clutching the pelt about her, and put her head to his feet.

She was slave.

To my surprise Kamchak, for no reason that he explained to me, did not clothe Elizabeth Cardwell Kajir, much to the irritation of other slave girls about the camp. Moreover, he did not brand her, nor fix in her nose the tiny golden ring of the Tuchuk women, nor did he even, incomprehensibly, put her in the Turian collar. He did not permit her, of course, to bind or dress her hair; it must be worn loose; that alone, naturally, was sufficient to mark her slave among the wagons.

For clothing he permitted her to cut and sew, as well as she could, a sleeveless garment from the pelt of the red larl. She did not sew well and it amused me to hear her cursing at the side of the wagon, bound now only by a collar and chain to the slave ring, time after time sticking the bone needle into her fingers as it emerged through the hide, or fouling the leather-threaded stitches, which would either be too tight, wrinkling and bunching the fur, or too loose, exposing what might eventually lie beneath it. I gathered that girls such as Elizabeth Cardwell, used to buying machine-made, presewn garments on Earth, were not as skilled as they might be in certain of the homely crafts which used to be associated with homemaking, crafts which might, upon occasion, it seemed, come in handy.

At last she had finished the garment, and Kamchak unchained her that she might rise and put it on.

Not surprisingly, but to my amusement, I noted that it hung serveral inches below her knees, indeed, only about four inches or so above her ankles. Kamchak took one look and, with a quiva, shortened it considerably, indeed, until it hung even more briefly than had the quite short, delightful yellow shift in which she had been captured.

"But it was the length of the leather dresses of the Tuchuk women," Elizabeth had dared to protest.

I translated.

"But you are slave," had said Kamchak.

I translated his remark.

She dropped her head, defeated.

Miss Cardwell had slim, lovely legs. Kamchak, a man, had desired to see them. Besides being a man, of course, Kamchak was her master; he owned the wench; thus he would have his desire. I will admit, if need be, that I was not displeased with his action. I did not particularly mind the sight of the lovely Miss Cardwell moving about the wagon.

Kamchak made her walk back and forth once or twice, and spoke to her rather sharply about her posture, then, to the surprise of both Miss Cardwell and myself, he did not chain her, but told her she might walk about the camp unattended, warning her only to return before dusk and the release of the herd sleen. She dropped her head shyly, and smiled, and sped from the wagon. I was pleased to see her that much free.

"You like her?" I asked.

Kamchak grinned. "She is only a little barbarian," he said. Then he looked at me. "It is Aphris of Turia I want," he said.

I wondered who she might be.

On the whole, it seemed to me that Kamchak treated his little barbarian slave notably well, considering that he was Tuchuk. This does not mean that she was not worked hard, nor that she did not receive a good drubbing now and then, but, on the whole, considering the normal lot of a Tuchuk slave girl, I do not think she was ill used. Once, it might be noted, she returned from searching for fuel with the dung sack, dragging behind her, only half full. "It is all I could find," she told Kamchak. He then, without ceremony, thrust her head first into the sack and tied it shut. He released her the next morning. Elizabeth Cardwell never again brought a half-filled dung sack to the wagon of Kamchak of the Tuchuks.

Now the Kassar, mounted on his kaiila, his lance under the tip of the girl's chin, who knelt before him, looking up at him, suddenly laughed and removed the lance.

I breathed a sign of relief.

He rode his kaiila to Kamchak. "What do you want for your pretty little barbarian slave?" he asked.

"She is not for sale," said Kamchak.

"Will you wager for her?" pressed the rider. He was Albrecht of the Kassars, and, with Conrad of the Kassars, had been riding against myself and Kamchak.

My heart sank.

Kamchak's eyes gleamed. He was Tuchuk. "What are your terms?" he asked.

"On the outcome of the sport," he said, and then pointed to two girls, both his, standing to the left in their furs, "against those two." The other girls were both Turian. They were not barbarians. Both were lovely. Both were, doubtless, well skilled in the art of pleasing the fancy of warriors of the Wagon Peoples.

Conrad, hearing the wager of Albrecht, snorted derisively.

"No," cried Albrecht, "I am serious!"

"Done!" cried Kamchak.

Watching us there were a few children, some men, some

slave girls. As soon as Kamchak had agreed to Albrecht's proposal the children and several of the slave girls immediately began to rush toward the wagons, delightedly crying "Wager! Wager!"

Soon, to my dismay, a large number of Tuchuks, male and female, and their male or female slaves, began to gather near the worn lane on the turf. The terms of the wager were soon well known. In the crowd, as well as Tuchuks and those of the Tuchuks, there were some Kassars, a Paravaci or two, even one of the Kataii. The slave girls in the crowd seemed particularly excited. I could hear bets being taken. The Tuchuks, not too unlike Goreans generally, are fond of gambling. Indeed, it is not unknown that a Tuchuk will bet his entire stock of bosk on the outcome of a single kaiila race; as many as a dozen slave girls may change hands on something as small as the direction that a bird will fly or the number of seeds in a tospit.

The two girls of Albrecht were standing to one side, their eyes shining, trying not to smile with pleasure. Some of the girls in the crowd looked enviously on them. It is a great honor to a girl to stand as a stake in Tuchuk gambling. To my amazement Elizabeth Cardwell, too, seemed rather pleased with the whole thing, though for what reason I could scarcely understand. She came over to me and looked up. She stood on tiptoes in her furred boots and held the stirrup. "You will win," she said.

I wished that I was as confident as she.

I was second rider to Kamchak, as Albrecht was to Conrad, he of the Kassars, the Blood People.

There is a priority of honor involved in being first rider, but points scored are the same by either rider, depending on his performance. The first rider is, commonly, as one might expect, the more experienced, skilled rider.

In the hour that followed I rejoiced that I had spent much of the last several months, when not riding with Kamchak in the care of his bosk, in the pleasant and, to a warrior, satisfying activity of learning Tuchuk weaponry, both of the hunt and war. Kamchak was a skilled instructor in these matters and, freely, hours at a time, until it grew too dark to see, supervised my practice with such fierce tools as the lance, the quiva and bola. I learned as well the rope and bow. The bow, of course, small, for use from the saddle, lacks the range and power of the Gorean longbow or crossbow; still, at close range, with considerable force, firing rapidly, arrow after arrow, it is a fearsome weapon. I was most fond, perhaps, of the balanced saddle knife, the quiva; it is about a foot in length, double edged; it tapers to a daggerlike point. I acquired, I think, skill in its use. At forty feet I could strike a thrown tospit; at one hundred feet I could strike a layered boskhide disk, about four inches in width, fastened to a lance thrust in the turf.

Kamchak had been pleased.

I, too, naturally had been pleased.

But if I had indeed acquired skills with those fierce articles, such skills, in the current contests, were to be tested to the utmost.

As the day grew late points were accumulated, but, to the zest and frenzy of the crowd, the lead in these contests of arms shifted back and forth, first being held by Kamchak and myself, then by Conrad and Albrecht.

In the crowd, on the back of a kaiila, I noted the girl Hereena, of the First Wagon, whom I had seen my first day in the camp of the Tuchuks, she who had almost ridden down Kamchak and myself between the wagons. She was a very exciting, vital, proud girl and the tiny golden nose ring, against her brownish skin, with her flashing black eyes, did not detract from her considerable but rather insolent beauty. She, and others like her, had been encouraged and spoiled from childhood in all their whims, unlike most other Tuchuk women, that they might be fit prizes, Kamchak had told me, in the games of Love War. Turian warriors, he told me, enjoy such women, the wild girls of the Wagons. A young man, blondish-haired with blue eyes, unscarred, bumped against the girl's stirrup in the press of the crowd. She struck him twice with the leather quirt in her hand, sharply, viciously. I could see blood on the side of his neck, where it joins the shoulder.

"Slave!" she hissed.

He looked up angrily. "I am not a slave," he said. "I am Tuchuk."

"Turian slave!" she laughed scornfully. "Beneath your furs you wear, I wager, the Kes!"

"I am Tuchuk," he responded, looking angrily away.

Kamchak had told me of the young man. Among the wagons he was nothing. He did what work he could, helping with the bosk, for a piece of meat from a cooking pot. He was called Harold, which is not a Tuchuk name, nor a name used among the Wagon Peoples, though it is similar to some of the Kassar names. It was an English name, but such are not unknown on Gor, having been passed down, perhaps, for more than a thousand years, the name of an ancestor, perhaps brought to Gor by Priest-Kings in what might have been the early Middle Ages of Earth. I knew the Voyages of Acquisition were of even much greater antiquity. I had determined, of course, to my satisfaction, having spoken with him once, that the boy, or young man, was indeed Gorean; his people and their people before them and as far back as anyone knew had been, as it is said, of the Wagons. The problem of the young man, and perhaps the reason that he had not yet won even the Courage Scar of the Tuchuks, was that he had fallen into the hands of Turian raiders in his youth and had spent several years in the city; in his adolescence he had, at great risk to himself, escaped from the city and made his way with great hardships across the plains to rejoin his people; they, of course, to his great disappointment, had not accepted him, regarding him as more Turian than Tuchuk. His parents and people had been slain in the Turian raid in which he had been captured, so he had no kin. There had been, fortunately for him, a Year Keeper who had recalled the family. Thus he had not been slain but had been allowed to remain with the Tuchuks. He did not have his own wagon or his own bosk. He did not even own a kaiila. He had armed himself with castoff weapons, with which he practiced in solitude. None of those, however, who led raids on enemy caravans or sorties against the city and its outlying fields, or retaliated upon their neighbors in the delicate matters of bosk stealing, would accept him in their parties. He had, to their satisfaction, demonstrated his prowess with weapons, but they would laugh at him. "You do not even own a kaiila," they would say. "You do not even wear the Courage Scar." I supposed that the young man would never be likely to wear the scar, without which, among the stern, cruel Tuchuks, he would be the continuous object of scorn, ridicule and contempt. Indeed, I knew that some among the wagons, the girl Hereena, for example, who seemed to bear him a great dislike, had insisted that he, though free, be forced to wear the Kes or the dress of a woman. Such would have been a great joke among the Tuchuks.

I dismissed the girl, Hereena, and the young man, Harold, from my mind.

Albrecht was rearing on his kaiila, loosening the bola at his saddle.

"Remove your furs," he instructed his two girls.

Immediately they did so and, in spite of the brisk, bright chilly afternoon, they stood in the grass, clad Kajir.

They would run for us.

Kamchak raced his kaiila over to the edge of the crowd, entering into swift negotiation with a warrior, one whose wagon followed ours in the march of the Tuchuks. Indeed, it had been from that warrior that Kamchak had rented the girls who had dragged Elizabeth Cardwell about the wagons, teaching her Gorean with thong and switch. I saw a flash of copper, perhaps a tarn disk from one of the distant cities, and one of the warrior's girls, an attractive Turian wench, Tuka, began to remove her fur.

She would run for one of the Kassars, doubtless Conrad.

Tuka, I knew, hated Elizabeth, and Elizabeth, I knew, reciprocated the emotion with vehemence. Tuka, in the matter of teaching Elizabeth the language, had been especially cruel. Elizabeth, bound, could not resist and did she try, Tuka's companions, the others of her wagon, would leap upon her with their switches flailing. Tuka, for her part, understandably had reason to envy and resent the young American slave. Elizabeth Cardwell, at least until now, had escaped, as Tuka had not, the brand, the nose ring and collar. Elizabeth was clearly some sort of favorite in her wagon. Indeed, she was the only girl in the wagon. That alone, though of course it meant she would work very hard, was regarded as a most enviable distinction. Lastly, but perhaps not least, Elizabeth Cardwell had been given for her garment the pelt of a larl, while she, Tuka, must go about the camp like all the others, clad Kajir.

I feared that Tuka would not run well, thus losing us the match, that she would deliberately allow herself to be easily snared.

But then I realized that this was not true. If Kamchak and her master were not convinced that she had run as well as she might, it would not go easily with her. She would have contributed to the victory of a Kassar over a Tuchuk. That night, one of the hooded members of the Clan of Torturers would have come to her wagon and fetched her away, never to be seen again. She would run well, hating Elizabeth or not. She would be running for her life.

Kamchak wheeled his kaiila and joined us. He pointed his lance to Elizabeth Cardwell. "Remove your furs," he said.

Elizabeth did so and stood before us in the pelt of the larl, with the other girls.

Although it was late in the afternoon the sun was still bright. The air was chilly. There was a bit of wind moving the grass.

A black lance was fixed in the prairie about four hundred yards away. A rider beside it, on a kaiila, marked its place. It was not expected, of course, that any of the girls would reach the lance. If one did, of course, the rider would decree her safe. In the run the important thing was time, the dispatch and the skill with which the thing was accomplished. Tuchuk girls, Elizabeth and Tuka, would run for the Kassars; the two Kassar girls would run for Kamchak and myself; naturally each slave does her best for her master, attempting to evade his competitor.

The time in these matters is reckoned by the heartbeat of a standing kaiila. Already one had been brought. Near the animal, on the turf, a long bosk whip was laid in a circle, having a diameter of somewhere between eight and ten feet. The girl begins her run from the circle. The object of the rider is to effect her capture, secure her and return her, in as little time as possible, to the circle of the whip.

Already a grizzled Tuchuk had his hand, palm flat, on the silken side of the standing kaiila.

Kamchak gestured and Tuka, barefoot, frightened, stepped into the circle.

Conrad freed his bola from the saddle strap. He held in his teeth a boskhide thong, about a yard in length. The saddle of the kaiila, like the tarn saddle, is made in such a way as to accommodate, bound across it, a female captive, rings being fixed on both sides through which binding fiber or thong may be passed. On the other hand, I knew, in this sport no time would be taken for such matters; in a few heartbeats of the kaiila the girl's wrists and ankles would be lashed together and she would be, without ceremony, slung over the pommel of the saddle, it the stake, her body the ring.

"Run," said Conrad quietly.

Tuka sped from the circle. The crowd began to cry out, to cheer, urging her on. Conrad, the thong in his teeth, the bola quiet at his side, watched her. She would receive a start of fifteen beats of the great heart of the kaiila, after which she would be about half way to the lance.

The judge, aloud, was counting.

At the count of ten Conrad began to slowly spin the bola.

It would not reach its maximum rate of revolution until he was in full gallop, almost on the quarry.

At the count of fifteen, making no sound, not wanting to warn the girl, Conrad spurred the kaiila in pursuit, bola swinging.

The crowd strained to see.

The judge had begun to count again, starting with one, the second counting, which would determine the rider's time.

The girl was fast and that meant time for us, if only perhaps a beat. She must have been counting to herself because only an instant or so after Conrad had spurred after her she looked over her shoulder, seeing-him approaching. She must then have counted about three beats to herself, and then she began to break her running pattern, moving to one side and the other, making it difficult to approach her swiftly.

"She runs well," said Kamchak.

Indeed she did, but in an instant I saw the leather flash of the bola, with its vicious, beautiful almost ten-foot sweep, streak toward the girl's ankles, and I saw her fall.

It was scarcely ten beats and Conrad had bound the struggling, scratching Tuka, slung her about the pommel, raced back, kaiila squealing, and threw the girl, wrists tied to her ankles, to the turf inside the circle of the boskhide whip.

"Thirty," said the judge.

Conrad grinned.

Tuka, as best she could, squirmed in the bonds, fighting them. Could she free a hand or foot, or even loosen the thong, Conrad would be disqualified.

After a moment or two, the judge said, "Stop," and Tuka obediently lay quiet. The judge inspected the thongs. "The wench is secured," he announced.

In terror Tuka looked up at Kamchak, mounted on his kaiila.

"You ran well," he told her.

She closed her eyes, almost fainting with relief.

She would live.

A Tuchuk warrior slashed apart the thongs with his quiva and Tuka, only too pleased to be free of the circle, leaped up and ran quickly to the side of her master. In a few moments, panting, covered with sweat, she had pulled on her furs.

The next girl, a lithe Kassar girl, stepped into the circle and Kamchak unstrapped his bola. It seemed to me she ran excellently but Kamchak, with his superb skill, snared her easily. To my dismay, as he returned racing toward the circle of the boskhide whip the girl, a fine wench, managed to sink her teeth into the neck of the kaiila causing it to rear squealing and hissing, then striking at her. By the time Kamchak had cuffed the girl from the animal's neck and struck the kaiila's snapping jaws from her twice-bitten leg and returned to the circle, he had used thirty-five beats.

He had lost.

When the girl was released, her leg bleeding, she was beaming with pleasure.

"Well done," said Albrecht, her master, adding with a grin, "—for a Turian slave."

The girl looked down, smiling.

She was a brave girl. I admired her. It was easy to see that she was bound to Albrecht the Kassar by more than a length of slave chain.

At a gesture from Kamchak Elizabeth Cardwell stepped into the circle of the whip.

She was now frightened. She, and I as well, had supposed that Kamchak would be victorious over Conrad. Had he been so, even were I defeated by Albrecht, as I thought likely, the points would have been even. Now, if I lost as well, she would be a Kassar wench.

Albrecht was grinning, swinging the bola lightly, not in a circle but in a gentle pendulum motion, beside the stirrup of the kaiila.

He looked at her. "Run," he said.

Elizabeth Cardwell, barefoot, in the larl's pelt, streaked for the black lance in the distance.

She had perhaps observed the running of Tuka and the Kassar girl, trying to watch and learn, but she was of course utterly inexperienced in this cruel sport of the men of the wagons. She had not, for example, timed her counting, for long hours, under the tutelage of a master, against the heartbeat of a kaiila, he keeping the beat but not informing her what it was, until she had called the beat. Some girls of the Wagon Peoples in fact, incredible though it seems, are trained exhaustively in the art of evading the bola, and such a girl is worth a great deal to a master, who uses her in wagering. One of the best among the wagons I had heard was a Kassar slave, a swift Turian wench whose name was Dina. She had run in actual competition more than two hundred times; almost always she managed to interfere with and postpone her return to the circle; and forty times, an incredible feat, she had managed to reach the lance itself.

At the count of fifteen, with incredible speed, Albrecht, bola now whirling, spurred silently after the fleeing Elizabeth Cardwell. She had misjudged the heartbeat or had not understood the swiftness of the kaiila, never having before observed it from the unenviable point of view of a quarry, because when she turned to see if her hunter had left the vicinity of the circle, he was upon her and as she cried out the bola struck her in an instant binding her legs and throwing her to the turf. It was hardly more than five or six beats, it seemed, before Elizabeth, her wrists lashed cruelly to her ankles, was thrown to the grass at the judge's feet.

"Twenty-five!" announced the judge.

There was a cheer from the crowd, which, though largely composed of Tuchuks, relished a splendid performance.

Weeping Elizabeth jerked and pulled at the thongs restraining her, helpless.

The judge inspected the bonds. "The wench is secured," he said.

Elizabeth moaned.

"Rejoice, Little Barbarian," said Albrecht, "tonight in Pleasure Silk you will dance the Chain Dance for Kassar Warriors."

The girl turned her head to one side, shuddering in the thongs. A cry of misery escaped her.

"Be silent," said Kamchak.

Elizabeth was silent and, fighting her tears, lay quietly waiting to be freed.

I cut the thongs from her wrists and ankles.

"I tried," she said, looking up at me, tears in her eyes. "I tried."

"Some girls," I told her, "have run from the bola more than a hundred times. Some are trained to do so."

"Do you concede?" Conrad asked Kamchak.

"No," said Kamchak. "My second rider must ride."

"He is not even of the Wagon Peoples," said Conrad.

"Nonetheless," said Kamchak, "he will ride."

"He will not beat twenty-five," said Conrad.

Kamchak shrugged. I knew myself that twenty-five was a remarkable time. Albrecht was a fine rider and skilled in this sport and, of course, this time, his quarry had been only an untrained barbarian slave, indeed, a girl who had never before run from the bola.

"To the circle," said Albrecht, to the other Kassar girl.

She was a beauty.

She stepped to the circle quickly, throwing her head back, breathing deeply.

She was an intelligent looking girl.

Black-haired.

Her ankles, I noted, were a bit sturdier than are thought desirable in a slave girl. They had withstood the shock of her body weight many times I gathered, in quick turnings, in leaps.

I wished that I had seen her run before, because most girls will have a running pattern, even in their dodging which, if you have seen it, several times, you can sense. Nothing simple, but something that, somehow, you can anticipate, if only to a degree. It is probably the result of gathering, from their running, how they think; then one tries to think with them and thus meet them with the bola. She was now breathing deeply, regularly. Prior to her entering the circle I had seen her moving about in the background, running a bit, loosening her legs, speeding the circulation of her blood.

It was my guess that this was not the first time she had run from the bola.

"If you win for us," Albrecht said to her, grinning down from the saddle of the kaiila, "this night you will be given a silver bracelet and five yards of scarlet silk."

"I will win for you, Master," she said.

I thought that a bit arrogant for a slave.

Albrecht looked at me. "This wench," he said, "has never been snared in less than thirty-two beats."

I noted a flicker pass through the eyes of Kamchak, but he seemed otherwise impassive.

"She is an excellent runner," I said.

The girl laughed.

Then, to my surprise, she looked at me boldly, though wearing the Turian collar; though she wore the nose ring; though she were only a branded slave clad Kajir.

"I wager," she said, "that I will reach the lance."

This irritated me. Moreover, I was not insensitive to the fact that though she were slave and I a free man, she had not addressed me, as the custom is, by the title of Master. I had no objection to the omission itself, but I did object to the affront therein implied. For some reason this wench seemed to me rather arrogant, rather contemptuous.

"I wager that you do not," I said.

"Your terms!" she challenged.

"What are yours?" I asked.

She laughed. "If I win," she said, "you give me your bola, which I will present to my master."

"Agreed," I said. "And if I should win?"

"You will not," she said.

"But if so?"

"Then," said she, "I will give you a golden ring and a silver cup."

"How is it that a slave has such riches?" I asked.

She tossed her head in the air, not deigning to respond.

"I have given her several such things," said Albrecht.

I now gathered that the girl facing me was not a typical slave, and that there must be a very good reason why she should have such things.

"I do not want your golden ring and silver cup," I said.

"What then could you want?" asked she.

"Should I win," I said, "I will claim as my prize the kiss of an insolent wench."

"Tuchuk sleen!" she cried, eyes flashing.

Conrad and Albrecht laughed. Albrecht said to the girl, "It is permitted."

"Very well, he-tharlarion," said the girl, "your bola—against a kiss." Her shoulders were trembling with rage. "I will show you how a Kassar girl can run!"

"You think well of yourself," I remarked. "You are not a Kassar girl—you are only a Turian slave of Kassars."

Her fists clenched.

In fury she looked at Albrecht and Conrad. "I will run as I have never run before," she cried.

My heart sank a bit. I recalled Albrecht had said that the girl had never been snared in less than thirty-two beats. Then she had doubtless run from the bola several times before, perhaps as many as ten or fifteen.

"I gather," I said to Albrecht, casually, "that the girl has run several times."

"Yes," said Albrecht, "that is true." Then he added, "You may have heard of her. She is Dina of Turia."

Conrad and Albrecht slapped their saddles and laughed uproariously. Kamchak laughed, too, so hard tears ran down the scarred furrows of his face. He pointed a finger at Conrad. "Wily Kassar!" he laughed. This was a joke. Even I had to smile. The Tuchuks were commonly called the Wily Ones. But, though the moment might have been amusing to those of the Wagon Peoples, even to Kamchak, I was not prepared to look on the event with such good humor. It might have been a good trick, but I was in no state of mind to relish it. How cleverly Conrad had pretended to mock Albrecht when he had bet two girls against one. Little did we know that one of those girls was Dina of Turia, who, of course, would run not for the skilled Kamchak, but for his awkward friend, the clumsy Tarl Cabot, not even of the Wagon Peoples, new to the kaiila and bola! Conrad and Albrecht had perhaps even come to the camp of the Tuchuks with this in mind. Undoubtedly! What could they lose? Nothing. The best that we might have hoped for was a tie, had Kamchak beaten Conrad. But he had not; the fine little Turian wench who had been able to bite the neck of the kaiila, thereby risking her life incidentally, had seen to that. Albrecht and Conrad had come for a simple purpose, to best a Tuchuk and, in the process, pick up a girl or two; Elizabeth Cardwell, of course, was the only one we had on hand.

Even the Turian girl, Dina, perhaps the best slave among all the wagons in this sport, was laughing, hanging on the stirrup of Albrecht, looking up at him. I noted that his kaiila was within the whip circle, within which the girl stood. Her feet were off the ground and she had the side of her head pressed against his furred boot.

"Run," I said.

She cried out angrily, as did Albrecht, and Kamchak laughed. "Run, you little fool," shouted Conrad. The girl had released the stirrup and her feet struck the ground. She was off balance but righted herself and with an angry cry she sped from the circle. By surprising her I had gained perhaps ten or fifteen yards.

I took the binding thong from my belt and put it in my teeth.

I began to swing the bola.

To my amazement, as I swung the bola in ever faster circles, never taking my eyes off her, she broke the straight running pattern only about fifty yards from the whip circle, and began to dodge, moving always, however, toward the lance. This puzzled me. Surely she had not miscounted, not Dina of Turia. As the judge counted aloud I observed the pattern, two left, then a long right to compensate, moving toward the lance; two left, then right; two left, then right.

"Fifteen!" called the judge, and I streaked on kaiila back from the circle of the boskhide whip.

I rode at full speed, for there was not a beat to lose. Even if by good fortune I managed to tie Albrecht, Elizabeth would still belong to the Kassars, for Conrad had a clear win over Kamchak. It is dangerous, of course, to approach any but a naive, straight-running, perhaps terrified, girl at full speed, for should she dodge or move to one side, one will have to slow the kaiila to turn it after her, lest one be carried past her too rapidly, even at the margins of bola range. But I could judge Dina's run, two left, one right, so I set the kaiila running at full speed for what would seem to be the unwilling point of rendezvous between Dina and the leather of the bola. I was surprised at the simplicity of her pattern. I wondered how it could be that such a girl had never been taken in less than thirty-two beats, that she had reached the lance forty times.

I would release the bola in another beat as she took her second sprint to the left.

Then I remembered the intelligence of her eyes, her confidence, that never had she been taken in less than thirty-two beats, that she had reached the lance forty times. Her skills must be subtle, her timing marvelous.

I released the bola, risking all, hurling it not to the expected rendezvous of the second left but to a first right, unexpected, the first break in the two-left, one-right pattern. I heard her startled cry as the weighted leather straps flashed about her thighs, calves and ankles, in an instant lashing them together as tightly as though by binding fiber. Hardly slackening speed I swept past the girl, turned the kaiila to face her, and again kicked it into a full gallop. I briefly saw a look of utter astonishment on her beautiful face. Her hands were out, trying instinctively to maintain her balance; the bola weights were still snapping about her ankles in tiny, angry circles; in an instant she would fall to the grass; racing past I seized her by the hair and threw her over the saddle; scarcely did she comprehend what was happening before she found herself my prisoner, while yet the kaiila did still gallop, bound about the pommel of the saddle. I had not taken even the time to dismount. Only perhaps a beat or two before the kaiila leapt into the circle had I finished the knots that confined her. I threw her to the turf at the judge's feet.

The judge, and the crowd, seemed speechless.

"Time!" called Kamchak.

The judge looked startled, as though he could not believe what he had seen. He took his hand from the side of the standing kaiila.

"Time!" called Kamchak.

The judge looked at him. "Seventeen," he whispered.

The crowd was silent, then, suddenly, as unexpectedly as a clap of thunder, they began to roar and cheer.

Kamchak was thumping a very despondent looking Conrad and Albrecht on the shoulders.

I looked down at Dina of Turia. Looking at me in rage, she began to pull and squirm in the thongs, twisting in the grass.

The judge allowed her to do so for perhaps a few Ihn, maybe thirty seconds or so, and then he inspected her bonds. He stood up, a smile on his face. "The wench is secured," he said.

There was another great cry and cheer from the crowd. They were mostly Tuchuks, and were highly pleased with what they had seen, but I saw, too, that even the Kassars and the one or two Paravaci present and the Kataii were unstinting in their acclaim. The crowd had gone mad.

Elizabeth Cardwell was leaping up and down clapping her hands.

I looked down at Dina, who lay at my feet, now no longer struggling.

I removed the bola from her legs.

With my quiva I slashed the thong on her ankles, permitting her to struggle to her feet.

She stood facing me, clad Kajir, her wrists still thonged behind her.

I refastened the bola at my saddle. "I keep my bola, it seems," I said.

She tried to free her wrists, but could not, of course, do so.

Helpless she stood waiting for me.

I then took Dina of Turia in my arms and, at some length, and with a certain admitted satisfaction, collected my winnings. Because she had annoyed me the kiss that was hers was that of master to a slave girl; yet was I patient because the kiss itself was not enough; I was not satisfied until, despite herself, I read in my arms her body's sudden, involuntary admission that I had conquered. "Master," she said, her eyes glazed, too weak to struggle against the thongs that encircled her wrists. With a cheerful slap I sped her back to Albrecht, who, angry, with the tip of his lance, severed the bonds that had confined her. Kamchak was laughing, and Conrad as well. And, too, many in the crowd. Elizabeth

Cardwell, however, to my surprise, seemed furious. She had pulled on her furs. When I looked at her, she looked away, angrily.

I wondered what was the matter with her.

Had I not saved her?

Were not the points between Kamchak and I, and Conrad and Albrecht even?

Was she not safe and the match at an end?

"The score is tied," said Kamchak, "and the wager is concluded. There is no winner."

"Agreed," said Conrad.

"No," said Albrecht.

We looked at him.

"Lance and tospit," he said.

"The match is at an end," I said.

"There is no winner," protested Albrecht.

"That is true," said Kamchak.

"There must be a winner," said Albrecht.

"I have ridden enough for today," said Kamchak.

"I, too," said Conrad. "Let us return to our wagons."

Albrecht pointed his lance at me. "You are challenged," he said. "Lance and tospit."

"We have finished with that," I said.

"The living wand!" shouted Albrecht.

Kamchak sucked in his breath.

Several in the crowd shouted out, "The living wand!"

I looked at Kamchak. I saw in his eyes that the challenge must be accepted. In this matter I must be Tuchuk.

Save for armed combat, lance and tospit with the living wand is the most dangerous of the sports of the Wagon Peoples.

In this sport, as might be expected, one's own slave must stand for one. It is essentially the same sport as lancing the tospit from the wand, save that the fruit is held in the mouth of a girl, who is slain should she move or in any way withdraw from the lance.

Needless to say many a slave girl has been injured in this cruel sport.

"I do not want to stand for him!" cried out Elizabeth Cardwell.

"Stand for him, Slave," snarled Kamchak.

Elizabeth Cardwell took her position, standing sideways, the tospit held delicately between her teeth.

For some reason she did not seem afraid but rather, to my

mind, incomprehensibly infuriated. She should have been shuddering with terror. Instead she seemed indignant.

But she stood like a rock and when I thundered past her the tip of my lance had been thrust through the tospit.

The girl who had bitten the neck of the kaiila, and whose leg had been torn by its teeth, stood for Albrecht.

With almost scornful ease he raced past her lifting the tospit from her mouth with the tip of his lance.

"Three points for each," announced the judge.

"We are finished," I said to Albrecht. "It is a tie. There is no winner."

He held his saddle on his rearing kaiila. "There will be a winner!" he cried. "Facing the lance!"

"I will not ride," I said.

"I claim victory and the woman!" shouted Albrecht.

"It will be his," said the judge, "if you do not ride."

I would ride.

Elizabeth, unmoving, faced me, some fifty yards away.

This is the most difficult of the lance sports. The thrust must be made with exquisite lightness, the lance loose in the hand, the hand not in the retaining thong, but allowing the lance to slip back, then when clear, moving it to the left and, hopefully, past the living wand. If well done, this is a delicate and beautiful stroke. If clumsily done the girl will be scarred, or perhaps slain.

Elizabeth stood facing me, not frightened, but seemingly rather put upon. Her fists were even clenched.

I hoped that she would not be injured. When she had stood sideways I had favored the left, so that if the stroke was in error, the lance would miss the tospit altogether; but now, as she faced me, the stroke must be made for the center of the fruit; nothing else would do.

The gait of the kaiila was swift and even.

A cry went up from the crowd as I passed Elizabeth, the tospit on the point of the lance.

Warriors were pounding on the lacquered shields with their lances. Men shouted. I heard the thrilled cries of slave girls.

I turned to see Elizabeth waver, and almost faint, but she did not do so.

Albrecht the Kassar, angry, lowered his lance and set out for his girl.

In an instant he had passed her, the tospit riding the lance tip.

The girl was standing perfectly still, smiling.

The crowd cheered as well for Albrecht.

Then they were quiet, for the judge was rushing to the lance of Albrecht, demanding it.

Albrecht the Kassar, puzzled, surrendered the weapon.

"There is blood on the weapon," said the judge.

"She was not touched," cried Albrecht.

"I was not touched!" cried the girl.

The judge showed the point of the lance. There was a tiny stain of blood at its tip, and too there was a smear of blood on the skin of the small yellowish-white fruit.

"Open your mouth, slave," demanded the judge.

The girl shook her head.

"Do it," said Albrecht.

She did so and the judge, holding her teeth apart roughly with his hands, peered within. There was blood in her mouth. The girl had been swallowing it, rather than show she had been struck.

It seemed to me she was a brave, fine girl.

It was with a kind of shock that I suddenly realized that she, and Dina of Turia, now belonged to Kamchak and myself.

The two girls, while Elizabeth Cardwell looked on angrily, knelt before Kamchak and myself, lowering their heads, lifting and extending their arms, wrists crossed. Kamchak, chuckling, leaped down from his kaiila and quickly, with binding fiber, bound their wrists. He then put a leather thong on the neck of each and tied the free ends to the pommel of his saddle. Thus secured, the girls knelt beside the paws of his kaiila. I saw Dina of Turia look at me. In her eyes, soft with tears, I read the timid concession that I was her master.

"I do not know what we need with all these slaves," Elizabeth Cardwell was saying.

"Be silent," said Kamchak, "or you will be branded."

Elizabeth Cardwell, for some reason, looked at me in fury, rather than Kamchak. She threw back her head, her little nose in the air, her brown hair bouncing on her shoulders.

Then for no reason I understood, I took binding fiber and bound her wrists before her body, and, as Kamchak had done with the other girls, put a thong on her neck and tied it to the pommel of my saddle.

It was perhaps my way of reminding her, should she forget, that she too was a slave.

"Tonight, Little Barbarian," said Kamchak, winking at her, "you will sleep chained under the wagon."

Elizabeth stifled a cry of rage.

Then Kamchak and I, on kaiila-back, made our way back to our wagon, leading the bound girls.

"The Season of Little Grass is upon us," said Kamchak. "Tomorrow the herds will move toward Turia."

I nodded. The Wintering was done. There would now be the third phase of the Omen Year, the Return to Turia.

It was now, perhaps, I hoped, that I might learn the answer to the riddles which had not ceased to disturb me, that I might learn the answer to the mystery of the message collar, perhaps the answer to the numerous mysteries which had attended it, and perhaps, at last, find some clue, as I had not yet with the wagons, to the whereabouts or fate of the doubtless golden spheroid that was or had been the last egg of Priest-Kings.

"I will take you to Turia," said Kamchak.

"Good," I said.

I had enjoyed the Wintering, but now it was done. The bosk were moving south with the coming of the spring. I and the wagons would go with them.

9

Aphris of Turia

There was little doubt that I, in the worn, red tunic of a warrior, and Kamchak, in the black leather of the Tuchuks, seemed somewhat out of place at the banquet of Saphrar, merchant of Turia.

"It is the spiced brain of the Torian vulo," Saphrar was explaining.

It was somewhat surprising to me that Kamchak and I, being in our way ambassadors of the Wagon Peoples, were entertained in the house of Saphrar, the merchant, rather than in the palace of Phanius Turmus, Administrator of Turia. Kamchak's explanation was reasonably satisfying. There were apparently two reasons, the official reason and the real reason. The official reason, proclaimed by Phanius Turmus, the Administrator, and others high in the government, was that those of the Wagon Peoples were unworthy to be entertained in the administrative palace; the real reason, apparently seldom proclaimed by anyone, was that the true power in Turia lay actually with the Caste of Merchants, chief of whom was Saphrar, as it does in many cities. The Administrator, however, would not be uninformed. His presence at the banquet was felt in the person of his plenipotentiary, Kamras, of the Caste of Warriors, a captain, said to be Champion of Turia.

I shot the spiced vulo brain into my mouth on the tip of a golden eating prong, a utensil, as far as I knew, unique to Turia. I took a large swallow of fierce Paga, washing it down as rapidly as possible. I did not much care for the sweet, syrupy wines of Turia, flavored and sugared to the point where one could almost leave one's fingerprint on their surface.

It might be mentioned, for those unaware of the fact, that the Caste of Merchants is not considered one of the traditional five High Castes of Gor—the Initiates, Scribes, Physicians, Builders and Warriors. Most commonly, and doubtless unfortunately, it is only members of the five high castes who occupy positions on the High Councils of the cities. Nonetheless, as might be expected, the gold of merchants, in most cities, exercises its not imponderable influence, not always in so vulgar a form as bribery and gratuities, but more often in the delicate matters of extending or refusing to extend credit in connection with the projects, desires or needs of the High Councils. There is a saying on Gor, "Gold has no caste." It is a saying of which the merchants are fond. Indeed, secretly among themselves, I have heard, they regard themselves as the highest caste on Gor, though they would not say so for fear of rousing the indignation of other castes. There would be something, of course, to be said for such a claim, for the merchants are often indeed in their way, brave, shrewd, skilled men, making long journeys, venturing their goods, risking caravans, negotiating commercial agreements, among themselves developing and enforcing a body of Merchant Law, the only common legal arrangements existing among the Gorean cities. Merchants also, in effect, arrange and administer the four great fairs that take place each year near the Sardar Mountains. I say "in effect" because the fairs are nominally under the direction of a committee of the Caste of Initiates, which, however, largely contents itself with its ceremonies and sacrifices, and is only too happy to delegate the complex management of those vast, commercial phenomena, the Sardar Fairs, to members of the lowly, much-despised Caste of Merchants, without which, incidentally, the fairs most likely could not exist, certainly not at any rate in their current form.

"Now this," Saphrar the merchant was telling me, "is the braised liver of the blue, four-spined Cosian wingfish."

This fish is a tiny, delicate fish, blue, about the size of a tarn disk when curled in one's hand; it has three or four slender spines in its dorsal fin, which are poisonous; it is capable of hurling itself from the water and, for brief distances, on its stiff pectoral fins, gliding through the air, usually to evade the smaller sea-tharlarions, which seem to be immune to the poison of the spines. This fish is also sometimes referred to as the songfish because, as a portion of its courtship rituals, the males and females thrust their heads from the water and utter a sort of whistling sound.

The blue, four-spined wingfish is found only in the waters of Cos. Larger varieties are found farther out to sea. The small blue fish is regarded as a great delicacy, and its liver as the delicacy of delicacies.

"How is it," I asked, "that here in Turia you can serve the livers of wingfish?"

"I have a war galley in Port Kar," said Saphrar the merchant, "which I send to Cos twice a year for the fish."

Saphrar was a short, fat, pinkish man, with short legs and arms; he had quick bright eyes and a tiny, roundish red-lipped mouth; upon occasion he moved his small, pudgy fingers, with rounded scarlet nails, rapidly, as though rubbing the gloss from a tarn disk or feeling the texture of a fine cloth; his head, like that of many merchants, had been shaved; his eyebrows had been removed and over each eye four golden drops had been fixed in the pinkish skin; he also had two teeth of gold, which were visible when he laughed, the upper canine teeth, probably containing poison; merchants are seldom trained in the use of arms. His right ear had been notched, doubtless in some accident. Such notching, I knew, is usually done to the ears of thieves; a second offense is normally punished by the loss of the right hand; a third offense by the removal of the left hand and both feet. There are few thieves, incidentally, on Gor. I have heard, though, there is a Caste of Thieves in Port Kar, a strong caste which naturally protects its members from such indignities as ear notching. In Saphrar's case, of course, he being of the Caste of Merchants, the notching of the ear would be a coincidence, albeit one that must have caused him some embarrassment. Saphrar was a pleasant, gracious fellow, a bit indolent perhaps, save for the eyes and rapid fingers. He was surely an attentive and excellent host. I would not have cared to know him better.

"How is it," I asked, "that a merchant of Turia has a war galley in Port Kar?"

Saphrar reclined on the yellow cushions, behind the low table covered with wines, fruits and golden dishes heaped with delicate viands.

"I did not realize Port Kar was on friendly terms with any of the inland cities," I said.

"She is not," said Saphrar.

"Then how?" I asked.

He shrugged. "Gold has no caste," he said.

I tried the liver of the wingfish. Then another swig of Paga.

Saphrar winced.

"Perhaps," he suggested, "you would like a piece of roasted bosk meat?"

I replaced the golden eating prong in its rack beside my place, shoved back the glittering dish in which lay several theoretically edible objects, carefully arranged by a slave to resemble a bouquet of wild flowers sprouting from a rock outcropping. "Yes," I said, "I think so."

Saphrar conveyed my wishes to the scandalized Feast Steward, and he, with a glare in my direction, sent two young slaves scampering off to scour the kitchens of Turia for a slice of bosk meat.

I looked to one side and saw Kamchak scraping another plate clean, holding it to his mouth, sliding and shoving the carefully structured design of viands into his mouth.

I glanced at Saphrar, who was now leaning on his yellow cushions, in his silken pleasure robes, white and gold, the colors of the Caste of Merchants. Saphrar, eyes closed, was nibbling on a tiny thing, still quivering, which had been impaled on a colored stick.

I turned away and watched a fire swallower perform to the leaping melodies of the musicians.

"Do not object that we are entertained in the house of Saphrar of the Merchants," Kamchak had said, "for in Turia power lies with such men."

I looked down the table a bit at Kamras, plenipotentiary of Phanius Turmus, Administrator of Turia. He was a large-wristed strong man with long, black hair. He sat as a warrior, though in robes of silk. Across his face there were two long scars, perhaps from their delicacy the scars of quiva wounds. He was said to be a great warrior, indeed, to be champion of Turia. He had not spoken with us nor acknowledged our presence at the feast.

"Besides," Kamchak had told me, nudging me in the ribs, "the food and the entertainment is better in the house of Saphrar than in the palace of Phanius Turmus."

I would still, I told myself, settle for a piece of bosk meat.

I wondered how the stomach of Kamchak could sustain the delightful injuries he was heaping into it with such gusto.

To be sure, it had not. The Turian feast usually consumes the better part of a night and can have as many as a hundred and fifty courses. This would be impractical, naturally, save for the detestable device of the golden bowl and tufted banquet stick, dipped in scented oils, by means of which the diner may, when he wishes, refresh himself and return with eagerness to the feast. I had not made use of this particular tool, and had contented myself with merely taking a bite or two, to satisfy the requirements of etiquette, from each course.

The Turians, doubtless, regarded this as a hopelessly barbarian inhibition on my part.

I had, perhaps, however, drunk too much Paga.

This afternoon Kamchak and I, leading four pack kaiila, had entered the first gate of nine-gated Turia.

On the pack animals were strapped boxes of precious plate, gems, silver vessels, tangles of jewelry, mirrors, rings, combs, and golden tarn disks, stamped with the signs of a dozen cities. These were brought as gifts to the Turians, largely as a rather insolent gesture on the part of the Wagon Peoples, indicating how little they cared for such things, that they would give them to Turians. Turian embassies to the Wagon Peoples, when they occurred, naturally strove to equal or surpass these gifts. Kamchak told me, a sort of secret I gather, that some of the things he carried had been exchanged back and forth a dozen times. One small, flat box, however, Kamchak would not turn over to the stewards of Phanius Turmus, whom he met at the first gate. He insisted on carrying that box with him and, indeed, it rested beside his right knee at the table now.

I was very pleased to enter Turia, for I have always been excited by a new city.

I found Turia to match my expectations. She was luxurious. Her shops were filled with rare, intriguing paraphernalia. I smelled perfumes that I had never smelled before. More than once we encountered a line of musicians dancing single file down the center of the street, playing on their flutes and drums, perhaps on their way to a feast. I was pleased to see again, though often done in silk, the splendid varieties of caste colors of the typical Gorean city, to hear once more the cries of peddlers that I knew so well, the cake sellers, the hawkers of vegetables, the wine vendor bending under a double verrskin of his vintage. We did not attract as much attention as I had thought we would, and I gathered that every spring, at least, visitors from the Wagon Peoples must come to the city. Many people scarcely glanced at us, in spite of the fact that we were theoretically blood foes. I suppose that life in high-walled Turia, for most of its citizens, went on from day to day in its usual patterns oblivious of the usually distant Wagon Peoples. The city had never fallen, and had not been under siege in more than a century. The average citizen worried about the Wagon Peoples, customarily, only when he was outside the walls. Then, of course, he worried a great deal, and, I grant him, wisely.

One disappointment to me in trekking through the streets of Turia was that a crier advanced before us, calling to the women of the city to conceal themselves, even the female slaves. Thus, unfortunately, save for an occasional furtive pair of dark eyes peering from behind a veil in a recessed casement, we saw in our journey from the gate of the city to the House of Saphrar none of the fabled, silken beauties of Turia.

I mentioned this to Kamchak and he laughed loudly.

He was right, of course. Among the Wagons, clad in a brief bit of cord and leather, branded, wearing nose ring and Turian collar, could be found many of the beauties of Turia. Indeed, to the annoyance of Elizabeth Cardwell, who had spent her nights under the wagon in the last weeks, there were two such in our own wagon, the girl Dina, whom I had snared in the contests of the bola, and her companion, the fine wench who had bitten the neck of Kamchak's kaiila and had attempted to conceal her injury by the lance of Albrecht; her name was Tenchika, a Tuchuk corruption of her Turian name, Tendite; she struggled to serve Kamchak well, but it was clear that she lamented her separation from Albrecht of the Kassars; he had, surprisingly, twice tried to buy his little slave back, but Kamchak was holding out for a higher price; Dina, on the other hand, served me skillfully and devotedly; once Albrecht, having a bola match planned, tried to buy her back, as well as Tenchika, but I had demurred.

"Does it mean," Dina had asked me that night, head to boot, "that Dina's master is pleased with her?"

"Yes," I said, "it does."

"I am happy," she had said.

"She has fat ankles," Elizabeth Cardwell had observed.

"Not fat," I said, "—strong, sturdy ankles."

"If you like fat ankles," Elizabeth had said, turning about, perhaps inadvertently revealing the delightful slimness of her own ankles, and leaving the wagon.

Suddenly I became aware again of the banquet of Saphrar of Turia.

My piece of bosk meat, roasted, had arrived. I picked it up and began to chew on it. I liked it better cooked over the open-fires on the prairie, but it was good bosk. I sank my teeth into the juicy meat, tearing it and chewing on it.

I observed the banquet tables, laid out in an open-ended rectangle, permitting slaves to enter at the open end, facilitating the serving, and, of course, allowing entertainers to perform among the tables. To one side there was a small altar to Priest-Kings, where there burned a small fire. On this fire, at the beginning of the feast the feast steward had scattered some grains of meal, some colored salt, some drops of wine. "Ta-Sardar-Gor," he had said, and this phrase had been repeated by the others in the room. "To the Priest-Kings of Gor." It had been the general libation for the banquet. The only one in the room who did not participate in this ceremony was Kamchak, who thought that such a libation, in the eyes of the sky, would not have been fitting. I partook of the libation out of respect for Priest-Kings, for one in particular, whose name was Misk.

A Turian sitting a few feet from me noted that I had partaken of the libation. "I see," he said, "that you were not raised among the wagons."

"No," I said.

"He is Tarl Cabot of Ko-ro-ba," Saphrar had remarked.

"How is it," I asked, "that you know my name?"

"One hears of such things," he said.

I would have questioned him on this matter, but he had turned to a man behind him and was talking with him, some matter I gathered pertaining to the feast.

I forgot about it.

If there had been no women for us to view in the streets of Turia, Saphrar, merchant of the city, had determined to make that omission good at his banquet. There were several women present at the tables, free women, and several others, slaves, who served. The free women, shamelessly to the mind of the rather prudish Kamchak, lowered their veils and threw back the hoods of their Robes of Concealment, enjoying the feast, eating with much the same Gorean gusto as their men. Their beauty and the sparkle of their eyes, their laughter and

conversation, to my mind, immeasurably improved the evening. Many were swift-tongued, witty wenches, utterly charm-
ing and uninhibited. I did think, however, that it was somewhat unusual that they should appear in public unveiled,
particularly with Kamchak and myself present. The women
in bondage present, who served us, each wore four golden
rings on each ankle and each wrist, locked on, which clashed
as they walked or moved, adding their sound to the slave
bells that had been fixed on their Turian collars, and that
hung from their hair; the ears of each, too, had been pierced
and from each ear hung a tiny slave bell. The single garment
of these women was the Turian camisk. I do not know
particularly why it is referred to as a camisk, save that it is a
simple garment for a female slave. The common camisk is a
single piece of cloth, about eighteen inches wide, thrown over
the girl's head and worn like a poncho. It usually falls a bit
above the knees in the front and back and is belted with cord
or chain. The Turian camisk, on the other hand, if it were to
be laid out on the floor, would appear somewhat like an
inverted "T" in which the bar of the "T" would be beveled
on each side. It is fastened with a single cord. The cord binds
the garment on the girl at three points, behind the neck,
behind the back, and in front at the waist. The garment
itself, as might be supposed, fastens behind the girl's neck,
passes before her, passes between her legs and is then lifted
and, folding the two sides of the T's bar about her hips, ties
in front. The Turian camisk, unlike the common camisk, will
cover a girl's brand; on the other hand, unlike the common
camisk, it leaves the back uncovered and can be tied, and is,
snugly, the better to disclose the girl's beauty.

We had been treated to exhibitions of juggling, fire swallowing, and acrobats. There had been a magician, who particularly pleased Kamchak, and a man who, whip in hand,
guided a dancing sleen through its paces.

I could pick up snatches of conversation between Kamchak and Saphrar, and I gathered from what was said that
they were negotiating places of meeting for the exchange
of goods. Then, later in the evening, when I was drunker on
Paga than I should have permitted myself to become, I heard
them discuss details which could only have pertained to what
Kamchak had called the games of Love War, details having
to do with specifications of time, weapons and judges, and
such. Then I heard the sentence, "If she is to participate, you
must deliver the golden sphere."

Abruptly, it seemed, I came awake, no longer half asleep, more than half drunk. It seemed suddenly I was shocked awake and sober. I began to tremble, but held the table, and, I believe, betrayed no sign of my inward excitement.

"I can arrange that she is chosen for the games," Saphrar was saying, "but it must be worth my while."

"How can you determine that she is selected?" Kamchak was asking.

"My gold can determine that," Saphrar was saying, "and further determine that she is ill defended."

Out of the corner of my eye I could see Kamchak's black eyes gleaming.

Then I heard the feast steward call out, his voice silencing all else, all conversation, even the musicians. The acrobats who were at the moment performing fled from between the tables. The feast steward's voice was heard, "The Lady Aphris of Turia."

I and all others turned our eyes to a wide, swirling marble stairway in the back and to the left of the lofty banquet hall in the house of Saphrar the merchant.

Down the stairway, slowly, in trailing white silk bordered with gold, the colors of the Merchants, there regally descended the girl who was Aphris of Turia.

Her sandals were of gold and she wore matching gloves of gold.

Her face could not be seen, for it was veiled, a white silken veil trimmed with gold, nor even her hair, for it was hidden in the folds of the free woman's Robes of Concealment, in her case, of course, done in the colors of the merchants.

Aphris of Turia, then, was of the caste of merchants.

I recalled Kamchak had spoken of her once or twice.

As the woman approached I suddenly became aware again of Saphrar speaking. "Behold my ward," he was saying, indicating the approaching girl.

"The richest woman in all Turia," Kamchak said.

"When she reaches her majority," Saphrar remarked.

Until then, I gathered, her means were in the doubtless capable hands of Saphrar the merchant.

This supposition was later confirmed by Kamchak. Saphrar was not related to the girl, but had been appointed by the Turian merchants, on whom he undoubtedly exercised considerable influence, the guardian of the girl following the death of her father in a Paravaci caravan raid several years before. The father of Aphris of Turia, Tethrar of Turia, had been the richest merchant in this city, itself one of the richest cities of Gor. There had been no surviving male heir and the considerable wealth of Tethrar of Turia was now that of his daughter, Aphris, who would assume control of these remarkable fortunes upon attaining her majority, which event was to occur this spring.

The girl, not unaware I am sure of the eyes upon her, stopped on the stairway and loftily surveyed the scene of the banquet. I could sense that she had almost immediately seen myself and Kamchak, strangers at the tables. Something in her carriage suggested that she might be amused.

I heard Saphrar whisper to Kamchak, whose eyes glowed as they rested on the figure in white and gold on the distant stairway.

"Is she not worth the golden sphere?" asked the merchant.

"It is hard to tell," said Kamchak.

"I have the word of her serving slaves," insisted Saphrar. "She is said to be marvelous."

Kamchak shrugged, his wily Tuchuk trading shrug. I had seen him use it several times while discussing the possible sale of little Tenchika to Albrecht in the wagon.

"The sphere is actually not of much value, Saphrar was saying, "it is not truly of gold—but only appears so."

"Still," Kamchak said, "the Tuchuks are fond of it."

"I would only wish it as a curiosity," Saphrar was saying.

"I must think on the matter," Kamchak was saying, not taking his eyes from Aphris of Turia.

"I know where it is," Saphrar was saying, his lips pulled back, revealing the golden canines, "I could send men for it."

Pretending not to listen I was, of course, as attentive as possible to their conversation. But few in that room would have noted my interest had I displayed it openly. All eyes, it seemed, were on the girl on the stairs, slim, said to be beautiful, veiled, clad in Robes of Concealment of white and gold. Even I was distracted by her. Even I, in spite of my preoccupation with the conversation of Kamchak and Saphrar, would have found it difficult, had I wished, to take my eyes from her. Now she descended the last three stairs and, stopping to nod her head and grace an eager fellow here and there along the tables with a word or gesture, she began to approach the head of the table. The musicians, at a signal from the feast steward, took up their instruments again and the acrobats rushed back among the tables, tumbling and leaping about.

"It is in the wagon of Kutaituchik," Saphrar was saying. "I could send mercenary tarnsmen from the north, but I would prefer not to have war."

Kamchak was still watching Aphris of Turia.

My heart was beating with great rapidity. I had learned now, if Saphrar was correct, that the golden sphere, undoubtedly the last egg of Priest-Kings, was in the wagon of Kutaituchik, said to be Ubar of the Tuchuks. At last, if Saphrar was correct, I knew its location.

I barely noticed, as Aphris of Turia made her way toward the head of the table, that she did not speak to nor acknowledge in any way any of the women present, though their robes suggested they must be of wealth and position. She gave them no sign that she recognized their existence. To a man here and there, however, she would nod her head or exchange a word or two. I thought perhaps Aphris was unwilling to acknowledge unveiled free women. Her own veil, of course, had not been lowered. Over the veil I could now see two black, deep, almond-shaped eyes; her skin, what I could see of it, was lovely and clear; her complexion was not so light as that of Miss Cardwell, but was lighter than that of the girl Hereena, of the First Wagon.

"The golden sphere for Aphris of Turia," Saphrar whispered to Kamchak.

Kamchak turned to the small, fat merchant and his scarred, furrowed face broke into a grin, bearing down on the round, pinkish face of the merchant. "The Tuchuks," he said, "are fond of the golden sphere."

"Very well," snapped Saphrar, "then you will not obtain the woman—I shall see to that—and somehow I shall have the sphere—understand that!"

Kamchak now turned to watch Aphris of Turia.

The girl now approached us, behind the tables, and Saphrar leaped to his feet and bowed low to her. "Honored Aphris of Turia, whom I love as my own daughter," he said.

The girl inclined her head to him, "Honored Saphrar," she said.

Saphrar gestured to two of the camisk-clad girls in the room, who brought cushions and a silken mat and placed them between Saphrar and Kamchak.

Aphris nodded her head to the feast steward and he sent the acrobats running and tumbling from the room and the musicians began to play soft, honeyed melodies. The guests at the banquet returned to their conversation and repast.

Aphris looked about her.

She lifted her head, and I could see the lovely line of her nose beneath the veil of white silk trimmed with gold. She sniffed twice. Then she clapped her little gloved hands two times and the feast steward rushed to her side.

"I smell bosk dung," she said.

The feast steward looked startled, then horrified, then knowledgeable, and then bowed and spread his hands. He smiled ingratiatingly, apologetically. "I am sorry, Lady Aphris," said he, "but under the circumstances—"

She looked about, and then it seemed she saw Kamchak. "Ah!" she said, "I see—a Tuchuk—of course."

Kamchak, though sitting cross-legged, seemed to bounce twice on the cushions, slapping the small table, rattling dishes for a dozen feet on either side. He was roaring with laughter.

"Superb!" he cried.

"Please, if you wish, Lady Aphris, join us," wheezed Saphrar.

Aphris of Turia, pleased with herself, assumed her place between the merchant and Kamchak, kneeling back on her heels in the position of the Gorean free woman.

Her back was very straight and her head high, in the Gorean fashion.

She turned to Kamchak. "It seems we have met before," she said.

"Two years ago," said Kamchak, "in such a place at such a time—you recall it was then you called me a Tuchuk sleen."

"I seem to recall," said Aphris, as though trying very hard to do so.

"I had brought you a five-belt necklace of diamonds," said Kamchak, "for I had heard you were beautiful."

"Oh," said Aphris, "yes—I gave it to one of my slaves."

Kamchak slapped the table in merriment again.

"It was then," he said, "that you turned away, calling me a Tuchuk sleen."

"Oh, yes!" laughed Aphris.

"And it was then," said Kamchak, still laughing, "that I vowed I would make you my slave."

Aphris stopped laughing.

Saphrar was speechless.

There was no sound at the tables.

Kamras, Champion of the City of Turia, rose to his feet.

He addressed Saphrar. "Permit me," he said, "to fetch weapons."

Kamchak was now swilling Paga and acted as though he had not heard the remark of Kamras.

"No, no, no!" cried Saphrar. "The Tuchuk and his friend are guests, and ambassadors of the Wagon Peoples—they must not come to harm!"

Aphris of Turia laughed merrily and Kamras, embarrassed, returned to his seat.

"Bring perfumes!" she called to the feast steward, and he sent forth the camisk-clad slave who carried the tiny tray of exotic Turian perfumes. She took one or two of these small bottles and held them under her nose, and then sprinkled them about the table and cushions. Her actions delighted the Turians, who laughed.

Kamchak now was still smiling, but he no longer laughed. "For that," he said, smiling, "you will spend your first night in the dung sack."

Again Aphris laughed merrily and was joined by those of the banquet.

The fists of Kamras were clenched on the table.

"Who are you?" asked Aphris, looking at me.

I was pleased to see that she, at least, did not know my name.

"I am Tarl Cabot," I said, "—of the city of Ko-ro-ba."

"It is in the far north," she said. "Even beyond Ar."

"Yes," I said.

"How comes it," asked she, "that a Koroban rides in the stinking wagon of a Tuchuk sleen?"

"The wagon does not stink," I said, "and Kamchak of the Tuchuks is my friend."

"You are an outlaw of course," she said.

I shrugged.

She laughed.

The girl turned to Saphrar. "Perhaps the barbarians would care to be entertained," she suggested.

I was puzzled at this, for throughout much of the evening there had been entertainment, the jugglers, the acrobats, the fellow who swallowed fire to music, the magician, the man with the dancing sleen.

Saphrar was looking down. He was angry. "Perhaps," he said. I supposed Saphrar was still irritated at Kamchak's refusal to give up, or arrange the transfer, of the golden sphere. I did not clearly understand Kamchak's motivations

in this matter—unless, of course, he knew the true nature of
the golden sphere, in which case, naturally, he would recognize it as priceless. I gathered he did not understand its true
value, seeing that he had apparently discussed its exchange
with some seriousness earlier in the evening—only that, apparently, he wanted more than Saphrar was offering, even
though that might be Aphris of Turia herself.

Aphris now turned to me. She gestured to the ladies at the
tables, with their escorts. "Are the women of Turia not
beautiful?" she asked.

"Indeed," I admitted, for there were none present who
were not, in their own ways, beautiful.

She laughed, for some reason.

"In my city," I said, "free women would not permit themselves to be seen unveiled before strangers."

The girl laughed merrily once more and turned to
Kamchak. "What think you, my colorful bit of bosk dung?"
she asked.

Kamchak shrugged. "It is well known," he said, "the wom-
en of Turia are shameless."

"I think not," snapped the angry Aphris of Turia, her eyes
flashing above the golden border of her white silken veil.

"I see them," said Kamchak, spreading his hands to both
sides, grinning.

"I think not," said the girl.

Kamchak looked puzzled.

Then, to my surprise, the girl clapped her hands sharply
twice and the women about the table stood, and together,
from both sides, moved swiftly to stand before us between
the tables. The drums and flutes of the musicians sounded, and
to my amazement the first girl, with a sudden, graceful swirl
of her body lifted away her robes and flung them high over
the heads of the guests to cries of delight. She stood facing
us, beautiful, knees flexed, breathing deeply, arms lifted over
her head, ready for the dance. Each of the women I had
thought free did the same, until each stood before us, a
collared slave girl clad only in the diaphanous, scarlet dancing silks of Gor. To the barbaric music they danced.

Kamchak was angry.

"Did you truly think," asked Aphris of Turia arrogantly,
"that a Tuchuk would be permitted to look upon the face of
a free woman of Turia?"

Kamchak's fists were clenched on the table, for no Tuchuk
likes to be fooled.

Kamras was laughing loudly and even Saphrar was giggling among the yellow cushions.

No Tuchuk, I knew, cares to be the butt of a joke, especially a Turian joke.

But Kamchak said nothing.

Then he took his goblet of Paga and drained it, watching the girls swaying to the caress of Turian melodies.

"Are they not delightful?" spurred Aphris, after a time.

"We have many girls among the wagons quite as good," said Kamchak.

"Oh?" asked Aphris.

"Yes," said Kamchak, "Turians—slaves—such as you will be."

"You are aware, of course," she said, "that if you were not an ambassador of the Wagon Peoples at this time I would order you slain."

Kamchak laughed. "It is one thing to order the death of a Tuchuk," he said. "It is another to kill him."

"I'm sure both could be arranged," remarked Aphris.

Kamchak laughed. "I shall enjoy owning you," he said.

The girl laughed. "You are a fool," she said. Then she added, unpleasantly, "But beware—for if you cease to amuse me—you will not leave these tables alive."

Kamchak was swilling down another bolt of Paga, part of it running out at the side of his mouth.

Aphris then turned to Saphrar. "Surely our guests would enjoy seeing the others?" she suggested.

I wondered what she meant.

"Please, Aphris," said Saphrar, shaking his fat, pinkish head, sweating. "No trouble, no trouble."

"Ho!" cried Aphris of Turia, summoning the feast steward to her, through the turning bodies of the girls dancing among the tables. "The others!" ordered Aphris, "—for the amusement of our guests!"

The feast steward turned a wary eye toward Saphrar, who, defeated, nodded his head.

The feast steward then clapped his hands twice, dismissing the girls, who rushed from the room; and then he clapped his hands twice more, paused a moment, then twice more.

I heard the sound of slave bells attached to ankle rings, to locked wrist bracelets, to Turian collars.

More girls approached rapidly, their feet taking small running steps in a turning line that sped forth from a small room in the back and to the right.

My hand clenched on the goblet. Aphris of Turia was bold indeed. I wondered if Kamchak would rise to do war in the very room.

The girls that now stood before us, barefoot, in swirling Pleasure Silks, belled and collared, were wenches of the Wagon Peoples, now, as could be determined even beneath the silks they wore, the branded slaves of Turians. Their leader, to her surprise, seeing Kamchak, fell in shame to her knees before him, much to the fury of the feast steward; the others did so as well.

The feast steward was handed a slave whip and stood towering over the leader of the girls.

His hand drew back but the blow never fell, for with a cry of pain he reeled away, the hilt of a quiva pressed against the inside of his forearm, the balance of the blade emerging on the other side.

Even I had not seen Kamchak throw the knife, Now, to my satisfaction, another of the blades was poised in his finger tips. Several of the men had leaped from behind the tables, including Kamras, but they hesitated, seeing Kamchak so armed. I, too, was on my feet. "Weapons," said Kamras, "are not permitted at the banquet."

"Ah," said Kamchak, bowing to him, "I did not know."

"Let us sit down and enjoy ourselves, recommended Saphrar. "If the Tuchuk does not wish to see the girls, let us dismiss them."

"I wish to see them perform," said Aphris of Turia, though she stood within arm's reach of Kamchak's quiva.

Kamchak laughed, looking at her. Then, to my relief, and doubtless to the relief of several at the table, he thrust the quiva in his sash and sat back down.

"Dance," ordered Aphris.

The trembling girl before her did not move.

"Dance!" screamed Aphris, rising to her feet.

"What shall I do?" begged the kneeling girl of Kamchak. She looked not too unlike Hereena, and was perhaps a similar sort of girl, raised and trained much the same. Like Hereena, of course, she wore the tiny golden nose ring.

Kamchak spoke to her, very gently. "You are slave," he said. "Dance for your masters."

The girl looked at him gratefully and she, with the others, rose to her feet and to the astounding barbarity of the music performed the savage love dances of the Kassars, the Paravaci, the Kataii, the Tuchuks.

They were magnificent.

One girl, the leader of the dancers, she who had spoken to Kamchak, was a Tuchuk girl, and was particularly startling, vital, uncontrollable, wild.

It was then clear to me why the Turian men so hungered for the wenches of the Wagon Peoples.

At the height of one of her dances, called the Dance of the Tuchuk Slave Girl, Kamchak turned to Aphris of Turia, who was watching the dance, eyes bright, as astounded as I at the savage spectacle. "I will see to it," said Kamchak, "when you are my slave, that you are taught that dance."

The back and head of Aphris of Turia was rigid with fury, but she gave no sign that she had heard him.

Kamchak waited until the girls of the Wagon Peoples had performed their dances and then, when they had been dismissed, he rose to his booted feet. "We must go," he said.

I nodded, and struggled to my feet, well ready to return to his wagon.

"What is in the box?" asked Aphris of Turia, as she saw Kamchak pick up the small black box which, throughout the banquet, he had kept at his right knee. The girl was clearly curious, female.

Kamchak shrugged.

I remembered that two years before, as I had learned, he had brought Aphris of Turia a five-string diamond necklace, which she had scorned, and had, according to her report at least, given to a slave. It had been at that time that she had called him a Tuchuk sleen, presumably because he had dared present her with a gift.

But, I could see, she was interested in the box. Indeed, at certain times during the evening, I had seen her casting furtive glances at it.

"It is nothing," said Kamchak, "only a trinket."

"But is it for someone?" she asked.

"I had thought," said Kamchak, "that I might give it to you."

"Oh?" asked Aphris, clearly intrigued.

"But you would not like it," he said.

"How do you know," she said, rather airily, "I have not seen it."

"I will take it home with me," said Kamchak.

"If you wish," she said.

"But you may have it if you wish," he said.

"Is it other," she asked, "than a mere necklace of dia-

monds?" Aphris of Turia was no fool. She knew that the
Wagon Peoples, plunderers of hundreds of caravans, occasionally possessed objects and riches as costly as any on Gor.

"Yes," said Kamchak, "it is other than a necklace of
diamonds."

"Ah!" she said. I then suspected that she had not actually
given the five-string diamond necklace to a slave. Undoubtedly it still reposed in one of her several chests of jewelry.

"But you would not like it," said Kamchak, diffidently.

"Perhaps I might," she said.

"No," said Kamchak, "you would not like it."

"You brought it for me, did you not?" she said.

Kamchak shrugged and looked down at the box in his
hand. "Yes," he said, "I brought it for you."

The box was about the size in which a necklace, perhaps
on black velvet, might be displayed.

"I want it," said Aphris of Turia.

"Truly?" asked Kamchak. "Do you want it?"

"Yes," said Aphris. "Give it to me!"

"Very well," said Kamchak, "but I must ask to place it on
you myself."

Kamras, the Champion of Turia, half rose from his position. "Bold Tuchuk sleen!" he hissed.

"Very well," said Aphris of Turia. "You may place it on
me yourself."

So then Kamchak bent down to where Aphris of Turia
knelt, her back straight, her head very high, before the low
table. He stepped behind her and she lifted her chin delicately. Her eyes were shining with curiosity. I could see the
quickness of her breath marked in the soft silk of her white
and gold veil.

"Now," said Aphris.

Kamchak then opened the box.

When Aphris heard the delicate click of the box lid it was
all she could do not to turn and regard the prize that was to
be hers, but she did not do so. She remained looking away,
only lifting her chin a bit more.

"Now!" said Aphris of Turia, trembling with anticipation.

What happened then was done very swiftly. Kamchak
lifted from the box an object indeed intended to grace the
throat of a girl. But it was a round metal ring, a Turian
collar, the collar of a slave. There was a firm snap of the
heavy lock in the back of the collar and the throat of Aphris
of Turia had been encircled with slave steel! At the same

instant Kamchak lifted her startled to her feet and turned her to face him, with both hands tearing the veil from her face! Then, before any of the startled Turians could stop him, he had purchased by his audacity a bold kiss from the lips of the astounded Aphris of Turia! Then he hurled her from him across and over the low table until she fell to the floor where Tuchuk slaves had danced for her pleasure. The quiva, appearing as if by magic in his hand, warned back those who would press in upon him to revenge the daughter of their city. I stood beside Kamchak, ready to defend him with my life, yet as startled as any in the room at what had been done.

The girl now had struggled to her knees tearing at the collar. Her tiny gloved fingers were locked in it, pulling at it, as though by brute force she would tear it from her throat.

Kamchak was looking at her. "Beneath your robes of white and gold," he said, "I smelled the body of a slave girl."

"Sleen! Sleen! Sleen!" she cried.

"Replace your veil!" ordered Saphrar.

"Remove the collar immediately," commanded Kamras, plenipotentiary of Phanius Turmus, Administrator of Turia.

Kamchak smiled. "It seems," he said, "that I have forgotten the key."

"Send for one of the Caste of Metal Workers!" cried Saphrar.

There were cries on all sides, "Slay the Tuchuk sleen!" "Torture for him!" "The oil of tharlarions!" "Leech plants!" "Impalement!" "Tongs and fire!" But Kamchak seemed unmoved. And none rushed upon him, for in his hand, and he was Tuchuk, there gleamed the quiva.

"Slay him!" screamed Aphris of Turia, "Slay him!"

"Replace your veil," repeated Saphrar to the girl. "Have you no shame?"

The girl attempted to rearrange the folds of the veil, but could only hold it before her face, for Kamchak had ripped away the pins by which it was customarily fastened.

Her eyes were wild with fury and tears.

He, a Tuchuk, had looked upon her face.

I was pleased, though I would not have admitted it, at Kamchak's boldness, for it was a face for which a man might risk much, even death in the torture dungeons of Turia, utterly beautiful though now, of course, transformed with rage, far more beautiful than had been that of the most beautiful of the slave girls who had served us or given us of the beauty of their dances.

"You recall, of course," Kamchak was saying, "that I am an ambassador of the Wagon Peoples and am entitled to the courtesies of your city."

"Impale him!" cried a number of voices.

"It is a joke," cried out Saphrar. "A joke! A Tuchuk joke!"

"Slay him!" screamed Aphris of Turia.

But no one would move against the quiva.

"Now, gentle Aphris," Saphrar was purring, "you must be calm—soon one from the Caste of Metal Workers will appear to free you—all will be well—return to your own chambers."

"No!" screamed Aphris. "The Tuchuk must be slain!"

"It is not possible, my dear," wheezed Saphrar.

"You are challenged!" said Kamras, spitting to the floor at Kamchak's booted feet.

For an instant I saw Kamchak's eyes gleam and thought he might at the very table at which he stood accept the challenge of the Champion of Turia, but instead, he shrugged and grinned. "Why should I fight?" he asked.

It did not sound like Kamchak speaking.

"You are a coward!" cried Kamras.

I wondered if Kamras knew the meaning of the word which he had dared to address to one who wore the Courage Scar of the Wagon Peoples.

But to my amazement, Kamchak only smiled. "Why should I fight?" he asked.

"What do you mean?" demanded Kamras.

"What is to be gained?" inquired Kamchak.

"Aphris of Turia!" cried the girl.

There were cries of horror, or protest, from the men crowded about.

"Yes!" cried Aphris of Turia. "If you will meet Kamras, Champion of Turia, I—Aphris of Turia—will stand at the stake in Love War!"

Kamchak looked at her. "I will fight," he said.

There was a silence in the room.

I saw Saphrar, a bit in the background, close his eyes and nod his head. "Wily Tuchuk," I heard him mutter. Yes, I said to myself, wily Tuchuk. Kamchak had, by means of the very pride of Aphris of Turia, of Kamras, and the offended Turians, brought the girl by her own will to the stake of Love War. It was something he would not buy with the golden sphere from Saphrar the merchant; it was something he was clearly capable of arranging, with Tuchuk cunning, by himself. I supposed, naturally, however, that Saphrar, guardian of Aphris of Turia, would not permit this to occur.

"No, my dear," Saphrar was saying to the girl, "you must not expect satisfaction for this frightful injury which has been wrought upon you—you must not even think of the games—you must forget this unpleasant evening—you must try not to think of the stories that will be told of you concerning this evening—what the Tuchuk did and how he was permitted to escape with impunity."

"Never!" cried Aphris. "I will stand, I tell you! I will! I will!"

"No," said Saphrar, "I cannot permit it—it is better that the people laugh at Aphris of Turia—and perhaps, in some years, they may forget."

"I demand to be permitted to stand," cried the girl. Then she cried, "I beg of you Saphrar—permit me!"

"But in a few days," said Saphrar, "you will attain your majority and receive your fortunes—then you may do as you wish."

"But it will be after the games!" cried the girl.

"Yes," said Saphrar, as though thinking, "that is true."

"I will defend her," said Kamras. "I will not lose."

"It is true you have never lost," wavered Saphrar.

"Permit it!" cried several of those present.

"Unless you permit this," wept Aphris, "my honor will be forever stained."

"Unless you permit it," said Kamras sternly, "I may never have an opportunity to cross steel with this barbaric sleen.'"

It then occurred to me, suddenly, that, following Gorean civic law, the properties and titles, assets and goods of a given individual who is reduced to slavery are automatically regarded as having been transferred to the nearest male relative—or nearest relative if no adult male relative is available—or to the city—or to, if pertinent, a guardian. Thus, if Aphris of Turia, by some mischance, were to fall to Kamchak, and surely slavery, her considerable riches would be immediately assigned to Saphrar, merchant of Turia. Moreover, to avoid legal complications and free the assets for investment and manipulation, the transfer is asymmetrical, in the sense that the individual, even should he somehow later recover his freedom, retains no legal claim whatsoever on the transferred assets.

"All right," said Saphrar, his eyes cast down, as though making a decision against his better judgment, "I will permit my ward, the Lady Aphris of Turia, to stand at the stake in Love War."

There was a cry of delight from the crowd, confident now that the Tuchak sleen would be fittingly punished for his bold use of the richest daughter of Turia.

"Thank you, my guardian," said Aphris of Turia, and with one last vicious look at Kamchak threw back her head and with a swirl of her white gown, bordered with gold, walked regally from between the tables.

"To see her walk," remarked Kamchak, rather loudly, "one would hardly suspect that she wears the collar of a slave."

Aphris spun to face him, her right fist clenched, her left hand muffling her veil about her face, her eyes flashing. The circle of steel gleamed on the silk at her throat.

"I meant only, little Aphris," said Kamchak, "—that you wear your collar well."

The girl cried out in helpless rage and turned, stumbling and clutching at the banister on the stairs. Then she ran up the stairs, weeping, veil disarranged, both hands jerking at the collar. With a cry she disappeared.

"Have no fear, Saphrar of Turia," Kamras was saying, "I shall slay the Tuchuk sleen—and I shall do so slowly."

10

Love War

It was early in the morning, several days after Saphrar's banquet, that Kamchak and myself, among some hundreds of others of the Four Wagon Peoples, came to the Plains of a Thousand Stakes, some pasangs distant from lofty Turia.

Judges and craftsmen from Ar, hundreds of pasangs away, across the Cartius, were already at the stakes, inspecting them and preparing the ground between them. These men, as in every year, I learned, had been guaranteed safe passage across the southern plains for this event. The journey, even so, was not without its dangers, but they had been well recompensed, from the treasure chests of both Turia and the Wagon Peoples. Some of the judges, now wealthy, had officiated several times at the games. The fee for even one of their accompanying craftsmen was sufficient to support a man for a year in luxurious Ar.

We moved slowly, walking the kaiila, in four long lines, the Tuchuks, the Kassars, the Kataii, the Paravaci, some two hundred or so warriors of each. Kamchak rode near the head of the Tuchuk line. The standard bearer, holding aloft on a lance a representation of the four bosk horns, carved from wood, rode near us. At the head of our line, on a huge kaiila, rode Kutaituchik, his eyes closed, his head nodding, his body swaying with the stately movement of the animal, a half-chewed string of kanda dangling from his mouth.

Beside him, but as Ubars, rode three other men, whom I took to be chief among the Kassars, the Kataii, the Paravaci. I could see, surprisingly near the forefront of their respective

105

lines, the other three men I had first seen on coming to the
Wagon Peoples, Conrad of the Kasars, Hakimba of the
Kataii and Tolnus of the Paravaci. These, like Kamchak,
rode rather near their respective standard bearers. The standard of the Kassars is that of a scarlet, three-weighted bola,
which hangs from a lance; the symbolic representation of a
bola, three circles joined at the center by lines, is used to
mark their bosk and slaves; both Tenchika and Dina wore
that brand; Kamchak had not decided to rebrand them, as is
done with bosk; he thought, rightly, it would lower their
value; also, I think he was pleased to have slaves in his
wagon who wore the brand of Kassars, for such might be
taken as evidence of the superiority of Tuchuks to Kassars,
that they had bested them and taken their slaves; similarly
Kamchak was pleased to have in his herd bosk, and he had
several, whose first brand was that of the three-weighted
bola; the standard of the Kataii is a yellow bow, bound
across a black lance; their brand is also that of a bow, facing
to the left; the Paravaci standard is a large banner of jewels
beaded on golden wires, forming the head and horns of a
bosk its value is incalculable; the Paravaci brand is a symbolic representation of a bosk head, a semicircle resting on an
inverted isoceles triangle.

Elizabeth Cardwell, barefoot, in the larl's pelt, walked
beside Kamchak's stirrup. Neither Tenchika nor Dina would
be with us. Yesterday afternoon, for an incredible forty
pieces of gold, four quivas and the saddle of a kaiila, Kachak
had sold Tenchika back to Albrecht. It was one of the
highest prices ever paid among the wagons for a slave and I
judged that Albrecht had sorely missed his little Tenchika;
the high price he was forced to pay for the girl was made
even more intolerable by Kamchak's amusement at his ex-
pense, roaring with laughter and slapping his knee because
only too obviously Albrecht had allowed himself to care for
the girl, and she only slave! Albrecht, while binding her wrists
and putting his thong on her neck, had angrily cuffed her two
or three times, calling her worthless and good for nothing;
she was laughing and leaping beside his kaiila, weeping with
joy; I last saw her running beside his stirrup, trying to press
her head against his fur boot. Dina, though she was slave, I
had placed on the saddle before me, her legs over the left
forequarters of the animal; and had ridden with her from the
wagons, until in the distance I could see the gleaming, white

walls of Turia. When I had come to this place I set her on the grass. She looked up at me, puzzled.

"Why have you brought me here?" she had asked.

I pointed into the distance. "It is Turia," I said, "your city."

She looked up at me. "Is it your wish," she asked, "that I run for the city?"

She referred to a cruel sport of the young men of the wagons who sometimes take Turian slave girls to the sight of Turia's walls and then, loosening bola and thong, bid them run for the city.

"No," I told her, "I have brought you here to free you."

The girl trembled.

She dropped her head. "I am yours—so much yours," she said, looking at the grass. "Do not be cruel."

"No," I said, "I have brought you here to free you."

She looked up at me. She shook her head.

"It is my wish," I said.

"But why?" she asked.

"It is my wish," I said.

"Have I not pleased you?" she asked.

"You have pleased me very much," I told her.

"Why do you not sell me?" she asked.

"It is not my wish," I said.

"But you would sell a bosk or kaiila," she said.

"Yes," I said.

"Why not Dina?" she asked.

"It is not my wish," I said.

"I am valuable," said the girl. She simply stated a fact.

"More valuable than you know," I told her.

"I do not understand," she said.

I reached into the pouch at my belt and gave her a piece of gold. "Take this," I said, "and go to Turia—find your people and be free."

Suddenly she began to shake with sobs and fell to her knees at the paws of the kaiila, the gold piece in her left hand. "If this is a Tuchuk joke," she wept, "kill me swiftly."

I sprang from the saddle of the kaiila and kneeling beside her held her in my arms, pressing her head against my shoulder. "No," I said, "Dina of Turia. I do not jest. You are free."

She looked at me tears in her eyes. "Turian girls are never freed," she said. "Never."

I shook her and kissed her. "You, Dina of Turia," I said,

"are free." Then I shook her again. "Do you want me to ride to the walls and throw you over?" I demanded.

She laughed through her tears. "No," she said, "no!"

I lifted her to her feet and she suddenly kissed me. "Tarl Cabot!" she cried. "Tarl Cabot!"

It seemed like lightning to us both that she had cried my name as might have a free woman. And indeed it was a free woman who cried those words, Dina, a free woman of Turia. "Oh, Tarl Cabot," she wept.

Then she regarded me gently. "But keep me a moment longer yours," she said.

"You are free," I said.

"But I would serve you," she said.

I smiled. "There is no place," I said.

"Ah, Tarl Cabot," she chided, "there is all the Plains of Turia."

"The Land of the Wagon Peoples, you mean."

She laughed. "No," she said, "the Plains of Turia."

"Insolent wench," I observed.

But she was kissing me and by my arms was being lowered to the grasses of the spring prairie.

When I had lifted her to her feet I noted, in the distance, a bit of dust moving from one of the gates of the city towards us, probably two or three warriors mounted on high tharlarion.

The girl had not yet seen them. She seemed to me very happy and this, naturally, made me happy as well. Then suddenly her eyes clouded and her face was transformed with distress. Her hands moved to her face, covering her mouth. "Oh!" she said.

"What's wrong?" I asked.

"I cannot go to Turia!" she cried.

"Why not?" I asked.

"I have no veil!" she cried.

I cried out in exasperation, kissed her, turned her about by the shoulders and with a slap, hardly befitting a free woman, started her on the way to Turia.

The dust was now nearing.

I leaped into the saddle and waved to the girl, who had run a few yards and then turned. She waved to me. She was crying.

An arrow swept over my head.

I laughed and wheeled the kaiila and raced from the

place, leaving the riders of the ponderous tharlarion far behind.

They circled back to find a girl, free though still clad Kajir, clutching in one hand a piece of gold, waving after a departed enemy, laughing and crying.

When I had returned to the wagon Kamchak's first words to me had been, "I hope you got a good price for her."

I smiled.

"Are you satisfied?" he asked.

I recalled the Plains of Turia. "Yes," I said, "I am well satisfied."

Elizabeth Cardwell, who had been fixing the fire in the wagon, had been startled when I had returned without Dina, but had not dared to ask what had been done with her. Now her eyes were on me, wide with disbelief. "You—sold—her?" she said, uncomprehendingly. "*Sold*?"

"You said she had fat ankles," I reminded her.

Elizabeth regarded me with horror. "She was a person—" said Elizabeth, "—a human person—"

"No!" said Kamchak, giving her head a shake. "An animal! A slave!" Then he added, giving her head another shake, "Like yourself!"

Elizabeth looked at him with dismay.

"I think—" said Kamchak, "I will sell you."

Elizabeth's face suddenly seemed terrified. She threw a wild, pleading look at me.

Kamchak's words had disturbed me as well.

I think it was then, perhaps the first time since her first coming to the Wagon Peoples, that she fully understood her plight—for Kamchak had, on the whole, been kind to her— he had not put the Tuchuk ring in her nose, nor had he clothed her Kajir, nor put the brand of the bosk horns on her thigh, nor even enclosed her lovely throat with the Turian collar. Now, again, Elizabeth, visibly shaken, ill, realized that she might, should it please Kamchak's whims, be sold or exchanged with the same ease as a saddle or a hunting sleen. She had seen Tenchika sold. Now she assumed that the disappearance of Dina from the wagon was to be similarly explained. She looked at me disbelievingly, shaking her head. For my part I did not think it would be a good idea to tell her that I had freed Dina. What good would that information do her? It might make her own bondage seem more cruel, or perhaps fill her with foolish hopes that Kamchak, her master, might someday bestow on her the same beautiful gift of freedom. I smiled at the thought. Kamchak! Free a slave! And, I told myself, even if I myself owned Elizabeth, and not Kamchak, I could not free her—for what would it be to free her? If she approached Turia she would fall slave to the first patrol that leashed and hooded her; if she tried to stay among the wagons, some young warrior, sensing she was undefended and not of the Peoples, would have his chain on her before nightfall. And I myself did not intend to stay among the wagons. I had now learned, if the information of Saphrar was correct, that the golden sphere, doubtless the egg of Priest-Kings, lay in the wagon of Kutaituchik. I must attempt to obtain it and return it to the Sardar. This, I knew, might well cost me my life. No, it was best that Elizabeth Cardwell believe I had callously sold the lovely Dina of Turia. It was best that she understand herself for what she was, a barbarian slave girl in the wagon of Kamchak of the Tuchuks.

"Yes," said Kamchak, "I think I will sell her."

Elizabeth shook with terror and put her head to the rug at Kamchak's feet. "Please," she said, in a whisper, "do not sell me, Master."

"What do you think she would bring?" asked Kamchak.

"She is only a barbarian," I said. I did not wish Kamchak to sell her.

"Perhaps I could have her trained—" mused Kamchak.

"It would considerably improve her price," I admitted. I also knew a good training would take months, though much can be done with an intelligent girl in only a few weeks.

"Would you like to learn," asked Kamchak of the girl, "to wear silk and bells, to speak, to stand, to walk, to dance—to drive men mad with the desire to own and master you?"

The girl said nothing but shuddered.

"I doubt if you could learn," said Kamchak.

Elizabeth said nothing, her head down.

"You are only a little barbarian," said Kamchak wearily. Then he winked at me. "But," said he, "she is a pretty little barbarian, is she not?"

"Yes," I said, "She is that indeed."

I saw Miss Cardwell's eyes close and her shoulders shake with shame. Her hands then covered her eyes.

I followed Kamchak out of the wagon. Once outside, to my astonishment, he turned to me and said, "You were a fool to free Dina of Turia."

"How do you know I freed her?" I asked.

"I saw you put her on your kaiila and ride toward Turia," he said. "She was not even running beside the kaiila bound." He grinned. "And I know that you liked her—that you would not wager for her—and," he added, nodding toward the pouch at my belt, "your pouch is no heavier now than when you left."

I laughed.

Kamchak pointed to the pouch. "You should have forty pieces of gold in that pouch," he said. "That much for her at least—maybe more—because she was skilled in the games of the bola." He chuckled. "A girl such as Dina of Turia is worth more than a kaiila," he said. "And, too," he added, "she was a beauty!" Kamchak laughed. "Albrecht was a fool," he said, "but Tarl Cabot was a bigger one!"

"Perhaps," I admitted.

"Any man who permits himself to care for a slave girl," said Kamchak, "is a fool."

"Perhaps someday," I said, "even Kamchak of the Tuchuks will care for a slave girl."

At this Kamchak threw back his head and roared, and then bent over slapping his knee.

"Then," I said, determinedly, "he may know how it feels."

At this Kamchak lost all control over himself and he leaned over backward slapping his thighs with the palms of his hands, laughing as though he were demented. He even reeled about roaring as though he were drunk and slapped the wheel of a neighbor's wagon for a minute or two until his laughter turned into spasmodic gasps and, making strange noises, he wheezingly fought to get a mouthful or two of air under his shaking ribs. I would not have much minded if he had asphyxiated himself on the spot.

"Tomorrow," I said, "you fight on the Plains of a Thousand Stakes."

"Yes," he said, "so tonight I will get drunk."

"It would be better," I said, "to get a good night's sleep."

"Yes," said Kamchak, "but I am Tuchuk—so I will get drunk."

"Very well," I said, "then I, too, shall get drunk."

We then spat to determine who would bargain for a bottle of Paga. By starting from the side and turning his head quickly, Kamchak bested me by some eighteen inches. In the light of his skill my own effort seemed depressingly naive, quite simple-minded, unimaginative and straightforward. I had not known about the head-twisting trick. The wily Tuchuk, of course, had had me spit first.

Now this morning we had come to the Plains of a Thousand Stakes.

For all his uproarious stomping about the wagon last night, Paga bottle in hand, singing gusty Tuchuk songs, half frightening Miss Cardwell to death, he seemed in good spirits, looking about, whistling, occasionally pounding a little rhythm on the side of his saddle. I would not tell Miss Cardwell but the rhythm was the drum rhythm of the Chain Dance. I gathered Kamchak had his mind on Aphris of Turia, and was, perilously to my mind, counting his wenches before he had won them.

I do not know if there are, by count, a thousand stakes or not on the Plains of a Thousand Stakes, but I would suppose that there are that many or more. The stakes, flat-topped, each about six and half feet high and about seven or eight inches in diameter, stand in two long lines facing one another in pairs. The two lines are separated by about fifty feet and each stake in a line is separated from the stake on its left and right by about ten yards. The two lines of stakes extended for more than four pasangs across the prairie. One of these lines is closest to the city and the other to the prairies beyond. The stakes had recently been, I observed, brightly painted, each differently, in a delightful array of colors; further, each was trimmed and decorated variously, depending on the whim of the workman, sometimes simply, sometimes fancifully, sometimes ornately. The entire aspect was one of color, good cheer, lightheartedness and gaiety. There was something of the sense of carnival in the air. I was forced to remind myself that between these two lines of stakes men would soon fight and die.

I noted some of the workmen still affixing small retaining rings to some of the stakes, bolting them one on a side, usually about five feet to five and a half feet from the ground. A workman sprang a pair shut, and then opened them with a key, which he subsequently hung from a tiny hook near the top of the stake.

I heard some musicians, come out early from Turia, playing a light tune behind the Turian stakes, about fifty yards or so away.

In the space between the two lines of stakes, for each pair of facing stakes, there was a circle of roughly eight yards in diameter. This circle, the grass having been removed, was sanded and raked.

Moving boldly now among the Wagon Peoples were vendors from Turia, selling their cakes, their wines and meats, even chains and collars.

Kamchak looked at the sun, which was now about a quarter of the way up the sky.

"Turians are always late," he said.

From the back of the kaiila I could now see dust from Turia. "They are coming," I said.

Among the Tuchuks, though dismounted, I saw the young man Harold, he whom Hereena of the First Wagon had so sorely insulted at the time of the wagering with Conrad and Albrecht. I did not, however, see the girl. The young man seemed to me a strong, fine fellow, though of course unscarred. He had, as I mentioned, blond hair and blue eyes, not unknown among the Tuchuks, but unusual. He carried weapons. He could not, of course, compete in these contests, for there is status involved in these matters and only warriors of repute are permitted to participate. Indeed, without the Courage Scar one could not even think of proposing oneself for the competition. It might be mentioned, incidentally, that without the Courage Scar one may not, among the Tuchuks, pay court to a free woman, own a wagon, or own more than five bosk and three kaiila. The Courage Scar thus has its social and economic, as well as its martial, import.

"You're right," said Kamchak, rising in the stirrups. "First the warriors."

On long lines of tharlarion I could see warriors of Turia approaching in procession the Plains of a Thousand Stakes. The morning sun flashed from their helmets, their long tharlarion lances, the metal embossments on their oval shields, unlike the rounded shields of most Gorean cities. I could hear, like the throbbing of a heart, the beating of the two tharlarion drums that set the cadence of the march. Beside the tharlarion walked other men-at-arms, and even citizens of Turia, and more vendors and musicians, come to see the games.

On the heights of distant Turia itself I could see the flutter of flags and pennons. The walls were crowded, and I supposed many upon them used the long glasses of the Caste of Builders to observe the field of the stakes.

The warriors of Turia extended their formation about two hundred yards from the stakes until in ranks of four or five

deep they were strung out in a line as long as the line of
stakes itself. Then they halted. As soon as the hundreds of
ponderous tharlarion had been marshaled into an order, a
lance, carrying a fluttering pennon, dipped and there was a
sudden signal on the tharlarion drums. Immediately the
lances of the lines lowered and the hundreds of tharlarion,
hissing and grunting, their riders shouting, the drums beating,
began to bound rapidly towards us.

"Treachery!" I cried.

There was nothing living on Gor I knew that could take
the impact of a tharlarion charge.

Elizabeth Cardwell screamed, throwing her hands before
her face.

To my astonishment the warriors of the Wagon Peoples
seemed to be paying very little attention to the bestial avalanche that was even then hurtling down upon them. Some
were haggling with the vendors, others were talking among
themselves.

I wheeled the kaiila, looking for Elizabeth Cardwell, who,
afoot, would be slain almost before the tharlarion had
crossed the lines of the stakes. She was standing facing the
charging tharlarion, as though rooted to the earth, her hands
before her face. I bent down in the saddle and tensed to kick
the kaiila forward to sweep her to the saddle, turn and race
for our lives.

"Really," said Kamchak.

I straightened up and saw that the lines of the tharlarion
lancers had, with much pounding and trampling of the earth,
with shouting, with the hissing of the great beasts, stopped
short, abruptly, some fifteen yards or so behind their line of
stakes.

"It is a Turian joke," said Kamchak. "They are as fond of
the games as we, and do not wish to spoil them."

I reddened. Elizabeth Cardwell's knees seemed suddenly
weak but she staggered back to us.

Kamchak smiled at me. "She is a pretty little barbarian,
isn't she," he said.

"Yes," I said, and looked away, confused.

Kamchak laughed.

Elizabeth looked up at us, puzzled.

I heard a cry from the Turians across the way. "The
wenches!" he cried, and this shout was taken up by many of
the others. There was much laughing and pounding of lances
on shields.

In a moment, to a thunder of kaiila paws on the turf, racing between the lines of stakes, scattering sand, there came a great number of riders, their black hair swirling behind them, who pulled up on their mounts, rearing and squealing, between the stakes, and leaped from the saddle to the sand, relinquishing the reins of their mounts to men among the Wagon Peoples.

They were marvelous, the many wild girls of the Wagons, and I saw that chief among them was the proud, beauteous Hereena, of the First Wagon. They were enormously excited, laughing. Their eyes shone. A few spit and shook their small fists at the Turians across the way, who reciprocated with good-natured shouts and laughter.

I saw Hereena notice the young man Harold among the warriors and she pointed her finger imperiously at him, gesturing him to her.

He approached her. "Take the reins of my kaiila, Slave," she said to him, insolently throwing him the reins.

He took them angrily and, to the laughter of many of the Tuchuks present, withdrew with the animal.

The girls then went to mingle with the warriors. There were between a hundred and a hundred and fifty girls there from each of the four Wagon Peoples.

"Hah!" said Kamchak, seeing now the lines of tharlarion part for a space of perhaps forty yards, through which could be seen the screened palanquins of Turian damsels, borne on the shoulders of chained slaves, among them undoubtedly men of the Wagon Peoples.

Now the excitement of the throng seemed mostly to course among the warriors of the Wagon Peoples as they rose in their stirrups to see better the swaying, approaching palanquins, each reputedly bearing a gem of great beauty, a fit prize in the savage contests of Love War.

The institution of Love War is an ancient one among the Turians and the Wagon Peoples, according to the Year Keepers antedating even the Omen Year. The games of Love War, of course, are celebrated every spring between, so to speak, the city and the plains, whereas the Omen Year occurs only every tenth year. The games of Love War, in themselves, do not constitute a gathering of the Wagon Peoples, for normally the herds and the free women of the peoples do not approach one another at these times; only certain delegations of warriors, usually about two hundred from a people, are sent in the spring to the Plains of a Thousand Stakes.

The theoretical justification of the games of Love War, from the Turian point of view, is that they provide an excellent arena in which to demonstrate the fierceness and prowess of Turian warriors, thus perhaps intimidating or, at the very least, encouraging the often overbold warriors of the Wagon Peoples to be wary of Turian steel. The secret justification, I suspect, however, is that the Turian warrior is fond of meeting the enemy and acquiring his women, particularly should they be striking little beasts, like Hereena of the First Wagon, as untamed and savage as they are beautiful; it is regarded as a great sport among Turian warriors to collar such a wench and force her to exchange riding leather for the bells and silks of a perfumed slave girl. It might also be mentioned that the Turian warrior, in his opinion, too seldom encounters the warrior of the Wagon Peoples, who tends to be a frustrating, swift and elusive foe, striking with great rapidity and withdrawing with goods and captives almost before it is understood what has occurred. I once asked Kamchak if the Wagon Peoples had a justification for the games of Love War. "Yes," he had said. And he had then pointed to Dina and Tenchika, clad Kajir, who were at that time busy in the wagon. "That is the justification," said Kamchak. And he had then laughed and pounded his knee. It was only then that it had occurred to me that both girls might have been acquired in the games; as a matter of fact, however, I later learned that only Tenchika had been so acquired; Dina had first felt the thongs of a master beside the burning wagons of a caravan in which she had purchased passage. Now, looking on the approaching palanquins, I supposed that so once, in veil and silks, had ridden the lovely Tenchika, and so, too, as far as I knew, might have ridden the lovely Dina, had she not fallen earlier and otherwise to the chains of Kassar warriors. I wondered how many of the proud beauties of Turia would this night tearfully serve barbarian masters; and how many of the wild, leather-clad girls of the Wagons, like Hereena, would find themselves this night naught but bangled, silken slaves locked behind the high walls of distant, lofty Turia.

One by one the screened palanquins of the damsels of Turia were placed on the grass and a serving slave placed before each a silken mat that the inmate of the palanquin, in stepping from her seclusion, might not soil the toe or heel of her sandal or slipper.

The wagon girls, watching this, some of them chewing on fruit or stalks of grass, jeered.

One by one, clad in the proud arrays of resplendent silks, each in the Robes of Concealment, the damsels of Turia, veiled and straight-standing, emerged from their palanquins, scarcely concealing their distaste for the noise and clamor about them.

Judges were now circulating, each with lists, among the Wagon Peoples and the Turians.

As I knew, not just any girl, any more than just any warrior, could participate in the games of Love War. Only the most beautiful were eligible, and only the most beautiful of these could be chosen.

A girl might propose herself to stand, as had Aphris of Turia, but this would not guarantee that she would be chosen, for the criteria of Love War are exacting and, as much as possible, objectively applied. Only the most beautiful of the most beautiful could stand in this harsh sport.

I heard a judge call, "First Stake! Aphris of Turia!"

"Hah!" yelled Kamchak, slapping me on the back, nearly knocking me from the back of my kaiila.

I was astonished. The Turian wench was beautiful indeed, that she could stand at the first stake. This meant that she was quite possibly the most beautiful woman in Turia, certainly at least among those in the games this year.

In her silks of white and gold, on cloths thrown before her, Aphris of Turia stepped disdainfully forward, guided by a judge, to the first of the stakes on the side of the Wagon Peoples. The girls of the Wagon Peoples, on the other hand, would stand at the stakes nearest Turia. In this way the Turian girls can see their city and their warriors, and the girls of the Wagons can see the plains and the warriors of the Wagon Peoples. I had also been informed by Kamchak that this places the girl farther from her own people. Thus, to interfere, a Turian would have to cross the space between the stakes, and so, too, would one of the Wagon Peoples, thus clearly calling themselves to the attention of the judges, those officials supervising the games.

The judges were now calling names, and girls, both of the Wagon Peoples and of Turia, were coming forward.

I saw that Hereena, of the First Wagon, stood Third Stake, though, as far as I could note, she was no less beautiful than the two Kassar girls who stood above her.

Kamchak explained that there was a slight gap between

two of her teeth on the upper right hand side in the back.
"Oh," I said.

I noted with amusement that she was furious at having
been chosen only third stake. "I, Hereena of the First Wagon, am superior," she was crying, "to those two Kassar
she-kaiila!"

But the judge was already four stakes below her.

The selection of the girls, incidentally, is determined by
judges in their city, or of their own people, in Turia by
members of the Caste of Physicians who have served in the
great slave houses of Ar; among the wagons by the masters
of the public slave wagons, who buy, sell and rent girls,
providing warriors and slavers with a sort of clearing house
and market for their feminine merchandise. The public slave
wagons, incidentally, also provide Paga. They are a kind of
combination Paga tavern and slave market. I know of nothing else precisely like them on Gor. Kamchak and I had
visited one last night where I had ended up spending four
copper tarn disks for one bottle of Paga. I hauled Kamchak
out of the wagon before he began to bid on a chained-up
little wench from Port Kar who had taken his eye.

I looked up and down the lines of stakes. The girls of the
Wagon Peoples stood proudly before their stakes, certain that
their champions, whoever they were to be, would be victorious and return them to their peoples; the girls of the city of
Turia stood also at their stakes, but with feigned indifference.

I supposed, in spite of their apparent lack of concern, the
hearts of most of the Turian girls were beating rapidly. This
could not be for them an ordinary day.

I looked at them, veiled and beautiful in their silks. Yet I
knew that beneath those Robes of Concealment many wore
the shameful Turian camisk, perhaps the only time the hated
garment would touch their bodies, for should their warrior
lose this match they knew they would not be permitted to
leave the stake in the robes in which they came. They would
not be led away as free women.

I smiled to myself, wondering if Aphris of Turia, standing
so loftily at the first stake, wore beneath the robes of white
and gold the camisk of a slave girl. I guessed not. She would
be too confident, too proud.

Kamchak was working his kaiila through the crowd
toward the first stake.

I followed him.

He leaned down from the saddle. "Good morning, little Aphris," he said cheerily.

She stiffened, and did not even turn to regard him. "Are you prepared to die, Sleen?" she inquired.

"No," Kamchak said.

I heard her laugh softly beneath the white veil, trimmed with silk.

"I see you no longer wear your collar," observed Kamchak.

She lifted her head and did not deign to respond.

"I have another," Kamchak assured her.

She spun to face him, her fists clenched. Those lovely almond eyes, had they been weapons, would have slain him in the saddle like a bolt of lightning.

"How pleased I shall be," hissed the girl, "to see you on your knees in the sand begging Kamras of Turia to finish you!"

"Tonight, little Aphris," said Kamchak, "as I promised you, you shall spend your first night in the dung sack."

"Sleen!" she cried. "Sleen! Sleen!"

Kamchak roared with laughter and turned the kaiila away.

"Are the women at stake?" called a judge.

From down the long lines, from other judges, came the confirming cry. "They are at stake."

"Let the women be secured," called the first judge, who stood on a platform near the beginning of the stake lines, this year on the side of the Wagon Peoples.

Aphris of Turia, at the request of one of the minor judges, irritably removed her gloves, of silk-lined white verrskin, trimmed with gold, and placed them in a deep fold of her robes.

"The retaining rings," prompted the judge.

"It is not necessary," responded Aphris. "I shall stand quietly here until the sleen is slain."

"Place your wrists in the rings," said the judge, "or it shall be done for you."

In fury the girl placed her hands behind her head, in the rings, one on each side of the stake. The judge expertly flipped them shut and moved to the next stake.

Aphris, not very obviously, moved her hands in the rings, tried to withdraw them. She could not, of course, do so. I thought I saw her tremble for just an instant, realizing herself secured, but then she stood quietly, looking about herself as though bored. The key to the rings hung, of course, on a small hook, about two inches above her head.

"Are the women secured?" called the first judge, he on the platform.

"They are secured," was relayed up and down the long lines.

I saw Hereena standing insolently at her stake, but her brown wrists, of course, were bound to it by steel.

"Let the matches be arranged," called the judge.

I soon heard the other judges repeating his cry.

All along the lines of stakes I saw Turian warriors and those of the Wagon Peoples press into the area between the stakes.

The girls of the wagons, as usual, were unveiled. Turian warriors walked along the line of stakes, examining them, stepping back when one spit or kicked at him. The girls jeered and cursed them, which compliment they received with good humor and pointed observations on the girls' real or imaginary flaws.

At the request of any warrior of the Wagon Peoples, a judge would remove the pins of the face veil of a Turian girl and push back the hood of her robes of concealment, in order that her head and face might be seen.

This aspect of the games was extremely humiliating for the Turian girls, but they understood its necessity; few men, especially barbarian warriors, care to fight for a woman on whose face they have not even looked.

"I would like to take a look at this one," Kamchak was saying, jerking a thumb in the direction of Aphris of Turia.

"Certainly," remarked the nearest judge.

"Can you not remember, Sleen," asked the girl, "the face of Aphris of Turia?"

"My memory is vague," said Kamchak. "There are so many faces."

The judge unpinned her white and gold veil and then, with a gentle hand, brushed back her hood revealing her long, lovely black hair.

Aphris of Turia was an incredibly beautiful woman.

She shook her hair as well as she could, bound to the post.

"Perhaps now you can remember?" she queried acidly.

"It's vague," muttered Kamchak, wavering, "I had in mind I think the face of a slave—there was, as I recall, a collar—"

"You tharlarion," she said. "You sleen!"

"What do you think?" asked Kamchak.

"She is marvelously beautiful," I said.

"There are probably several better among the stakes," said Kamchak. "Let's take a look."

He started off, and I followed him.

I suddenly glimpsed the face of Aphris of Turia contort with rage and she tried to free herself. "Come back here!" she cried. "You sleen! You filthy sleen! Come back! Come back!" I heard her pulling at the rings and kicking at the post.

"Stand quietly," the judge warned her, "or you will be forced to drink a sedative."

"The sleen!" she cried.

But already several of the other warriors of the Wagon Peoples were inspecting the unveiled Aphris of Turia.

"Aren't you going to fight for her?" I asked Kamchak.

"Certainly," said Kamchak.

But he and I, before we finished, had looked over each of the Turian beauties.

At last he returned to Aphris.

"It's a sorry lot this year," he told her.

"Fight for me!" she cried.

"I do not know if I will fight for any of them," he said, "they are all she-sleen, she-kaiila."

"You must fight!" she cried. "You must fight for me!"

"Do you ask it?" inquired Kamchak, interested.

She shook with rage. "Yes," she said, "I ask it."

"Very well," said Kamchak, "I will fight for you."

It seemed then Aphris of Turia leaned back for an instant in exhausted relief against the stake. Then she regarded Kamchak with pleasure. "You will be slain by inches at my feet," she said.

Kamchak shrugged, not dismissing the possibility. Then he turned to the judge. "Do any wish to fight for her but me?" he asked.

"No," said the judge.

When more than one wish to fight for a given woman, incidentally, the Turians decide this by rank and prowess, the Wagon Peoples by scars and prowess. In short, in their various ways, something like seniority and skills determines, of two or more Turians, or two or more warriors of the Wagons, who will take the field. Sometimes men fight among themselves for this honor, but such combat is frowned upon by both the Turians and those of the Wagons, being regarded as somewhat disgraceful, particularly in the presence of foes.

"She must be plain indeed," remarked Kamchak, looking closely again at Aphris.

"No," said the judge, "it is because she is defended by Kamras, Champion of Turia."

"Oh, no!" cried Kamchak, throwing his fist to his forehead in mock despair.

"Yes," said the judge, "he."

"Surely you recall?" laughed Aphris merrily.

"I had had much Paga at the time," admitted Kamchak.

"You need not meet him if you wish," said the judge.

I thought that a humane arrangement—that two men must understand who it is they face before entering the circle of sand. It would indeed be unpleasant if one suddenly, unexpectedly, found oneself facing a superb, famed warrior, say, a Kamras of Turia.

"Meet him!" cried Aphris.

"If no one meets him," said the judge, "the Kassar girl will be his by forfeit."

I could see that the Kassar girl, a beauty, at the stake opposite Aphris of Turia was distressed, and understandably so. It appeared she was to depart for Turia without so much as a handful of sand kicked about on her behalf.

"Meet him, Tuchuk!" she cried.

"Where are your Kassars?" asked Kamchak.

I thought it an excellent question. I had seen Conrad about, but he had picked out a Turian wench to fight for some six or seven stakes away. Albrecht was not even at the games. I supposed he was home with Tenchika.

"They are fighting elsewhere!" she cried. "Please, Tuchuk!" she wept.

"But you are only a Kassar wench," pointed out Kamchak.

"Please!" she cried.

"Besides," said Kamchak, "you might look well in Pleasure Silk."

"Look at the Turian wench!" cried the girl. "Is she not beautiful? Do you not want her?"

Kamchak looked at Aphris of Turia.

"I suppose," he said, "she is no worse than the rest."

"Fight for me!" cried Aphris of Turia.

"All right," said Kamchak. "I will."

The Kassar girl put her back against the stake, trembling with relief.

"You are a fool," said Kamras of Turia.

I was a bit startled, not realizing he was so close. I looked

at him. He was indeed an impressive warrior. He seemed
strong and fast. His long black hair was now tied behind his
head. His large wrists had been wrapped in boskhide straps.
He wore a helmet and carried the Turian shield, which is
oval. In his right hand there was a spear. Over his shoulder
was slung the sheath of a short sword.

Kamchak looked up at him. It was not that Kamchak was
particularly short, but rather that Kamras was a very large
man.

"By the sky," said Kamchak, whistling, "you are a big
fellow indeed."

"Let us begin," proposed Kamras.

At this word the judge called out to clear the space
between the stakes of Aphris of Turia and the lovely Kassar
wench. Two men, from Ar, I took it, came forward with
rakes and began to smooth the circle of sand between the
stakes, for it had been somewhat disturbed in the inspection
of the girls.

Unfortunately for Kamchak, I knew that this was the year
in which the Turian foeman might propose the weapon of
combat. Fortunately, however, the warrior of the Wagon
Peoples could withdraw from the combat any time before his
name had actually been officially entered in the lists of the
games. Thus if Kamras chose a weapon with which Kamchak
did not feel at ease, the Tuchuk might, with some grace,
decline the combat, in this forfeiting only a Kassar girl,
which I was sure would not overly disturb the philosophical
Kamchak.

"Ah, yes, weapons," Kamchak was saying, "what shall it
be—the kaiila lance, a whip and bladed bola—perhaps the
quiva?"

"The sword," said Kamras.

The Turian's decision plunged me into despair. In all my
time among the wagons I had not seen one of the Gorean
short swords, so fierce and swift and common a weapon
among those of the cities. The warrior of the Wagon Peoples
does not use the short sword, probably because such a weapon could not be optimally used from the saddle of the
kaiila; the saber, incidentally, which would be somewhat
more effective from kaiilaback, is almost unknown on Gor;
its role, I gather, is more than fulfilled by the lance, which
may be used with a delicacy and address comparable to that
of a blade, supplemented by the seven quiva, or saddle
knives; it might further be pointed out that a saber would

barely reach to the saddle of the high tharlarion; the warrior of the Wagon Peoples seldom approaches an enemy more closely than is required to bring him down with the bow, or, if need be, the lance; the quiva itself is regarded, on the whole, as more of a missile weapon than a hand knife. I gather that the Wagon Peoples, if they wanted sabers or regarded them as valuable, would be able to acquire them, in spite of the fact that they have no metalworking of their own; there might be some attempt to prevent them from falling into the hands of the Wagon Peoples, but where there are gold and jewels available merchants, in Ar and elsewhere, would see that they were manufactured and reached the southern plains. Most quivas, incidentally, are wrought in the smithies of Ar. The fact that the saber is not a common weapon of Wagon Peoples is a reflection of the style, nature and conditions of warfare to which they are accustomed, a matter of choice on their part rather than the result of either ignorance or technological limitation. The saber, incidentally, is not only unpopular among the Wagon Peoples but among the warriors of Gor generally; it is regarded as being too long and clumsy a weapon for the close, sharp combat so dear to the heart of the warrior of the cities; further it is not of much use from the saddle of a tarn or tharlarion. The important point, however, in the circumstances was that Kamras had proposed the sword as the weapon of his encounter with Kamchak, and poor Kamchak was almost certain to be as unfamiliar with the sword as you or I would be with any of the more unusual weapons of Gor, say, the whip knife of Port Kar or the trained varts of the caves of Tyros. Incidentally, Turian warriors, in order to have the opportunity to slay a foe, as well as acquire his woman, customarily choose as the weapon of combat in these encounters, buckler and dagger, ax and buckler, dagger and whip, ax and net, or the two daggers, with the reservation that the quiva, if used, not be thrown. Kamras, however, appeared adamant on the point. "The sword," he repeated.

"But I am only a poor Tuchuk," wailed Kamchak.

Kamras laughed. "The sword," he said, yet again.

I thought, all things considered, that the stipulation of Kamras regarding weapons was cruel and shameful.

"But how would I, a poor Tuchuk," Kamchak was moaning, "know anything of the sword?"

"Then withdraw," said Kamras, loftily, "and I will take this Kassar wench slave to Turia."

The girl moaned.

Kamras smiled with contempt. "You see," he said, "I am Champion of Turia and I have no particular wish to stain my blade with the blood of an urt."

The urt is a loathsome, horned Gorean rodent; some are quite large, the size of wolves or ponies, but most are very small, tiny enough to be held in the palm of one hand.

"Well," said Kamchak, "I certainly would not want that to happen either."

The Kassar girl cried out in distress.

"Fight him, filthy Tuchuk!" screamed Aphris of Turia, pulling against the retaining rings.

"Do not be uneasy, gentle Aphris of Turia," said Kamras. "Permit him to withdraw branded braggart and coward. Let him live in his shame, for so much the richer will be your vengeance."

But the lovely Aphris was not convinced. "I want him slain," she cried, "cut into tiny pieces, the death of a thousand cuts!"

"Withdraw," I advised Kamchak.

"Do you think I should," he inquired.

"Yes," I said, "I do."

Kamras was regarding Aphris of Turia. "If it is truly your wish," he said, "I will permit him to choose weapons agreeable to us both."

"It is my wish," she said, "that he be slain!"

Kamras shrugged. "All right," he said, "I will kill him." He then turned to Kamchak. "All right, Tuchuk," he said, "I will permit you to choose weapons agreeable to us both."

"But perhaps I will not fight," said Kamchak warily.

Kamras clenched his fists. "Very well," he said, "as you wish."

"But then again," mused Kamchak, "perhaps I shall."

Aphris of Turia cried out in rage and the Kassar wench in distress.

"I will fight," announced Kamchak.

Both girls cried out in pleasure.

The judge now entered the name of Kamchak of the Tuchuks on his lists.

"What weapon do you choose?" asked the judge. "Remember," cautioned the judge, "the weapon or weapons chosen must be mutually agreeable."

Kamchak seemed lost in thought and then he looked up

brightly. "I have always wondered," he said, "what it would be like to hold a sword."

The judge nearly dropped the list.

"I will choose the sword," said Kamchak.

The Kassar girl moaned.

Kamras looked at Aphris of Turia, dumbfounded. The girl herself was speechless. "He is mad," said Kamras of Turia.

"Withdraw," I urged Kamchak.

"It is too late now," said the judge.

"It is too late now," said Kamchak, innocently.

Inwardly I moaned, for in the past months I had come to respect and feel an affection for the shrewd, gusty brawny Tuchuk.

Two swords were brought, Gorean short swords, forged in Ar.

Kamchak picked his up as though it were a wagon lever, used for loosening the wheels of mired wagons.

Kamras and I both winced.

Then Kamras, and I give him credit, said to Kamchak, "Withdraw." I could understand his feelings. Kamras was, after all, a warrior, and not a butcher.

"A thousand cuts!" cried the gentle Aphris of Turia. "A piece of gold to Kamras for every cut!" she cried.

Kamchak was running his thumb on the blade. I saw a sudden, bright drop of blood on his thumb. He looked up. "Sharp," he said.

"Yes," I said in exasperation. I turned to the judge. "May I fight for him?" I demanded.

"It is not permitted," said the judge.

"But," said Kamchak, "it was a good idea."

I seized Kamchak by the shoulders. "Kamras has no real wish to kill you," I said. "It is enough for him to shame you. Withdraw."

Suddenly the eyes of Kamchak gleamed. "Would you see me shamed?" he asked.

I looked at him, "Better, my friend," I said, "that than death."

"No," said Kamchak, and his eyes were like steel, "better death than shame."

I stepped back. He was Tuchuk. I would sorely miss my friend, the ribald, hard-drinking, stomping, dancing Kamchak of the Tuchuks.

In the last moment I cried out to Kamchak, "For the sake of Priest-Kings, hold the weapon thus!" trying to teach him the simplest of the commoner grips for the hilt of the short sword, permitting a large degree of both retention and flexibility. But when I stepped away he was now holding it like a Gorean angle saw.

Even Kamras closed his eyes briefly, as though to shut out the spectacle. I now realized Kamras had only wished to drive Kamchak from the field, a chastened and humiliated man. He had little more wish to slay the clumsy Tuchuk than he would have a peasant or a potmaker.

"Let the combat begin," said the judge.

I stepped away from Kamchak and Kamras approached him, by training, cautiously.

Kamchak was looking at the edge of his sword, turning it about, apparently noting with pleasure the play of sunlight on the blade.

"Watch out!" I cried.

Kamchak turned to see what I had in mind and to his great good fortune, as he did so, the sun flashed from the blade into the eyes of Kamras, who suddenly threw his arm up, blinking and shaking his head, for the instant blinded.

"Turn and strike now!" I screamed.

"What?" asked Kamchak.

"Watch out!" I cried, for now Kamras had recovered, and was once again approaching.

Kamras, of course, had the sun at his back, using it as naturally as the tarn to protect his advance.

It had been incredibly fortunate for Kamchak that the blade had flashed precisely at the time it had in the way it had.

It had quite possibly saved his life.

Kamras lunged and it looked like Kamchak threw up his arm at the last instant as though he had lost balance, and indeed he was now tottering on one boot. I scarcely noticed the blow had been smartly parried. Kamras then began to chase Kamchak about the ring of sand. Kamchak was nearly stumbling over backward and kept trying to regain his balance. In this chase, rather undignified, Kamras had struck a dozen times and each time, astoundingly, the off-balance Kamchak, holding his sword now like a physician's pestle, had managed somehow to meet the blow.

"Slay him!" screamed Aphris of Turia.

I was tempted to cover my eyes.

The Kassar girl was wailing.

Then, as though weary, Kamchak, puffing, sat down in the

sand. His sword was in front of his face, apparently blocking
his vision. With his boots he kept rotating about, always
facing Kamras no matter from which direction he came.
Each time the Turian struck and I would have thought
Kamchak slain, somehow, incomprehensibly, at the last instant, nearly causing my heart to stop, with a surprised,
weary little twitch, the blade of the Tuchuk would slide the
Turian steel harmlessly to the side. It was only about this
time that it dawned on me that for three or four minutes
Kamchak had been the object of the ever-more-furious assault of Turia's champion and was, to this instant, un-
scratched.

Kamchak then struggled wearily to his feet.

"Die, Tuchuk!" cried Kamrus, now enraged, rushing upon
him. For more than a minute, while I scarcely dared to
breathe and there was silence all about save for the ring of
steel, I watched Kamchak stand there, heavy in his boots, his
head seeming almost to sit on his shoulders, his body hardly
moving save for the swiftness of a wrist and the turn of a
hand.

Kamras, exhausted, scarcely able to lift his arm, staggered
backward.

Once again, expertly, the sun flashed from the sword of
Kamchak in his eyes.

In terror Kamras blinked and shook his head, thrashing
about wearily with his sword.

Then, foot by booted foot, Kamchak advanced toward
him. I saw the first blood leap from the cheek of Kamras,
and then again from his left arm, then from the thigh, then
from an ear.

"Kill him!" Aphris of Turia was screaming. "Kill him!"

But now, almost like a drunk man, Kamras was fighting
for his life and the Tuchuk, like a bear, scarcely moving
more than arm and wrist, followed him about, shuffling
through the sand after him, touching him again and again
with the blade.

"Slay him!" howled Aphris of Turia!

For perhaps better than fifteen minutes, patiently, not
hurrying, Kamchak of the Tuchuks shuffled after Kamras of
Turia, touching him once more and ever again, each time
leaving a quick, bright stain of blood on his tunic or body.
And then, to my astonishment, and that of the throng who
had gathered to witness the contest, I saw Kamras, Champion of Turia, weak from the loss of blood, fall to his knees

before Kamchak of the Tuchuks. Kamras tried to lift his sword but the boot of Kamchak pressed it into the sand, and Kamras lifted his eyes to look dazed into the scarred, inscrutable countenance of the Tuchuk. Kamchak's sword was at his throat. "Six years," said Kamchak, "before I was scarred was I mercenary in the guards of Ar, learning the walls and defenses of that city for my people. In that time of the guards of Ar I became First Sword."

Kamras fell in the sand at the feet of Kamchak, unable even to beg for mercy.

Kamchak did not slay him.

Rather he threw the sword he carried into the sand and though he threw it easily it slipped through almost to the hilt. He looked at me and grinned. "An interesting weapon," he said, "but I prefer lance and quiva."

There was an enormous roar about us and the pounding of lances on leather shields. I rushed to Kamchak and threw my arms about him laughing and hugging him. He was grinning from ear to ear, sweat glistening in the furrows of his scars.

Then he turned and advanced to the stake of Aphris of Turia, who stood there, her wrists bound in steel, regarding him, speechless with horror.

11

Bells and Collar

Kamchak regarded Aphris of Turia.

"Why is a slave," he asked, "masquerading in the robes of a free woman?"

"Please, no, Tuchuk," she said. "Please, no!"

And in a moment the lovely Aphris of Turia stood at the stake revealed to the eyes of her master.

She threw back her head and moaned, wrists still locked in the retaining rings.

She had not, as I had suspected, deigned to wear the shameful camisk beneath her robes of white and gold.

The Kassar wench, who had been bound across from her to the opposing stake, had now been freed by a judge and she strode to where Aphris was still confined.

"Well done, Tuchuk!" said the girl, saluting Kamchak.

Kamchak shrugged.

Then the girl, with vehemence, spat in the face of the lovely Aphris. "Slave girl!" hissed the girl. "Slave! Slave girl!"

She then turned and strode away, looking for warriors of the Kassars.

Kamchak laughed loudly.

"Punish her!" demanded Aphris.

Kamchak suddenly cuffed Aphris of Turia. Her head snapped sideways and there was a streak of blood at the corner of her mouth. The girl looked at him in sudden fear. It might have been the first time she had ever been struck. Kamchak had not hit her hard, but sharply enough to instruct her. "You will take what abuse any free person of the Wagon Peoples cares to inflict upon you," he said.

"I see," said a voice, "you know how to handle slaves."

I turned to see, only a few feet away, on the shoulders of slaves standing on the bloodied sand, the open, bejeweled, cushioned palanquin of Saphrar of the Caste of Merchants.

Aphris blushed from head to toe, enfolded transparent in the crimson flag of her shame.

Saphrar's round, pinkish face was beaming with pleasure, though I would have thought this day a tragic one for him. The tiny red-lipped mouth was spread wide with benign satisfaction. I saw the tips of the two golden canines.

Aphris suddenly pulled at the retaining rings, trying to rush to him, now oblivious of the riches of her beauty revealed even to the slaves who carried his palanquin. To them, of course, she was now no more than they, save perhaps that her flesh would not be used to bear the poles of palanquins, to carry boxes nor dig in the earth, but would be appointed its own tasks, lighter and more suitable, doubtless even more pleasing than theirs to a master. "Saphrar!" she cried. "Saphrar!"

Saphrar looked on the girl. He took from a silken pouch lying before him on the palanquin a small glass, with glass petal edges like a flower, mounted on a silver stem about which curled silver leaves. Through this he looked on her more closely.

"Aphris!" he cried, as though horrified, but yet smiling.

"Saphrar," she wept, "free me!"

"How unfortunate!" wailed Saphrar. I could still see the tips of the golden teeth.

Kamchak had his arm about my shoulder, chuckling. "Aphris of Turia," he said, "has a surprise coming."

Aphris turned her head to Kamchak. "I am the richest woman in all Turia," she said. "Name your price!"

Kachak looked at me. "Do you think five gold pieces would be too much?" he asked.

I was startled.

Aphris nearly choked. "Sleen," she wept. Then she turned to Saphrar. "Buy me!" she demanded. "If necessary, use all my resources, all! Free me!"

"But Aphris," Saphrar was purring, "I am in charge of your funds and to barter them—and all your properties and goods—for one slave would be a most unwise and absurd decision on my part, irresponsible even."

Aphris suddenly looked at him, dumbfounded.

"It is—or was—true that you were the richest woman in all Turia," Saphrar was saying, "but your riches are not yours to manage—but mine—not, that is, until you would have reached your majority, some days from now I believe."

"I do not wish to remain a slave for even a day!" she cried.

"Is it my understanding," asked Saphrar, the golden drops over his eyes rising, "that you would—upon reaching your majority—transfer your entire fortunes to a Tuchuk, merely to obtain your freedom."

"Of course!" she wept.

"How fortunate then," observed Saphrar, "that such a transaction is precluded by law."

"I don't understand," said Aphris.

Kamchak squeezed my shoulder and rubbed his nose.

"Surely you are aware," said Saphrar, "that a slave cannot own property—any more than a kaiila, a tharlarion or sleen."

"I am the richest woman in Turia!" she cried.

Saphrar reclined a bit more on his cushions. His little round pinkish face shone. He pursed his lips and then smiled. He poked his head forward and said, very quickly, "You are a slave!" He then giggled.

Aphris of Turia threw back her head and screamed.

"You do not even have a name," hissed the little merchant.

It was true. Kamchak would undoubtedly continue to call her Aphris, but it would be now his name for her and not her own. A slave, not being a person in the eyes of Gorean law, cannot possess a name in his own right, any more than an animal. Indeed, in the eyes of Gorean law, unfortunately, slaves are animals, utterly and unqualifiedly at the disposition of their masters, to do with as he pleases.

"I think," roared Kamchak, "I will call her Aphris of Turia!"

"Free me, Saphrar," cried the girl piteously, "free me!"

Saphrar laughed.

"Sleen!" she screamed at him. "You stinking sleen!"

"Be careful," warned Saphrar, "how you speak to the richest man in Turia!"

Aphris wept and pulled at the retaining rings.

"You understand, of course," continued Saphrar, "that at the instant you became slave all your properties and riches, your wardrobes and jewels, your investments and assets, chattels and lands, became mine."

Aphris was weeping uncontrollably at the stake. Then she lifted her head to him, her eyes bright with tears. "I beg you, noble Saphrar," she wept, "I beg of you—I beg of you to free me. Please! Please! Please!"

Saphrar smiled at her. He then turned to Kamchak, "What, Tuchuk, did you say her price was?"

"I have lowered it,'" said Kamchak. "I will let you have her for one copper tarn disk."

Saphrar smiled. "The price is too high," he said.

Aphris cried out in distress.

Saphrar then again lifted the tiny glass through which he had regarded her, and examined her with some care. Then he shrugged and gestured for his slaves to turn the palanquin.

"Saphrar!" cried out the girl one last time.

"I do not speak to slaves," said he, and the merchant, on the palanquin, moved away toward the walls of distant Turia.

Aphris was looking after him, numbly, her eyes red, her cheeks stained with tears.

"It does not matter," said Kamchak soothingly to the girl. "Even had Saphrar been a worthy man you would not now be free."

She turned her beautiful head to stare at him, blankly.

"No,". said Kamchak, taking her hair and giving her head a friendly shake, "I would not have sold you for all the gold in Turia."

"But why?" she whispered.

"Do you recall," asked Kamchak, "one night two years ago when you spurned my gift and called me sleen?"

The girl nodded, her eyes frightened.

"It was on that night," said Kamchak, "that I vowed to make you my slave."

She dropped her head.

"And it is for that reason," said Kamchak, "that I would not sell you for all the gold of Turia."

She looked up, red-eyed.

"It was on that night, little Aphris," said Kamchak, "that I decided I wanted you—and would have you—slave."

The girl shuddered and dropped her head.

The laugh of Kamchak of the Tuchuks was loud.

He had waited long to laugh that laugh, waited long to see

his fair enemy thus before him, thus bound and shamed, his, a slave.

In short order then Kamchak took the key over the head of Aphris of Turia and sprang open the retaining rings. He then led the numb, unresisting Turian maiden to his kaiila.

There, beside the paws of the animal, he made her kneel. "Your name is Aphris of Turia," he said to her, giving her a name.

"My name is Aphris of Turia," she said, accepting her name at his hands.

"Submit," ordered Kamchak.

Trembling Aphris of Turia, kneeling, lowered her head and extended her arms, wrists crossed. Kamchak quickly and tightly thonged them together.

She lifted her head. "Am I to be bound across the saddle?" she asked numbly.

"No," said Kamchak, "there is no hurry."

"I don't understand," said the girl.

Already Kamchak was placing a thong on her neck, the loose end of which he looped several times about the pommel of his saddle. "You will run alongside," he informed her.

She looked at him in disbelief.

Elizabeth Cardwell, unbound, had already taken her position on the other side of Kamchak's kaiila, beside his right stirrup. Then Kamchak, with his two women, and I, left the Plains of a Thousand Stakes and set out for the wagons of the Tuchuks.

Behind us we could hear still the sounds of combat, the cries of men.

Some two hours later we reached the encampment of the Tuchuks and made our way among the wagons and the cooking pots and playing children. Slave girls ran beside us, jeering at Kamchak's tethered prize; free women looked up from their ladles and kettles to stare with jaundiced eye at yet another Turian woman brought to the camp.

"She was First Stake," called Kamchak to the jeering girls. "What were you?" Then he turned his kaiila suddenly toward them and they would break and run screaming and laughing and then, like a flock of birds, take up once more the pursuit. Kamchak was grinning from ear to ear. "First stake!" he called out to a warrior, jerking his thumb at the stumbling, gasping Aphris. The warrior laughed. "It is true!" roared Kamchak, grinning and slapping the side of the saddle.

To be sure there might have been some doubt that the miserable wench thonged behind Kamchak's kaiila could have been first stake. She was gasping and stumbling; her body glistened with perspiration; her legs were black with wet dust; her hair was tangled and thick with dust; her feet and ankles were bleeding; her calves were scratched and speckled with the red bites of rennels. When Kamchak reached his wagon, the poor girl, gasping for breath, legs trembling, fell exhausted to the grass, her entire body shaking with the ordeal of her run. I supposed that Aphris of Turia had done little in her life that was more strenuous than stepping in and out of a scented bath. Elizabeth Cardwell, on the other hand, I was pleased to see, ran well, breathing evenly, showing few signs of fatigue. She had, of course, in her time with the wagons, become used to this form of exercise. I had rather come to admire her. The life in the open air, the work, had apparently been good for her. She was trim, vital, buoyant. I wondered how many of the girls in her New York office could have run as she beside the stirrup of a Tuchuk warrior.

Kamchak leaped down from the saddle of the kaiila, puffing a bit.

"Here, here!" he cried cheerily, hauling the exhausted Aphris to her knees. "There is work to be done, Wench!"

She looked up at him, the thong still on her neck, her wrists bound. Her eyes seemed dazed.

"There are bosk to be groomed," he informed her, "and their horns and hoofs must be polished—there is fodder to be fetched and dung to be gathered—the wagon must be wiped and the wheels greased—and there is water to be brought from the stream some four pasangs away and meat to hammer and cook for supper—hurry—hurry, Lazy Girl!"

Then he leaned back and laughed his Tuchuk laugh, slapping his thighs.

Elizabeth Cardwell was removing the thong from the girl's neck and unbinding her wrists. "Come along," she said, kindly. "I will show you."

Aphris stood up, wobbling, still dazed. She turned her eyes on Elizabeth, whom she seemed to see then for the first time. "Your accent," said Aphris, slowly. "You are barbarian." She said it with a kind of horror.

"You will see," said Kamchak, "that she wears the pelt of a larl—that she is not collared, that she does not wear the nose ring, that she does not wear the brand." And then he added, "—as you will."

Aphris trembled, her eyes pleading.

"Do you wonder, Little Aphris," asked Kamchak, "why the barbarian—though slave—is not clad Kajir, why she does not wear ring, brand and collar?"

"Why?" asked Aphris, frightened.

"So that there will be one higher than you in the wagon," said Kamchak.

I had wondered why Kamchak had not treated Elizabeth Cardwell as any other enslaved wench of Tuchuks.

"For," said Kamchak, "among your other tasks, my dear, you will perform for this barbarian the duties of a female serving slave."

This struck fire in Aphris of Turia. She suddenly straightened indignantly and cried out. "Not I—not Aphris of Turia!"

"You," said Kamchak.

"A serving slave to a barbarian!"

"Yes," said Kamchak.

"Never!" cried the girl.

"Yes," roared Kamchak, thowing back his head and guffawing, "Aphris of Turia, in my wagon, will be a barbarian's serving slave!"

The girl's fists were clenched.

"And I shall see," said Kamchak, "that word of this reaches Turia!" He then bent over and started cracking his knees with his fists, so amused he was.

Aphris of Turia trembled with rage before him.

"Please," said Elizabeth, "come away." She tried to take Aphris by the arm.

Aphris of Turia shrugged away her touch arrogantly, not wishing to feel her hand. But then, head in the air, she deigned to accompany Elizabeth from where we stood.

"If she does not work well," called Kamchak cheerily, "beat her."

Aphris turned to face him, fists clenched.

"You will learn, Little Aphris," said he, "who is master here."

The girl lifted her head. "Is a Tuchuk too poor," she asked, "to clothe a miserable slave?'"

"I have many diamonds in the wagon," said Kamchak, "which you may wear if you wish—but nothing else will you wear until it pleases me."

She turned in fury and followed Elizabeth Cardwell away.

After this Kamchak and I left the wagon and wandered about, stopping at one of the slave wagons for a bottle of Paga, which, while wandering about, we killed between us.

This year, as it turned out, the Wagon Peoples had done exceedingly well in the games of Love War—a bit of news we picked up with the Paga—and about seventy percent of the Turian maidens had been led slave from the stakes to which they had been manacled. In some years I knew the percentages were rather the other way about. It apparently made for zestful competition. We also heard that the wench Hereena, of the First Wagon, had been won by a Turian officer representing the house of Saphrar of the Merchants, to whom, for a fee, he presented her. I gathered that she would become another of his dancing girls. "A bit of perfume and silk will be good for that wench," stated Kamchak. It seemed strange to think of her, so wild and insolent, arrogant on the back of her kaiila, now a perfumed, silken slave of Turians. "She could use a bit of whip and steel, that wench," Kamchak muttered between swallows of Paga, pretty much draining the bottle. It was too bad, I thought, but at least I supposed there would be one fellow among the wagons, the young man Harold, he whom the girl had so abused, he who had not yet won the Courage Scar, who would be just as pleased as not that she, with all her contempt and spleen, was now delightfully salted away in bangles and bells behind the high, thick walls of a Turian's pleasure garden.

Kamchak had circled around and we found ourselves back at the slave wagon.

We decided to wager to see who would get the second bottle of Paga.

"What about the flight of birds?" asked Kamchak.

"Agreed," I said, "but I have first choice."

"Very well," he said.

I knew, of course, that it was spring and, in this hemisphere, most birds, if there were any migrating, would be moving south. "South," I said.

"North," he said.

We then waited about a minute, and I saw several birds—river gulls—flying north.

"Those are Vosk gulls," said Kamchak, "In the spring, when the ice breaks in the Vosk, they fly north."

I fished some coins out of my pouch for the Paga.

"The first southern migrations of meadow kites," he said, "have already taken place. The migrations of the forest hurlit and the horned gim do not take place until later in the spring. This is the time that the Vosk gulls fly."

"Oh," I said.

Singing Tuchuk songs, we managed to make it back to the wagon.

Elizabeth had the meat roasted, though it was now considerably overdone.

"The meat is overdone," said Kamchak.

"They are both stinking drunk," said Aphris of Turia.

I looked at her. Both of them were beautiful. "No," I corrected her, "gloriously inebriated."

Kamchak was looking closely at the girls, leaning forward, squinting.

I blinked a few times.

"Is anything wrong?" asked Elizabeth Cardwell.

I noted that there was a large welt on the side of her face, that her hair was ripped up a bit and that there were five long scratches on the left side of her face.

"No," I said.

Aphris of Turia appeared in even worse shape. She had surely lost more than one handful of hair. There were teeth marks in her left arm and, if I was not mistaken, her right eye was ringed and discolored.

"The meat is overdone," grumbled Kamchak. A master takes no interest in the squabbles of slaves, it being beneath him. He of course would not have approved had one of the girls been maimed, blinded or disfigured.

"Have the bosk been tended?" asked Kamchak.

"Yes," said Elizabeth firmly.

Kamchak looked at Aphris. "Have the bosk been tended?" he asked.

She looked up suddenly, her eyes bright with tears. She cast an angry look at Elizabeth. "Yes," she said, "they have been tended."

"Good," said Kamchak, "good." Then he pointed at the meat. "It is overdone," he said.

"You were hours late," said Elizabeth.

"Hours," repeated Aphris.

"It is overdone," said Kamchak.

"I shall roast fresh meat," said Elizabeth, getting up, and she did so. Aphris only sniffed.

When the meat was ready Kamchak ate his fill, and drank

down, too, a flagon of bosk milk; I did the same, though the milk, at least for me, did not sit too well with the Paga of the afternoon.

Kamchak, as he often did, was sitting on what resembled a gray rock, rather squarish, except that the corners tended to be a bit rounded. When I had first seen this thing, heaped with other odds and ends in one corner of the wagon, some of the odds and ends being tankards of jewels and small, heavy chests filled with golden tarn disks, I had thought it merely a rock. Once, when rummaging through his things, Kamchak had kicked it across the rug for me to look at. I was surprised at the way it bounced on the rug and, when I picked it up, I was interested to see how light it was. It was clearly not a rock. It was rather leathery and had a grained surface. I was a bit reminded of some of the loose, tumbled rocks I had once glimpsed in certain abandoned portions of the place of Priest-Kings, far beneath the Sardar. Among such rocks it would not have been noticed. "What do you make of it?" Kamchak asked.

"Interesting," I observed.

"Yes," said he, "I thought so." He held out his hands and I tossed the object back. "I have had it for some time," he said. "It was given to me by two travelers."

"Oh," I said.

When Kamchak had finished his freshly roasted meat and his flagon of bosk milk, he shook his head and rubbed his nose.

He looked at Miss Cardwell. "Tenchika and Dina are gone," said he. "You may sleep once more in the wagon."

Elizabeth cast a grateful look at him. I gathered that the ground under the wagon was hard.

"Thank you," she said.

"I thought he was your master," remarked Aphris.

"Master," added Elizabeth, with a withering look at Aphris, who smiled.

I now began to understand why there were often problems in a wagon with more than one girl. Still, Tenchika and Dina had not quarreled very much. Perhaps this was because Tenchika's heart was elsewhere, in the wagon of Albrecht of the Kassars.

"Who, may I ask," asked Aphris, "were Tenchika and Dina?"

"Slaves, Turian wenches," said Kamchak.

"They were sold," Elizabeth informed Aphris.

"Oh," said Aphris. Then she looked at Kamchak. "I do not suppose I shall be fortunate enough to be sold?"

"She would probably bring a high price," pointed out Elizabeth, hopefully.

"Higher than a barbarian surely," remarked Aphris.

"Do not fret, Little Aphris," said Kamchak, "when I am finished with you I shall—if it pleases me—put you on the block in the public slave wagon."

"I shall look forward to the day," she said.

"On the other hand," said Kamchak, "I may feed you to the kaiila."

At this the Turian maiden trembled slightly, and looked down.

"I doubt that you are good for much," Kamchak said, "but kaiila feed."

Aphris looked up angrily.

Elizabeth laughed and clapped her hands.

"You," said Kamchak, glaring at Elizabeth, "you stupid little barbarian—you cannot even dance!"

Elizabeth looked down, confused, rather shamed. It was true, what Kamchak had said.

The voice of Aphris was timid and quiet. "I can't either," she said.

"What!" howled Kamchak.

"No," cried Aphris, "I never learned!"

"Kaiila feed!" cried Kamchak.

"I'm sorry," said Aphris, now a bit irritated, "I just never planned on becoming a slave."

"You should have learned anyway," cried the disappointed Kamchak.

"Nonsense," said Aphris.

"It will cost money," grumbled Kamchak, "but you will learn—I will have you taught."

Aphris sniffed and looked away.

Elizabeth was looking at me. Then she turned to Kamchak. To my astonishment, she asked, "Could I, too, be taught?"

"Why?" he asked.

She looked down, blushing.

"She is only a barbarian," said Aphris, "—all knees and elbows—she could never learn."

"Hah!" laughed Kamchak. "The Little Barbarian does not wish to become second girl in the wagon!" He gave Elizabeth's head a rough, affectionate shake. "You will fight for your place! Excellent!"

"She can be first girl if she wishes," sniffed Aphris. "I shall excape at the first opportunity and return to Turia."

"Beware of the herd sleen," said Kamchak.

Aphris turned white.

"If you attempt to leave the wagons at night they will sense you out and rip my pretty little slave girl in pieces."

"It is true," I warned Aphris of Turia.

"Nonetheless," said Aphris, "I will escape."

"But not tonight!" guffawed Kamchak.

"No," said Aphris acidly, "not tonight." Then she looked about herself, disdainfully at the interior of the wagon. Her gaze rested for a moment on the kaiila saddle which had been part of the spoils which Kamchak had acquired for Tenchika. In the saddle, in their sheaths, were seven quivas. Aphris turned again to face Kamchak. "This slave," she said, indicating Elizabeth, "would not give me anything to eat."

"Kamchak must eat first, Slave," responded Elizabeth.

"Well," said Aphris, "he has eaten."

Kamchak then took a bit of meat that was left over from the fresh-roasted meat that Miss Cardwell had prepared. He held it out in his hand. "Eat," he said to Aphris, "but do not touch it with your hands."

Aphris looked at him in fury, but then smiled. "Certainly," she said and the proud Aphris of Turia, kneeling, bent forward, to eat the meat held in the hand of her master. Kamchak's laugh was cut short when she sank her fine white teeth into his hand with a savage bite.

"Aiii!" he howled, jumping up and sticking his bleeding hand into his mouth, sucking the blood from the wound.

Elizabeth had leaped up and so had I.

Aphris had sprung to her feet and ran to the side of the wagon where there lay the kaiila saddle with its seven sheathed quivas. She jerked one of the quivas from its saddle sheath and stood with the blade facing us. She was bent over with rage.

Kamchak sat down again, still sucking his hand. I also sat down, and so, too, did Elizabeth Cardwell.

We left Aphris standing there, clutching the knife, breathing deeply.

"Sleen!" cried the girl. "I have a knife!"

Kamchak paid her no attention now but was looking at his hand. He seemed satisfied that the wound was not serious, and picked up the piece of meat which he had dropped, which he tossed to Elizabeth, who, in silence, ate it. He then pointed at the remains of the overdone roast, indicating that she might eat it.

"I have a knife!" cried Aphris in fury.

Kamchak was now picking his teeth with a fingernail. "Bring wine," he said to Elizabeth, who, her mouth filled with meat, went and fetched a small skin of wine and a cup, which she filled for him. When Kamchak had drunk the cup of wine he looked again at Aphris. "For what you have done," he said, "it is common to call for one of the Clan of Torturers."

"I will kill myself first," cried Aphris, posing the quiva over her heart.

Kamchak shrugged.

The girl did not slay herself. "No," she cried, "I will slay you."

"Much better," said Kamchak, nodding. "Much better."

"I have a knife!" cried out Aphris.

"Obviously," said Kamchak. He then got up and walked rather heavily over to one wall of the wagon and took a slave whip from the wall.

He faced Aphris of Turia.

"Sleen!" she wept. She threw back her hand with the knife to rush forward and thrust it into the heart of Kamchak but the coil of the whip lashed forth and I saw its stinging tip wrap four times about the wrist and forearm of the Turian girl who cried out in sudden pain and Kamchak had stepped to the side and with a motion of his hand had thrown her off balance and then by the whip dragged her rudely over the rug to his feet. There he stepped on her wrist and removed the knife from her open hand. He thrust it in his belt.

"Slay me!" wept the girl. "I will not be your slave!"

But Kamchak had hauled her to her feet and then flung her back to where she had stood before. Dazed, holding her right arm, on which could be seen four encircling blazes of scarlet, she regarded him. Kamchak then removed the quiva from his belt and hurled it across the room until it struck in one of the poles of the frame supporting the wagon hides, two inches in the wood, beside the throat of the girl.

"Take the quiva," said Kamchak.

The girl shook with fear.

"Take it," ordered Kamchak.

She did so.

"Now," he said, "replace it."

Trembling, she did so.

"Now approach me and eat," said Kamchak. Aphris of

Turia did so, defeated, kneeling before him and turning her head delicately to take the meat from his hand. "Tomorrow," said Kamchak, "you will be permitted—after I have eaten—to feed yourself."

Suddenly Elizabeth Cardwell said, perhaps unwisely. "You are cruel."

Kamchak looked at her in surprise. "I am kind," he said.

"How is that?" I asked.

"I am permitting her to live," he said.

"I think," I said, "that you have won this night but I warn you that the girl from Turia will think again of the quiva and the heart of a Tuchuk warrior."

"Of course," smiled Kamchak, feeding Aphris, "she is superb."

The girl looked at him with wonder.

"For a Turian slave," he added. He fed her another piece of meat. "Tomorrow, Little Aphris," said he, "I will give you something to wear."

She looked at him gratefully.

"Bells and collar," said he.

Tears appeared in her eyes.

"Can I trust you?" he asked.

"No," she said.

"Bells and collar," said he. "But I shall wind them about with strings of diamonds—that those who see will know that your master can well afford the goods you will do without."

"I hate you," she said.

"Excellent," said Kamchak. "Excellent."

When the girl had finished and Elizabeth had given her a dipper of water from the leather bucket that hung near the door, Aphris extended her wrists to Kamchak.

The Tuchuk looked puzzled.

"Surely," she said, "you will lock me in slave bracelets and chain me tonight?"

"But it is rather early," pointed out Kamchak.

The girl's eyes showed a moment of fear but then she seemed resolved. "You have made me your slave," she said, "but I am still Aphris of Turia. You may, Tuchuk, slay Aphris of Turia if it pleases you, but know that she will never serve your pleasure—never."

"Well," said the Tuchuk, "tonight I am pretty drunk."

"Never," said Aphris of Turia.

"I note," said Kamchak, "that you have never called me Master."

"I call no man Master," said the girl.

"I am tired tonight," said Kamchak, yawning. "I have had a hard day."

Aphris trembled in anger, her wrists still forward.

"I would retire," she said.

"Perhaps then," said Kamchak, "I should have sheets of crimson silk brought, and the furs of the mountain larl."

"As you wish," said the girl.

Kamchak clapped her on the shoulders. "Tonight," he said, "I will not chain you nor put you in the bracelets."

Aphris was clearly surprised. I saw her eyes furtively dart toward the kaiila saddle with its seven quivas.

"As Kamchak wishes," she said.

"Do you not recall," asked Kamchak, "the banquet of Saphrar?"

"Of course," she said, warily.

"Do you not recall," asked Kamchak, "the affair of the tiny bottles of perfume and the smell of bosk dung—how nobly you attempted to rid the banquet hall of that most unpleasant and distasteful odor?"

"Yes," said the girl, very slowly.

"Do you not recall," asked Kamchak, "what I then said to you—what I said at that time?"

"No!" cried the girl leaping up, but Kamchak had jumped toward her, scooped her up and threw her over his shoulder. She squirmed and struggled on his shoulder, kicking and pounding on his back. "Sleen!" she cried. "Sleen! Sleen! Sleen!"

I followed Kamchak down the steps of the wagon and, blinking and still sensible of the effects of the Paga, gravely held open the large dung sack near the rear left wheel of the wagon. "No, Master!" the girl wept.

"You call no man Master," Kamchak was reminding her.

And then I saw the lovely Aphris of Turia pitched head first into the large, leather sack, screaming and sputtering, thrashing about.

"Master!" she cried. "Master! Master!"

Sleepily I could see the sides of the sack bulging out wildly here and there as she squirmed about.

Kamchak then tied shut the end of the leather sack and wearily stood up. "I am tired," he said. "I have had a difficult and exhausting day."

I followed him into the wagon where, in a short time, we had both fallen asleep.

12

The Quiva

In the next days I several times wandered into the vicinity of the huge wagon of Kutaituchik, called Ubar of the Tuchuks. More than once I was warned away by guards. I knew that in that wagon, if the words of Saphrar were correct, there lay the golden sphere, doubtless the egg of Priest-Kings, which he had, for some reason, seemed so anxious to obtain.

I realized that I must, somehow, gain access to the wagon and find and carry away the sphere, attempting to return it to the Sardar. I would have given much for a tarn. Even on my kaiila I was certain I could be outdistanced by numerous riders, each leading, in the Tuchuk fashion, a string of fresh mounts. Eventually my kaiila would tire and I would be brought down on the prairie by pursuers. The trailing would undoubtedly be done by trained herd sleen.

The prairie stretched away for hundreds of pasangs in all directions. There was little cover.

It was possible, of course, that I might declare my mission to Kutaituchik or Kamchak, and see what would occur—but I knew that Kamchak had said to Saphrar of Turia that the Tuchuks were fond of the golden sphere—and I had no hopes that I might make them part with it—and surely I had no riches comparable to those of Saphrar with which to purchase it—and Saphrar's own attempts to win the sphere by purchase, I reminded myself, had failed.

Yet I was hesitant to make the strike of a thief at the wagon of Kutaituchik—for the Tuchuks, in their bluff way, had made me welcome, and I had come to care for some of them, particularly the gruff, chuckling, wily Kamchak, whose wagon I shared. It did not seem to me a worthy thing to betray the hospitality of Tuchuks by attempting to purloin an object which obviously they held to be of great value. I wondered if any in the camp of the Tuchuks realized how actually great indeed was the value of that golden sphere, containing undoubtedly the last hope of the people called Priest-Kings.

In Turia I had learned nothing, unfortunately, of the answers to the mystery of the message collar—or to the appearance of Miss Elizabeth Cardwell on the southern plains of Gor. I had, however, inadvertently, learned the location of the golden sphere, and that Saphrar, a man of power in Turia, was also interested in obtaining it. These bits of information were acquisitions not negligible in their value. I wondered if Saphrar himself might be the key to the mysteries that confronted me. It did not seem impossible. How was it that he, a merchant of Turia, knew of the golden sphere? How was it that he, a man of shrewdness and intelligence, seemed willing to barter volumes of gold for what he termed merely a curiosity? There seemed to be something here at odds with the rational avarice of mercantile calculation, something extending even beyond the often irresponsible zeal of the dedicated collector—which he seemed to claim to be. Yet I knew that whatever Saphrar, merchant of Turia, might be, he was no fool. He, or those for whom he worked, must have some inkling—or perhaps know—of the nature of the golden sphere. If this was true, and I thought it likely, I realized I must obtain the egg as rapidly as possible and attempt to return it to the Sardar. There was no time to lose. And yet how could I succeed?

I resolved that the best time to steal the egg would be during the days of the Omen Taking. At that time Kutaituchik and other high men among the Tuchuks, doubtless including Kamchak, would be afield, on the rolling hills surrounding the Omen Valley, in which on the hundreds of smoking altars, the haruspexes of the four peoples would be practicing their obscure craft, taking the omens, trying to determine whether or not they were favorable for the election of a Ubar San, a One Ubar, who would be Ubar of all the Wagons. If such were to be elected, I trusted, at least for the sake of the Wagon Peoples, that it would not be Kutaituchik. Once he might have been a great man and warrior but now, somnolent and fat, he thought of little save the contents of a golden kanda box. But, I reminded myself, such a choice, if choice there must be, might be best for the cities of Gor, for under Kutaituchik the Wagons would not be likely to move northward, nor even to the gates of Turia. But, I then reminded myself even more strongly, there would be no choice—there had been no Ubar San for a hundred years or more—the Wagon Peoples, fierce and independent, did not wish a Ubar San.

I noted, following me, as I had more than once, a masked figure, one wearing the hood of the Clan of Torturers. I supposed he was curious about me, not a Tuchuk, not a merchant or singer, yet among the Wagons. When I would look at him, he would turn away. Indeed, perhaps I only imagined he followed me. Once I thought to turn and question him, but he had disappeared.

I turned and retraced my steps to the wagon of Kamchak. I was looking forward to the evening.

The little wench from Port Kar, whom Kamchak and I had seen in the slave wagon when we had bought Paga the night before the games of Love War, was this night to perform the chain dance. I recalled that he might have, had it not been for me, even purchased the girl. She had surely taken his eye and, I shall admit, mine as well.

Already a large, curtained enclosure had been set up near the slave wagon. For a fee, the proprietor of the wagon would permit visitors. These arrangements irritated me somewhat, for customarily the chain dance, the whip dance, the love dance of the newly collared slave girl, the brand dance, and so on, are performed openly by firelight in the evening, for the delight of any who care to watch. Indeed, in the spring, with the results of caravan raids already accumulating, it is a rare night on which one cannot see one or more such dances performed. I gathered that the little wench from Port Kar must be superb. Kamchak, not a man to part easily with a tarn disk, had apparently received inside word on the matter. I resolved not to wager with him to see who would pay the admission.

When I returned to the wagon I saw the bosk had already been tended, though it was early in the day, and that there was a kettle on an outside fire boiling. I also noted that the dung sack was quite full.

I bounded up the stairs and entered the wagon.

The two girls were there, and Aphris was kneeling behind Elizabeth, combing Elizabeth's hair.

Kamchak, as I recalled, had recommended a thousand strokes a day.

The pelt of the larl which Elizabeth wore had been freshly brushed.

Both girls had apparently washed at the stream some four pasangs away, taking the opportunity to do so while fetching water.

They seemed rather excited. Perhaps Kamchak would permit them to go somewhere.

Aphris of Turia wore bells and collar, about her neck the Turian collar hung with bells, about each wrist and ankle, locked, a double row of bells. I could hear them move as she combed Elizabeth's hair. Aside from the bells and collar she wore only several strings of diamonds wrapped about the collar, some dangling from it, with the bells.

"Greetings, Master," said both girls at the same time.

"Ow!" cried Elizabeth as Aphris' comb apparently suddenly caught in a snarl in her hair.

"Greetings," I said. "Where is Kamchak?"

"He is coming," said Aphris.

Elizabeth turned her head over her shoulder. "I will speak with him," she said. "I am First Girl."

The comb caught in Elizabeth's hair again and she cried out.

"You are only a barbarian," said Aphris sweetly.

"Comb my hair, Slave," said Elizabeth, turning away.

"Certainly—Slave," said Aphris, continuing her work.

"I see you are both in a pleasant mood," I said. Actually, as a matter of fact, both were. Each seemed rather excited and happy, their bickering notwithstanding.

"Master," said Aphris, "is taking us tonight to see a Chain Dance, a girl from Port Kar."

I was startled.

"Perhaps I should not go," Elizabeth was saying, "I would feel too sorry for the poor girl."

"You may remain in the wagon," said Aphris.

"If you see her," I said, "'I think you will not feel sorry for her.' I didn't really feel like telling Elizabeth that no one ever feels sorry for a wench from Port Kar. They tend to be superb, feline, vicious, startling. They are famed as dancers throughout all the cities of Gor.

I wondered casually why Kamchak was taking the girls,

for the proprietor of the slave wagon would surely want his fee for them as well as us.

"Ho!" cried Kamchak, stomping into the wagon. "Meat!" he cried.

Elizabeth and Aphris leaped up to tend the pot outside.

He then settled down cross-legged on the rug, not far from the brass and copper grating.

He looked at me shrewdly and, to my surprise, drew a tospit out of his pouch, that yellowish-white, bitter fruit, looking something like a peach but about the size of a plum. He threw me the tospit.

"Odd or even?" he asked.

I had resolved not to wager with Kamchak, but this was indeed an opportunity to gain a certain amount of vengeance which, on my part, would be sorely appreciated. Usually, in guessing tospit seeds, one guesses the actual number, and usually both guessers opt for an odd number. The common tospit almost invariably has an odd number of seeds. On the other hand the rare, long-stemmed tospit usually has an even number of seeds. Both fruits are indistinguishable outwardly. I could see that, perhaps by accident, the tospit which Kamchak had thrown me had had the stem twisted off. It must be then, I surmised, the rare, long-stemmed tospit.

"Even," I said.

Kamchak looked at me as though pained. "Tospits almost always have an odd number of seeds," he said.

"Even," I said.

"Very well," said he, "eat the tospit and see."

"Why should I eat it?" I asked. The tospit, after all, is quite bitter. And why shouldn't Kamchak eat it? He had suggested the wager.

"I am a Tuchuk," said Kamchak, "I might be tempted to swallow seeds."

"Let's cut it up," I proposed.

"One might miss a seed that way," said Kamchak.

"Perhaps we could mash the slices," I suggested.

"But would that not be a great deal of trouble," asked Kamchak, "and might one not stain the rug?"

"Perhaps we could mash them in a bowl," I suggested.

"But then a bowl would have to be washed," said Kamchak.

"That is true," I admitted.

"All things considered," said Kamchak, "I think the fruit should be eaten."

"I guess you are right," I said.

I bit into the fruit philosophically. It was indeed bitter.

"Besides," said Kamchak, "I do not much care for tospits."

"I am not surprised," I said.

"They are quite bitter," said Kamchak.

"Yes," I said.

I finished the fruit and, of course, it had seven seeds.

"Most tospits," Kamchak informed me, "have an odd number of seeds."

"I know," I said.

"Then why did you guess even?" he asked.

"I supposed," I grumbled, "that you would have found a long-stemmed tospit."

"But they are not available," he said, "until late in the summer."

"Oh," I said.

"Since you lost," pointed out Kamchak, "I think it only fair that you pay the admission to the performance."

"All right," I said.

"The slaves," mentioned Kamchak, "will also be coming."

"Of course," I said, "naturally."

I took out some coins from my pouch and handed them to Kamchak who slipped them in a fold of his sash. As I did so I glowered significantly at the tankards of jewels and chests of golden tarn disks in the corner of the wagon.

"Here come the slaves," said Kamchak.

Elizabeth and Aphris entered, carrying the kettle between them, which they sat on the brass and copper grating over the fire bowl in the wagon.

"Go ahead and ask him," prompted Elizabeth, "Slave."

Aphris seemed frightened, confused.

"Meat!" said Kamchak.

After we had eaten and the girls had eaten with us, there not being that night much time for observing the amenities, Elizabeth poked Aphris, "Ask him," she said.

Aphris lowered her head and shook it.

Elizabeth looked at Kamchak. "One of your slaves," she said, "would like to ask you something."

"Which one?" inquired Kamchak.

"Aphris," said Elizabeth firmly.

"No," said Aphris, "no, Master."

"Give him Ka-la-na wine," prompted Elizabeth.

Aphris got up and fetched not a skin, but a bottle, of wine,

Ka-la-na wine, from the Ka-la-na orchards of great Ar itself. She also brought a black, red-trimmed wine crater from the isle of Cos.

"May I serve you?" she asked.

Kamchak's eyes glinted. "Yes," he said.

She poured wine into the crater and replaced the bottle. Kamchak had watched her hands very carefully. She had had to break the seal on the bottle to open it. The crater had been upside down when she had picked it up. If she had poisoned the wine she had certainly done so deftly.

Then she knelt before him in the position of the Pleasure Slave and, head down, arms extended, offered him the crater.

He took it and sniffed it and then took a wary sip.

Then he threw back his head and drained the crater. "Hah!" said he when finished.

Aphris jumped.

"Well," said Kamchak, "what is it that a Turian wench would crave of her master?"

"Nothing," said Aphris.

"If you do not ask him, I shall," said Elizabeth.

"Speak, Slave!" shouted Kamchak and Aphris went white and shook her head.

"She found something today," said Elizabeth, "that someone had thrown away."

"Bring it!" said Kamchak.

Timidly Aphris rose and went to the thin rep-cloth blanket that was her bedding near the boots of Kamchak. Hidden in the blanket there was a faded yellow piece of cloth, which she had folded very small.

She brought it to Kamchak and held it out to him.

He took it and whipped it out. It was a worn, stained Turian camisk, doubtless one that had been worn by one of the Turian maidens acquired in Love War.

Aphris had her head to the rug, trembling.

When she looked up at Kamchak there were tears in her eyes. She said, very softly, "Aphris of Turia, the slave girl, begs her master that she might clothe herself."

"Aphris of Turia," laughed Kamchak, "begs to be permitted to wear a camisk!"

The girl nodded and swiftly put her head down.

"Come here, Little Aphris," said Kamchak.

She came forward.

He put his hands in the strings of diamonds on her throat. "Would you rather wear diamonds or the camisk?" he asked.

"Please, Master," she said, "the camisk."

Kamchak jerked the diamonds from her collar and threw them to the side of the room. Then he withdrew from his pouch the key to her collar and bells and, lock by lock, removed them from her. She could hardly believe her eyes.

"You were very noisy," Kamchak said to her, sternly.

Elizabeth clapped her hands with pleasure and began to consider the camisk.

"A slave girl is grateful to her master," said Aphris, tears in her eyes.

"Properly so," agreed Kamchak.

Then, delighted, Aphris, assisted by Elizabeth Cardwell, donned the yellow camisk. Against her dark almond eyes and long black hair the yellow camisk was exceedingly lovely.

"Come here," commanded Kamchak, and Aphris ran lightly to him, timidly.

"I will show you how to wear a camisk," said Kamchak, taking the cord and adjusting it with two or three pulls and jerks that just about took the wind out of the Turian girl. He then tied it tightly about her waist. "There," he said, "that is how a camisk is worn." I saw that Aphris of Turia would be marvelously attractive in the garment.

Then, to my surprise, she walked a bit in the wagon and twirled twice before Kamchak. "Am I not pretty, Master?" she asked.

"Yes," said Kamchak, nodding.

She laughed with delight, as proud of the worn camisk as she might have been once of robes of white and gold.

"For a Turian slave," added Kamchak.

"Of course," she laughed, "for a Turian slave!"

"We will be late for the performance," said Elizabeth, "if we do not hurry."

"I thought you were staying in the wagon," said Aphris.

"No," said Elizabeth, "I have decided to come."

Kamchak was fishing about among his paraphernalia and he came up with two wrist-ankle hobbles.

"What are those for?" asked Aphris.

"So that you will not forget you are slave girls," growled Kamchak. "Come along."

Kamchak, with my money, fairly won in wager of course, paid our admission and we found our way within the curtained enclosure.

Several men, and some of the their girls, were there. I saw

among them even some Kassars and Paravaci, and one of the rare Kataii, seldom seen in the encampments of the other peoples. The Tuchuks, of course, were most in evidence, sitting cross-legged in circles rather about a large fire near the center of the enclosure. They were in good humor and were laughing and moving their hands about as they regaled one another with accounts of their recent deeds, of which there were plainly a great many, it being the most active season for caravan raiding. The fire, I was pleased to note, was not of bosk dung but wood, timber and planking, I was less pleased to note, torn and splintered from a merchant's wagon.

To one side, across a clearing from the fire, a bit in the background, was a group of nine musicians. They were not as yet playing, though one of them was absently tapping a rhythm on a small hand drum, the kaska; two others, with stringed instruments, were tuning them, putting their ears to the instruments. One of the instruments was an eight-stringed czehar, rather like a large flat oblong box; it is held across the lap when sitting cross-legged and is played with a horn pick; the other was the kalika, a six-stringed instrument; it, like the czehar, is flat-bridged and its strings are adjusted by means of small wooden cranks; on the other hand, it less resembles a low, flat box and suggests affinities to the banjo or guitar, though the sound box is hemispheric and the neck rather long; it, too, of course, like the czehar, is plucked; I have never seen a bowed instrument on Gor; also, I might mention, I have never on Gor seen any written music; I do not know if a notation exists; melodies are passed on from father to son, from master to apprentice. There was another kalika player, as well, but he was sitting there holding his instrument, watching the slave girls in the audience. The three flutists were polishing their instruments and talking together; it was shop talk I gathered, because one or the other would stop to illustrate some remark by a passage on his flute, and then one of the others would attempt to correct or improve on what he had done; occasionally their discussion grew heated. There was also a second drummer, also with a kaska, and another fellow, a younger one, who sat very seriously before what appeared to me to be a pile of objects; among them was a notched stick, played by sliding a polished tem-wood stick across its surface; cymbals of various sorts; what was obviously a tambourine; and several other instruments of a percussion variety, bits of metal on

wires, gourds filled with pebbles, slave bells mounted on hand
rings, and such. These various things, from time to time,
would be used not only by himself but by others in the
group, probably the second kaska player and the third flutist.
Among Gorean musicians, incidentally, czehar players have
the most prestige; there was only one in this group, I noted,
and he was their leader; next follow the flutists and then the
players of the kalika; the players of the drums come next;
and the farthest fellow down the list is the man who keeps
the bag of miscellaneous instruments, playing them and par-
celing them out to others as needed. Lastly it might be
mentioned, thinking it is of some interest, musicians on Gor
are never enslaved; they may, of course, be exiled, tortured,
slain and such; it is said, perhaps truly, that he who makes
music must, like the tarn and the Vosk gull, be free.

Inside the enclosure, over against one side, I saw the slave
wagon. The bosk had been unhitched and taken elsewhere. It
was open and one could go in and purchase a bottle of Paga
if one cared to do so.

"One is thirsty," said Kamchak.

"I'll buy the Paga," I said.

Kamchak shrugged. He had, after all, bought the admis-
sions.

When I returned with the bottle I had to step through,
over, and once or twice on, Tuchuks. Fortunately my clum-
siness was not construed as a challenge. One fellow I stepped
on was even polite enough to say, "Forgive me for sitting
where you are stepping." In Tuchuk fashion, I assured him
that I had taken no offense, and, sweating, I at last made my
way to Kamchak's side. He had rather good seats, which
hadn't been there before, obtained by the Tuchuk method of
finding two individuals sitting closely together and then sitting
down between them. He had also parked Aphris on his right
and Elizabeth on his left. I bit out the cork in the Paga and
passed it past Elizabeth to Kamchak, as courtesy demanded.
About a third of the bottle was missing when Elizabeth,
looking faint at having smelled the beverage, returned it to
me.

I heard two snaps and I saw that Kamchak had put a
hobble on Aphris. The slave hobble consists of two rings, one
for a wrist, the other for an ankle, joined by about seven
inches of chain. In a right-handed girl, such as either Aphris
or Elizabeth, it locks on the right wrist and left ankle. When
the girl kneels, in any of the traditional positions of the

Gorean woman, either slave or free, it is not uncomfortable. In spite of the hobble, Aphris, in the yellow camisk, black hair flowing behind her, was kneeling alertly by Kamchak's side, looking about her with great interest. I saw several of the Tuchuks present eye her with admiration. Female slaves on Gor, of course, are used to being eyed boldly. They expect this and relish it. Aphris, I discovered, to my delight, was no exception.

Elizabeth Cardwell also had her head up, kneeling very straight, obviously not unconscious that she herself was the object of a look or two.

I noted that, in spite of the fact that Aphris had now been in the wagon for several days, Kamchak had not yet called for the Iron Master. The girl had neither been branded nor had the Tuchuk nose ring been affixed. This seemed to me of interest. Moreover, after the first day or two he had hardly cuffed the girl, though he had once beaten her rather severely when she had dropped a cup. Now I saw that, though she had been only a few days his slave, already he was permitting her to wear the camisk. I smiled rather grimly to myself and took a significant swallow of Paga. "Wily Tuchuk, eh?" I thought to myself.

Aphris, for her part, though the quivas were still available, seemed, shortly after having begun to sleep at Kamchak's boots, for some reason to have thought the better of burying one in his heart. It would not have been wise, of course, for even were she successful, her consequent hideous death at the hands of the Clan of Torturers would probably, all things considered, have made her act something of a bad bargain. On the other hand she may have feared that Kamchak would simply turn around and seize her. After all, it is difficult to sneak up on a man while wearing collar and bells. Also, she may have feared more than death that if she failed in an attempt to slay him she would be plunged in the sack again which lay ever ready near the back, left wheel of the wagon. That seemed to be an experience which she, no more than Elizabeth Cardwell, was not eager to repeat.

Well did I recall the first day following the first night of Aphris as the slave of Kamchak. We had slept late that day and finally when Kamchak managed to be up and around, after a late breakfast served rather slowly by Elizabeth, and had recollected Aphris and had opened the end of her sleeping quarters and she had crawled out backward and had begged, head to boot, to be allowed to draw water for the bosk, though it was early, it seemed evident to all that the lovely wench from Turia would not, could she help it, spend a night again similar to her first in the encampment of Tuchuks. "Where will you sleep tonight, Slave?" Kamchak had demanded. "If my master will permit," said the girl, with great apparent sincerity, "at his feet." Kamchak laughed. "Get up, Lazy Girl," said he, "the bosk need watering." Gratefully Aphris of Turia had taken up the leather buckets and hurried away to fetch water.

I heard a bit of chain and looked up. Kamchak tossed me the other hobble. "Secure the barbarian," he said.

This startled me, and startled Elizabeth as well.

How was it that Kamchak would have me secure his slave? She was his, not mine. There is a kind of implicit claim of ownership involved in putting a wench in slave steel. It is seldom done save by a master.

Suddenly Elizabeth was kneeling terribly straight, looking ahead, breathing very quickly.

I reached around and took her right wrist, drawing it behind her body. I locked the wrist ring about her wrist. Then I took her left ankle in my hand and lifted it a bit, slipping the open ankle ring under it. Then I pressed the ring shut. It closed with a small, heavy click.

Her eyes suddenly met mine, timid, frightened.

I put the key in my pouch and turned my attention to the crowd. Kamchak now had his right arm about Aphris.

"In a short time," he was telling her, "you will see what a real woman can do."

"She will be only a slave such as I," Aphris was responding.

I turned to face Elizabeth. She was regarding me, it seemed, with incredible shyness. "What does it mean," she asked, "that you have chained me?"

"Nothing," I said.

Her eyes dropped. Without looking up, she said, "He likes her."

"Aphris the Slave?" I scoffed.

"Will I be sold?" she asked.

I saw no reason to hide this from the girl. "It is possible," I said.

She looked up, her eyes suddenly moist. "Tarl Cabot," she said, whispering, "if I am to be sold—buy me."

I looked at her with incredulity.

"Why?" I asked.

She dropped her head.

Kamchak reached across Elizabeth and dragged the Paga bottle out of my hand. Then he was wrestling with Aphris and had her head back, fingers pinching her nose, the neck of the bottle thrust between her teeth. She was struggling and laughing and shaking her head. Then she had to breathe and a great draught of Paga burned its way down her throat making her gasp and cough. I doubt that she had ever before experienced a drink stronger than the syrupy wines of Turia. She was now gasping and shaking her head and Kamchak was pounding her on the back.

"Why?" I again asked Elizabeth.

But Elizabeth, with her free left hand had seized the Paga bottle from Kamchak, and, to his amazement, had thrown back her head and taken, without realizing the full import of her action, about five lusty, guzzling swallows of Paga. Then, as I rescued the bottle, her eyes opened very wide and then blinked about ten times. She exhaled slowly as if fire might be sizzling out instead of breath and then she shook, a delayed reaction, as if she had been thumped five times and then began to cough spasmodically and painfully until I, fearing she might suffocate, pounded her several times on the back. At last, bent over, gasping for breath, she seemed to be coming around. I held her by the shoulders and suddenly she turned herself in my hands and, as I was sitting cross-legged, threw herself on her back across my lap, her right wrist still chained to her left ankle. She stretched insolently, as well as she could. I was astounded. She looked up at me. "Because I am better than Dina and Tenchika," she said.

"But not better than Aphris," called Aphris.

"Yes," said Elizabeth, "better than Aphris."

"Get up, Little She-Sleen," said Kamchak, amused, "or to preserve my honor I must have you impaled."

Elizabeth looked up at me.

"She's drunk," I told Kamchak.

"Some men might like a barbarian girl," Elizabeth said.

I hoisted Elizabeth back up on her knees. "No one will buy me," she wailed.

There were immediate offers from three or four of the Tuchuks gathered about, and I was afraid that Kamchak might, if the bids improved, part with Miss Cardwell on the spot.

"Sell her," advised Aphris.

"Be quiet, Slave," said Elizabeth.

Kamchak was roaring with laughter.

The Paga had apparently hit Miss Cardwell swiftly and hard. She seemed barely able to kneel and, at last, I permitted her to lean against me, and she did, her chin on my right shoulder.

"You know," said Kamchak, "the Little Barbarian wears your chain well."

"Nonsense," I said.

"I saw," said Kamchak, "how at the games when you thought the men of Turia charging you were prepared to rescue the wench."

"I wouldn't have wanted your property damaged," I said.

"You like her," annnounced Kamchak.

"Nonsense," I said to him.

"Nonsense," said Elizabeth, sleepily.

"Sell her to him," recommended Aphris, hiccuping.

"You only want to be First Girl," said Elizabeth.

"I'd give her away myself," said Aphris. "She is only a barbarian."

Elizabeth lifted her head from my shoulder and regarded me. She spoke in English. "My name is Miss Elizabeth Cardwell, Mr. Cabot," she said, "would you like to buy me?"

"No," I said, in English.

"I didn't think so," she said, again in English, and put her head back on my shoulder.

"Did you not observe," asked Kamchak, "how she moved and breathed when you locked the steel on her?"

I hadn't thought much about it. "I guess not," I said.

"Why do you think I let you chain her?" asked Kamchak.

"I don't know," I said.

"To see," he said. "And it is as I thought—your steel kindles her."

"Nonsense," I said.

"Nonsense," said Elizabeth.

"Do you want to buy her?" suddenly asked Kamchak.

"No," I said.

"No," said Elizabeth.

The last thing I needed in the dangerous mission ahead was to be burdened with a slave girl.

"Will the performance start soon?" asked Elizabeth of Kamchak.

"Yes," he said.

"I do not know," said Elizabeth, "if I should watch."

"Permit her to return to the wagon," suggested Aphris.

"I suppose," said Elizabeth, "I could hop all the way on one foot."

I myself doubted that this would be feasible, particularly in her condition.

"You probably could," said Aphris, "you have muscular legs—"

I did not regard Miss Cardwell's legs as muscular. She was, however, a good runner.

Miss Cardwell lifted her chin from my shoulder. "Slave," she said.

"Barbarian," retorted Aphris.

"Release her," said Kamchak.

I reached into the pouch at my belt to secure the key to the hobble.

"No," said Elizabeth, "I will stay."

"If Master permits," added Aphris.

"Yes," said Elizabeth, glowering, "if Master permits."

"All right," said Kamchak.

"Thank you, Master," said Elizabeth politely, and once more put her head on my shoulder.

"You should buy her!" said Kamchak.

"No," I said.

"I will give you a good price," he said.

Oh, yes, I said to myself, a good price, and ho, ho, ho.

"No," I said.

"Very well," said Kamchak.

I breathed more easily.

About that time the black-clad figure of a woman appeared on the steps of the slave wagon. I heard Kamchak hush up Ahpris of Turia and he gave Elizabeth a poke in the ribs that she might bestir herself. "Watch, you miserable cooking-pot wenches," he said, "and learn a thing or two!"

A silence came over the crowd. Almost without meaning to, I noticed, over to one side, a hooded member of the Clan of Torturers. I was confident it was he who had often followed me about the camp.

But this matter was dismissed from my mind by the performance which was about to begin. Aphris was watching intently, her lips parted. Kamchak's eyes were gleaming. Even Elizabeth had lifted her head now from my shoulder and was rising on her knees a bit for a clearer view.

The figure of the woman, swathed in black, heavily veiled, descended the steps of the slave wagon. Once at the foot of the stairs she stopped and stood for a long moment. Then the musicians began, the hand-drums first, a rhythm of heartbeat and flight.

To the music, beautifully, it seemed the frightened figure ran first here and then there, occasionally avoiding imaginary objects or throwing up her arms, ran as though through the crowds of a burning city—alone, yet somehow suggesting the presence about her of hunted others. Now, in the background, scarcely to be seen, was the figure of a warrior in scarlet cape. He, too, in his way, though hardly seeming to move, approached, and it seemed that wherever the girl might flee there was found the warrior. And then at last his hand was upon her shoulder and she threw back her head and lifted her hands and it seemed her entire body was wretchedness and despair. He turned the figure to him and, with both hands, brushed away hood and veil.

There was a cry of delight from the crowd.

The girl's face was fixed in the dancer's stylized moan of terror, but she was beautiful. I had seen her before, of course, as had Kamchak, but it was startling still to see her thus in the firelight—her hair was long and silken black, her eyes dark, the color of her skin tannish.

She seemed to plead with the warrior but he did not move. She seemed to writhe in misery and try to escape his grip but she did not.

Then he removed his hands from her shoulders and, as the crowd cried out, she sank in abject misery at his feet and performed the ceremony of submission, kneeling, lowering the head and lifting and extending the arms, wrists crossed.

The warrior then turned from her and held out one hand.

Someone from the darkness threw him, coiled, the chain and collar.

He gestured for the woman to rise and she did so and stood before him, head lowered.

He pushed up her head and then, with a click that could be heard throughout the enclosure, closed the collar—a Turian collar—about her throat. The chain to which the collar was attached was a good deal longer than that of the Sirik, containing perhaps twenty feet of length.

Then, to the music, the girl seemed to twist and turn and move away from him, as he played out the chain, until she stood wretched some twenty feet from him at the chain's length. She did not move then for a moment, but stood crouched down, her hands on the chain.

I saw that Aphris and Elizabeth were watching fascinated. Kamchak, too, would not take his eyes from the woman.

The music had stopped.

Then with a suddenness that almost made me jump and the crowd cry out with delight the music began again but this time as a barbaric cry of rebellion and rage and the wench from Port Kar was suddenly a chained she-larl biting and tearing at the chain and she had cast her black robes from her and stood savage revealed in diaphanous, swirling yellow Pleasure Silk. There was now a frenzy and hatred in the dance, a fury even to the baring of teeth and snarling. She turned within the collar, as the Turian collar is designed to permit. She circled the warrior like a captive moon to his imprisoning scarlet sun, always at the length of the chain. Then he would take up a fist of chain, drawing her each time inches closer. At times he would permit her to draw back again, but never to the full length of the chain, and each time he permitted her to withdraw, it was less than the last. The dance consists of several phases, depending on the general orbit allowed the girl by the chain. Certain of these phases are very slow, in which there is almost no movement, save perhaps the turning of a head or the movement of a hand; others are defiant and swift; some are graceful and pleading; some stately, some simple; some proud, some piteous; but each time, as the common thread, she is drawn closer to the caped warrior. At last his fist was within the Turian collar itself and he drew the girl, piteous and exhausted, to his lips, subduing her with his kiss, and then her arms were about his neck and unresisting, obedient, her head to his chest, she was lifted lightly in his arms and carried from the firelight.

Kamchak and I, and others, threw coins of gold into the sand near the fire.

"She was beautiful," cried out Aphris of Turia.

"I never knew a woman," said Elizabeth, her eyes blazing, showing few signs of the Paga, "could be so beautiful!"

"She was marvelous," I said.

"And I," howled Kamchak, "have only miserable cooking-pot wenches!"

Kamchak and I were standing up. Aphris suddenly put her head to his thigh, looking down. "Tonight," she whispered, "make me a slave."

Kamchak put his fist in her hair and lifted her head to stare up at him. Her lips were parted.

"You have been my slave for days," said he.

"Tonight," she begged, "please, Master, tonight!"

With a roar of triumph Kamchak swept her up and slung her, hobbled as she was, over his shoulder and she cried out and he, singing a Tuchuk song, was stomping away with her from the curtained enclosure.

At the exit he stopped briefly and, Aphris over his shoulder, turned and faced Elizabeth and myself. He threw up his right hand in an expansive gesture. "For the night," he cried, "the Little Barbarian is yours!" Then he turned again and, singing, disappeared through the curtain.

I laughed.

Elizabeth Cardwell was staring after him. Then she looked up at me. "He can do that, can't he?" she asked.

"Of course," I said.

"Of course," she said, numbly. "Why not?" Then suddenly she jerked at the hobble but could not rise and nearly fell, and pounded her left fist into the dirt before her. "I don't want to be a slave!" she cried. "I don't want to be a slave!"

"I'm sorry," I said.

She looked up at me. There were tears in her eyes. "He has no right!" she cried.

"He has the right," I said.

"Of course," she wept, putting her head down. "It is like a book—a chair—an animal. She is yours! Take her! Keep her until tomorrow! Return her in the morning—when you are finished with her!"

Head down she laughed and sobbed.

"I thought you wished," I said, "that I might buy you." I thought it well to jest with her.

"Don't you understand?" she asked. "It could have been anyone to whom I was given—not just to you—but to anyone, anyone!"

"That is true," I said.

"To anyone!" she wept. "Anyone! Anyone!"

"Do not be distraught," I said.

She shook her head, the hair swirling behind her, and looked up at me, and through the tears smiled. "It seems— Master—" she said, "that for the hour I am yours."

"It would appear so," I said.

"Will you carry me over your shoulder to the wagon," she asked, lightly, "like Aphris of Turia?"

"I'm sorry," I said.

I bent to the girl's shackles and removed them.

She stood up and faced me. "What are you going to do with me?" she asked. She smiled. "—Master?"

I smiled. "Nothing," I told her. "Do not fear."

"Oh?" she asked, one eyebrow rising skeptically. Then she dropped her head. "Am I truly so ugly?" she asked.

"No," I said, "you are not ugly."

"But you do not want me?" she asked.

"No," I said.

She looked at me boldly, throwing back her head. "Why not?" she asked.

What could I tell her? She was lovely, but yet in her condition piteous. I felt moved on her behalf. The little secretary, I thought to myself, so far from her pencils, the typewriter, the desk calendars and steno pads—so far from her world—so helpless, so much at Kamchak's mercy and this night, should I choose, at mine.

"You are only a little barbarian," I said to her. Somehow I thought of her still as the frightened girl in the yellow shift—caught up in games of war and intrigue beyond her comprehension and, to a great extent, mine. She was to be protected, sheltered, treated with kindness, reassured. I could not think of her in my arms—nor of her ignorant, timid lips on mine—for she was always and would remain only the unfortunate Elizabeth Cardwell, the innocent and unwitting victim of an inexplicable translocation and an unexpected, unjust reduction to shameful bondage. She was of Earth and knew not the flames which her words might have evoked in the breast of a Gorean warrior—nor did she understand herself truly nor the relation in which she, slave girl, stood to a free man to whom she had been for the hour given—I could not tell her that another warrior might at her very glance, have dragged her helpless to the darkness between the high wheels of the slave wagon itself. She was gentle, not understanding, naive, in her way foolish—a girl of Earth but not on Earth—not a woman of Gor female on her own barbaric world—she would always be of Earth—the bright, pretty girl with the stenographer's pad—like many girls of Earth, not men but not yet daring to be woman. "But," I admitted to her, giving her head a shake, "you are a pretty little barbarian."

She looked into my eyes for a long moment and then suddenly dropped her head weeping. I gathered her into my arms to comfort her but she pushed me away, and turned and ran from the enclosure.

I looked after her, puzzled.

Then, shrugging, I too left the enclosure, thinking that perhaps I should wander among the wagons for a few hours, before returning.

I recalled Kamchak. I was happy for him. Never before had I seen him so pleased. I was, however, confused about Elizabeth, for it seemed to me she had behaved strangely this night. I supposed that, on the whole, she was perhaps distraught because she feared she might soon be supplanted as first girl in the wagon; indeed, that she might soon be sold. To be sure, having seen Kamchak with his Aphris, it did not seem to me that either of these possibilities were actually unlikely. Elizabeth had reason to fear. I might, of course, and would, encourage Kamchak to sell her to a good master, but Kamchak, cooperative to a point, would undoubtedly have his eye fixed most decisively on the price to be obtained. I might, of course, if I could find the money, buy her myself and attempt to find her a kind master. I thought perhaps Conrad of the Kassars might be a just master. He had, however, I knew, recently won a Turian girl in the games. Moreover, not every man wants to own an untrained barbarian slave, for such, even if given to them, must be fed—and, this spring, as I could tell from walking about the camp, there was no shortage of girls, freshly collared and branded perhaps, untrained perhaps, but yet, and most importantly, Gorean, which—most significantly—Elizabeth Cardwell was not, and in my opinion could never be.

For no reason that I am quite sure of I unwisely puchased another bottle of Paga, perhaps for company in my lonely walk.

I was only about a quarter of the way through the bottle and was passing the side of a wagon when I saw a swift flicker of a shadow suddenly leap on the lacquered boards and by instinct I threw my head to one side as a quiva flashed past and buried itself three inches deep in the timber side of the wagon. Flinging the Paga bottle aside, a swirl of the liquid flying out of it, I whirled and saw, some fifty feet away, between two wagons, the dark figure of the hooded man, he of the Clan of Torturers, who had been following me. He turned and ran, and I, drawing my sword, ran stumbling after him but in less than a moment or two I found my pursuit cut short by a string of tied kaiila being returned after having been released to hunt on the plains. By the time I could manage to avoid their buffeting bodies and crawl under the rope that joined them, my assailant was gone. All I received for my trouble were the angry shouts of the man leading the kaiila string. Indeed, one of the vicious beasts even snapped at me, ripping the sleeve on my shoulder.

Angry I returned to the wagon and drew the quiva from the boards.

By this time the owner of the wagon, who was naturally curious about the matter, was beside me. He held a small torch, lit from the fire bowl within the wagon. He was examining, not happily, the cut in his planking. "A clumsy throw," he remarked, I thought a bit ill-humoredly.

"Perhaps," I admitted.

"But," he added, turning and looking at me, "I suppose under the circumstances it was just as well."

"Yes," I said, "I think so."

I found the Paga bottle and noted that there was a bit of liquid left in it, below the neck of the bottle. I wiped off the neck and handed it to the man. He took about half of it and then wiped his mouth and handed it back. I then finished the bottle. I flung it into a refuse hole, dug and periodically cleaned by male slaves.

"It is not bad Paga," said the man.

"No," I said, "I think it is pretty good."

"May I see the quiva?" asked the man.

"Yes," I said.

"Interesting," said he.

"What?" I asked.

"The quiva," said he.

"But what is interesting about it?" I asked.

"It is Paravaci," he said.

13

The Attack

In the morning, to my dismay, Elizabeth Cardwell was not to be found.

Kamchak was beside himself with fury. Aphris, knowing the ways of Gor and the temper of Tuchuks, was terrified, and said almost nothing.

"Do not release the hunting sleen," I pleaded with Kamchak.

"I shall keep them leashed," he responded grimly.

With misgivings I observed the two, six-legged, sinuous, tawny hunting sleen on their chain leashes. Kamchak was holding Elizabeth's bedding—a rep-cloth blanket—for them to smell. Their ears began to lay back against the sides of their triangular heads; their long, serpentine bodies trembled; I saw claws emerge from their paws, retract, emerge again and then retract; they lifted their heads, sweeping them from side to side, and then thrust their snouts to the ground and began to whimper excitedly; I knew they would first follow the scent to the curtained enclosure within which last night we had observed the dance.

"She would have hidden among the wagons last night," Kamchak said.

"I know," I said, "—the herd sleen." They would have torn the girl to pieces on the prairie in the light of the three Gorean moons.

"She will not be far," said Kamchak.

He hoisted himself to the saddle of his kaiila, a prancing and trembling hunting sleen on each side of the animal, the chains running to the pommel of the saddle.

"What will you do to her?" I asked.

"Cut off her feet," said Kamchak, "and her nose and ears, and blind her in one eye—then release her to live as she can among the wagons."

Before I could remonstrate with the angry Tuchuk the hunting sleen suddenly seemed to go wild, rearing on their hind legs, scratching in the air, dragging against the chains. It was all Kamchak's kaiila could do to brace itself against their sudden madness.

"Hah!" cried Kamchak.

I spied Elizabeth Cardwell approaching the wagon, two leather water buckets fastened to a wooden yoke she carried over her shoulders. Some water was spilling from the buckets.

Aphris cried out with delight and ran to Elizabeth, to my astonishment, to kiss her and help with the water.

"Where have you been?" asked Kamchak.

Elizabeth lifted her head innocently and gazed at him frankly. "Fetching water," she said.

The sleen were trying to get at her and she had backed away against the wagon, watching them warily. "They are vicious beasts," she observed.

Kamchak threw back his head and roared with laughter. Elizabeth did not so much as look at me.

Then Kamchak seemed sober and he said to the girl. "Go into the wagon. Bring slave bracelets and a whip. Then go to the wheel."

She looked at him, but did not appear afraid. "Why?" she asked.

Kamchak dismounted. "You were overly long in fetching water," he said.

Elizabeth and Aphris had gone into the wagon.

"She was wise to return," said Kamchak.

I agreed with him but would not say so. "It seems she was fetching water," I pointed out.

"You like her, don't you?" asked Kamchak.

"I feel sorry for her," I said.

"Did you enjoy her yesterday?" asked Kamchak.

"I did not see her after she left the enclosure of the dance," I said.

"If I had known that," said Kamchak, "I would have had the sleen out last night."

"Then," I said, "it is fortunate for the girl that you did not know it."

"Agreed," smiled Kamchak. "Why did you not make use of her?" he inquired.

"She is only a girl," I said.

"She is a woman," said Kamchak, "with blood."

I shrugged.

By this time Elizabeth had returned with the whip and bracelets, and had handed them to Kamchak. She then went to stand by the left, rear wheel of the wagon. There Kamchak braceleted her wrists high over her head about the rim and over one of the spokes. She faced the wheel.

"There is no escape from the wagons," he said.

Her head was high. "I know," she said.

"You lied to me," he said, "saying you went to fetch water."

"I was afraid," said Elizabeth.

"Do you know who fears to tell the truth?" he asked.

"No," she said.

"A slave," said Kamchak.

He ripped the larl's pelt from her and I gathered that she would wear the garment no longer.

She stood well, her eyes closed, her right cheek pressed against the leather rim of the wheel. Tears burst from between the tightly pressed lids of her eyes but she was superb, restraining her cries.

She had still uttered no sound when Kamchak, satisfied, had released her, but fastening her wrists before her body with the bracelets. She stood trembling, her head down. Then he took her braceleted hands and with one hand raised her hands over her head. She stood so, her knees slightly flexed, head down.

"You think," said Kamchak to me, "she is only a girl."

I said nothing.

"You are a fool, Tarl Cabot," said he.

I did not respond.

Coiled, in his right hand, Kamchak still held the slave whip.

"Slave," said Kamchak.

Elizabeth looked at him.

"Do you wish to serve men?" he asked.

Tears in her eyes she shook her head, no, no, no. Then her head fell again to her breast.

"Observe," said Kamchak to me.

Then, before I could realize what he intended, he had subjected Miss Cardwell to what, among slavers, is known as the Whip Caress. Ideally it is done, as Kamchak had, unexpectedly, taking the girl unawares. Elizabeth suddenly cried out throwing her head to one side. I observed to my amazement the sudden, involuntary, uncontrollable response to the touch. The Whip Caress is commonly used among Slavers to force a girl to betray herself.

"She is a woman," said Kamchak. "Did you not see the secret blood of her? —That she is eager and ready—that she is fit prize for the steel of a master—that she is female, and," he added, "slave?"

"No!" cried Elizabeth Cardwell. "No!" But Kamchak was pulling her by the bracelets toward an empty sleen cage mounted on a low cart near the wagon, into which, still braceleted, he thrust her, then closing the door, locking it.

She could not stand in the low, narrow cage, and knelt, wrists braceleted, hands on the bars. "It is not true!" she screamed.

Kamchak laughed at her. "Female slave," he said. She buried her head in her hands and wept. She knew, as well as we, that she had showed herself—that her blood had leaped within her and its memory must now mock the hysteria of her denial—that she had acknowledged to us and to herself, perhaps for the first time, the incontrovertible splendor of her beauty and its meaning.

Her response had been that of an utter woman.

"It's not true!" she whispered over and over, sobbing as she had not from the cruel strokes of the whip. "It's not true!"

Kamchak looked at me. "Tonight," he said, "I shall call the Iron Master."

"Don't," I said.

"I shall," he said.

"Why?" I asked.

He smiled at me grimly. "She was too long in fetching water."

I said nothing. Kamchak, for a Tuchuk, was not unkind. The punishment of a runaway slave is often grievous, sometimes culminating in death. He would do no more to Elizabeth Cardwell than was commonly done to female slaves among the wagons, even those who had never dared to speak back or disobey in the least particular. Elizabeth, in her way, was fortunate. As Kamchak might have said, he was permitting her to live. I did not think she would be temped to run away again.

I saw Aphris sneaking to the cage to bring Elizabeth a dipper of water. Aphris was crying.

Kamchak, if he saw, did not stop her. "Come along," he said. "There is a new kaiila I want to see near the wagon of Yachi of the Leather Workers' Clan."

It was a busy day for Kamchak.

He did not buy the kaiila near the wagon of Yachi of the Leather Workers though it was apparently a splendid beast. At one point, he wrapped a heavy fur and leather robe about his left arm and struck the beast suddenly on the snout with his right hand. It had not struck back at him swiftly enough to please him, and there were only four needlelike scratches in the arm guard before Kamchak had managed to leap back and the kaiila, lunging against its chain, was snapping at him. "Such a slow beast," said Kamchak, "might in battle cost a man his life." I supposed it true. The kaiila and its master fight in battle as one unit, seemingly a single savage animal, armed with teeth and lance. After looking at the kaiila Kamchak visited a wagon where he discussed the crossing of one of his cows with the owner's bull, in exchange for a similar favor on his own part. This matter was arranged to their mutual satisfaction. At another wagon he haggled over a set of quiva, forged in Ar, and, obtaining his price, arranged to have them, with a new saddle, brought to his wagon on the morrow. We lunched on dried bosk meat and Paga and then he trooped to the wagon of Kutaituchik, where he exchanged pleasantries with the somolent figure on the robe of gray boskhide, about the health of the bosk, the sharpness of quivas and the necessity of keeping wagon axles greased, and certain other matters. While near Kutaituchik's wagon, on the dais, he also conferred with several other high men among the Tuchuks. Kamchak, as I had learned before, held a position of some importance with the Tuchuks. After seeing Kutaituchik and the others, Kamchak stopped by an Iron Master's wagon, and, to my irritation, arranged for the fellow to come by the wagon that very night. "I can't keep her in a sleen cage forever," Kamchak said. "There is work to be done about the wagon." Then, to my delight, Kamchak, borrowing two kaiila, which he seemed to have no difficulty doing—from a Tuchuk warrior I had not even seen before—rode with me to the Omen Valley.

Coming over a low, rolling hill, we saw a large number of tents pitched in a circle, surrounding a large grassy area. In the grassy area, perhaps about two hundred yards in diameter, there were literally hundreds of small, stone altars. There was a large circular stone platform in the center of the field.

On the top of this platform was a huge, four-sided altar which was approached by steps on all four sides. On one side of this altar I saw the sign of the Tuchuks, and on the others, that of the Kassars, the Kataii and the Paravaci. I had not mentioned the matter of the Paravaci quiva which had almost struck me last night, having been in the morning disturbed about the disappearance of Elizabeth Cardwell and in the afternoon busy following Kamchak about in his rounds. I resolved to mention the matter to him sometime—but not this evening—for I was convinced this would not be a good evening for anyone in the wagon, except perhaps for Kamchak, who seemed pleased about the arrangements he had made with the herder pertaining to crossing livestock and the bargain, it seemed, he had contracted with the fellow with the quivas and saddle.

There were a large number of tethered animals about the outer edge of the circle, and, beside them, stood many haruspexes. Indeed, I supposed there must be one haruspex at least for each of the many altars in the field. Among the animals I saw many verrs; some domestic tarsks, their tusks sheathed; cages of flapping vulos, some sleen, some kaiila, even some bosk; by the Paravaci haruspexes I saw manacled male slaves, if such were to be permitted; commonly, I understood from Kamchak, the Tuchuks, Kassars and Kataii rule out the sacrifice of slaves because their hearts and livers are thought to be, fortunately for the slaves, untrustworthy in registering portents; after all, as Kamchak pointed out, who would trust a Turian slave in the kes with a matter so important as the election of a Ubar San; it seemed to me good logic and, of course, I am sure the slaves, too, were taken with the cogency of the argument. The animals sacrificed, incidentally, are later used for food, so the Omen Taking, far from being a waste of animals, is actually a time of feasting and plenty for the Wagon Peoples, who regard the Omen Taking, provided it results that no Ubar San is to be chosen, as an occasion for gaiety and festival. As I may have mentioned, no Ubar San had been chosen for more than a hundred years.

As yet the Omen Taking had not begun. The haruspexes had not rushed forward to the altars. On the other hand on each altar there burned a small bosk-dung fire into which, like a tiny piece of kindling, had been placed an incense stick.

Kamchak and I dismounted and, from outside the circle,

watched the four chief haruspexes of the Wagon Peoples approach the huge altar in the center of the field. Behind them another four haruspexes, one from each People, carried a large wooden cage, made of sticks lashed together, which contained perhaps a dozen white vulos, domesticated pigeons. This cage they placed on the altar. I then noted that each of the four chief haruspexes carried, about his shoulder, a white linen sack, somewhat like a peasant's rep-cloth seed bag.

"This is the first Omen," said Kamchak, "—the Omen to see if the Omens are propitious to take the Omens."

"Oh," I said.

Each of the four haruspexes then, after intoning an involved entreaty of some sort to the sky, which at the time was shining beneficiently, suddenly cast a handful of something—doubtless grain—to the pigeons in the stick cage.

Even from where I stood I could see the pigeons pecking at the grain in reassuring frenzy.

The four haruspexes turned then, each one facing his own minor haruspexes and anyone else who might be about, and called out, "It is propitious!"

There was a pleased cry at this announcement from the throng.

"This part of the Omen Taking always goes well," I was informed by Kamchak.

"Why is that?" I asked.

"I don't know," he said. Then he looked at me. "Perhaps," he proposed, "it is because the vulos are not fed for three days prior to the taking of the Omen."

"Perhaps," I admitted.

"I," said Kamchak, "would like a bottle of Paga."

"I, too," I admitted.

"Who will buy?" he asked.

I refused to speak.

"We could wager," he suggested.

"I'll buy it," I said.

I could now see the other haruspexes of the peoples pouring with their animals toward the altars. The Omen Taking as a whole lasts several days and consumes hundreds of animals. A tally is kept, from day to day. One haruspex, as we left, I heard cry out that he had found a favorable liver. Another, from an adjoining altar had rushed to his side. They were engaged in dispute. I gathered that reading the signs was a subtle business, calling for sophisticated interpretation and the utmost delicacy and judgment. Even as we made our way back to the kaiila I could hear two more haruspexes crying out that they had found livers that were clearly unfavorable. Clerks, with parchment scrolls, were circulating among the altars, presumably, I would guess, noting the names of haruspexes, their peoples, and their findings. The four chief haruspexes of the peoples remained at the huge central altar, to which a white bosk was being slowly led.

It was toward dark when Kamchak and I reached the slave wagon to buy our bottle of Paga.

On the way we passed a girl, a girl from Cos taken hundreds of pasangs away in a raid on a caravan bound for Ar. She had been bound across a wagon wheel lying on the ground, her body over its hub. Her clothing had been removed. Fresh and clean on her burned thigh was the brand of the four bosk horns. She was weeping. The Iron Master affixed the Turian collar. He bent to his tools, taking up a tiny, open golden ring, a heated metal awl, a pair of pliers. I turned away. I heard her scream.

"Do not Korobans brand and collar slaves?" asked Kamchak.

"Yes," I admitted, "they do."

I could not rid my mind of the image of the girl from Cos weeping bound on the wheel. Such tonight, or on another night, would be the lovely Elizabeth Cardwell. I threw down a wild swallow of Paga. I resolved I would somehow release the girl, somehow protect her from the cruelty of the fate decreed for her by Kamchak.

"You do not much speak," said Kamchak, taking the bottle, puzzled.

"Must the Iron Master be called," I asked, "to the wagon of Kamchak."

Kamchak looked at me. "Yes," he said.

I glared down at the polished boards of the wagon floor.

"Have you no feeling for the barbarian?" I asked.

Kamchak had never been able to pronounce her name, which he regarded as of barbarian length and complexity. "E-liz-a-beth-card-vella" he would try to say, adding the "a" sound because it is a common ending of feminine names on Gor. He could never, like most native speakers of Gorean, properly handle the "w" sound, for it is extremely rare in Gorean, existing only in certain unusual words of obviously barbarian origin. The "w" sound, incidentally, is a complex one, and, like many such sounds, is best learned only during the brief years of childhood when a child's linguistic flexibility

is at its maximum—those years in which it might be trained
to speak any of the languages of man with native fluency—a
capacity which is, for most individuals at least, lost long prior
to attaining their majority. On the other hand, Kamchak
could say the sound I have represented as "vella" quite easily
and would upon occasion use this as Elizabeth's name. Most
often, however, he and I simply referred to her as the Little
Barbarian. I had, incidentally, after the first few days, refused to speak English to her, thinking it would be more
desirable for her to learn to speak, think and hear in Gorean
as rapidly as possible. She could now handle the language
rather well. She could not, of course, read it. She was
illiterate.

Kamchak was looking at me. He laughed and leaned over
and slapped me on the shoulder. "She is only a slave!" he
chuckled.

"Have you no feeling for her?" I demanded.

He leaned back, serious for a moment. "Yes," he said, "I
am fond of the Little Barbarian."

"Then why?" I demanded.

"She ran away," said Kamchak.

I did not deny it.

"She must be taught."

I said nothing.

"Besides," said Kamchak, "the wagon grows crowded—
and she must be readied for sale."

I took back the Paga bottle and threw down another
swallow.

"Do you want to buy her?" he asked.

I thought of the wagon of Kutaituchik and the golden
sphere. The Omen Taking had now begun. I must attempt—
this night or some other in the near future—to purloin the
sphere, to return it somehow to the Sardar. I was going to
say, "No," but then I thought of the girl from Cos, bound on
the wheel, weeping. I wondered if I could meet Kamchak's
price. I looked up.

Suddenly Kamchak lifted his hand, alert, gesturing for
silence.

I noted, too, the other Tuchuks in the wagon. Suddenly
they were not moving.

Then I too heard it, the winding of a bosk horn in the
distance, and then another.

Kamchak leaped to his feet. "The camp is under attack!"
he cried.

14

Tarnsmen

Outside, as Kamchak and I bounded down the steps of the slave wagon, the darkness was filled with hurrying men, some with torches, and running kaiila, already with their riders. War lanterns, green and blue and yellow, were already burning on poles in the darkness, signaling the rallying grounds of the Orlus, the Hundreds, and the Oralus, the Thousands. Each warrior of the Wagon Peoples, and that means each able-bodied man, is a member of an Or, or a Ten; each ten is a member of an Orlu, or Hundred; each Orlu is a member of an Oralu, a Thousand. Those who are unfamiliar with the Wagon Peoples, or who know them only from the swift raid, sometimes think them devoid of organization, sometimes conceive of them as mad hordes or aggregates of wild warriors, but such is not the case. Each man knows his position in his Ten, and the position of his Ten in the Hundred, and of the Hundred in the Thousand. During the day the rapid movements of these individually maneuverable units are dictated by bosk horn and movements of the standards; at night by the bosk horns and the war lanterns slung on high poles carried by riders.

Kamchak and I mounted the kaiila we had ridden and, as rapidly as we could, pressed through the throngs toward our wagon.

When the bosk horns sound the women cover the fires and prepare the men's weapons, bringing forth arrows and bows, and lances. The quivas are always in the saddle sheaths. The bosk are hitched up and slaves, who might otherwise take advantage of the tumult, are chained.

Then the women climb to the top of the high sides on the wagons and watch the war lanterns in the distance, reading them as well as the men. Seeing if the wagons must move, and in what direction.

I heard a child screaming its disgust at being thrust in the wagon.

In a short time Kamchak and I had reached our wagon. Aphris had had the good sense to hitch up the bosk. Kamchak kicked out the fire at the side of the wagon. "What is it?" she cried.

Kamchak took her roughly by the arm and shoved her stumbling toward the sleen cage where, holding the bars, frightened, knelt Elizabeth Cardwell. Kamchak unlocked the cage and thrust Aphris inside with Elizabeth. She was slave and would be secured, that she might not seize up a weapon or try to fight or burn wagons. "Please!" she cried, thrusting her hands through the bars. But already Kamchak had slammed shut the door and twisted the key in the lock. "Master!" she cried. It was better, I knew, for her to be secured as she was rather than chained in the wagon, or even to the wheel. The wagons, in Turian raids, are burned.

Kamchak threw me a lance, and a quiver with forty arrows and a bow. The kaiila I rode already had, on the saddle, the quivas, the rope and bola. Then he bounded from the top step of the wagon onto the back of his kaiila and sped toward the sound of the bosk horns. "Master!" I heard Aphris cry.

In no more than a few Gorean Ihn we had come to the interior edge of the herds. There on a front pasangs in length, already the Thousands had nearly formed, and long lines of riders, few gaps in their ranks, waited, lance in hand, their eyes on the war lanterns.

Among these but to no Ten or Hundred did Kamchak ride. Rather, to my astonishment, he rode before them all, racing his kaiila to the center of the line where some five or ten warriors, on kaiilaback, waited. With these he hurriedly conferred and then I saw him lift his arm and red war lanterns were moved on ropes to the top of poles, and to my amazement, aisles seemed to open in the densely packed bosk before the men, herdsmen and herd sleen moving the animals back to clear long grassy passages between their lumbering, shaggy hulks. And then, following the war lanterns, filing out of their ranks with a swiftness and precision that was incredible, long, flying columns of warriors flowed like rivers between the beasts.

I rode at Kamchak's side and in an instant it seemed we had passed through the bellowing, startled herd and had emerged on the plain beyond. In the light of the Gorean moons we saw slaughtered bosk, some hundreds of them, and, some two hundred yards away, withdrawing, perhaps a thousand warriors mounted on tharlarion.

Suddenly, instead of giving pursuit, Kamchak drew his mount to a halt and behind him the rushing cavalries of the Tuchuks snarled pawing to a halt, holding their ground. I saw that a yellow lantern was halfway up the pole below the two red lanterns.

"Give pursuit!" I cried.

"Wait!" he cried. "We are fools! Fools!"

I drew back the reins on my kaiila to keep the beast quiet.

"Listen!" said Kamchak, agonized.

In the distance we heard a sound like a thunder of wings and then, against the three white moons of Gor, to my dismay, we saw tarnsmen pass overhead, striking toward the camp. There were perhaps eight hundred to a thousand of them. I could hear the notes of the tarn drum above controlling the flight of the formation.

"We are fools!" cried Kamchak, wheeling his kaiila.

In an instant we were hurtling through ranks of men back toward the camp. When we had passed through the ranks, which had remained still, those thousands of warriors simply turned their kaiila, the last of them now first, and followed us.

"Each to his own wagon and war!" cried Kamchak.

I saw two yellow lanterns and a red lantern on the high pole.

I was startled by the appearance of tarnsmen on the southern plains. The nearest tarn cavalries as far as I knew were to be found in distant Ar.

Surely great Ar was not at war with the Tuchuks of the southern plains.

They must be mercenaries!

Kamchak did not return to his own wagon but now raced his kaiila, followed by a hundred men, toward the high ground on which stood the standard of the four bosk horns, on which stood the huge wagon of Kutaituchik, called Ubar of the Tuchuks.

Among the wagons the tarnsmen would have found only
slaves, women and children, but not a wagon had been
burned or looted.,

We heard a new thunder of wings and looking overhead
saw the tarnsmen, like a black storm, drum beating and tarns
screaming, streak by overhead.

A few arrows from those who followed us looped weakly
up after them, falling then among the wagons.

The sewn, painted boskhides that had covered the domed
framework over the vast wagon of Kutaituchik hung slashed
and rent from the joined tem-wood poles of the framework.
Where they were not torn I saw that they had been pierced
as though a knife had been driven through them again and
again, only inches apart.

There were some fifteen or twenty guards slain, mostly by
arrows. They lay tumbled about, several on the dais near the
wagon. In one body there were six arrows.

Kamchak leaped from the back of his kaiila and, seizing a
torch from an iron rack, leaped up the stairs and entered the
wagon.

I followed him, but then stopped, startled at what I saw.
Literally thousands of arrows had been fired through the
dome into the wagon. One could not step without breaking
and snapping them. Near the center of the wagon, alone, his
head bent over, on the robe of gray boskhide, sat Kutaituchik, perhaps fifteen or twenty arrows imbedded in his
body. At his right knee was the golden kanda box. I looked
about. The wagon had been looted, the only one that had
been as far as I knew.

Kamchak had gone to the body of Kutaituchik and sat
down across from it, cross-legged, and had put his head in his
hands.

I did not disturb him.

Some others pressed into the wagon behind us, but not
many, and those who did remained in the background.

I heard Kamchak moan. "The bosk are doing as well as
might be expected," he said. "The quivas—I will try to keep
them sharp. I will see that the axles of the wagons are
greased." Then he bent his head down and sobbed, rocking
back and forth.

Aside from his weeping I could hear only the crackle of
the torch that lit the interior of the rent dome. I saw here
and there, among the rugs and polished wood bristling with
white arrows, overturned boxes, loose jewels scattered, torn

robes and tapestries. I did not see the golden sphere. If it had been there, it was now gone.

At last Kamchak stood up.

He turned to face me. I could still see tears in his eyes. "He was once a great warrior," he said.

I nodded.

Kamchak looked about himself, and picked up one of the arrows and snapped it.

"Turians are responsible for this," he said.

"Saphrar?" I asked.

"Surely," said Kamchak, "for who could hire tarnsmen but Saphrar of Turia—or arrange for the diversion that drew fools to the edge of the herds?"

I was silent.

"There was a golden sphere," said Kamchak. "It was that which he wanted."

I said nothing.

"Like yourself, Tarl Cabot," added Kamchak.

I was startled.

"Why else," asked he, "would you have come to the Wagon Peoples?"

I did not respond. I could not.

"Yes," I said, "it is true—I want it for Priest-Kings. It is important to them."

"It is worthless," said Kamchak.

"Not to Priest-Kings," I said.

Kamchak shook his head. "No, Tarl Cabot," said he, "the golden sphere is worthless."

The Tuchuk then looked around himself, sadly, and then again gazed on the sitting, bent-over figure of Kutaituchik.

Suddenly tears seemed to burst from Kamchak's eyes and his fists were clenched. "He was a great man!" cried Kamchak. "Once he was a great man!"

I nodded. I knew Kutaituchik, of course, only as the huge, somnolent mass of man who sat cross-legged on a robe of gray boskhide, his eyes dreaming.

Suddenly Kamchak cried out in rage and seized up the golden kanda box and hurled it away.

"There will now have to be a new Ubar of the Tuchuks," I said, softly.

Kamchak turned and faced me. "No," he said.

"Kutaituchik," I said, "is dead."

Kamchak regarded me evenly. "Kutaituchik," he said, "was not Ubar of the Tuchuks."

"I don't understand," I said.

"He was called Ubar of the Tuchuks," said Kamchak, "but he was not Ubar."

"How can this be?" I asked.

"We Tuchuks are not such fools as Turians would believe," said Kamchak. "It was for such a night as this that Kutaituchik waited in the Wagon of the Ubar."

I shook my head in wonder.

"He wanted it this way," said Kamchak. "He would have it no other." Kamchak wiped his arm across his eyes. "He said it was now all he was good for—for this—and for nothing else."

It was a brilliant strategy.

"Then the true Ubar of the Tuchuks is not slain," I said.

"No," said Kamchak.

"Who knows who the Ubar truly is?" I asked.

"The Warriors know," said Kamchak. "The warriors."

"Who is Ubar of the Tuchuks?" I asked.

"I am," said Kamchak.

15

Harold

Turia, to some extent, now lay under seige, though the Tuchuks alone could not adequately invest the city. The other Wagon Peoples regarded the problem of the slaying of Kutaituchik and the despoiling of his wagon as one best left to the resources of the people of the four bosk horns. It did not concern, in their opinion, the Kassars, the Kataii or the Paravaci. There had been Kassars who had wanted to fight and some Kataii, but the calm heads of the Paravaci had convinced them that the difficulty lay between Turia and the Tuchuks, not Turia and the Wagon Peoples generally. Indeed, envoys had flown on tarnback to the Kassars, Kataii and Paravaci, assuring them of Turia's lack of hostile intentions towards them, envoys accompanied by rich gifts.

The cavalries of the Tuchuks, however, managed to maintain a reasonably effective blockade of land routes to Turia. Four times masses of tharlarion cavalry had charged forth from the city but each time the Hundreds withdrew before them until the charge had been enveloped in the swirling kaiila, and then its riders were brought down swiftly by the flashing arrows of the Tuchuks, riding in closely, almost to lance range and firing again and again until striking home.

Several times also, hosts of tharlarion had attempted to protect caravans leaving the city, or advanced to meet scheduled caravans approaching Turia, but each time in spite of this support, the swift, harrying, determined riders of the Tuchuks had forced the caravans to turn back, or man by

181

man, beast by beast, left them scattered across pasangs of prairie.

The mercenary tarnsmen of Turia were most feared by the Tuchuks, for such could, with relative impunity, fire upon them from the safety of their soaring height, but even this dread weapon of Turia could not, by itself, drive the Tuchuks from the surrounding plains. In the field the Tuchuks would counter the tarnsmen by breaking open the Hundreds into scattered Tens and presenting only erratic, swiftly moving targets; it is difficult to strike a rider or beast at a distance from tarnback when he is well aware of you and ready to evade your missile; and, of course, did the tarnsman approach too closely, then he himself and his mount were exposed to the return fire of the Tuchuks, in which case of proximity, the Tuchuk could use his small bow to fierce advantage. The archery of tarnsmen, of course, is most effective against massed infantry or clusters of the ponderous tharlarion. Also, perhaps not unimportantly, many of Turia's mercenary tarnsmen found themselves engaged in the time-consuming, distasteful task of supplying the city from distant points, often bringing food and arrow wood from as far away as the valleys of the eastern Cartius. I presume that the mercenaries, being tarnsmen—a proud, headstrong breed of men—made the Turians pay highly for the supplies they carried, the indignities of bearing burdens being lessened somewhat by the compensating weight of golden tarn disks. There was no problem of water in the city, incidentally, for Turia's waters are supplied by deep, tile-lined wells, some of them hundreds of feet deep; there are also siege reservoirs, filled with the melted snows of the winter, the rains of the spring.

Kamchak, on kaiilaback, would sit in fury regarding the distant, white walls of Turia. He could not prevent the supplying of the city by air. He lacked siege engines, and the men, and the skills, of the northern cities. He stood as a nomad, in his way baffled at the walls raised against him.

"I wonder," I said, "why the tarnsmen have not struck at the wagons—with fire arrows—why they do not attack the bosk themselves, slaying them from the air, forcing you to withdraw to protect the beasts."

It seemed to be a simple, elementary strategy. There was, after all, no place on the prairies to hide the wagons or the bosk, and tarnsmen could easily reach them anywhere within a radius of several hundred pasangs.

"They are mercenaries," growled Kamchak.

"I do not understand your meaning," I said.

"We have paid them not to burn the wagons nor slay the bosk," said he.

"They are being paid by both sides?" I asked.

"Of course," said Kamchak, irritably.

For some reason this angered me, though, naturally, I was pleased that the wagons and bosk were yet safe. I suppose I was angered because I myself was a tarnsman, and it seemed somehow improper for warriors astride the mighty tarns to barter their favors indiscriminately for gold to either side.

"But," said Kamchak, "I think in the end Saphrar of Turia will meet their price—and the wagons will be fired and the bosk slain—" He gritted his teeth. "He has not yet met it," said Kamchak, "because we have not yet harmed him—nor made him feel our presence."

I nodded.

"We will withdraw," said Kamchak. He turned to a subordinate. "Let the wagons be gathered," he said, "and the bosk turned from Turia."

"You are giving up?" I asked.

Kamchak's eyes briefly gleamed. Then he smiled. "Of course," he said.

I shrugged.

I knew that I myself must somehow enter Turia, for in Turia now lay the golden sphere. I must somehow attempt to seize it and return it to the Sardar. Was it not for this purpose that I had come to the Wagon Peoples? I cursed the fact that I had waited so long—even to the time of the Omen Taking—for thereby had I lost the opportunity to try for the sphere myself in the wagon of Kutaituchik. Now, to my chagrin, the sphere lay not in a Tuchuk wagon on the open prairie but, presumably, in the House of Saphrar, a merchant stronghold, behind the high, white walls of Turia.

I did not speak to Kamchak of my intention, for I was confident that he would have, and quite properly, objected to so foolish a mission, and perhaps even have attempted to prevent my leaving the camp.

Yet I did not know the city. I could not see how I might enter. I did not know how I might even attempt to succeed in so dangerous a task as that which I had set myself.

The afternoon among the wagons was a busy one, for they were preparing to move. Already the herds had been eased

westward, away from Turia toward Thassa, the distant sea.
There was much grooming of wagon bosk, checking of harness and wagons, cutting of meat to be dried hanging from
the sides of the moving wagons in the sun and wind. In the
morning the wagons, in their long lines, would follow the
slowly moving herds away from Turia. Meanwhile the Omen
Taking, even with the participation of the Tuchuk haruspexes,
continued—for the haruspexes of the people would remain
behind until even the final readings had been completed. I
had heard, from a master of hunting sleen, that the Omens
were developing predictably, several to one against the choice
of a Ubar San. Indeed, the difficulty of the Tuchuks with the
Turians had possibly, I guessed, exerted its influence on an
omen or two in passing. One could hardly blame the Kassars,
the Kataii and Paravaci for not wanting to be led by a
Tuchuk against Turia—or for not wanting to acquire the
Tuchuk troubles by uniting with them in any fashion. The
Paravaci were particularly insistent on maintaining the inde-
pendence of the peoples.

Since the death of Kutaituchik, Kamchak had turned ugly
in manner. Now he seldom drank or joked or laughed. I
missed his hitherto frequent proposals of contests, races and
wagers. He now seemed dour, moody, consumed with hatred
for Turia and Turians. He seemed particularly vicious with
Aphris. She was Turian. When he returned that night from
the wagon of Kutaituchik to his own wagon he strode angrily
to the sleen cage where he had confined Aphris with Elizabeth during the putative attack. He unlocked the door and
ordered the Turian maiden forth, commanding her to stand
before him, head down. Then, without speaking, to her
consternation he tore swiftly away the yellow camisk and
fastened slave bracelets on her wrists. "I should whip you,"
he said. The girl trembled. "But why, Master?" she asked.
"Because you are Turian," he said. The girl looked at him
with tears in her eyes. Roughly Kamchak took her by the
arm and thrust her into the sleen cage beside the miserable
Elizabeth Cardwell. He shut the door and locked it. "Master?" questioned Aphris. "Silence, Slave," he said. The girl
dared not speak. "There both of you will wait for the Iron
Master," he snarled, and turned abruptly, and went to the
stairs to the wagon. But the Iron Master did not come that
night, or the next, or the next. In these days of siege and war
there were more important matters to attend to than the
branding and collaring of female slaves. "Let him ride with

his Hundred," Kamchak said. "They will not run away—let
them wait like she-sleen in their cage—not knowing on which
day the iron will come." Also, perhaps for no reason better
than his suddenly found hatred for Aphris of Turia, he
seemed in no hurry to free the girls from their confinement.
"Let them crawl out," he snarled, "begging for a brand."
Aphris, in particular, seemed utterly distraught by Kamchak's
unreasoning cruelty, his callous treatment of herself and Elizabeth—perhaps most by his sudden, seeming indifference to
her. I suspected, though the girl would not have dreamed of
making the admission, that her heart as well as her body
might now rightfully have been claimed as his by the cruel
Ubar of the Tuchuks. Elizabeth Cardwell refused to meet my
eyes, and would not so much as speak to me. "Go away!" she
would cry. "Leave me!" Kamchak, once a day, at night, the
hour in which sleen are fed, would throw the girls bits of
bosk meat and fill a pan of water kept in the cage. I
remonstrated with him frequently in private but he was
adamant. He would look at Aphris and then return to the
wagon and sit cross-legged, not speaking, for hours, staring at
the side of the wagon. Once he pounded the rug on the
polished floor in front of him and cried out angrily, as though
to remind himself of some significant and inalterable fact,
"She is Turian! Turian!" The work of the wagon was done by
Tuka and another girl, whom Kamchak hired for the purpose. When the wagons were to move, Tuka was to walk
beside the cart of the sleen cage, drawn by a single bosk, and
with a bosk stick guide the animal. I once spoke harshly to
her when I saw her cruelly poke Elizabeth Cardwell through
the bars with the bosk stick. Never did she do so again when I
was nearby. She seemed to leave the distressed, red-eyed
Aphris of Turia alone, perhaps because she was Turian,
perhaps because she had no grievance against her. "Where
now is the pelt of the red larl, Slave?" Tuka would taunt
Elizabeth, threatening her with the bosk stick. "You will look
pretty with a ring in your nose!" she would cry. "You will
like your collar! Wait until you feel the iron, Slave—like
Tuka!" Kamchak never reproved Tuka, but I would silence
her when I was present. Elizabeth endured the insults as
though paying no attention, but sometimes at night I could
hear her sobbing.

I searched among the wagons long before I found, sitting
cross-legged beneath a wagon, wrapped in a worn bosk robe,

his weapons at hand folded in leather, the young man whose name was Harold, the blond-haired, blue-eyed fellow who had been so victimized by Hereena, she of the First Wagon, who had fallen spoils to Turia in the games of Love War.

He was eating a piece of bosk meat in the Tuchuk fashion, holding the meat in his left hand and between his teeth, and cutting pieces from it with a quiva scarcely a quarter inch from his lips, then chewing the severed bite and then again holding the meat in his hand and teeth and cutting again.

Without speaking I sat down near him and watched him eat. He eyed me warily, and neither did he speak. After a time I said to him, "How are the bosk?"

"They are doing as well as might be expected," he said.

"Are the quivas sharp?" I inquired.

"We try to keep them that way," he said.

"It is important," I observed, "to keep the axles of wagons greased."

"Yes," he said, "I think so."

He handed me a piece of meat and I chewed on it.

"You are Tarl Cabot, the Koroban," he said.

"Yes," I said, "and you are Harold—the Tuchuk."

He looked at me and smiled. "Yes," he said, "I am Harold—the Tuchuk."

"I am going to Turia," I said.

"That is interesting," said Harold, "I, too, am going to Turia."

"On an important matter?" I inquired.

"No," he said.

"What is it you think to do?" I asked.

"Acquire a girl," he said.

"Ah," I said.

"What is it you wish in Turia?" inquired Harold.

"Nothing important," I remarked.

"A woman?" he asked.

"No," I said, "a golden sphere."

"I know of it," said Harold, "it was stolen from the wagon of Kutaituchik." He looked at me. "It is said to be worthless."

"Perhaps," I admitted, "but I think I shall go to Turia and look about for it. Should I chance to see it I might pick it up and bring it back with me."

"Where do you think this golden sphere will be lying about?" asked Harold.

"I expect," I said, "it might be found here or there in the House of Saphrar, a merchant of Turia."

"That is interesting," said Harold, "for I had thought I might try chain luck in the Pleasure Gardens of a Turian merchant named Saphrar."

"That is interesting indeed," I said, "perhaps it is the same."

"It is possible," granted Harold. "Is he the smallish fellow, rather fat, with two yellow teeth."

"Yes," I said.

"They are poison teeth," remarked Harold, "a Turian affectation—but quite deadly, being filled with the venom of the Ost."

"Then I shall attempt not to be bitten," I said.

"I think that is a good idea," granted Harold.

Then we sat there together for a time, not speaking further, he eating, I watching while he cut and chewed the meat that was his supper. There was a fire nearby, but it was not his fire. The wagon over his head was not his wagon. There was no kaiila tethered at hand. As far as I could gather Harold had little more than the clothes on his back, a boskhide robe, his weapons and his supper.

"You will be slain in Turia," said Harold, finishing his meat and wiping his mouth in Tuchuk fashion on the back of his right sleeve.

"Perhaps," I admitted.

"You do not even know how to enter the city," he said.

"That is true," I admitted.

"I can enter Turia when I wish," he said. "I know a way."

"Perhaps," I suggested, "I might accompany you."

"Perhaps," he granted, carefully wiping the quiva on the back of his left sleeve.

"When are you going to Turia?" I asked.

"Tonight," he said.

I looked at him. "Why have you not gone before?" I asked.

He smiled. "Kamchak," he said, "told me to wait for you."

16

I Find the Golden Sphere

It was not a pleasant path to Turia that Harold the Tuchuk showed to me, but I followed him.

"Can you swim?" he asked.

"Yes," I said. Then I inquired, "How is it that you, a Tuchuk, can swim?" I knew few Tuchuks could, though some had learned in the Cartius.

"I learned in Turia,' said Harold, "in the public baths where I was once a slave."

The baths of Turia were said to be second only to those of Ar in their luxury, the number of their pools, their temperatures, the scents and oils.

"Each night the baths were emptied and cleaned and I was one of many who attended to this task," he said. "I was only six years of age when I was taken to Turia, and I did not escape the city for eleven years." He smiled. "I cost my master only eleven copper tarn disks," he said, "and so I think he had no reason to be ill satisfied with his investment."

"Are the girls who attend to the baths during the day as beautiful as it is said?" I inquired. The bath girls of Turia are almost as famous as those of Ar.

"Perhaps," he said, "I never saw them—during the day I and the other male slaves were chained in a darkened chamber that we might sleep and preserve our strength for the work of the night." Then he added, "Sometimes one of the girls, to discipline her, would be thrown amongst us—but we had no way of knowing if she were beautiful or not."

"How is it," I asked, "that you managed to escape?"

"At night, when cleaning the pools, we would be unchained, in order to protect the chain from dampness and rust—we were then only roped together by the neck—I had not been put on the rope until the age of fourteen, at which time I suppose my master adjudged it wise—prior to that I had been free a bit to sport in the pools before they were drained and sometimes to run errands for the Master of the Baths—it was during those years that I learned how to swim and also became familiar with the streets of Turia—one night in my seventeenth year I found myself last man on the rope and I chewed through it and ran—I hid by seizing a well rope and descending to the waters below—there was movement in the water at the foot of the well and I dove to the bottom and found a cleft, through which I swam underwater and emerged in a shallow pool, the well's feed basin—I again swam underwater and this time emerged in a rocky tunnel, through which flowed an underground stream—fortunately in most places there were a few inches between the level of the water and the roof of the tunnel—it was very long—I followed it."

"And where did you follow it to?" I asked.

"Here," said Harold, pointing to a cut between two rocks, only about eight inches wide, through which from some underground source a flow of water was emerging, entering and adding to the small stream at which, some four pasangs from the wagons, Aphris and Elizabeth had often drawn water for the wagon bosk.

Not speaking further, Harold, a quiva in his teeth, a rope and hook on his belt, squeezed through and disappeared. I followed him, armed with quiva and sword.

I do not much care to recall that journey. I am a strong swimmer but it seemed we must confront and conquer the steady press of flowing water for pasangs—and indeed we did so. At last, at a given point in the tunnel, Harold disappeared beneath the surface and I followed him. Gasping, we emerged in the tiny basin area fed by the underground stream. Here, Harold disappeared again under the water and once more I followed him. After what seemed to me an uncomfortably long moment we emerged again, this time at the bottom of a tile-lined well. It was a rather wide well, perhaps about fifteen feet in width. A foot or so above the surface hung a huge, heavy drum, now tipped on its side. It would contain literally hundreds of gallons of water when filled. Two ropes led to the drum, a small rope to control its filling, and a large one to support it; the large rope, incidentally, has a core of chain; the rope itself, existing primarily to protect the chain, is treated with a waterproof glue made from the skins, bones and hoofs of bosk, secured by trade with the Wagon Peoples. Even so the rope and chain must be replaced twice a year. I judged that the top of the well might lie eight or nine hundred feet above us.

I heard Harold's voice in the darkness, sounding hollow against the tiled walls and over the water. "The tiles must be periodically inspected," he said, "and for this purpose there are foot knots in the rope."

I breathed a sigh of relief. It is one thing to descend a long rope and quite another, even in the lesser gravity of Gor, to climb one—particularly one as long as that which I now saw dimly above me.

The foot knots were done with subsidiary rope but worked into the fiber of the main rope and glued over so as to be almost one with it. They were spaced about every ten feet on the rope. Still, even resting periodically, the climb was an exhausting one. More disturbing to me was the prospect of bringing the golden sphere down the rope and under the water and through the underground stream to the place where we had embarked on this adventure. Also, I was not clear how Harold, supposing him to be successful in his shopping amongst the ferns and flowers of Saphrar's Pleasure Gardens, intended to conduct his squirming prize along this unscenic, difficult and improbable route.

Being an inquisitive chap, I asked him about it, some two or three hundred feet up the drum rope.

"In escaping," he informed me, "we shall steal two tarns and make away."

"I am pleased to see," I said, "that you have a plan."

"Of course," he said, "I am Tuchuk."

"Have you ever ridden a tarn before?" I asked him.

"No," he said, still climbing somewhere above me.

"Then how do you expect to do so?" I inquired, hauling myself up after him.

"You are a tarnsman, are you not?" he asked.

"Yes," I said.

"Very well," said he, "you will teach me."

"It is said," I muttered, "that the tarn knows who is a tarnsman and who is not—and that it slays him who is not."

"Then," said Harold, "I must deceive it."

"How do you expect to do that?" I asked.

"It will be easy," said Harold. "I am a Tuchuk."

I considered lowering myself down the rope and returning to the wagons for a bottle of Paga. Surely tomorrow would be as propitious a day as any for my mission. Yet I did not care to pursue again that underground stream nor, particularly, on some new trip to Turia, to swim once more against it. It is one thing to roll about in a public bath or splash about in some pool or stream, but quite another to struggle for pasangs against a current in a tunnel channel with only a few inches between the water and the roof of the tunnel.

"It should be worth the Courage Scar," said Harold from above, "don't you think so?"

"What?" I asked.

"Stealing a wench from the House of Saphrar and returning on a stolen tarn."

"Undoubtedly," I grumbled. I found myself wondering if the Tuchuks had an Idiocy Scar. If so, I might have nominated the young man hoisting himself up the rope above me as a candidate for the distinction.

Yet, in spite of my better judgment, I found myself somehow admiring the confident young fellow.

I suspected that if anyone could manage the madness on his mind it would surely be he, or someone such as he, someone quite as courageous, or daft.

On the other hand, I reminded myself, my own probabilities of success and survival were hardly better—and here I was, his critic—climbing up the drum rope, wet, cold, puffing, a stranger to the city of Turia, intending to steal an object—the egg of Priest-Kings—which was undoubtedly, by now, as well guarded as the Home Stone of the city itself. I decided that I would nominate both Harold and myself for an Idiocy Scar and let the Tuchuks take their pick.

It was with a feeling of relief that I finally got my arm over the crossbar of the windlass and drew myself up. Harold had already taken up a position, looking about, near the edge of the well. The Turian wells, incidentally, have no raised wall, but are, save for a rim of about two inches in height, flat with the level. I joined Harold. We were in an inclosed well yard, surrounded by walls of about sixteen feet in height, with a defender's catwalk about the inside. The walls provide a means for defending the water and also, of course, considering the number of wells in the city, some of which, by the way, are fed by springs, provide a number of defensible enclaves should portions of the city fall into enemy

hands. There was an archway leading from the circular well
yard, and the two halfs of the timbered, arched gate were
swung back and fastened on both sides. It was necessary only
to walk through the archway and find ourselves on one of the
streets of Turia. I had not expected the entry to the city to
be so easy—so to speak.

"The last time I was here," said Harold, "was over five
years ago."

"Is it far to the House of Saphrar?" I asked.

"Rather far," he said. "But the streets are dark."

"Good," I said. "Let us be on our way." I was chilly in the
spring night and my clothes, of course, were soaked. Harold
did not seem to notice or mind this inconvenience. The
Tuchuks, to my irritation, tended on the whole not to notice
or mind such things. I was pleased the streets were dark and
that the way was long.

"The darkness," I said, "will conceal somewhat the wetness
of our garments—and by the time we arrive we may be
rather dry."

"Of course," said Harold. "That was part of my plan."

"Oh," I said.

"On the other hand," said Harold, "I might like to stop by
the baths."

"They are closed at this hour, are they not?" I asked.

"No," said he, "not until the twentieth hour." That was
midnight of the Gorean day.

"Why do you wish to stop by the baths?" I asked.

"I was never a customer," he said, "and I often wondered—
like yourself apparently—if the bath girls of Turia are as
lovely as it is said."

"That is all well and good," I said, "but I think it would be
better to strike out for the House of Saphrar."

"If you wish," said Harold. "After all, I can always visit
the baths after we take the city."

"Take the city?" I asked.

"Of course," said Harold.

"Look," I said to him, "the bosk are already moving
away—the wagons will withdraw in the morning. The siege is
over. Kamchak is giving up."

Harold smiled. He looked at me. "Oh, yes," he said.

"But," I said, "if you like I will pay your way to the
baths."

"We could always wager," he suggested.

"No," I said firmly, "let me pay."

"If you wish—" he said.

I told myself it might be better, even, to come to the House of Saphrar late, rather than possibly before the twentieth hour. In the meantime it seemed reasonable to while away some time and the baths of Turia seemed as good a place as any to do so.

Arm in arm, Harold and I strode under the archway leading from the well yard.

We had scarcely cleared the portal and set foot in the street when we heard a swift rustle of heavy wire and, startled, looking up, saw the steel net descend on us.

Immediately we heard the sound of several men leaping down to the street and the draw cords on the wire net—probably of the sort often used for snaring sleen—began to tighten. Neither Harold nor myself could move an arm or hand and, locked in the net, we stood like fools until a guardsman kicked the feet out from under us and we rolled, entrapped in the wire, at his feet.

"Two fish from the well," said a voice.

"This means, of course," said another voice, "that others know of the well."

"We shall double the guard," said a third voice.

"What shall we do with them?" asked yet another man.

"Take them to the House of Saphrar," said the first man.

I twisted around as well as I could. "Was this," I asked Harold, "a part of your plan?"

He grinned, pressing against the net, trying its strength. "No," he said.

I, too, tried the net. The thick woven wire held well.

Harold and I had been fastened in a Turian slave bar, a metal bar with a collar at each end and, behind the collar, manacles which fasten the prisoner's hands behind his neck.

We knelt before a low dais, covered with rugs and cushions, on which reclined Saphrar of Turia. The merchant wore his Pleasure Robes of white and gold and his sandals, too, were of white leather bound with golden straps. His toenails, as well as the nails of his hands, were carmine in color. His small, fat hands moved with delight as he observed us. The golden drops above his eyes rose and fell. He was smiling and I could see the tips of the golden teeth which I had first noticed on the night of the banquet.

Beside him, on each side, cross-legged, sat a warrior. The warrior on his right wore a robe, much as one might when emerging from the baths. His head was covered by a hood, such as is worn by members of the Clan of Torturers. He was toying with a Paravaci quiva. I recognized him, some- how in the build and the way he held his body. It was he who had hurled the quiva at me among the wagons, who would have been my assassin save for the sudden flicker of a shadow on a lacquered board. On the left of Saphrar there sat another warrior, in the leather of a tarnsman, save that he wore a jeweled belt, and about his neck, set with dia- monds, there hung a worn tarn disk from the city of Ar. Beside him there rested, lying on the dais, spear, helmet and shield.

"I am pleased that you have chosen to visit us, Tarl Cabot of Ko-ro-ba," said Saphrar. "We expected that you would soon try, but we did not know that you knew of the Passage Well."

Through the metal bar I felt a reaction on the part of Harold. He had apparently, when fleeing years ago, stumbled on a route in and out of the city which had not been unknown to certain of the Turians. I recalled that the Turians, because of the baths, are almost all swimmers.

The fact that the man with the Paravaci quiva wore the robe now seemed to be significant.

"Our friend," said Saphrar, gesturing to his right, "with the hood preceded you tonight in the Passage Well. Since we have been in touch with him and have informed him of the well, we deemed it wise to mount a guard nearby— fortunately, as it seems."

"Who is the traitor to the Wagon Peoples?" asked Harold.

The man in the hood stiffened.

"Of course," said Harold, "I see now—the quiva—he is Paravaci, naturally."

The man's hand went white on the quiva, and I feared he might leap to his feet and thrust the quiva to its hilt in the breast of the Tuchuk youth.

"I have often wondered," said Harold , "where the Parava- ci obtained their riches."

With a cry of rage the hooded figure leaped to his feet, quiva raised.

"Please," said Saphrar, lifting his small fat hand. "Let there be no ill will among friends."

Trembling with rage, the hooded figure resumed his place on the dais.

The other warrior, a strong, gaunt man, scarred across the

left cheekbone, with shrewd, dark eyes, said nothing, but watched us, considering us, as a warrior considers an enemy.

"I would introduce our hooded friend," explained Saphrar, "but even I do not know his name nor face—only that he stands high among the Paravaci and accordingly has been of great use to me."

"I know him in a way," I said. "He followed me in the camp of the Tuchuks—and tried to kill me."

"I trust," said Saphrar, "that we shall have better fortune."

I said nothing.

"Are you truly of the Clan of Torturers?" asked Harold of the hooded man.

"You shall find out," he said.

"Do you think," asked Harold, "you will be able to make me cry for mercy?"

"If I choose," said the man.

"Would you care to wager?" asked Harold.

The man leaned forward and hissed. "Tuchuk sleen!"

"May I introduce," inquired Saphrar, "Ha-Keel of Port Kar, chief of the mercenary tarnsmen."

"Is it known to Saphrar," I inquired, "that you have received gold from the Tuchuks?"

"Of course," said Ha-Keel.

"You think perhaps," said Saphrar, chuckling, "that I might object—and that thus you might sow discord amongst us, your enemies. But know, Tarl Cabot, that I am a merchant and understand men and the meaning of gold—I no more object to Ha-Keel dealing with Tuchuks than I would to the fact that water freezes and fire burns—and that no one ever leaves the Yellow Pool of Turia alive."

I did not follow the reference to the Yellow Pool of Turia. I glanced, however, at Harold, and it seemed he had suddenly paled.

"How is it," I asked, "that Ha-Keel of Port Kar wears about his neck a tarn disk from the city of Ar?"

"I was once of Ar," said scarred Ha-Keel. "Indeed, I can remember you, though as Tarl of Bristol, from the siege of Ar."

"It was long ago," I said.

"Your swordplay with Pa-Kur, Master of the Assassins, was superb."

A nod of my head acknowledged his compliment.

"You may ask," said Ha-Keel, "how it is that I, a tarnsman of Ar, ride for merchants and traitors on the southern plains?"

"It saddens me," I said, "that a sword that was once raised in defense of Ar is raised now only by the beck and call of gold."

"About my neck," he said, "you see a golden tarn disk of glorious Ar. I cut a throat for that tarn disk, to buy silks and perfumes for a woman. But she had fled with another. I, hunted, also fled. I followed them and in combat slew the warrior, obtaining my scar. The wench I sold into slavery. I could not return to Glorious Ar." He fingered the tarn disk. "Sometimes," said he, "it seems heavy."

"Ha-Keel," said Saphrar, "wisely went to the city of Port Kar, whose hospitality to such as he is well known. It was there we first met."

"Ha!" cried Ha-Keel. "The little urt was trying to pick my pouch!"

"You were not always a merchant, then?" I asked Saphrar.

"Among friends," said Saphrar, "perhaps we can speak frankly, particularly seeing that the tales we tell will not be retold. You see, I know I can trust you."

"How is that?" I asked.

"Because you are to be slain," he said.

"I see," I said.

"I was once," continued Saphrar, "a perfumer of Tyros— but I one day left the shop it seems inadvertently with some pounds of the nectar of talenders concealed beneath my tunic in a bladder—and for that my ear was notched and I was exiled from the city. I found my way to Port Kar, where I lived unpleasantly for some time on garbage floating in the canals and such other tidbits as I could find about."

"How then are you a rich merchant?" I asked.

"A man met me," said Saphrar, "a tall man—rather dreadful actually—with a face as gray as stone and eyes like glass."

I immediately recalled Elizabeth's description of the man who had examined her for fitness to bear the message collar— on Earth!

"I have never seen that man," said Ha-Keel. "I wish that I might have."

Saphrar shivered. "You are just as well off," he said.

"Your fortunes turned," I said, "when you met that man?"

"Decidedly," he said. "In fact," continued the small merchant, "it was he who arranged my fortunes and sent me, some years ago, to Turia."

"What is your city?" I demanded.

He smiled. "I think—" he said, "Port Kar."

That told me what I wanted to know. Though raised in Tyros and successful in Turia, Saphrar the merchant thought of himself as one of Port Kar. Such a city, I thought, could stain the soul of a man.

"That explains," I said, "how it is that you, though in Turia, can have a galley in Port Kar."

"Of course," said he.

"Also," I cried, suddenly aware, "the rence paper in the message collar, paper from Port Kar!"

"Of course," he said.

"The message was yours," I said.

"The collar was sewn on the girl in this very house," said he, "though the poor thing was anesthetized at the time and unaware of the honor bestowed upon her." Saphrar smiled. "In a way," he said, "it was a waste—I would not have minded keeping her in my Pleasure Gardens as a slave." Saphrar shrugged and spread his hands. "But he would not hear of it—it must be she!"

"Who is 'he'?" I demanded.

"The gray fellow," said Saphrar, "who brought the girl to the city, drugged on tarnback."

"What is his name?" I demanded.

"Always he refused to tell me," said Saphrar.

"What did you call him?" I asked.

"Master," said Saphrar. "He paid well," he added.

"Fat little slave," said Harold.

Saphrar took no offense but arranged his robes and smiled. "He paid very well," he said.

"Why," I asked, "did he not permit you to keep the girl as a slave?"

"She spoke a barbarous tongue," said Saphrar, "like yourself apparently. The plan was, it seems, that the message would be read, and that the Tuchuks would then use the girl to find you and when they had they would kill you. But they did not do so."

"No," I said.

"It doesn't matter—now," said Saphrar.

I wondered what death he might have in mind for me.

"How was it," I asked, "that you, who had never seen me, knew me and spoke my name at the banquet?"

"You had been well described to me by the gray fellow,"
said Saphrar. "Also, I was certain there could not have been
two among the Tuchuks with hair such as yours."

I bristled slightly. For no rational reason I am sometimes
angered when enemies or strangers speak of my hair. I
suppose this dates back to my youth when my flaming hair,
perhaps a deplorably outrageous red, was the object of dozens of derisive comments, each customarily engendering its
own rebuttal, both followed often by a nimble controversy,
adjudicated by bare knuckles. I recalled, with a certain
amount of satisfaction, even in the House of Saphrar, that I
had managed to resolve most of these disputes in my favor.
My aunt used to examine my knuckles each evening and
when they were skinned—which was not seldom—I trooped
away to bed with honor rather than supper.

"It was an amusement on my part," smiled Saphrar, "to
speak your name at that time—to see what you would
do—to give you something, so to speak, to stir in your
wine."

It was a Turian saying. They used wines in which, as a
matter of fact, things could be and were, upon occasion,
stirred—mostly spices and sugars.

"Let us kill him," said the Paravaci.

"No one has spoken to you, Slave," remarked Harold.

"Let me have this one," begged the Paravaci of Saphrar,
pointing the tip of his quiva at Harold.

"Perhaps," said Saphrar. Then the little merchant stood up
and clapped his hands twice. From a side, from a portal
which had been concealed behind a hanging, two men-at-
arms came forth, followed by two others. The first two
carried a platform, draped in purple. On this platform, nes-
tled in the folds of the purple, I saw the object of my
quest—what I had come so far to find—that for which I had
risked and, apparently, lost my life—the golden sphere.

It was clearly an egg. Its longest axis was apparently about
eighteen inches. It was, at its widest point, about a foot
thick.

"You are cruel to show it to him," said Ha-Keel.

"But he has come so far and risked so much," said Saphrar
kindly. "Surely he is entitled to a glimpse of our precious
prize."

"Kutaituchik was killed for it," I said.

"Many more than he," said Saphrar, "and perhaps in the
end even more will die."

"Do you know what it is?" I asked.

"No," said Saphrar, "but I know it is important to Priest-Kings." He stood up and went to the egg, putting his finger on it. "Why, though," he said, "I have no idea—it is not truly of gold."

"It appears to be an egg," said Ha-Keel.

"Yes," said Saphrar, "whatever it is, it has the shape of an egg."

"Perhaps it is an egg," suggested Ha-Keel.

"Perhaps," admitted Saphrar, "but what would Priest-Kings wish with such an egg?"

"Who knows?" asked Ha-Keel.

"It was this, was it not," asked Saphrar, looking at me, "that you came to Turia to find?"

"Yes," I admitted. "That is what I came to find."

"See how easy it was!" he laughed.

"Yes," I said, "very easy."

Ha-Keel drew his sword. "Let me slay him as befits a warrior," he said.

"No," cried the Paravaci, "let me have him as well as the other."

"No," said Saphrar firmly. "They are both mine."

Ha-Keel angrily rammed his sword back into the sheath. He had clearly wanted to kill me honorably, swiftly. Clearly he had little stomach for whatever games the Paravaci or Saphrar might have in mind. Ha-Keel might have been a cutthroat and a thief but, too, he was of Ar—and a tarnsman.

"You have secured the object," I inquired, "to give it to the gray man?"

"Yes," said Saphrar.

"He will then return it to Priest-Kings?" I asked innocently.

"I do not know what he will do with it," said Saphrar. "As long as I receive my gold—and the gold will perhaps make me the richest man on Gor—I do not care."

"If the egg is injured," I said, "the Priest-Kings might be angry."

"For all I know," said Saphrar, "the man is a Priest-King. How else would he dare to use the name of Priest-Kings on the message in the message collar?"

I knew, of course, that the man was not a Priest-King. But I could now see that Saphrar had no idea who he was—or for whom, if anyone, he was working. I was confident that the man was the same as he who had brought Elizabeth Cardwell to this world—he who had seen her in New York and decided she would play her role in his perilous sport—and that thus he had at his disposal an advanced technology—certainly to the level of at least space flight. I did not know, of course, if the technology at his disposal was his own, or that of his kind, or if it were furnished by others—unknown—not seen—who had their own stake in these games of two worlds, perhaps more. He might well be, and I supposed it true, merely an agent—but for whom, or what?—something that would challenge even Priest-Kings—but, it must be, something that feared Priest-Kings, or it would already have struck—this world, or Earth—something that wanted Priest-Kings to die—that the one world, or two, or perhaps even the system of our sun, would be freed for their taking.

"How did the gray man know where the golden sphere was?" I asked.

"He said once," said Saphrar, "that he was told—"

"By whom?" I asked.

"I do not know," said Saphrar.

"You know no more?"

"No," said Saphrar.

I speculated. The Others—those of power, not Priest-Kings, must, to some extent, understand or sense the politics, the needs and policies of the remote denizens of the Sardar—they were probably not altogether unaware of the business of Priest-Kings, particularly not now, following the recent War of Priest-Kings, after which many humans had escaped the Place of Priest-Kings and now wandered free, if scoffed at and scorned for the tales they might bear—possibly from these, or from spies or traitors in the Nest itself, the Others had learned—the Others, I was sure, would neither jeer nor scoff at the stories told by vagabonds of Priest-Kings.

They could have learned of the destruction of much of the surveillance equipment of the Sardar, of the substantial reduction in the technological capabilities of Priest-Kings, at least for a short time—and, most importantly, that the War had been fought, in a way, over the succession of dynasties—thus learning that generations of Priest-Kings might be in the offing. If there had been rebels—those wanting a new generation—there must have been the seeds of that generation. But in a Place of Priest-Kings there is only one bearer of young, the Mother, and she had died shortly before the War. Thus, the Others might well infer that there was one, or nore, concealed eggs, hidden away, which must now be ecured that the new generation might be inaugurated, but idden away quite possibly not in the Place of Priest-Kings self, but elsewhere, out of the home of Priest-Kings, beyond ven the black Sardar itself. And they might have learned, as vell, that I had been in the War of Priest-Kings a lieutenant o Misk, the Fifth Born, Chief of the Rebels, and that I had ow made my way to the southern plains, to the land of the Wagon Peoples. It would not then have required great intelli-ence to suspect that I might have come to fetch the egg or ggs of Priest-Kings.

If they had reasoned thus, then their strategy would seem ikely to have been, first, to see that I did not find the egg, nd, secondly, to secure it for themselves. They could uarantee their first objective, of course, by slaying me. The natter of the message collar had been a clever way of ttempting to gain that end but, because of the shrewdness of 'uchuks, who seldom take anything at its face value, it had ailed; they had then attempted to bring me down among the vagons with a Paravaci quiva, but that, too, had failed; I rimly reminded myself, however, that I was now in the ower of Saphrar of Turia. The second objective, that of btaining the egg for themselves, was already almost accom-lished; Kutaituchik had been killed and it had been stolen rom his wagon; there was left only to deliver it to the gray nan, who would, in turn, deliver it to the Others—whoever r whatever they might be. Saphrar, of course, had been in 'uria for years. This suggested to me that possibly the Others ad even followed the movements of the two men who had rought the egg from the Sardar to the Wagon Peoples. Perhaps they had now struck more openly and quickly— mploying Gorean tarnsmen—fearing that I might myself eize the egg first and return it to the Sardar. The attempt on ny life took place one night and the raid on Kutaituchik's vagon the next. Saphrar, too, I reminded myself, had known hat the golden sphere was in the wagon of Kutaituchik. I vas puzzled a bit that he had had this information. Tuchuks lo not make good spies, for they tend to be, albeit fierce and ruel, intensely loyal; and there are few strangers allowed in he wagon of a Tuchuk Ubar. It occurred to me that perhaps he Tuchuks had made no secret of the presence of the golden sphere in Kutaituchik's wagon. That puzzled me. On he other hand they may well not have understood its true alue. Kamchak himself had told me the golden sphere was

worthless—poor Tuchuk! But now, I said to myself, poor
Cabot! However it came about—and I could not be sure—
Others than Priest-Kings had now entered the games of
Gor—and these Others knew of the egg and wanted it—and,
it seemed, would have it. In time Priest-Kings, those remain-
ing, would die. Their weapons and devices would rust and
crumble in the Sardar. And then, one day, like the pirates of
Port Kar in their long galleys, unannounced, unexpected,
Others would cross the seas of space and bring their craft to
rest on the shores and sands of Gor.

"Would you like to fight for your life?" asked Saphrar of
Turia.

"Of course," I said.

"Excellent," said Saphrar. "You may do so in the Yellow
Pool of Turia."

17

The Yellow Pool of Turia

At the edge of the Yellow Pool of Turia Harold and I stood, now freed of the slave bar, but with wrists tied behind our backs. I had not been given back my sword but the quiva I had carried was now thrust in my belt.

The pool is indoors—in a spacious chamber in the House of Saphrar—with a domed ceiling of some eighty feet in height. The pool itself, around which there is a marble walkway some seven or eight feet in width, is roughly circular in shape and has a diameter of perhaps sixty or seventy feet.

The room itself is very lovely and might have been one of the chambers in the renowned baths of Turia. It was decorated with numerous exotic floral designs, done primarily in greens and yellows, representing the vegetation of a tropical river, perhaps the tropical belt of the Cartius, or certain of its tributaries far to the north and west. Besides the designs there were also, growing from planting areas recessed here and there in the marble walkway, broad-leafed, curling plants; vines; ferns; numerous exotic flowers; it was rather beautiful, but in an oppressive way, and the room had been heated to such an extent that it seemed almost steamy; I gathered the temperature and humidity in the room were desirable for the plantings, or were supposed to simulate the climate of the tropical area represented.

The light in the room came, interestingly, from behind a translucent blue ceiling, probably being furnished by energy bulbs. Saphrar was a rich man indeed to have energy bulbs in his home; few Goreans can afford such a luxury; and, indeed, few care to, for Goreans, for some reason, are fond of the light of flame, lamps and torches and such; flames must be made, tended, watched; they are more beautiful, more alive.

Around the edge of the pool there were eight large columns, fashioned and painted as though the trunks of trees, one standing at each of the eight cardinal points of the Gorean compass; from these, stretching often across the pool, were vines, so many that the ceiling could be seen only as a patchwork of blue through vinous entanglements. Some of the vines hung so low that they nearly touched the surface of the pool. A slave, at a sort of panel fixed with wires and levers, stood at one side. I was puzzled by the manner in which the heat and humidity were introduced to the room, for I saw no vents nor cauldrons of boiling water, or devices for releasing drops of water on heated plates or stones. I had been in the room for perhaps three or four minutes before I realized that the steam rose from the pool itself. I gathered that it was heated. It seemed calm. I wondered what I was expected to meet in the pool. I would have at least the quiva. I noted that the surface of the pool, shortly after we had entered, began to tremble slightly, and it was then once again calm. I supposed something, sensing our presence, had stirred in its depths, and was now waiting. Yet the motion had been odd for it was almost as if the pool had lifted itself, rippled, and then subsided.

Harold and I, though bound, were each held by two men-at-arms, and another four, with crossbows, had accompanied us.

"What is the nature of the beast in the pool?" I asked.

"You will learn," Saphrar laughed.

I conjectured it would be a water animal. Nothing had yet broken the surface. It would probably be a sea-tharlarion, or perhaps several such; sometimes the smaller sea-tharlarion, seemingly not much more than teeth and tail, fluttering in packs beneath the waves, are even more to be feared than their larger brethren, some of whom in whose jaws an entire galley can be raised from the surface of the sea and snapped in two like a handful of dried reeds of the rence plant. It might, too, be a Vosk turtle. Some of them are gigantic, almost impossible to kill, persistent, carnivorous. Yet, if it had been a tharlarion or a Vosk turtle, it might well have broken the surface for air. It did not. This reasoning also led me to suppose that it would not be likely to be anything like a water sleen or a giant urt from the canals of Port Kar. These two, even before the tharlarion or the turtle, would by now, presumably, have surfaced to breathe.

Therefore whatever lay in wait in the pool must be truly aquatic, capable of absorbing its oxygen from the water itself. It might be gilled, like Gorean sharks, probably descendants of Earth sharks placed experimentally in Thassa millenia ago by Priest-Kings, or it might have the gurdo, the layered, ventral membrane, shielded by porous plating, of several of the marine predators perhaps native to Gor, perhaps brought to Gor by Priest-Kings from some other, more distant world than Earth. Whatever it was, I would soon learn.

"I do not care to watch this," Ha-Keel said, "so with your permission, I shall withdraw."

Saphrar looked pained, but not much more so than was required by courtesy. He benignly lifted his small fat hand with the carmine fingernails and said, "By all means, my dear Ha-Keel, withdraw if you so wish."

Ha-Keel nodded curtly and turned abruptly and angrily strode from the room.

"Am I to be thrown bound into the pool?" I asked.

"Certainly not," said Saphrar. "That would hardly be fair."

"I am pleased to see that you are concerned with such matters," I said.

"Such matters are very important to me," said Saphrar.

The expression on his face was much the same as that I had seen at the banquet, when he had prepared to eat the small, quivering thing impaled on the colored stick.

I heard the Paravaci, behind the hood, snicker.

"Fetch the wooden shield," commanded Saphrar. Two of the men-at-arms left the room.

I studied the pool. It was beautiful, yellow, sparkling as though filled with gems. There seemed to be wound through its fluids ribbons and filaments and it was dotted here and there with small spheres of various colors. I then became aware that the steam that rose from the pool did so periodically, rather than continuously. There seemed to be a rhythm in the rising of the steam from the pool. I noted, too, that the surface of the pool licking at the marble basin in which it lay trapped seemed to rise slightly and then fall with the discharge of the steam.

This train of observation was interrupted by the arrival of

Saphrar's two men-at-arms bearing a wooden barrier of
sorts, about four and a half feet high and twelve feet wide,
which they set between myself and my captors, and Saphrar,
the Paravaci and those with the crossbow. Harold and his
captors, as well, were not behind the barricade. It was, like
the curving wall of the room, decorated in exotic floral
patterns.

"What is the shield for?" I asked.

"It is in case you might feel tempted to hurl the quiva at
us," said Saphrar.

That seemed foolish to me, but I said nothing. I certainly
had nothing in mind so ridiculous as to hurl at enemies the
one weapon which might mean life or death to me in my
struggle in the Yellow Pool of Turia.

I turned about, as well as I could, and examined the pool
again. I still had seen nothing break the surface to breathe,
and now I was determined that my unseen foe must indeed
be aquatic. I hoped it would be only one thing. And, too,
larger animals usually move more slowly than smaller ones.
If it were a school of fifteen-inch Gorean pike, for example, I
might kill dozens and yet die half eaten within minutes.

"Let me be sent first to the pool," said Harold.

"Nonsense," said Saphrar. "But do not be impatient—for
your turn will come."

Though it might have been my imagination it seemed that
the pool's yellow had now become enriched and that the
shifting fluid hues that confronted me had achieved new
ranges of brilliance. Some of the filamentous streamers
beneath the surface now seemed to roil beneath the surface
and the colors of the spheres seemed to pulsate. The rhythm
of the steam seemed to increase in tempo and I could now
detect, or thought I could, more than simple moisture in that
steam, perhaps some other subtle gas or fume, perhaps
hitherto unnoticed but now increasing in its volume.

"Let him be untied," said Saphrar.

While two men-at-arms continued to hold me, another
undid the bonds on my wrists. Three men-at-arms, with
crossbows, stood ready, the weapons trained on my back.

"If I succeed in slaying or escaping the monster in the
pool," I said, casually, "I take it that I am then, of course,
free."

"That is only fair," said Saphrar.

"Good," I said.

The Paravaci, in the hood, threw back his head and laughed. The crossbowmen also smiled.

"None has, of course," said Saphrar, "ever succeeded in doing either."

"I see," I said.

I now looked across the surface of the pool. Its appearance was now truly remarkable. It was almost as if it were lower in the center and the edges higher near the marble basin, inching as high as they could toward our sandals. I took it that this was an optical illusion of some sort. The pool was now, it seemed, literally coruscating, glistening with a brilliance of hues that was phenomenal, almost like hands lifting and spilling gems in sunlit water. The filamentous strands seemed to go mad with movement and the spheres of various colors were almost phosphorescent, pulsating beneath the surface. The steam rhythm was now swift, and the gases or fumes mixed with that moisture, noxious. It was almost as though the pool itself respired.

"Enter the pool," commanded Saphrar.

Feet first, quiva in hand, I plunged into the yellow fluid.

To my surprise the pool, at least near the edge, was not deep. I stood in the fluid only to my knees. I took a few more steps out into the pool. It became deeper toward the center. About a third of the way toward the center I was entered into the pool to my waist.

I looked about, searching for whatever it was that would attack me. It was difficult to look into the fluid because of the yellow, the glistening brilliance of the surface troubled by my passage.

I noted that the steam, and gas or fumes, no longer rose from the pool. It was quiet.

The filamentous threads did not approach me, but now seemed quiet, almost as if content. The spheres, too, seemed quiescent. Some of them, mostly whitish, luminescent ones, had seemed to float nearer, and hovered slightly beneath the surface, in a ring about me, some ten feet away. I took a step towards the ring and the spheres, doubtless moved by the fluids displaced in my step, seemed to slowly disperse and move away. The yellow of the pool's fluid, though rich, no longer seemed to leap and startle me with its vibrance.

I waited for the attack of the monster.

I stood so, in the fluid to my waist, for perhaps two or three minutes.

Then, angrily, thinking perhaps the pool was empty, or I

had been made fool of, I cried out to Saphrar. "When is it that I meet the monster?"

Over the surface I heard Saphrar, standing behind the wooden shield, laugh. "You have met it," he said.

"You lie!" I cried.

"No," he responded, amused, "you have met it."

"What is the monster?" I cried.

"The pool!" he shouted.

"The pool?" I asked.

"Yes," said Saphrar, gleefully. "It is alive!"

18

The Pleasure Gardens

At the very instant that Saphrar had called out there was a great blast of steam and fumes that seemed to explode from the fluid about me as though the monster in which I found myself had now, its prey satisfactorily entrapped, dared to respire and, at the same time, I felt the yellow fluid about my body begin to thicken and gell. I cried out suddenly in alarm horrified at my predicament and struggled to turn back and wade to the edge of the marbled basin that was the cage of the thing in which I was, but the fluid, tightening about me, now seemed to have the consistency of a rich yellow, hot mud and then, by the time I had reached a level where it rose to a point midway between my knees and waist the fluid had become as resistant as wet, yellow cement and I could move no further. My legs began to tingle and sting, and I could feel the skin beginning to be etched and picked by the corrosive elements now attacking them.

I heard Saphrar remark, "It sometimes takes hours to be fully digested."

Wildly, with the useless quiva, I began to slash and pick at the damp, thick stuff about me. The blade would sink in fully, as though in a tub of wet cement, leaving a mark, but when it was withdrawn the mark would be erased by the material flowing in to fill the aperture.

"Some men," said Saphrar, "those who do not struggle— have lived for as much as three hours—long enough in some cases to see their own bones."

I saw one of the vines hanging near me. My heart leaped

wildly at this chance. If I could but reach it! With all my strength I moved towards it—an inch—and then another inch—my fingers stretched, my arms and back aching, until in another inch I might have grasped it and then, to my horror, as I reached in agony for the vine, it rustled and lifted itself just beyond my reach. I moved toward it again, and again it did this. I howled with rage. I was going to try again when I saw the slave I had noticed earlier watching me, his hands on certain of the levers in the panel on the curving wall. I stood in the coagulating, tightening fluid, held fast a prisoner, and threw back my head in despair. He had, of course, controlled the movement of the vine from the panel, undoubtedly by wires.

"Yes, Tarl Cabot," wheezed Saphrar, giggling, "and yet you will, in an hour or so, when you are mad with pain and fear, try yet again and again to touch and grasp a vine, knowing that you will not succeed but yet again and again trying, believing that once somehow you will be successful. But you will not!" Saphrar now giggled uncontrollably. "I have even seen them reach for vines a spear's length above their head and think they could reach them!" Saphrar's two golden teeth, like yellow fangs, showed as he put back his head and howled with pleasure, his fat little hands pounding on the wood of the shield.

The quiva had turned itself in my hand and my arm flew back, that I might take with me in my death the tormentor, Saphrar of Turia.

"Beware!" cried the Paravaci and Saphrar suddenly stopped laughing and observed me warily.

If my arm should fly forward he would have time to leap below the wooden frame.

Now he was putting his chin on the wooden shield and watching me again, once more giggling.

"Many have used the quiva before now," he said, "but usually to plunge it into their own heart."

I looked at the blade.

"Tarl Cabot," I said, "does not slay himself."

"I did not think so," said Saphrar. "And that is why you were permitted to keep the quiva." Then he threw back his head and laughed again.

"You fat, filthy urt!" cried Harold, struggling in his bonds with the two men-at-arms who held him.

"Be patient," giggled Saphrar. "Be patient, my impetuous young friend. Your turn will come!"

I stood as still as I could. My feet and legs felt cold and yet as if they were burning—presumably the acids of the pool were at work. As nearly as I could determine the pool was thick, rubbery, gelatinous, only in the area near to my body. I could see it rippling, and splashing a bit against the edge of the marbled basin. Indeed, it was even lower toward the edge now, and had humped itself in my vicinity, as though in time it might climb my body and, in some hours perhaps, engulf me. But doubtless by then I would have been half digested, much of me little more than a cream of fluids and proteins then mixing with and nourishing the substance of my devourer—the Yellow Pool of Turia.

I pushed now, with all my might, not toward the edge of the marbled basin, but rather toward the deepest part of the pool. To my satisfaction I found that I could move, though barely, in this direction. The pool was content that I should enter it more deeply, perhaps it even desired that I do so, that its meal might be even more readily obtained.

"What is he doing?" cried the Paravaci.

"He is mad," said Saphrar.

Each inch I moved toward the center of the pool my journey became easier. Then suddenly, the yellow, encircling cementlike substance had oozed from my limbs and I could take two or three free steps. The fluid was now, however, to my armpits. One of the luminescent, white spheres floated by, quite close to me. To my horror I saw it change its shade as it neared the surface, more closely approaching the light. As it had risen toward the surface, just beneath which it now rested, its pigmentation had changed from a luminescent white to a rather darkish gray. It was clearly photosensitive. I reached out and slashed at it with the quiva, cutting it, and it withdrew suddenly, rolling in the fluid, and the pool itself seemed suddenly to churn with steam and light. Then it was quiet again. Yet somehow I knew now the pool, like all forms of life, had some level of irritability. More of the luminescent, white orbs now floated about me, circling me, but none of them now approached closely enough to allow me to use the quiva.

I splashed across the center of the pool, literally swimming. As soon as I had crossed the center I felt the fluids of the pool once again begin to gell and tighten. By the time I had reached the level of my waist on the opposite side I could, once again, no longer move toward the edge of the pool. I tried this twice more, in different directions, with

identically the same result. Always, the luminescent, photosensitive orbs seemed to float behind me and around me in
the fluid. Then I was swimming freely in the yellow fluid at
the center of the pool. Beneath me, vaguely, several feet
under the surface, I could see a collection, almost like
threads and granules in a transparent bag, of intertwined,
writhing filaments and spheres, imbedded in a darkish yellow
jelly, walled in by a translucent membrane.

Quiva in my teeth I dove toward the deepest part of the
Yellow Pool of Turia, where glowed the quickness and substance of the living thing in which I swam.

Almost instantly as I submerged the fluid beneath me
began to jell, walling me away from the glowing mass at the
bottom of the pool but, hand over hand, pulling at it and
thrusting my way, I forced my way deeper and deeper into it.
Finally I was literally digging in it feet below the surface. My
lungs began to scream for air. Still I dug in the yellow fluid,
hands and fingernails bleeding, and then, when it seemed my
lungs would burst and darkness was engulfing me and I
would lose consciousness, I felt a globular, membranous
tissue, wet and slimy, recoil spasmodically from my touch.
Upside down, locked in the gelling fluid, I took the quiva
from my mouth and, with both hands, pressed down with the
blade against that twitching, jerking, withdrawing membrane.
It seemed that the living, amorphous globe of matter which I
struck began to move away, slithering away in the yellow
fluids, but I pursued it, one hand in the torn membrane and
continued to slash and tear at it. Crowded about my body
now were entangling filaments and spheres trying, like hands
and teeth, to tear me from my work, but I struck and tore
again and again and then entered the secret world beneath
the membrane slashing to the left and right and suddenly the
fluid began to loosen and withdraw above me and within the
membranous chamber it began to solidify against me and
push me out—I stayed as long as I could but, lungs wrenching,
at last permitted myself to be thrust from the membranous
chamber and hurled into the loose fluid above. Now below me
the fluid began to gell swiftly almost like a rising floor and
it loosened and withdrew on all sides and suddenly my
head broke the surface and I breathed. I now stood on
the hardened surface of the Yellow Pool of Turia and saw
the fluids of the sides seeping into the mass beneath me and
hardening almost instantly. I stood now on a warm, dry

globular mass, almost like a huge, living shell. I could not have scratched the surface with the quiva.

"Kill him!" I heard Saphrar cry, and there was suddenly the hiss of a crossbow quarrel which streaked past me and shattered on the curving wall behind me. Standing now on the high, humped dried thing—lofty on that protective coating—I leaped easily up and seized one of the low hanging vines and climbed rapidly toward the blue ceiling of the chamber. I heard another hiss and saw a bolt from the crossbow shatter through the crystalline blue substance. One of the crossbowmen had leaped to the now dry floor of the marble basin and stood almost beneath me, his crossbow raised. I knew I would not be able to elude his quarrel. Then suddenly I heard his agonized cry and saw that beneath me, once again, there glistened the yellow fluids of the pool, moving about him, for the thing—perhaps thermotropic— had again, as rapidly as it had hardened, liquified and swirled about him, the luminescent spheres and filaments visible beneath its surface. The crossbow bolt went wild, again shattering the blue surface of the dome. I heard the wild, eerie cry of the luckless man beneath me and then, with my fist, broke the blue surface and climbed through, grasping the iron of a reticulated framework supporting numerous energy bulbs.

Far off, it seemed, I could hear Saphrar screeching for more guards.

I ran over the iron framework until, judging by the distance and curve of the dome, I had reached a point above where Harold and I had waited at the edge of the pool. There, quiva in hand, uttering the war cry of Ko-ro-ba, feet first, I leaped from the framework and shattered through the blue surface landing among my startled enemies. The crossbowmen were each winding their string tight for a new quarrel. The quiva had sought and found the heart of two before even they realized I was upon them. Then another fell. Harold, wrists still bound behind his back, hurled himself against two men and, screaming, they pitched backward into the Yellow Pool of Turia. Saphrar cried out and darted away.

The remaining two guardsmen, who had no crossbows, simultaneously whipped out their swords. Behind them, quiva poised in his fingertips, I could see the hooded Paravaci.

I shielded myself from the flight of the Paracaci quiva by rushing towards the two guardsmen. But before I reached them my quiva, with the underhand hilt cast, had struck the guardsman on my left. I moved to his right and from his strengthless hand, even before he fell, tore his weapon.

"Down!" cried Harold, and I fell to the floor barely sensible of the silverish quiva of the Paravaci speeding overhead. I took the attack of the second guardsman by rolling on my back and flinging up my blade in defense. Four times he struck and each time I parried and then I had regained my feet. He fell back from my blade, turned once and fell into the glistening, living liquid of the Yellow Pool of Turia.

I spun to face the Paravaci but he, weaponless, with a curse, turned and fled from the room.

From the breast of the first guardsman I removed the quiva, wiping it on his tunic.

I stepped to Harold and with one motion severed the bonds that constrained him.

"Not badly done for a Koroban," he granted.

We heard running feet approaching, those of several men, the clank of arms, the high-pitched, enraged screaming of Saphrar of Turia.

"Hurry!" I cried.

Together we ran about the perimeter of the pool until we came to a tangle of vines depending from the ceiling, up which we climbed, broke through the blue substance, and cast wildly about for an avenue of escape. There would be such, for the ceiling had been unbroken by a door or panel, and there must surely be some provision for the rearrangement and replacement of energy bulbs. We quickly found the exit, though it was only a panel some two feet by two feet, of a size for slaves to crawl through. It was locked but we kicked it open, splintering the bolt from the wood, and emerged on a narrow, unrailed balcony.

I had the guardsman's sword and my quiva, Harold his quiva alone.

He had, running swiftly, climbed up the outside of a dome concentric to the one below, and was there looking about.

"There it is!" he cried.

"What?" I demanded. "Tarns! Kaiila!"

"No," he cried, "Saphrar's Pleasure Gardens!" and disappeared down the other side of the dome.

"Come back!" I cried.

But he was gone.

Angry, I sped about the dome, not wishing to silhouette

myself against the sky on its curve, lest there be enemy bowmen within range.

About a hundred and fifty yards away, over several small roofs and domes, all within the vast compound that was the House of Saphrar of Turia, I saw the high walls of what was undoubtedly a Pleasure Garden. I could see, here and there, on the inside, the tops of graceful flower trees.

I could also see Harold bounding along, from roof to roof, in the light of the three moons.

Furious I followed him.

Could I have but put my hands on him at the time I might have wrung a Tuchuk neck.

I now saw him leap to the wall and, scarcely looking about, run along and then leap to the swaying trunk of one of the flower trees and descend swiftly into the darkness of the gardens.

In a moment I followed him.

19

Harold Finds A Wench

I had no difficulty finding Harold. Indeed, coming down the segmented trunk of the flower tree, I almost landed on top of him. He was sitting with his back to the tree, puffing, resting.

"I have formed a plan," he said to me.

"That is good news indeed," I responded. "Does it include some provision for escaping?"

"I have not yet formed that part of it," he admitted.

I leaned back against the tree, breathing heavily. "Would it not have been a good idea to reach the streets immediately?" I asked.

"The streets will be searched," puffed Harold, "—immediately—by all the guardsmen and men-at-arms in the city." He took two or three deep breaths. "It will never occur to them to search the Pleasure Gardens," he said. "Only fools would try to hide there."

I closed my eyes briefly. I felt ready to concede his last point.

"You are aware, of course," I mentioned, "that the Pleasure Gardens of so rich a man as Saphrar of Turia may contain a large number of female slaves—not all of whom might be trusted to keep silent—and some of whom will undoubtedly notice something as unusual as two strange warriors wandering about among the shrubs and ferns?"

"That is true," said Harold, "but I do not expect to be here by morning." He picked up a stalk of a patch of violet grass, one of several hues used in such gardens, and began to chew on it. "I think," said he, "an hour or so will be sufficient—perhaps less."

"Sufficient for what?" I asked.

"For tarnsmen to be called in to aid in the search," he said. "Their movements will undoubtedly be coordinated in the house of Saphrar—and some tarns and their riders, if only messengers or officers—will surely be available."

Suddenly there seemed to me a real possibility in Harold's plan. Undoubtedly tarnsmen, mounted, would come from time to time during the night to the House of Saphrar.

"You are clever," I said.

"Of course," he said, "I am a Tuchuk."

"But I thought you told me," I said, "that your plan did not yet contain a provision for escape."

"At the time," he said, "it did not—but while sitting here I formed it."

"Well," I said, "I am glad."

"Something always comes to me," he said. "I am a Tuchuk."

"What do you suggest we do now?" I asked.

"For the time," said Harold, "let us rest."

"Very well," I said.

And so we sat with our backs against the flower tree in the House of Saphrar, merchant of Turia. I looked at the lovely, dangling loops of interwoven blossoms which hung from the curved branches of the tree. I knew that the clusters of flowers which, cluster upon cluster, graced those linear, hanging stems, would each be a bouquet in itself, for the trees are so bred that the clustered flowers emerge in subtle, delicate patterns of shades and hues. Besides several of the flower trees there were also some Ka-la-na trees, or the yellow wine trees of Gor; there was one large-trunked, reddish Tur tree, about which curled its assemblage of Tur-Pah, a vinelike tree parasite with curled, scarlet, ovate leaves, rather lovely to look upon; the leaves of the Tur-Pah incidentally are edible and figure in certain Gorean dishes, such as sullage, a kind of soup; long ago, I had heard, a Tur tree was found on the prairie, near a spring, planted perhaps long before by someone who passed by; it was from that Tur tree that the city of Turia took its name; there was also, at one side of the garden, against the far wall, a grove of tem-wood, linear, black, supple. Besides the trees there were numerous shrubs and plantings, almost all flowered, sometimes fantastically; among the trees and the colored grasses there wound curved, shaded walks. Here and there I could hear the flowing of water, from miniature artificial waterfalls and fountains. From where I sat I could see two lovely pools, in which lotuslike plants floated; one of the pools was large enough for swimming; the other, I supposed, was stocked with tiny, bright fish from the various seas and lakes of Gor.

Then I became aware of the flickerings and reflections of light from over the wall, against some of the higher buildings about. I also heard the running of feet, the sound of arms. I could hear someone shouting. Then the noise, the light, passed.

"I have rested," said Harold.

"Good," I said.

"Now," said he, looking about, "I must find myself a wench."

"A wench!" I cried, almost a shout.

"Shhhh," said he, cautioning me to silence.

"Have we not enough troubles?" I inquired.

"Why do you think I came to Turia?" he asked.

"For a wench," I said.

"Certainly," said he, "and I do not intend to depart without one."

I gritted my teeth. "Well," I said, "I am sure there are many about."

"Doubtless," said Harold, getting to his feet, as though he must now be back to work.

I, too, got to my feet.

He had no binding fiber, no slave hood, no tarn. Yet this absence of equipment did not deter him, nor did he seem to regard his deprivations in these particulars as worthy of note.

"It may take a moment to pick out one I like," he apologized.

"That is all right," I assured him, "take your time."

I then followed Harold along one of the smooth, stone paths leading among the trees, brushing our way through the clusters of blossoms, skirting the edge of the nearer blue pool. I could see the three moons of Gor reflected in its surface. They were beautiful shining among the green and white blossoms on the water.

The masses of flowers and vegetation in Saphrar's Pleasure Gardens filled the air with mingled, heavy sweet frangrances. Also the fountains had been scented and the pools.

Harold left the walk and stepped carefully to avoid trampling a patch of talenders, a delicate yellow flower, often associated in the Gorean mind with love and beauty. He made his way across some dark blue and yellowish orange grass and came to the buildings set against one wall of the gardens. Here we climbed several low, broad marble steps and passed down a columned porch and entered the central building, finding ourselves in a dim, lamp-lit hall, bestrewn with carpets and cushions and decorated, here and there, with carved, reticulated white screening.

There were seven or eight girls, clad in Pleasure Silks, sleeping in this hall, scattered about, curled up on cushions. Harold inspected them, but did not seem satisfied. I looked them over and would have thought that any one of them would have been a prize, presuming it could be safely transported somehow to the wagons of the Tuchuks. One poor girl slept naked on the tiles by the fountain. About her neck was a thick metal collar to which a heavy iron chain had been fastened; the chain itself was attached to a large iron ring placed in the floor. I supposed she was being disciplined. I immediately began to worry that that girl would be the one who would strike Harold's eye. To my relief, he examined her briefly and passed on.

Soon Harold had left the central hall and was making his way down a long, carpeted, lamp-hung corridor. He entered various rooms off this corridor and, after, I suppose, inspecting their contents, always emerged and trekked off again.

We then examined other corridors and other rooms, and finally returned to the main hall and started off down another way, again encountering corridors and rooms; this we did four times, until we were moving down one of the last corridors, leading from one of the five main corridors off the central hall. I had not kept count but we must have passed by more than seven or eight hundred girls, and still, among all these riches of Saphrar, he could not seem to find the one for which he searched. Several times, one girl or another, would roll over or shift in her sleep, or throw out an arm, and my heart would nearly stop, but none of the wenches awakened and we would troop on to the next room.

At last we came to a largish room, but much smaller than the main hall, in which there were some seventeen beauties strewn about, all in Pleasure Silk. The light in the room was furnished by a single tharlarion-oil lamp which hung from the ceiling. It was carpeted by a large red rug on which were several cushions of different colors, mostly yellows and oranges. There was no fountain in the room but, against one wall, there were some low tables with fruits and drinks upon them. Harold looked the girls over and then he went to the low table and poured himself a drink, Ka-la-na wine by the smell of it. He then picked up a juicy, red larma fruit, biting into it with a sound that seemed partly crunching as he went through the shell, partly squishing as he bit into the fleshy, segmented endocarp. He seemed to make a great deal of noise. Although one or two of the girls stirred uneasily, none, to my relief, awakened.

Harold was now fishing about, still chewing on the fruit, in a wooden chest at one end of the table. He drew out of the chest some four silken scarves, after rejecting some others which did not sufficiently please him.

Then he stood up and went to where one of the girls lay curled on the thick red carpet.

"I rather like this one," he said, taking a bite out of the fruit, spitting some seeds to the rug.

She wore yellow Pleasure Silk, and, beneath her long black hair, on her throat, I glimpsed a silverish Turian collar. She lay with her knees drawn up and her head resting on her left elbow. Her skin color was tannish, not too unlike the girl I had seen from Port Kar. I bent more closely. She was a beauty, and the diaphanous Pleasure Silk that was the only garment permitted her did not, by design, conceal her charms. Then, startled, as she moved her head a bit, restlessly on the rug, I saw that in her nose was the tiny golden ring of a Tuchuk girl.

"This is the one," Harold said.

It was, of course, Hereena, she of the First Wagon.

Harold tossed the emptied, collapsed shell of the larma fruit into a corner of the room and whipped one of the scarfs from his belt.

He then gave the girl a short, swift kick, not to hurt her, but simply, rather rudely, to startle her awake.

"On your feet, Slave Girl," he said.

Hereena struggled to her feet, her head down, and Harold had stepped behind her, pulling her wrists behind her back and tieing them with the scarf in his hand.

"What is it?" she asked.

"You are being abducted," Harold informed her.

The girl's head flew up and she spun to face him, pulling to free herself. When she saw him her eyes were as wide as larma fruit and her mouth flew open.

"It is I," said Harold, "Harold the Tuchuk."

"No!" she said. "Not you!"

"Yes," he said, "I," turning her about once again, routinely checking the knots that bound her wrists, taking her wrists in his hands, trying to separate them, examining the knots for slippage; there was none. He permitted her to turn and face him again.

"How did you get in here?" she demanded.

"I chanced by," said Harold.

She was trying to free herself. After an instant she realized that she could not, that she had been bound by a warrior. Then she acted as though she had not noticed that she had been perfectly secured, that she was his prisoner, the prisoner of Harold of the Tuchuks. She squared her small shoulders and glared up at him.

"What are you doing here?" she demanded.

"Stealing a slave girl," he said.

"Who?" she asked.

"Oh, come now," said Harold.

"Not I!" she said.

"Of course," said he.

"But I am Hereena," she cried, "of the First Wagon!"

I feared the girl's voice might awaken the others, but they seemed still to sleep.

"You are only a little Turian slave girl," said Harold, "who has taken my fancy."

"No!" she said.

Then Harold had his hands in her mouth, holding it open. "See," he said to me.

I looked. To be sure, there was a slight gap between two of the teeth on the upper right.

Hereena was trying to say something. It is perhaps just as well she could not.

"It is easy to see," said Harold, "why she was not chosen First Stake."

Hereena struggled furiously, unable to speak, the young Tuchuk's hands separating her jaws.

"I have seen kaiila with better teeth," he said.

Hereena made an angry noise. I hoped that the girl would not burst a blood vessel. Then Harold removed his hands deftly, narrowly missing what would have been a most savage bite.

"Sleen!" she hissed.

"On the other hand," said Harold, "all things considered— she is a not unattractive little wench."

"Sleen! Sleen!" cursed the girl.

"I shall enjoy owning you," said Harold, patting her head.

"Sleen! Sleen! Sleen!" cursed the girl.

Harold turned to me. "She is—is she not—all things considered—a pretty little wench?"

I could not help but regard the angry, collared Hereena, furious in the swirling Pleasure Silk.

"Yes," I said, "very."

"Do not fret, little Slave Girl," said Harold to Hereena. "You will soon be able to serve me—and I shall see that you shall do so superbly."

Irrationally, like a terrified, vicious little animal, Hereena struggled again to free herself.

Harold stood by, patiently, making no attempt to interfere.

At last, trembling with rage, she approached him, her back to him, holding her wrists to him. "Your jest has gone far enough," she said. "Free me."

"No," said Harold.

"Free me!" commanded the girl.

"No," said Harold.

She spun to face him again, tears of rage in her eyes.

"No," said Harold.

She straightened herself. "I will never go with you," she hissed. "Never! Never! Never!"

"That is interesting," said Harold. "How do you propose to prevent it?"

"I have a plan," she said.

"Of course," he said, "you are Tuchuk." He looked at her narrowly. "What is your plan?"

"It is a simple one," she responded.

"Of course," said Harold, "though you are Tuchuk, you are also female."

One of Hereena's eyebrows rose skeptically. "The simplest plans," she remarked, "are often the best."

"Upon occasion," granted Harold. "What is your plan?"

"I shall simply scream," she said.

Harold thought for a moment. "That is an excellent plan," he admitted.

"So," said Hereena, "free me—and I will give you ten Ihn to flee for your lives."

That did not seem to me like much time. The Gorean Ihn, or second, is only a little longer than the Earth second. Regardless of the standard employed, it was clear that Hereena was not being particularly generous.

"I do not choose to do so," remarked Harold.

She shrugged. "Very well," she said.

"I gather you intend to put your plan into effect," said Harold.

"Yes," she said.

"Do so," said Harold.

She looked at him for a moment and then put back her head and sucked in air and then, her mouth open, prepared to utter a wild scream.

My heart nearly stopped but Harold, at the moment just before the girl could scream, popped one of the scarves into her mouth, wadding it up and shoving it between her teeth. Her scream was only a muffled noise, hardly more than escaping air.

"I, too," Harold informed her, "had a plan—a counterplan."

He took one of the two remaining scarves and bound it across her mouth holding the first scarf well inside her mouth.

"My plan," said Harold, "which I have now put into effect, was clearly superior to yours."

Hereena made some muffled noises. Her eyes regarded him wildly over the colored scarf and her entire body began to squirm savagely.

"Yes," said Harold, "clearly superior."

I was forced to concede his point. Standing but five feet away I could barely hear the tiny, angry noises she made.

Harold then lifted her from her feet and, as I winced, simply dropped her on the floor. She was, after all, a slave. She said something that sounded like "Ooof," when she hit the floor. He then crossed her ankles, and bound them tightly with the remaining scarf.

She glared at him in pained fury over the colored scarf.

He scooped her up and put her over his shoulder. I was forced to admit that he had handled the whole affair rather neatly.

In a short while Harold, carrying the struggling Hereena, and I had retraced our steps to the central hall and descended the steps of the porch and returned by means of the curving walks between the shrubs and pools to the flower tree by means of which we had originally entered the Pleasure Gardens of Saphrar of Turia.

20

The Keep

"By now," said Harold, "guardsmen will have searched the roofs, so it should be safe to proceed across them to our destination."

"And where is that?" I asked.

"Wherever the tarns happen to be," he responded.

"Probably," I said, "on the highest roof of the highest building in the House of Saphrar."

"That would be," suggested Harold, "the keep."

I agreed with him. The keep, in the private houses of Goreans, is most often a round, stone tower, built for defense, containing water and food. It is difficult to fire from the outside, and the roundness—like the roundness of Gorean towers in general—tends to increase the amount of oblique hits from catapult stones.

Making our way up the flower tree with Hereena, who fought like a young she-larl, was not easy. I went part way up the tree and was handed the girl, and then Harold would go up above me and I would hoist her up a way to him, and then I would pass him, and so on. Occasionally, to my irritation, we became entangled in the trailing, looped stems of the tree, each with its richness of clustered flowers, whose beauty I was no longer in a mood to appreciate. At last we got Hereena to the top of the tree.

"Perhaps," puffed Harold, "you would like to go back and get another wench—one for yourself?"

"No," I said.

"Very well," he said.

Although the wall was several feet from the top of the tree I managed, by springing on one of the curved branches, to build up enough spring pressure to leap to where I could get my fingers over the edge of the wall. I slipped with one hand and hung there, feet scraping the wall, some fifty feet from the ground, for a nasty moment, but then managed to get both hands on the edge of the wall and hoist myself up.

"Be careful," advised Harold.

I was about to respond when I heard a stifled scream of horror and saw that Harold had hurled Hereena in my direction, across the space between the tree and the wall. I managed to catch her. She was now covered with a cold sweat and was trembling with terror. Perched on the wall, holding the girl with one hand to prevent her tumbling off, I watched Harold springing up and down and then he was leaping towards me. He, too, slipped, as I was not displeased to note, but our hands met and he was drawn to safety.

"Be careful," I advised him, attempting not to let a note of triumph permeate my admonition.

"Quite right," wheezed Harold, "as I myself earlier pointed out."

I considered pushing him off the wall, but, thinking of the height, the likelihood of breaking his neck and back and such, and consequently thereby complicating our measures for escape, I dismissed the notion as impractical, however tempting.

"Come along," he said, flinging Hereena across his shoulders like a thigh of bosk meat, and starting along the wall. We soon came, to my satisfaction, to an easily accessible, flat roof and climbed onto it. Harold laid Hereena down on the roof to one side and sat cross-legged for a minute, breathing heavily. I myself was almost winded as well.

Then overhead in the darkness we heard the beat of a tarn's wings and saw one of the monstrous birds pass above us. In a short moment we heard it flutter to alight somewhere beyond. Harold and I then got up and, with Hereena under one of his arms, we circumspectly made our way from roof to roof until we saw the keep, rising like a dark cylinder against one of Gor's three moons. It stood some seventy feet from any of the other buildings in the compound that was the House of Saphrar, but now, swaying, formed of rope and sticks, a removable footbridge extended from an open door in its side to a porch some several feet below us. The bridge permitted access to the tower from the building on the roof

of which we stood. Indeed, it provided the only access, save
on tarnback, for there are no doors at ground level in a
Gorean keep. The first sixty feet or so of the tower would
presumably be solid stone, to protect the tower from forced
entrance or the immediate, efficient use of battering rams.
The tower itself was some one hundred and forty feet in
height and had a diameter of about fifty feet. It was furnished with numerous ports for the use of bowmen. The roof
of the tower, which might have been fortified with impaling
spears and tarn wire, was now clear, to permit the descent of
tarns and their riders.

On the roof, as we lay there, we could hear, now and
then, someone run along the footbridge. Then there was
someone shouting. From time to time a tarn would descend
or take flight from the roof of the keep.

When we were sure there were at least two tarns on the
roof of the keep I leaped down from the roof and landed on
the light bridge, struggling to retain my footing as it began to
swing under my feet. Almost immediately I heard a shout
from the building. "There's one of them!"

"Hurry!" I cried to Harold.

He threw Hereena down to me and I caught her on the
bridge. I saw briefly the wild, frightened look in her eyes,
heard what might have been a muffled plea. Then Harold
had sprung down beside me on the bridge, seizing the hand
rope to keep from tumbling off.

A guardsman had emerged, carrying a crossbow, framed in
the light of the threshold at the entrance to the bridge from
the building. There was a quarrel on the guide and he threw
the weapon to his shoulder. Harold's arm flashed past me
and the fellow stood suddenly still, then his knees gave slowly
way beneath him and he fell to the flooring of the porch, a
quiva hilt protruding from his chest, the crossbow clattering
beside him.

"Go ahead," I commanded Harold.

I could now hear more men coming, running.

Then to my dismay I saw two more crossbowmen, this
time on a nearby roof.

"I see them!" one of them cried.

Harold sped along the bridge, Hereena in his arms, and
disappeared into the keep.

Two swordsmen now rushed from the building, leaping
over the fallen crossbowman, and raced along the bridge
toward me. I engaged them, dropping one and wounding the

other. A quarrel from one of the crossbowmen on the roof suddenly shattered through the sticks of the bridge at my feet, splintering them not six inches from where I stood.

I backed rapidly along the bridge and another quarrel sped past me, striking sparks from the stone tower behind me. Now I could see several more guardsmen rushing toward the bridge. It would be eleven or twelve seconds before the crossbowmen would be ready to fire again. I turned and began to hack at the ropes that bound the swaying bridge to the tower. Inside I could hear a startled guard demanding to know who Harold was.

"Is it not obvious!" Harold was yelling at him. "You see I have the girl!"

"What girl?" the guard was asking.

"A wench from the Pleasure Gardens of Saphrar, you fool!" Harold was crying at him.

"But why should you be bringing such a wench here?" the guard was asking.

"You are dull, are you not!" demanded Harold. "Here—take her!"

"Very well," said the guard.

I then heard a sudden, sharp crack, as of a fist meeting bone.

The bridge began to rock and sag on its ropes and several men from the building began to thunder across towards me. Then there was a horrified cry as one rope was cut and the flooring of the bridge suddenly pitched, throwing several of the guardsmen to the ground below. A quarrel now struck the flooring of the tower at my feet and skidded into the building. I struck again and the other rope burst from my stroke and the bridge swung rapidly back against the wall of the building opposite with a clatter of sticks and cries, knocking the remaining, clinging guardsmen from it, dropping them like wood senseless to the foot of the wall. I leaped inside the door of the keep and swung it shut. Just as I did so the bolt of a crossbow struck the door and splintered through it, its head projecting some six inches on my side. I then flung the two bars in position, which locked the door, lest men on ladders from the ground attempt to force it.

The room in which I found myself contained an unconscious guard, but no further sign of Harold or Hereena. I then climbed up a wooden ladder to the next level, which was empty, and then another level and another, and another. Then I emerged in the chamber below the roof of the keep

and there found Harold, sitting on the bottom rung of the
last ladder, breathing heavily, Hereena lying squirming at his
feet. "I have been waiting for you," said Harold, gasping.

"Let us proceed," I said, "lest the tarns be flown from the
roof and we be isolated in the tower."

"My plan exactly," said Harold, "but first should you not
teach me to master the tarn?"

I heard Hereena moan with horror and she began to
struggle madly to free herself of the scarves that bound her.

"Normally," I said, "it takes years to become a skilled
tarnsman."

"That is all well and good," responded Harold, "but can
you not impart certain important information relating to the
matter in a briefer span?"

"Come to the roof!" I cried.

I preceded Harold up the ladder and thrust up the trap
admitting us to the roof. On the roof there were five tarns.
One guard was even then approaching the trap. The other
was releasing the tarns one by one.

I was ready to engage the first guard, half on the ladder,
but Harold's head emerged from the opening behind me.
"Don't fight," he called to the guard. "It is Tarl Cabot of
Ko-ro-ba, you fool!"

"Who is Tarl Cabot of Ko-ro-ba?" asked the guard, startled.

"I am," I responded, not knowing much what else to say.

"This is the girl," Harold was saying. "Hurry, take her!"

The guard sheathed his sword. "What is the trouble below?" he asked. "Who are you?"

"Do not ask questions," snapped Harold, "here is the
girl—take her!"

The guard shrugged and as he took Hereena from Harold
I winced as the young man felled him with a blow that might
have broken the skull of a bosk. Deftly, before she had
fallen, Harold nipped Hereena from the guard's arms. He
then tumbled the guard down the trap to the level below.

The other guard, across the dark roof, was bending to
work with the tarn hobbles. He had already released two of
the great birds, driving them from the roof with a tarn goad.

"You there!" cried Harold. "Release one more tarn!"

"Very well," called the man. He sent one more of the
great birds winging from the roof.

"Come here!" cried Harold.

The fellow came running across the roof. "Where is Kuurus?" he asked.

"Below," Harold informed him.

"Who are you?" asked the guard. "What is going on here?"

"I am Harold of the Tuchuks," responded Harold of the Tuchuks.

"What are you doing here?" asked the guard.

"Are you not Ho-bar?" inquired Harold. It was a common name in Ar, whence many of the mercenaries had come.

"I know of no Ho-bar," said the man. "Is he Turian?"

"I had hoped to find Ho-bar," said Harold, "but perhaps you will do."

"I shall try," said the guard.

"Here," said Harold. "Take the wench."

Hereena shook her head violently at the guard, protesting through the muffling folds of the scarf wadded in her mouth.

"What will I do with her?" asked the guard.

"Just hold her," said Harold.

"Very well," said the guard.

I closed my eyes and it was over in a second. Harold once more had Hereena over his shoulder and was boldly approaching the tarns.

There were two of the great birds left on the roof, both fine specimens, huge, vicious, alert.

Harold dropped Hereena to the floor of the roof and strode to the first tarn. I shut my eyes as he vigorously struck it once, authoritatively, across the beak. "I am Harold of the Tuchuks," he said, "I am a skilled tarnsman—I have ridden over a thousand tarns—I have spent more time in the tarn saddle than most men on their feet—I was conceived on tarnback—I was born on tarnback—I eat tarns—fear me! I am Harold of the Tuchuks!"

The bird, if such emotions it could have, was looking at him, askance and baffled. Any instant I expected it to pick Harold from the roof with its beak, bite him in two and eat the pieces. But the bird seemed utterly startled, if possible, dumbfounded.

Harold turned to face me. "How do you ride a tarn?" he asked

"Get into the saddle," I said.

"Yes!" he said, and climbed up, missing one of the rungs of the rope ladder at the saddle and slipping his leg through it. I then managed to get him to the saddle and made sure he

fastened the safety strap. As swiftly as I could I then explained to him the guidance apparatus, the main saddle ring
and its six straps.

When I handed Hereena to him the poor girl was shivering
and moaning in terror, uncontrollably trembling. She, a girl
of the plains, familiar with fierce kaiila, herself a proud,
spirited wench, brave and daring, was yet—like many
women—utterly for some reason terrified of a tarn. I felt
genuine pity for the Tuchuk girl. On the other hand Harold
seemed quite pleased that she was beside herself with terror.
The slave rings on the tarn saddle are similar to those on the
kaiila saddle and in a trice Harold, using the thongs streaming from the slave rings, one on each side of the saddle, had
bound the girl on her back across the saddle in front of him.
Then, without waiting, uttering a great cry, he hauled on the
one-strap. The tarn did not move but, I thought, though it
was undoubtedly not the case, turned and regarded him
skeptically, reproachfully.

"What is the matter?" asked Harold.

"It is still hobbled," I said.

I bent to the tarn hobble and opened it. Immediately the
huge bird's wings began to beat and it sprang skyward.
"Aiii!" I heard Harold cry, and could well imagine what had
happened to his stomach.

As quickly as I could I then unhobbled the other bird and
climbed to the saddle, fastening the broad safety strap. Then
I hauled on the one-strap and seeing Harold's bird wheeling
about in circles against one of the Gorean moons sped to his
side.

"Release the straps!" I called to him. "The bird will follow
this one!"

"Very well," I heard him call, cheerily.

And in a moment we were speeding high over the city of
Turia. I took one long turn, seeing the torches and lights in
the House of Saphrar below, and then guided my bird out
over the prairie in the direction of the wagons of the
Tuchuks.

I was elated that we had managed to escape alive from the
House of Saphrar, but I knew that I must return to the city,
for I had not obtained the object for which I had come—the
golden sphere—which still resided in the merchant stronghold.

I must manage to seize it before the man with whom

Saphrar had had dealings—the gray man with eyes like glass—could call for it—and destroy it or carry it away.

As we sped high over the prairie I wondered at how it was that Kamchak was withdrawing the wagons and bosk from Turia—that he would so soon abandon the siege.

Then, in the dawn, we saw the wagons below us, and the bosk beyond them. Already fires had been lit and there was much activity in the camp of the Tuchuks, the cooking, the checking of wagons, the gathering and hitching up of the wagon bosk. This, I knew, was the morning on which the wagons moved away from Turia, toward distant Thassa, the Sea. Risking arrows, I, followed by Harold, descended to alight among the wagons.

21

Kamchak Enters Turia

I had now been in the city of Turia some four days, having
returned on foot in the guise of a peddler of small jewels. I
had left the tarn with the wagons. I had spent my last tarn
disk to buy a couple of handfuls of tiny stones, many of them
of little or no value; yet their weight in my pouch gave me
some pretext for being in the city.

I had found Kamchak, as I had been told I would, at the
wagon of Kutaituchik, which, drawn up on its hill near the
standard of the four bosk horns, had been heaped with what
wood was at hand and filled with dry grass. The whole was
then drenched in fragrant oils, and that dawn of the retreat,
Kamchak, by his own hand, hurled the torch into the wagon.
Somewhere in the wagon, fixed in a sitting position, weapons
at hand, was Kutaituchik, who had been Kamchak's friend,
and who had been called Ubar of the Tuchuks. The smoke of
the wagon must easily have been seen from the distant walls
of Turia.

Kamchak had not spoken but sat on his kaiila, his face
dark with resolve. He was terrible to look upon and I, though
his friend, did not dare to speak to him. I had not returned
to the wagon I had shared with him, but had come immediately to the wagon of Kutaituchik, where I had been informed he was to be found.

Clustered about the hill, in ranks, on their kaiila, black
lances in the stirrup, were several of the Tuchuk Hundreds.
Angrily they watched the wagon burn.

I wondered that such men as Kamchak and these others
would so willingly abandon the siege of Turia.

At last when the wagon had burned and the wind moved about the blackened beams and scattered ashes across the green prairie, Kamchak raised his right hand. "Let the standard be moved," he cried.

I observed a special wagon, drawn by a dozen bosk, being pulled up the hill, into which the standard, when uprooted, would be set. In a few minutes the great pole of the standard had been mounted on the wagon and was descending the hill, leaving on the summit the burned wood and the black ashes that had been the wagon of Kutaituchik, surrendering them now to the wind and the rain, to time and the snows to come, and to the green grass of the prairie.

"Turn the wagons!" called Kamchak.

Slowly, wagon by wagon, the long columns of the Tuchuk retreat were formed, each wagon in its column, each column in its place, and, covering pasangs of prairie, the march from Turia had begun.

Far beyond the wagons I could see the herds of bosk, and the dust from their hoofs stained the horizon.

Kamchak rose in his stirrups. "The Tuchuks ride from Turia!" he cried.

Rank by rank the warriors on the kaiila, dour, angry, silent, turned their mounts away from the city and slowly went to find their wagons, save for the Hundreds that would flank the withdrawal and form its rear guard.

Kamchak rode his kaiila up the hill until he stood, that cold dawn, at the edge of the burned wood and ashes of Kutaituchik's wagon. He stayed there for some time, and then turned his mount away, and came slowly down the hill.

Seeing me, he stopped. "I am pleased to see you live," he said.

I dropped my head, acknowledging the bond he had acknowledged. My heart felt grateful to the stern, fierce warrior, though he had been in the past days harsh and strange, half drunk with hatred for Turia. I did not know if the Kamchak I had known would ever live again. I feared that part of him—perhaps that part I had loved best—had died the night of the raid, when he had entered the wagon of Kutaituchik.

Standing at his stirrup I looked up. "Will you leave like this?" I asked. "Is it enough?"

He looked at me, but I could read no expression on his face. "The Tuchuks ride from Turia," he said. He then rode away, leaving me standing on the hill.

Somewhat to my surprise I had no difficulty the next morning, after the withdrawal of the wagons, in entering the city. Before leaving the wagons I had joined them briefly on their march, long enough to purchase my peddler's disguise and the pound or so of stones which was to complete it. I purchased these things from the man from whom Kamchak had, on a happier afternoon, obtained a new saddle and set of quivas. I had seen many things in the man's wagon and I had gathered, correctly it seems, that he was himself a peddler of sorts. I then, on foot, following for a time the tracks of the departing wagons, then departing from them, returned to the vicinity of Turia. I spent the night on the prairie and then, on what would have been the second day of the retreat, entered the city at the eighth hour. My hair was concealed in the hood of a thin, ankle-length rep-cloth garment, a dirty white through which ran flecks of golden thread, a fit garment, in my opinion, for an insignificant merchant. Beneath my garment, concealed, I carried sword and quiva.

I was hardly questioned by guards at the gates of Turia, for the city is a commercial oasis in the plains and during a year hundreds of caravans, not to mention thousands of small merchants, on foot or with a single tharlarion wagon, enter her gates. To my great surprise the gates of Turia stood open after the withdrawal of the wagons and the lifting of the siege. Peasants streamed through them returning to their fields and also hundreds of townsfolk for an outing, some of them to walk even as far as the remains of the old Tuchuk camp, hunting for souvenirs. As I entered I regarded the lofty double gates, and wondered how long it would take to close them.

As I hobbled through the city of Turia, one eye half shut, staring at the street as though I hoped to find a lost copper tarn disk among the stones, I made my way toward the compound of Saphrar of Turia. I was jostled in the crowds, and twice nearly knocked down by officers in the guard of Phanius Turmus, Ubar of Turia.

I was vaguely conscious, from time to time, that I might be followed. I dismissed this possibility, however, for, glancing about, I could find no one I might fear. The only person I saw more than once was a slip of a girl in Robes of Concealment and veil, a market basket on her arm, who the second time passed me, not noticing me. I breathed a sigh of relief. It is a nerve-wracking business, the negotiation of an enemy city, knowing that discovery might bring torture or sudden death, at best perhaps an impalement by sundown on the city's walls, a warning to any other who might be similarly tempted to transgress the hospitality of a Gorean city.

I came to the ring of flat, cleared ground, some hundred feet or so wide, which separates the walled compound of buildings which constitutes the House of Saphrar of Turia from all the surrounding structures. I soon learned, to my irritation, that one could not approach the high compound wall more closely than ten spear lengths.

"Get away you!" cried a guard from the wall, with a crossbow. "There is no loitering here!"

"But master!" I cried. "I have gems and jewels to show the noble Saphrar!"

"Approach then the nearer gate!" he called. "And state your business."

I found a rather small gate in the wall, heavily barred, and begged admittance to show my wares to Saphrar. I hoped to be ushered into his presence and then, on the threat of slaying him, secure the golden sphere and a tarn for escape.

To my chagrin I was not admitted into the compound, but my pitiful stock of almost worthless stones was examined outside the gate by a steward in the company of two armed warriors. It took him only a few moments to discover the value of the stones and, when he did, with a cry of disgust, he hurled them away from the gate into the dust, and the two warriors, while I pretended fright and pain, belabored me with the hilts of their weapons. "Be gone, Fool!" they snarled.

I hobbled after the stones, and fell to my knees in the dust, scrabbling after them, moaning and crying aloud.

I heard the guards laugh.

I had just picked up the last stone and tucked it back in my pouch and was about to rise from my knees when I found myself staring at the high, heavy sandals, almost boots, of a warrior.

"Mercy, Master," I whined.

"Why are you carrying a sword beneath your robe?" he asked.

I knew the voice. It was that of Kamras of Turia, Champion of the City, whom Kamchak had so sorely bested in the games of Love War.

I lunged forward seizing him by the legs and upended him

in the dust and then leaped to my feet and ran, the hood flying off behind me.

I heard him cry. "Stop that man! Stop him! I know him! He is Tarl Cabot of Ko-ro-ba! Stop him!"

I stumbled in the long robe of the merchant and cursed and leaped up and ran again. The bolt of a crossbow splattered into a brick wall on my right, gouging a cupful of masonry loose in chips and dust.

I darted down a narrow street. I could hear someone, probably Kamras, and then one or two others running after me. Then I heard a girl cry out, and scream, and two men curse. I glanced behind me to see that the girl who carried the market basket had inadvertently fallen in front of the warriors. She was crying angrily at them and waving her broken basket. They pushed her rudely to one side and hurried on. By that time I had rounded a corner and leaped to a window, pulled myself up to the next window, and hauled myself up again and onto the flat roof of a shop. I heard the running feet of the two warriors, and then of six more men, pass in the street below. Then some children, screaming, ran after the soldiers. I heard some speculative conversation in the street below, between two or three passersby, then it seemed quiet.

I lay there scarcely daring to breathe. The sun on the flat roof was hot. I counted five Gorean Ehn, or minutes. Then I decided I had better move across the roofs in the opposite direction, find a sheltered roof, stay there until nightfall and then perhaps try to leave the city. I might go after the wagons, which would be moving slowly, obtain the tarn I had left with them, and then return on tarnback to Saphrar's house. It would be extremely dangerous, of course, to leave the city in the near future. Certainly word would soon be at the gates to watch for me. I had entered Turia easily. I did not expect I would leave as easily as I had entered. But how could I stay in the city until vigilance at the gates might be relaxed, perhaps three or four days from now? Every guardsman in Turia would be on the lookout for Tarl Cabot, who unfortunately, was not difficult to recognize.

About this time I heard someone coming along the street whistling a tune. I had heard it. Then I realized that I had heard it among the wagons of the Tuchuks. It was a Tuchuk tune, a wagon tune, sometimes sung by the girls with the bosk sticks.

I picked up the melody and whistled a few bars, and then

the person below joined me and we finished the tune together.

Cautiously I poked my head over the edge of the roof. The street was deserted save for a girl, who was standing below, looking up toward the roof. She was dressed in veil and Robes of Concealment. It was she whom I had seen before, when I had thought I might be followed. It was she who had inadvertently detained my pursuers. She carried a broken market basket.

"You make a very poor spy, Tarl Cabot," she said.

"Dina of Turia!" I cried.

I stayed four days in the rooms above the shop of Dina of Turia. There I dyed my hair black and exchanged the robes of the merchant for the yellow and brown tunic of the Bakers, to which caste her father and two brothers had belonged.

Downstairs the wooden screens that had separated the shop from the street had been splintered apart; the counter had been broken and the ovens ruined, their oval domes shattered, their iron doors twisted from their hinges; even the top stones on the two grain mills had been thrown to the floor and broken.

At one time, I gathered from Dina, her father's shop had been the most famed of the baking shops of Turia, most of which are owned by Saphrar of Turia, whose interests range widely, though operated naturally, as Gorean custom would require, by members of the Caste of Bakers. Her father had refused to sell the shop to Saphrar's agents, and take his employment under the merchant. Shortly thereafter some seven or eight ruffians, armed with clubs and iron bars, had attacked the shop, destroying its equipment. In attempting to defend against this attack both her father and her two older brothers had been beaten to death. Her mother had died shortly thereafter of shock. Dina had lived for a time on the savings of the family, but had then taken them, sewn in the lining of her robes, and purchased a place on a caravan wagon bound for Ar, which caravan had been ambushed by Kassars, in which raid she herself, of course, had fallen into their hands.

"Would you not like to hire men and reopen the shop?" I asked.

"I have no money," she said.

"I have very little," I said, taking the pouch and spilling

the stones in a glittering if not very valuable heap on the small table in her central room.

She laughed and poked through them with her fingers. "I learned something of jewels," she said, "in the wagons of Albrecht and Kamchak—and there is scarcely a silver tarn disk's worth here."

"I paid a golden tarn disk for them," I asserted.

"But to a Tuchuk—" she said.

"Yes," I admitted.

"My dear Tarl Cabot," she said, "my sweet dear Tarl Cabot." Then she looked at me and her eyes saddened. "But," said she, "even had I the money to reopen the shop— it would mean only that the men of Saphrar would come again."

I was silent. I supposed what she said was true.

"Is there enough there to buy passage to Ar?" I asked.

"No," she said. "But I would prefer in any case to remain in Turia—it is my home."

"How do you live?" I asked.

"I shop for wealthy women," said she, "for pastries and tarts and cakes—things they will not trust their female slaves to buy."

I laughed.

In answer to her questions I told her the reason for which I had entered the city—to steal an object of value from Saphrar of Turia, which he himself had stolen from the Tuchuks. This pleased her, as I guessed anything would which was contrary to the interests of the Turian merchant, for whom she entertained the greatest hatred.

"Is this truly all you have?" she asked, pointing at the pile of stones.

"Yes," I said.

"Poor warrior," said she, her eyes smiling over the veil, "you do not even have enough to pay for the use of a skilled slave girl."

"That is true," I admitted.

She laughed and with an easy motion dropped the veil from her face and shook her head, freeing her hair. She held out her hands. "I am only a poor free woman," said she, "but might I not do?"

I took her hands and drew her to me, and into my arms. "You are very beautiful, Dina of Turia," I said to her.

For four days I remained with the girl, and each day, once at noon and once in the evening, we would stroll by one or more of the gates of Turia, to see if the guards might now be less vigilant than they had been the time before. To my disappointment, they continued to check every outgoing person and wagon with great care, demanding proof of identity and business. When there was the least doubt, the individual was detained for interrogation by an officer of the guard. On the other hand I noted, irritably, that incoming individuals and wagons were waved ahead with hardly a glance. Dina and myself attracted little attention from guardsmen or men-at-arms. My hair was now black; I wore the tunic of the Bakers; and I was accompanied by a woman.

Several times criers had passed through the streets shouting that I was still at large and calling out my description.

Once two guardsmen came to the shop, searching it as I expect most other structures in the city were searched. During this time I climbed out a back window facing another building, and hoisted myself to the flat roof of the shop, returning by the same route when they had gone.

I had, almost from the first in Kamchak's wagon, been truly fond of Dina, and I think she of me. She was truly a fine, spirited girl, quick-witted, warm-hearted, intelligent and brave. I admired her and feared for her. I knew, though I did not speak of it with her, that she was willingly risking her life to shelter me in her native city. Indeed, it is possible I might have died the first night in Turia had it not been that Dina had seen me, followed me and in my time of need boldly stood forth as my ally. In thinking of her I realized how foolish are certain of the Gorean prejudices with respect to the matter of caste. The Caste of Bakers is not regarded as a high caste, to which one looks for nobility and such; and yet her father and her brothers, outnumbered, had fought and died for their tiny shop; and this courageous girl, with a valor I might not have expected of many warriors, weaponless, alone and friendless, had immediately, asking nothing in return, leaped to my aid, giving me the protection of her home, and her silence, placing at my disposal her knowledge of the city and whatever resources might be hers to command.

When Dina was about her own business, shopping for her clients, usually in the early morning and the late afternoon, I would remain in the rooms above the shop. There I thought long on the matter of the egg of Priest-Kings and the House of Saphrar. In time I would leave the city—when I thought it safe—and return to the wagons, obtain the tarn and then make a strike for the egg. I did not give myself, however, much hope of success in so desperate a venture. I lived in constant fear that the gray man—he with eyes like glass—would come to Turia on tarnback and acquire, before I could act, the golden sphere—for which so much had been risked, for which apparently more than one man had died.

Sometimes Dina and I, in our walking about the city, would ascend the high walls and look out over the plains. There was no objection to this on the part of anyone, provided entry into the guard stations was not attempted. Indeed, the broad walk, some thirty feet wide, within the high walls of Turia, with the view over the plains, is a favorite promenade of Turian couples. During times of danger or siege, of course, none but military personnel or civilian defenders are permitted on the walls.

"You seem troubled, Tarl Cabot," said Dina, by my side, looking with me out over the prairie.

"It is true, my Dina," said I.

"You fear the object you seek will leave the city before you can obtain it?" she asked.

"Yes," I said, "I fear that."

"You wish to leave the city tonight?" she asked.

"I think perhaps I shall," I said.

She knew as well as I that the guards were still questioning those who would depart from Turia, but she knew too, as I, that each day, each hour, I remained in Turia counted against me.

"It is my hope that you will be successful," she said.

I put my arm about her and together we looked out over the parapet.

"Look," I said, "there comes a single merchant wagon—it must be safe now on the plains."

"The Tuchuks are gone," she said. And she added, "I shall miss you, Tarl Cabot."

"I shall miss you, too, my Dina of Turia," I told her.

In no hurry to depart from the wall, we stood together there. It was shortly before the tenth Gorean hour, or noon of the Gorean day.

We stood on the wall near the main gate of Turia, through which I had entered the city some four days ago, the morning after the departure of the Tuchuk wagons for the pastures this side of the Ta-Thassa Mountains, beyond which lay the vast, gleaming Thassa itself.

I watched the merchant wagon, large and heavy, wide,

with planked sides painted alternately white and gold, covered with a white and gold rain canvas. It was drawn not by the draft tharlarion like most merchant wagons but, like some, by four brown bosk.

"How will you leave the city?" asked Dina.

"By rope," I said. "And on foot."

She leaned over the parapet, looking skeptically down at the stones some hundred feet below.

"It will take time," she said, "and the walls are patrolled closely after sundown, and lit by torches." She looked at me. "And you will be on foot," she said. "You know we have hunting sleen in Turia?"

"Yes," I said, "I know."

"It is unfortunate," she said, "that you do not have a swift kaiila and then you might, in broad daylight, hurtle past the guards and make your way into the prairie."

"Even could I steal a kaiila or tharlarion," I said, "there are tarnsmen—"

"Yes," she said, "that is true."

Tarnsmen would have little difficulty in finding a rider and mount on the open prairie near Turia. It was almost certain they would be flying within minutes after an alarm was sounded, even though they need be summoned from the baths, the Paga taverns, the gaming rooms of Turia, in which of late, the siege over, they had been freely spending their mercenary gold, much to the delight of Turians. In a few days, their recreations complete, I expected Ha-Keel would weigh up his gold, marshal his men and withdraw through the clouds from the city. I, of course, did not wish to wait a few days—or more—or however long it might take Ha-Keel to rest his men, square his accounts with Saphrar and depart.

The heavy merchant wagon was near the main gate now and it was being waved forward.

I looked out over the prairie, in the direction that had been taken by the Tuchuk wagons. Some five days now they had been gone. It had seemed strange to me that Kamchak, the resolute, implacable Kamchak of the Tuchuks, had so soon surrendered his assault on the city—not that I expected it would have been, if prolonged, successful. Indeed, I respected his wisdom—withdrawing in the face of a situation in which there was nothing to be gained and, considering the vulnerability of the wagons and bosk to tarnsmen, much to be lost. He had done the wise thing. But how it must have hurt him—he, Kamchak—to turn the wagons and withdraw from Turia, leaving Kutaituchik unrevenged and Saphrar of Turia triumphant. It had been, in its way, a courageous thing for him to do. I would rather have expected Kamchak to have stood before the walls of Turia, his kaiila saddled, his arrows at hand, until the winds and snows had at last driven him, the Tuchuks, the wagons and the bosk away from the gates of the beleaguered city, the nine-gated, high-walled stronghold of Turia, inviolate and never conquered.

This train of thought was interrupted by the sounds of an altercation below, the shouting of an annoyed guardsman at the gate, the protesting cries of the driver of the merchant wagon. I looked down from the wall, and to my amusement, though I felt sorry for the distraught driver, saw that the right, rear wheel of the wide, heavy wagon had slipped the axle and that the wagon, obviously heavily loaded, was now tilting crazily, and then the axle struck the dirt, imbedding itself.

The driver had immediately leaped down and was gesticulating wildly beside the wheel. Then, irrationally, he put his shoulder under the wagon box and began to push up, trying to right the wagon, surely an impossible task for one man.

This amused several of the guards and some of the passersby as well, who gathered to watch the driver's discomfiture. Then the officer of the guard, nearly beside himself with rage, ordered several of his amused men to put their shoulders to the wagon as well. Even the several men, together with the driver, could not right the wagon, and it seemed that levers must be sent for.

I looked away, across the prairie, bemused. Dina was still watching the broil below and laughing, for the driver seemed so utterly distressed and apologetic, cringing and dancing about and scraping before the irate officer. Then I noted, across the prairie, hardly remarking it, a streak of dust in the sky.

Even the guards and townsfolk here and there on the wall seemed now to be watching the stalled wagon below.

I looked down again. The driver I noted was a young man, well built. He had blond hair. There seemed to be something familiar about him.

Suddenly I wheeled and gripped the parapet. The streak of dust was now more evident. It was approaching the main gate of Turia.

I seized Dina of Turia in my arms.

"What's wrong!" she said.

I whispered to her, fiercely. "Return to your home and lock yourself in. Do not go out into the streets!"

"I do not understand," said she. "What are you talking about?"

"Do not ask questions," I ordered her. "Do as I say! Go home, bolt the door to your rooms, do not leave the house!"

"But, Tarl Cabot," she said.

"Hurry!" I said.

"You're hurting my arms," she cried.

"Obey me!" I commanded.

Suddenly she looked out over the parapet. She, too, saw the dust. Her hand went to her mouth. Her eyes widened in fear.

"You can do nothing," I said. "Run!"

I kissed her savagely and turned her about and thrust her a dozen feet down the walkway inside the wall. She stumbled a few feet and turned. "What of you?" she cried.

"Run!" I commanded.

And Dina of Turia ran down the walkway, along the rim of the high wall of Turia.

Beneath the unbelted tunic of the Bakers, slung under my left arm, its lineaments concealed largely by a short brown cloak worn over the left shoulder, there hung my sword and with it, the quiva. I now, not hurrying, removed the weapons from my tunic, removed the cloak and wrapped them inside it.

I then looked once more over the parapet. The dust was closer now. In a moment I would be able to see the kaiila, the flash of light from the lance blades. Judging from the dust, its dimensions, its speed of approach, the riders, perhaps hundreds of them, the first wave, were riding in a narrow column, at full gallop. The narrow column, and probably the Tuchuk spacing, a Hundred and then the space for a Hundred, open, and then another Hundred, and so on, tends to narrow the front of dust, and the spaces between Hundreds gives time for some of the dust to dissipate and also, incidentally, to rise sufficiently so that the progress of the consequent Hundreds is in no way impeded or handicapped. I could now see the first Hundred, five abreast, and then the open space behind them, and then the second Hundred. They were approaching with great rapidity. I now saw a sudden flash of light as the sun took the tips of Tuchuk lances.

Quietly, not wishing to hurry, I descended from the wall and approached the stalled wagon, the open gate, the guards.

Surely in a moment someone on the wall would give the alarm.

At the gate the officer was still berating the blond-haired fellow. He had blue eyes, as I had known he would, for I had recognized him from above.

"You will suffer for this!" the commander of the guard was crying. "You dull fool!"

"Oh mercy, master!" whined Harold of the Tuchuks.

"What is your name?" demanded the officer.

At that moment there was a long, wailing cry of horror from the wall above. "Tuchuks!" The guards suddenly looked about themselves startled. Then two more people on the wall took up the cry, pointing wildly out over the wall. "Tuchuks! Close the gates!"

The officer looked up in alarm, and then he cried out to the men on the windlass platform. "Close the gates!"

"I think you will find," said Harold, "that my wagon is in the way."

Suddenly understanding, the officer cried out in rage and whipped his sword from his sheath but before he could raise his arm the young man had leaped to him and thrust a quiva into his heart. "My name," he said, "is Harold—of the Tuchuks!"

There was now screaming on the walls, the rushing of guardsmen toward the wagon. The men on the windlass platform were slowly swinging the great double gates shut as much as possible. Harold had withdrawn his quiva from the breast of the officer. Two men leaped toward him with swords drawn and I leaped in front of him and engaged them, dropping one and wounding the other.

"Well done, Baker," he cried.

I gritted my teeth and met the attack of another man. I could now hear the drumming of kaiila paws beyond the gate, perhaps no more than a pasang away. The double gate had closed now save for the wagon wedged between the two parts of the gate. The wagon bosk, upset by the running men, the shouting and the clank of arms about them, were bellowing wildly and throwing their heads up and down, stomping and pawing in the dust.

My Turian foe took the short sword under the heart. I kicked him from the blade barely in time to meet the attack of two more men.

I heard Harold's voice behind me. "I suppose while the bread is baking," he was saying, "there is little to do but stand about and improve one's swordplay."

I might have responded but I was hard pressed.

"I had a friend," Harold was saying, "whose name was Tarl Cabot. By now he would have slain both of them."

I barely turned a blade from my heart.

"And quite some time ago," Harold added.

The man on my left now began to move around me to my left while the other continued to press me from the front. It should have been done seconds ago. I stepped back, getting my back to the wagon, trying to keep their steel from me.

"There is a certain resemblance between yourself and my friend Tarl Cabot," Harold was saying, "save that your swordplay is decidedly inferior to his. Also he was of the caste of warriors and would not permit himself to be seen on his funeral pyre in the robes of so low a caste as that of the Bakers. Moreover, his hair was red—like a larl from the sun—whereas yours is a rather common and, if I may say so, a rather uninspired black."

I managed to slip my blade through the ribs of one man and twist to avoid the thrust of the other. In an instant the position of the man I had felled was filled by yet another guardsman.

"It would be well to be vigilant also on the right," remarked Harold.

I spun to the right just in time to turn the blade of a third man.

"It would not have been necessary to tell Tarl Cabot that," Harold said.

Some passersby were now fleeing past, crying out. The great alarm bars of the city were now ringing, struck by iron hammers.

"I sometimes wonder where old Tarl Cabot is," Harold said wistfully.

"You Tuchuk idiot!" I screamed.

Suddenly I saw the faces of the men fighting me turn from rage to fear. They turned and ran from the gate.

"It would now be well," said Harold, "to take refuge under the wagon." I then saw his body dive past, scrambling under the wagon. I threw myself to the ground and rolled under with him.

Almost instantly there was a wild cry, the war cry of the Tuchuks, and the first five kaiila leaped from outside the gate onto the top of the wagon, finding firm footing on what I had taken to be simple rain canvas, but actually was canvas stretched over a load of rocks and earth, accounting for the

incredible weight of the wagon, and then bounded from the
wagon, two to one side, two the other, and the middle rider
actually leaping from the top of the wagon to the dust beyond
the harnessed bosk. In an instant another five and then
another and another had repeated this maneuver and soon,
sometimes with squealing of kaiila and dismounting of riders
as one beast or another would be crowded between the gates
and the others, a Hundred and then another Hundred had
hurtled howling into the city, black lacquered shields on the
left arms, lance seized in the right hand. About us there were
the stamping paws of kaiila, the crying of men, the sound of
arms, and always more and more Tuchuks striking the top of
the wagon and bounding into the city uttering their war cry.
Each of the Hundreds that entered turned to its own destination, taking different streets and turns, some dismounting and
climbing to command the roofs with their small bows. Already I could smell smoke.

Under the wagon with us, crouching, terrified, were three
Turians, civilians, a wine vendor, a potter and a girl. The
wine vendor and the potter were peeping fearfully from
between the wheels at the riders thundering into the streets.
Harold, on his hands and knees, was looking into the eyes of
the girl who knelt, too, numb with terror. "I am Harold of
the Tuchuks," he was telling her. He deftly removed the veil
pins and she scarcely noticed, so terrified was she. "I am not
really a bad fellow," he was informing her. "Would you like
to be my slave?" She managed to shake her head, No, a tiny
motion, her eyes wide with fear. "Ah, well," said Harold,
repinning her veil. "It is probably just as well anyway. I
already have one slave and two girls in one wagon—if I had
a wagon—would probably be difficult." The girl nodded her
head affirmatively. "When you leave the wagon," Harold told
her, "you might be stopped by Tuchuks—nasty fellows—who
would like to put your pretty little throat in a collar—you
understand?" She nodded, Yes. "So you tell them that you
are already the slave of Harold the Tuchuk, understand?"
She nodded again. "It will be dishonest on your part," said
Harold apologetically, "but these are hard times." There were
tears in her eyes. "Then go home and lock yourself in the
cellar," he said. He glanced out. There were still riders
pouring into the city. "But as yet," he said, "you cannot
leave." She nodded, Yes. He then unpinned her veil and took
her in his arms, improving the time.

I sat cross-legged under the wagon, my sword across my

knees, watching the paws and legs of the swirling kaiila bounding past. I heard the hiss of crossbow quarrels and one rider and his mount stumbled off the wagon top, falling and rolling to one side, others bounding over him. Then I heard the twang of the small horn bows of Tuchuks. Somewhere, off on the other side of the wagon, I heard the heavy grunting of a tharlarion and the squealing of a kaiila, the meeting of lances and shields. I saw a woman, unveiled, hair streaming behind her, twisting, buffeted, among the kaiila, somehow managing to find her way among them and rush between two buildings. The tolling of the alarm bars was now fearful throughout the city. I could hear screaming some hundred yards away. The roof of a building on the left was afire and smoke and sparks were being hurled into the sky and swept by the wind across the adjoining buildings. Some dozen dismounted Tuchuks were now at the great windlass on its platform slowly opening the gates to their maximum width, and when they had done so the Tuchuks, howling and waving their lances, entered the city in ranks of twenty abreast, thus only five ranks to the Hundred. I could now see smoke down the long avenue leading from the gate, in a dozen places. Already I saw a Tuchuk with a dozen silver cups tied on a string to his saddle. Another had a screaming woman by the hair, running her beside his stirrup. And still more Tuchuks bounded into the city. The wall of a building off the main avenue collapsed flaming to the street. I could hear in three or four places the clash of arms, the hiss of the bolts of crossbows, the answering featherswift flight of the barbed Tuchuk war arrows. Another wall, on the other side of the avenue, tumbled downward, two Turian warriors leaping from it, being ridden down by Tuchuks, leaping over the burning debris on kaiilaback, lance in hand.

Then in the clearing inside the gate, on his kaiila, lance in his right fist, turning and barking orders, I saw Kamchak of the Tuchuks, waving men to the left and right, and to the roof tops. His lance point was red. The black lacquer of his shield was deeply cut and scraped. The metal net that depended from his helmet had been thrown back and his eyes and face were fearful to behold. He was flanked by officers of the Tuchuks, commanders of Thousands, mounted as he was and armed. He turned his kaiila to face the city and it reared and he lifted his shield on his left arm and his lance in his right fist. "I want the blood of Saphrar of Turia," he cried.

22

Kamchak's Feast

It had, of course, been the Tuchuk turn.

One makes a pretext of seriously besieging a city, spending several days, sometimes weeks, in the endeavor, and then, apparently, one surrenders the seige and withdraws, moving away slowly with the wagons and bosk for some days—in this case four—and then, the bosk and wagons removed from probable danger, swiftly, in a single night, under the cover of darkness, sweeping back to the city, taking it by surprise.

It had worked well.

Much of Turia was in flames. Certain of the Hundreds, delegated the task, had immediately, almost before the alarm bars could sound, seized many of the wells, granaries and public buildings, including the very palace of Phanius Turmus itself. The Ubar, and Kamras, his highest officer, had fallen captive almost immediately, each to a Hundred set that purpose. Most of the High Council of Turia, too, now reposed in Tuchuk chains. The city was largely without leadership, though here and there brave Turians had gathered guardsmen and men-at-arms and determined civilians and sealed off streets, forming fortresses within the city against the invaders. The compound of the House of Saphrar, however, had not fallen, protected by its numerous guardsmen and its high walls, nor had the tower elsewhere that sheltered the tarn cots and warriors of Ha-Keel, the mercenary from Port Kar.

Kamchak had taken up quarters in the palace of Phanius Turmus, which, save for the looting and the ripping down of tapestries, the wanton defacing of wall mosaics, was unharmed. It was from this place that he directed the occupation of the city.

Harold, after the Tuchuks had entered the city, insisted on squiring the young woman home whom he had encountered under the wagon, and, for good measure, the wine vendor and potter as well. I accompanied him, stopping only long enough to rip away most of the upper partions of the baker's tunic and rinse the dye from my hair in a street fountain. I had no wish to be brought down with a Tuchuk arrow in the streets as a Turian civilian. Also I knew many of the Tuchuks were familiar with my perhaps too red hair and might, seeing it, generously refrain from firing on its owner. It seemed to me that for once my hair might actually prove useful, a turnabout I contemplated with pleasure. Do not take me wrong—I am rather fond, on the whole, of my hair—it is merely that one must, to be objective about such matters, recognize that it has, from time to time, involved me in various difficulties—beginning about my fourth year. Now, however, it might not hurt at all to be promptly and accurately identified by means of it.

When I lifted my head from the fountain in the Turian street Harold cried out in amazement, "Why you ARE Tarl Cabot!"

"Yes," I had responded.

After we had taken the girl and the potter and wine vendor to whatever safety their homes might afford, we set out for the House of Saphrar, where, after some examination of the scene, I convinced myself there was nothing immediately to be done. It was invested by better than two of the Thousands. No assault of the place had yet begun. Doubtless rocks and large pieces of building stone had already been piled behind the gates. I could smell tharlarion oil on the walls, waiting to be fired and poured on those who might attempt to dig at the walls or mount ladders against them. Occasional arrows and crossbow bolts were exchanged. One thing troubled me. The standing wall about the compound kept the Tuchuk bowmen far enough from the roof of the keep within that tarns might, without too great a danger, enter and leave the compound. Saphrar, if he chose, could escape on tarnback. As yet, cut off, he probably had no way of knowing how serious his danger was. Within he undoubtedly had ample food and water to withstand a long siege. It seemed to me he could fly with safety when he chose, but that he had merely not yet chosen.

I then wished to proceed immediately to the palace of Phanius Turmus, where Kamchak had set up his headquarters, to place myself at his disposal, but Harold insisted rather on trooping about the city, here and there examining pockets of Turian resistance.

"Why?" I asked.

"We owe it to our importance," he said.

"Oh," I said.

At last it was night and we were making our way through the streets of Turia, sometimes between burning buildings.

We came to a high, walled structure and began walking about it.

I could hear occasional shouts inside. Also, at one point, the wailing of women carried to my ears.

· "What place is this?" I asked.

"The palace of Phanius Turmus," he said.

"I heard the crying of women," I said.

"Turian women," said Harold, "taken by Tuchuks." Then he added, "Much of the richest booty of Turia lies behind these walls."

I was astonished when, at the gate to the palace of Phanius Turmus, the four Tuchuk guards smote their lances three times on their leather shields. The lance strikes the shield once for the commander of a Ten; twice for the commander of a Hundred; three times for the commander of a Thousand. "Pass, Commanders," said the chief of the four guards, and they stepped aside.

Naturally I inquired of Harold, shortly after entering, the meaning of the guards' salutation. I had expected to be challenged and then perhaps, if all went well, wrangled inside on some strategem dreamed up by Harold on the spur of the moment.

"It means," remarked Harold, looking about the courtyard, "that you have the rank of a Commander of a Thousand."

"I don't understand," I said.

"It is a gift of Kamchak," said Harold. "I suggested it as appropriate in view of your manly, if somewhat clumsy, efforts at the gate."

"Thank you," I said.

"I of course recommended the same rank for myself," said Harold, "inasmuch as I am the one who really carried the thing off."

·"Naturally," I said.

"You do not, of course, have a Thousand to command," pointed out Harold.

"Nonetheless," I said, "there is considerable power in the rank itself."

"That is true," he said.

Indeed it was true, for the next level beneath a Ubar among the Wagon Peoples is that of the Commander of a Thousand.

"Why did you not tell me?" I asked.

"It did not seem to me important," remarked the young man.

I clenched my fists and considered punching him in the nose, moderately hard.

"Korobans, though," remarked Harold, "are probably more impressed with such things than Tuchuks."

By this time I had followed Harold over to a corner of the courtyard wall, which was heaped high, banked into the corner, with precious metals, plates, cups; bowls of jewels; necklaces and bracelets; boxes of coins and, in heavy, wooden crates, numerous stacked cubes of silver and gold, each stamped with its weight, for the palace of a Ubar is also the mint of a city, where its coins are struck one at a time by a hammer pounding on the flat cap of a die. Incidentally, Gorean coins are not made to be stacked and accordingly, because of the possible depth of the relief and the consequent liberties accorded to the artist, the Gorean coin is almost always more beautiful than the machine-milled, flat, uniform coins of Earth. Some Gorean coins are drilled, incidentally, to allow stringing, the coins of Tharna, for example; Turian coins, and most others, are not.

Further on down the wall there were great piles of cloth, mostly silk; I recognized them as Robes of Concealment. Beyond them, again in a large heap, were numerous weapons, saddles and harnesses. Beyond them I saw numerous rugs and tapestries, rolled, for transport from the city.

"As a commander," said Harold, "you may take what you want of any of this."

I nodded.

We now entered yet another courtyard, an inner courtyard, between the palace and the inside wall of the outer courtyard.

Here I saw, along one wall, a long line of Turian women, unclothed, who were kneeling, fastened together in various ways, some by chains, some by thongs. The wrists of each,

however, were bound, one girl's before her body and the next
behind her back, alternately. It was these women whom I
had heard outside the wall. Some were sobbing, others
wailing, but most were silent, numb with shock, staring at the
ground. Two Tuchuk guards stood over them. One carried a
slave whip and, occasionally, should the cries of one of the
girls grow too obtrusive, he would silence her with the lash.

"You are the commander of a Thousand," said Harold. "If
one of the girls pleases you, let the guard know and he will
mark her for you."

"No," I said. "Let us proceed directly to Kamchak."

At that moment there was a scuffle and commotion at the
gate to the inner courtyard and two Tuchuks, one laughing
and with a bloody shoulder, were dragging a fiercely resisting, unveiled but clothed girl between them.

It was Dina of Turia!

The laughing Tuchuk, he with the bloody shoulder, hauled
her before us.

"A beauty," said he, "Commander!" He nodded to his
shoulder. "Marvelous! A fighter!"

Suddenly Dina stopped pulling and kicking and scratching
She flung up her head and looked at me, breathing hard,
startled.

"Do not add her to the chain," I said. "Neither remove her
clothing nor put her in bonds. Permit her to veil herself if she
wishes. She is to be treated in all respects as a free woman.
Take her back to her home and while we remain in the city
guard her with your lives."

The two men were startled, but Tuchuk discipline is re-
lentless. "Yes, Commander!" they both cried, releasing her.
"With our lives!"

Dina of Turia looked at me, gratitude in her eyes.

"You will be safe," I assured her.

"But my city burns," she said.

"I am sorry," I said, and turned swiftly away, to enter the
palace of Phanius Turmus.

I knew that while the Tuchuks remained in Turia there
would be in all the city no woman more safe than lovely
Dina, she only of the Caste of Bakers.

I sprang up the steps, followed by Harold, and we soon
found ourselves in the marbled entry hall of the palace
Kaiila were stabled there.

Directed by Tuchuks we soon made our way to the throne
room of Phanius Turmus, where, to my surprise, a banquet

was in progress. At one end of the room, on the throne of the Ubar, a purple robe thrown over his black leather, sat dour Kamchak of the Tuchuks, his shield and lance leaning against the throne, an unsheathed quiva on the right arm of the throne. At the low tables, perhaps brought from various places in the palace, there sat many Tuchuk officers, and even some men without rank. With them, now freed of collars, were exuberant Tuchuk girls bedecked in the robes of free women. All were laughing and drinking. Only Kamchak seemed solemn. Near him, in places of honor, at a long, low table, above the bowls of yellow and red salt, on each side, sat many of the high men of Turia, clad in their finest robes, their hair oiled, scented and combed for the banquet. I saw among them Kamras, Champion of Turia, and another, on Kamchak's right hand, a heavy, swollen, despondent man, who could only have been Phanius Turmus himself. Behind them stood Tuchuk guards, quivas in their right hands. At a sign from Kamchak, as the men well knew, their throats would be immediately cut.

Kamchak turned to them. "Eat," he said.

Before them had been placed large golden dishes heaped with delicacies prepared by the kitchens of the Ubar, tall precious goblets filled with Turian wines, the small bowls of spices and sugars with their stirring spoons at hand.

The tables were served by naked Turian girls, from the highest families of the city.

There were musicians present and they, to the best of their ability under the circumstances, attempted to provide music for the feast.

Sometimes one of the serving girls would be seized by an ankle or arm and dragged screaming to the cushions among the tables, much to the amusement of the men and the Tuchuk girls.

"Eat," ordered Kamchak.

Obediently the captive Turians began to put food in their mouths.

"Welcome, Commanders," said Kamchak, turning and regarding us, inviting us to sit down.

"I did not expect to see you in Turia," I said.

"Neither did the Turians," remarked Harold, reaching over the shoulder of one of the high council of Turia and taking a candied verr chop.

But Kamchak was looking away disconsolately toward the rug before the throne, now stained with spilled beverages,

cluttered with the thrown garbage of the feast. He hardly
seemed aware of what was taking place. Though this should
have been a night of triumph for him, he did not seem
pleased.

"The Ubar of the Tuchuks does not appear happy," I
observed.

Kamchak turned and looked at me again.

"The city burns," I said.

"Let it burn," said Kamchak.

"It is yours," I said.

"I do not want Turia," he said.

"What is it you seek?" I asked.

"Only the blood of Saphrar," said he.

"All this," I asked, "is only to avenge Kutaituchik?"

"To avenge Kutaituchik," said Kamchak, "I would burn a
thousand cities."

"How is that?" I asked.

"He was my father," said Kamchak, and turned away.

During the meal, from time to time, messengers, from
various parts of the city, and even from the distant wagons,
hours away by racing kaiila, would approach Kamchak,
speak with him and hastily depart.

More foods and wines were served, and even the high men
of Turia, at quiva point, were forced to drink heavily and
some began to mumble and weep, while the feasters grew, to
the barbaric melodies of the musicians, ever more merry and
wild. At one point three Tuchuk girls, in swirling silks,
switches in their hands, came into the room dragging a
wretched, stripped Turian girl. They had found a long piece
of rope and tied her hands behind her back and then had
wound the same rope three or four times about the girl's
waist, had securely knotted it, and were leading her about by
it. "She was our mistress!" cried one of the Tuchuk girls
leading the Turian girl, and struck her sharply with the
switch, at which information the Tuchuk girls at the tables
clapped their hands with delight. Then, two or three other
groups of Tuchuk girls straggled in, each leading some
wretched wench who had but hours before owned them.
These girls they forced to comb their hair and wash their feet
before the tables, performing the duties of serving slaves.
Later they made some of them dance for the men. Then one
of the Tuchuk girls pointed to her ex-mistress and cried out,
"What am I offered for this slave!" and one of the men,
joining in the sport, would cry out a price, some figure in

terms of copper tarn disks. The Tuchuk girls would shriek with delight and each joined in inciting buyers and auctioning their mistresses. One beautiful Turian girl was thrown, weeping and bound, into the arms of a leather-clad Tuchuk for only seven copper tarn disks. At the height of such festivities, a distraught messenger rushed to Kamchak. The Ubar of the Tuchuks listened impassively and then arose. He gestured at the captive Turian men. "Take them away," he said, "put them in the Kes and chain them—put them to work." Phanius Turmus, Kamras and the others were dragged from the tables by their Tuchuk guards. The feasters were now watching Kamchak. Even the musicians were now silent.

"The feast is done," said Kamchak.

The guests and the captives, led by those who would claim them, faded from the room.

Kamchak stood before the throne of Phanius Turmus, the purple robe of the Ubar over one shoulder, and looked at the overturned tables, the spilled cups, the remains of the feast. Only he, Harold and I remained in the great throne room.

"What is the matter?" I asked him.

"The wagons and bosk are under attack," he said.

"By whom?" cried Harold.

"Paravaci," said Kamchak.

23

The Battle at the Wagons

Kamchak had had his flying columns followed by some two dozen of the wagons, mostly containing supplies. On one of these wagons, with the top removed, were the two tarns Harold and I had stolen from the roof of Saphrar's keep. They had been brought for us, thinking that they might be of use in the warfare in the city or in the transportation of goods or men. A tarn can, incidentally, without difficulty, carry a knotted rope of seven to ten men.

Harold and I, mounted on kaiila, raced toward these wagons. Thundering behind each of us was a Thousand, which would continue on toward the main Tuchuk encampment, several Ahn away. Harold and I would take a tarn each and he would go to the Kassars and I to the Kataii, begging their help. I had little hope that either of these peoples would come to the aid of Tuchuks. Then, on the path to the main Tuchuk encampment, Harold and I were each to join our Thousand, subsequently doing what we could to protect the bosk and wagons. Kamchak would meanwhile marshal his forces within the city, preparing to withdraw, Kutaituchik unavenged, to ride back against the Paravaci.

I had learned to my surprise that the Ubars of the Kassars, Kataii and Paravaci were, respectively, Conrad, Hakimba and Tolnus, the very three I had first encountered with Kamchak on the plains of Turia when first I came to the Wagon Peoples. What I had taken to be merely a group of four outriders had actually been a gathering of Ubars of the Wagon Peoples. I should have known that no four common warriors of the four peoples would have ridden together. Further, the Kassars, the Kataii and the Paravaci did not reveal their true Ubars with any greater willingness than the Tuchuks had. Each people, as the Tuchuks had, had its false Ubar, its decoy to protect the true Ubar from danger or assassination. But, Kamchak had assured me, Conrad, Hakimba and Tolnus were indeed the true Ubars of their peoples.

I was nearly slain by arrows when I dropped the tarn amidst the startled blacks of the Kataii, but my black jacket with the emblem of the four bosk horns, emblem of the Tuchuk courier, soon proved its worth and I was led to the dais of the Ubar of the Kataii. I was permitted to speak directly to Hakimba, when I made it clear to my escort that I knew the identity of their true Ubar and that it was with him I must speak.

As I expected, Hakimba's brown eyes and richly scarred countenance showed little interest in my presentation of the plight of the Tuchuks.

It was little to him, apparently, that the Paravaci should raid the herds and wagons of the Tuchuks when most of the Tuchuk warriors were engaged in Turia. He did not, on the other hand, approve of the fact that the raid had taken place during the Omen Year, which is a time of general truce among the Wagon Peoples. I sensed, however, that he was angry when I spoke of the probable complicity of the Paravaci with the Turians, striking when and how they did, even during the Omen Year, presumably to draw the Tuchuks away from Turia. In short, though Hakimba did not approve of the Paravaci action and was incensed at their presumed league with the Turians, he did not feel sufficiently strongly to invest his own men in a struggle that did not seem to concern him directly.

"We have our own wagons," said Hakimba, at last. "Our wagons are not the wagons of the Tuchuks—or of the Kassars—or of the Paravaci. If the Paravaci attack our wagons, we will fight. We will not fight until then."

Hakimba was adamant and it was with a heavy heart that I climbed once more to the saddle of my tarn.

In the saddle I said to him, "I have heard that the Paravaci are killing bosk."

Hakimba looked up. "Killing bosk?" he asked, skeptically.

"Yes," I said, "and cutting out the nose rings to sell in Turia after the Tuchuks withdraw."

"That is bad," said Hakimba, "killing bosk."

"Will you help?" I asked.

"We have our own wagons," said Hakimba. "We will watch our own wagons."

"What will you do," I asked, "if in another year the Paravaci and the Turians turn on the Kataii—and kill their bosk?"

"The Paravaci," said Hakimba slowly, "would like to be the one people—and own the grass of all the prairie—and all the bosk."

"Will you not fight?" I demanded.

"If the Paravaci attack us," said Hakimba, "then we will fight." Hakimba looked up. "We have our own wagons," he said. "We will watch our own wagons."

I drew on the one-strap and took the tarn into the air, striking out across the prairie skies to intercept my Thousand on its way to the wagons of the Tuchuks.

In my flight I could see at one point the Omen Valley, where the haruspexes were still working about their numerous, smoking altars. I laughed bitterly.

In a few Ehn I had overtaken my Thousand and given the tarn over to five men, who would keep it until its wagon should, following the tracks of the riders, reach them.

Within perhaps the Ahn a grim, angry Harold brought his tarn down between the two columns, that of his Thousand and of mine. It took only a moment for him to give the tarn into the keeping of some five warriors and leap on the back of his kaiila. I had noted, to my satisfaction, that he now handled the tarn rather well. He had apparently, in the past several days since our escape from Saphrar's keep, been familiarizing himself with the saddle straps and the bird's habits and responses. But he was not elated as he rode beside me nor did he speak lightly.

Like my own mission to the Kataii, Harold's mission to the Kassars had been fruitless. For much the same reasons as the Kataii, Conrad was unwilling to commit his forces to the defense of Tuchuk herds. Indeed, as we rode together, we wondered that Kamchak had even sent us on an errand so unlikely of success, an errand in its way, considering the temper of the Wagon Peoples, so foolish.

Our kaiila were spent when we reached the wagons of the Tuchuks and the herds, and we were only two thousand. Hundreds of the wagons were burning and fighting was taking place among them. We found thousands of bosk slain in the grass, their throats cut, their flesh rotting, the golden nose rings chopped or torn away.

The men behind us cried out with rage.

Harold took his Thousand into the Wagons, engaging the Paravaci wherever he could find them. I knew that in little more than fifteen or twenty Ehn his forces would be lost, dissipated among the wagons, and yet surely the Paravaci must be met and fought there as well as on the prairie. I swept with my Thousand about the outskirts of the herds until we found some hundred or two hundred Paravaci engaged in the grisly work of destroying Tuchuk bosk. These two hundred, afoot, suddenly looking up with their quivas and axes, startled, screaming, were ridden down in a matter of an Ehn. But then we could see, forming on the crest of a hill, thousands of Paravaci warriors, apparently held in readiness in case reinforcements should come. Already they were mounting their fresh, rested kaiila. We could hear the bosk horns forming their Hundreds, see the movements of the sunlight on their arms.

Raising my arm and shouting, I led the Thousand toward them, hoping to catch them before they could form and charge. Our bosk horns rang out and my brave Thousand, worn in the saddle, weary, on spent kaiila, without a murmur or a protest, turned and following my lead struck into the center of the Paravaci forces.

In an instant we were embroiled among angry men—the half-formed, disorganized Hundreds of the Paravaci—striking to the left and right, shouting the war cry of the Tuchuks. I did not wish to remain on the crest of the hill long enough to allow the left and right flanks of the Paravaci—rapidly assembling—to fold about my men and so, in less than four Ehn—as their disorganized, astonished center fell back—our bosk horn sounded our retreat and our men, as one, withdrew to the herds—only a moment before the left and right flanks of the Paravaci would have closed upon us. We left them facing one another, cursing, while we moved slowly back through our bosk, keeping them as a shield. We would remain close enough that small parties would not be able to approach the bosk with impunity again. If they sent archers forth to slay the beasts, we could, from within the herd, answer their fire, or, if we wished, open the herd and ride forth, scattering the archers.

Among the bosk I ordered my men to rest.

But the Paravaci neither sent forth small groups nor con-

tingents of archers, but formed and, en masse, riding over the
bodies of their fallen comrades, began to approach the herd
slowly, to move through it, slaying them as they went, and
close with us.

Once again our bosk horns sounded and this time my
Thousand began to cry out and jab the animals with their
lances, turning them toward the Paravaci. Thousands of
animals were already turned toward the approaching enemy
and beginning to walk toward them when the Paravaci suddenly realized what was happening. Now the bosk began to
move more swiftly, bellowing and snorting. And then, as the
Paravaci bosk horns sounded frantically, our bosk began to
run, their mighty heads with the fearsome horns nodding up
and down, and the earth began to tremble and my men cried
out more and jabbed animals, riding with the flood and the
Paravaci with cries of horror that coursed the length of their
entire line tried to stop and turn their kaiila but the ranks
behind them pressed on and they were milling there before
us, confused, trying to make sense out of the wild signals of
their own bosk horns when the herd, horns down, now
running full speed, struck them.

It was the vengeance of the bosk and the frightened,
maddened animals thundered into the Paravaci lines goring
and trampling both kaiila and riders, and the Paravaci who
could manage turned their animals and rode for their lives.

In a moment, maintaining my saddle in spite of the leaping
and stumbling of my kaiila over the slain bosk, fallen kaiila
and screaming men, I gave orders to turn the bosk back and
reform them near the wagons. The escaping Paravaci could
now, on their kaiila, easily outdistance the herd and I did not
wish the animals to be strung out over the prairie, at the
mercy of the Paravaci when they should at last turn and take
up the battle again.

By the time the Paravaci had reformed my Tuchuks had
managed to swing the herd, slow it, get it milling about and
then drive it back to a perimeter about the wagons.

It was now near nightfall and I was confident the Paravaci, who greatly outnumbered us, perhaps in the order of ten
or twenty to one, would wait until morning before pressing
the advantage of their numbers. When, on the whole, the
long-term balance of battle would seem to lie with them,
there would be little point in their undertaking the risk of
darkness.

In the morning, however, they would presumably avoid the

herd, find a clear avenue of attack, and strike, perhaps even through the wagons, pinning us against our own herd.

That night I met with Harold, whose men had been fighting among the wagons. He had cleared several areas of Paravaci but they were still, here and there, among the wagons. Taking council with Harold, we dispatched a rider to Kamchak in Turia, informing him of the situation, and that we had little hope of holding out.

"It will make little difference," said Harold. "It will take the rider, if he gets through, seven Ahn to reach Turia and even if Kamchak rides with his full force the moment the rider comes to the gates of the city, it will be eight Ahn before their vanguard can reach us—and by then it will be too late."

It seemed to me that what Harold said was true, and that there was little point in discussing it much further. I nodded wearily.

Both Harold and I then spoke with our men, each issuing orders that any man with us who wished might now withdraw from the wagons and rejoin the main forces in Turia. Not a man of either Thousand moved.

We set pickets and took what rest we could, in the open, the kaiila saddled and tethered at hand.

In the morning, before dawn, we awakened and fed on dried bosk meat, sucking the dew from the prairie grass.

Shortly after dawn we discovered the Paravaci forming in their Thousands away from the herd, preparing to strike the wagons from the north, pressing through, slaying all living things they might encounter, save women, slave or free. The latter would be driven before the warriors through the wagons, both slave girls and free women stripped and bound together in groups, providing shields against arrows and lance charges on kaiilaback for the men advancing behind them. Harold and I determined to appear to meet the Paravaci in the open—before the wagons—and then, when they charged, to withdraw among the wagons, and close the wagons on their attacking front, halting the charge, then at almost point-blank range hopefully taking heavy toll of their forces by our archers. It would be, of course, only a matter of time before our barricade would be forced or outflanked, perhaps from five pasangs distant, in an undefended sector.

The battle was joined at the seventh Gorean hour and, as planned, as soon as the Paravaci center was committed, the bulk of our forces wheeled and retreated among the wagons, the rest of our forces then turning and pushing the wagons together. As soon as our men were through the barricade they leaped from their kaiila, bow and quiver in hand, and took up prearranged positions under the wagons, between them, on them, and behind the wagon box planking, taking advantage of the arrow ports therein.

The brunt of the Paravaci charge almost tipped and broke through the wagons, but we had lashed them together and they held. It was like a flood of kaiila and riders, weapons flourishing, that broke and piled against the wagons, the rear ranks pressing forward on those before them. Some of the rear ranks actually climbed fallen and struggling comrades and leaped over the wagons to the other side, where they were cut down by archers and dragged from their kaiila to be flung beneath the knives of free Tuchuk women.

At a distance of little more than a dozen feet thousands of arrows were poured into the trapped Paravaci and yet they pressed forward, on and over their brethren, and then arrows spent, we met them on the wagons themselves with lances in our hands, thrusting them back and down.

About a pasang distant we could see new forces of the Paravaci forming on the crest of a sweeping gradient.

The sound of their bosk horns was welcome to us, signaling the retreat of those at the wagons.

Bloody, covered with sweat, gasping, we saw the living Paravaci draw back, falling back between the newly forming lines on the gradient above.

I issued orders swiftly and exhausted men poured from beneath and between the wagons to haul as many of the fallen kaiila and riders as possible from the wagons, that there might not be a wall of dying animals and men giving access to the height of our wagons.

Scarcely had we cleared the ground before the wagons when the Paravaci bosk horns sounded again and another wave of kaiila and riders, lances set, raced towards us. Four times they charged thus and four times we held them back.

My men and those of Harold had now been decimated and there were few that had not lost blood. I estimated that there was scarcely a quarter of those living who had ridden with us to the defense of the herds and wagons.

Once again Harold and I issued our orders that any wishing to depart might now do so.

Again no man moved.

"Look," cried an archer, pointing to the gradient.

There we could see new thousands forming, the standards of Hundreds and Thousands taking up their position.

"It is the Paravaci main body," said Harold. "It is the end."

I looked to the left and right over the torn, bloody barricade of wagons, at the remains of my men, wounded and exhausted, many of them lying on the barricade or on the ground behind it, trying to gain but a moment's respite. Free women, and even some Turian slave girls, went to and fro, bringing water and, here and there, where there was point in it, binding wounds. Some of the Tuchuks began to sing the Blue Sky Song, the refrain of which is that though I die, yet there will be the bosk, the grass and sky.

I stood with Harold on a planked platform fixed across the wagon box of the wagon at our center, whose domed framework had been torn away. Together we looked out over the field. We watched the milling of kaiila and riders in the distance, the movement of standards.

"We have done well," said Harold.

"Yes," I said, "I think so."

We heard the bosk horns of the Paravaci signaling to the assembled Thousands.

"I wish you well," said Harold.

I turned and smiled at him. "I wish you well," I said.

Then again we heard the bosk horns and the Paravaci, in vast ranks, like sweeping crescents, like steel scythes of men and animals and arms, far extending beyond our own lines, began to move slowly towards us, gaining steadily in momentum and speed with each traversed yard of stained prairie.

Harold and I, and those of our men that remained, stood with the wagons, watching the nearing waves of warriors, observing the moment when the chain face guards of the Paravaci helmets were thrown forward, the moment when the lances, like that of a single man, were leveled. We could now hear the drumming of the paws of the kaiila, growing ever more rapid and intense, the squealing of animals here and there along the line, the rustle of weapons and accouterments.

"Listen!" cried Harold.

I listened, but seemed to hear only the maddeningly intensifying thunder of the Paravaci kaiila sweeping towards us, but then I heard, from the far left and right, the sound of distant bosk horns.

"Bosk horns!" cried Harold.

"What does it matter?" I asked.

I wondered how many Paravaci there could possibly be.

I watched the nearing warriors, lances ready, the swiftness of the charge hurtling into full career.

"Look!" cried Harold, sweeping his hand to the left and right.

My heart sank. Suddenly rising over the crest of rolling hills, like black floods, from both the left and the right, I saw on racing kaiila what must have been thousands of warriors, thousands upon thousands.

I unsheathed my sword. I supposed it would be the last time I would do so.

"Look!" cried Harold.

"I see," I said, "what does it matter?"

"Look!" he screamed, leaping up and down.

And I looked and saw suddenly and my heart stopped beating and then I uttered a wild cry for from the left, riding with the Thousands sweeping over the hills, I saw the standard of the Yellow Bow, and on the right, flying forward with the hurtling Thousands, its leather streaming behind its pole, I saw the standard of the Three-Weighted Bola.

"Kataii!" screamed Harold, hugging me. "Kassars!"

I stood dumbfounded on the planking and saw the two great wedges of the Kataii and the Kassars close like tongs on the trapped Paravaci, taking them in the unprotected flanks, crushing the ranks before them with the weight of their charge. And even the sky seemed dark for a moment as, from the left and right, thousands upon thousands of arrows fell like dark rain among the startled, stumbling, turning Paravaci.

"We might help," remarked Harold.

"Yes!" I cried.

"Korobans are slow to think of such matters," he remarked.

I turned to the men. "Open the wagons!" I cried. "To your animals!"

And in an instant it seemed the wagon lashing had been cut by quivas and our hundreds of warriors, the pitiful remnant of our two Thousands, swept forth upon the Paravaci, riding as though they had been fresh rested and ready, shouting the wild war cry of the Tuchuks.

It was not until late that afternoon that I met with Hakimba of the Kataii and Conrad of the Kassars. On the field we met and, as comrades in arms, we embraced one another.

"We have our own wagons," said Hakimba, "but yet we are of the Wagon Peoples."

"It is so, too, with us," said Conrad, he of the Kassars.

"I regret only," I said, "that I sent word to Kamchak and even now he has withdrawn his men from Turia and is returning to the wagons."

"No," said Hakimba, "we sent riders to Turia even as we left our own camp. Kamchak knew of our movements long before you."

"And of ours," said Conrad, "for we too sent him word—thinking it well to keep him informed in these matters."

"For a Kataii and a Kassar," said Harold, "you two are not bad fellows." And then he added. "See that you do not ride off with any of our bosk or women."

"The Paravaci left their camp largely unguarded," said Hakimba. "Their strength was brought here."

I laughed.

"Yes," said Conrad, "most of the Paravaci bosk are now in the herds of the Kataii and Kassars."

"Reasonably evenly divided I trust," remarked Hakimba.

"I think so," said Conrad. "If not, we can always iron matters out with a bit of bosk raiding."

"That is true," granted Hakimba, the yellow and red scars wrinkling into a grin on his lean, black face.

"When the Paravaci—those who escaped us—return to their wagons," remarked Conrad, "they will find a surprise in store for them."

"Oh?" I inquired.

"We burned most of their wagons—those we could," said Hakimba."

"And their goods and women?" inquired Harold.

"Those that pleased us—both of goods and women," remarked Conrad, "we carried off—of goods that did not please us, we burned them—of women that did not please us, we left them stripped and weeping among the wagons."

"This will mean war," I said, "for many years among the Wagon Peoples."

"No," said Conrad, "the Paravaci will want back their bosk and women—and perhaps they may have them—for a price."

"You are wise," said Harold.

"I do not think they will slay bosk or join with Turians again," said Hakimba.

I supposed he was right. Later in the afternoon the last of

the Paravaci had been cleared from the Tuchuk wagons, wherever they might be found. Harold and I sent a rider back to Kamchak with news of the victory. Following him, in a few hours, would be a Thousand each from the Kataii and the Kassars, to lend him what aid they might in his work in Turia.

In the morning the warriors remaining of the two Thousands who had ridden with Harold and I would, with the help of other Tuchuks surviving among the wagons, move the wagons and the bosk from the field. Already the bosk were growing uneasy at the smell of death and already the grass about the camp was rustling with the movements of the tiny brown prairie urts, scavengers, come to feed. Whether, after we had moved the wagons and bosk some pasangs away, we should remain there, or proceed toward the pastures this side of the Ta-Thassa Mountains, or return toward Turia, was not decided. In the thinking of both Harold and myself, that decision was properly Kamchak's. The Kataii main force and the Kassar main force camped separately some pasangs from the Tuchuk camp and the field and would, in the morning, return to their own wagons. Each had exchanged riders who, from time to time, would report to their own camp from that of the other. Each had also, as had the Tuchuks, set their own pickets. Neither wished the other to withdraw secretly and do for them what they together had done for the Paravaci, and what the Paravaci had attempted to do to the Tuchuks. It was not that they, on this night, truly distrusted one another so much as the fact that a lifetime of raiding and war had determined each to be, as a simple matter of course, wary of the other.

I myself was anxious to return to Turia as soon as it could be well managed. Harold, willingly enough, volunteered to remain in the camp until the commander of a Thousand could be sent from Turia to relieve him. I appreciated this very much on his part, for I keenly wished to return to Turia as soon as it would be at all practical—I had pressing and significant business yet unfinished behind its walls.

I would leave in the morning.

That night I found Kamchak's old wagon, and though it had been looted, it had not been burned.

There was no sign of either Aphris or Elizabeth, either about the wagon, or in the overturned, broken sleen cage in which, when I had last seen them, Kamchak had confined them. I was told by a Tuchuk woman that they had not been in the cage when the Paravaci had struck—but rather that Aphris had been in the wagon and the barbarian, as she referred to Miss Cardwell, had been sent to another wagon, the whereabouts she did not know. Aphris had, according to the woman, fallen into the hands of the Paravaci who had looted Kamchak's wagon; Elizabeth's fate she did not know; I gathered, of course, from the fact that Elizabeth had been sent to another wagon that Kamchak had sold her. I wondered who her new master might be and hoped, for her sake, that she would well please him. She might, of course, have also fallen, like Aphris, into the hands of the Paravaci. I was bitter and sad as I looked about the interior of Kamchak's wagon. The covering on the framework had been torn in several places and the rugs ripped or carried away. The saddle on the side had been cut and the quivas had been taken from their sheaths. The hangings were torn down, the wood of the wagon scratched and marred. Most of the gold and jewels, and precious plate and cups and goblets, were missing, except where here and there a coin or stone might lie missed at the edge of the wagon hides or at the foot of one of the curved wagon poles. Many of the bottles of wine were gone and those that were not had been shattered against the floor, or against the wagon poles, leaving dark stains on the poles and on the hides behind them. The floor was littered with broken glass. Some things, of little or no worth, but which I remembered fondly, were still about. There was a brass ladle that Aphris and Elizabeth had used in cooking and a tin box of yellow Turian sugar, dented in now and its contents scattered; and the large, gray leathery object which I had upon occasion seen Kamchak use as a stool, that which he had once kicked across the floor for my inspection; he had been fond of it, that curiosity, and would perhaps be pleased that it had not been, like most of his things, carried away in the leather loot sacks of Paravaci raiders. I wondered on the fate of Aphris of Turia. Kamchak, I knew, however, cared little for the slave, and would not be much concerned; yet her fate concerned me, and I hoped that she might live, that her beauty if not compassion or justice might have won her life for her, be it only as a Paravaci wagon slave; and then, too, I wondered again on the fate of Miss Elizabeth Cardwell, the lovely young New York secretary, so cruelly and so far removed from her own world; and then, exhausted, I lay down on the boards of Kamchak's looted wagon and fell asleep.

24

The Wagon of a Commander

Turia was now largely under the control of Tuchuks. For days it had been burning.

The morning after the Battle at the Wagons I had mounted a rested kaiila and set forth for Turia. Some Ahn after departing from the Tuchuk camp I encountered the wagon that carried my tarn, and its guard, still advancing toward the camp. The wagon carrying Harold's tarn and its guard accompanied it. I left the kaiila with the Tuchuks and mounted my tarn, and in less than an Ahn, saw the shimmering walls of Turia in the distance, and the veils of smoke rising over the city.

The House of Saphrar still stood, and the tower that had been fortified by Ha-Keel's tarnsmen. Aside from these there remained few pockets of organized resistance in the city, though here and there, in alleys and on roof tops, small groups of Turians furtively and sporadically attempted to carry the war to the invaders. I and Kamchak expected Saphrar to flee by tarn at any moment, for it must now be clear to him that the strike of the Paravaci against the Tuchuk wagons and herds had not forced Kamchak to withdraw; indeed, his forces were now supplemented by Kataii and Kassars, a development which must have horrified him. The only reason that occurred to me why Saphrar had not yet fled was that he was waiting in Turia for an excellent reason—quite possibly the arrival on tarnback of the gray man—with whom he had negotiated apparently to secure the golden sphere. I reminded myself, beyond this, that if his house should actually be forced, and himself threatened, he could always flee, with relative safety, at the last moment, abandoning his men, his servants and slaves to the mercies of ravaging Tuchuks.

I knew that Kamchak was in constant touch, by means of riders, with the wagons of the Tuchuks, and so I did not speak with him of the looting of his wagon, nor of the fate of Aphris of Turia, nor did I deem it well to speak to him of Elizabeth Cardwell, for it seemed evident that he had sold her, and that my inquiry, to a Tuchuk mind, might thus appear prying or impertinent; I would discover, if possible, her master and his whereabouts independently; indeed, for all I knew, perhaps she had been abducted by raiding Paravaci, and none among the Tuchuks would even know.

I did ask Kamchak why, considering the probabilities that the Kataii and the Kassars would not have come to the aid of the Tuchuks, he had not abandoned Turia and returned with his main forces to the wagons. "It was a wager," said he, "which I had made with myself."

"A dangerous wager," I had remarked.

"Perhaps," he said, "but I think I know the Kataii and the Kassars."

"The stakes were high," I said.

"They are higher than you know," he said.

"I do not understand," I said.

"The wager is not yet done," he said, but would speak no more.

On the day following my arrival in Turia, Harold, on tarnback, relieved at his request of the command of the wagons and herds, joined me in the palace of Phanius Turmus.

During the day and night, taking hours of sleep where we could, sometimes on the rugs of the palace of Phanius Turmus, sometimes on the stones of the streets by watch fires, Harold and I, at Kamchak's orders, performed a variety of tasks, sometimes joining in the fighting, sometimes acting as liaison between him and other commanders, sometimes merely positioning men, checking outposts and reconnoitering. Kamchak's forces, on the whole, were so disposed as to push the Turians toward two gates which he had left open and undefended, thus providing a route of escape for civilians and soldiers who would make use of it. From certain positions on the walls we could see the stream of refugees fleeing the burning city. They carried food and what possessions they could. The time of the year was the late spring and the prairie's climate was not unkind, though occasionally long rains must have made the lot of the refugees fleeing toward other cities miserable. There were occasional small creeks across the paths of the refugees and water was available. Also, Kamchak, to my pleasure but surprise, had had his men drive verr flocks and some Turian bosk after the refugees.

I asked him about this, for Tuchuk warfare, as I understood it, was complete, leaving no living thing in its wake, killing even domestic animals and poisoning wells. Certain cities, burned by the Wagon Peoples more than a hundred years ago, were still said to be desolate ruins between their broken walls, silent save for the wind and the occasional footfall of a prowling sleen hunting for urts.

"The Wagon Peoples need Turia," said Kamchak, simply.

I was thunderstruck. Yet it seemed to me true, for Turia was the main avenue of contact between the Wagon Peoples and the other cities of Gor, the gate through which tradegoods flowed to the wilderness of grasses that was the land of the riders of the kaiila and the herders of bosk. Without Turia, to be sure, the Wagon Peoples would undoubtedly be the poorer.

"And," said Kamchak, "the Wagon Peoples need an enemy."

"I do not understand," I said.

"Without an enemy," said Kamchak, "they will never stand together—and if they fail to stand together, someday they will fall."

"Has this something to do with the 'wager' you spoke of?" I asked.

"Perhaps," said Kamchak.

Still I was not altogether satisfied, for, on the whole, it seemed to me that Turia might yet have survived even had Kamchak's forces wrought much greater destruction than they had—for example, opening but a single gate and permitting only a few hundred, rather than thousands to escape the city. "Is that all?" I asked. "Is that the only reason that so many of Turia yet live beyond the city?"

He looked at me, without expression. "Surely, Commander," he said, "you have duties elsewhere."

I nodded curtly and turned and left the room, dismissed. Long ago I had learned not to press the Tuchuk when he did not wish to speak. But as I left I wondered at his comparative lenience. He professed a cruel hatred of Turia and

Turians, and yet he had, considering the normal practices of the Wagon Peoples, not noted for their mercy to helpless foes, treated the unarmed citizens of the city with unique indulgence, permitting them, on the whole, to keep their lives and freedom, though only as refugees beyond the walls. The clearest exception to this, of course, lay in the case of the more beautiful of the city's women, who were treated by Gorean custom, as portions of the booty.

I spent what free time I could in the vicinity of Saphrar's compound. The structures about the compound had been fortified by Tuchuks, and walls of stone and wood had been thrown into the streets and openings between the buildings, thus enclosing the compound. I had been training some hundred Tuchuks in the use of the crossbow, dozens of which had now fallen into our hands. Each warrior had at his disposal five crossbows and four Turian slaves, for winding and loading the bows. These warriors I stationed on roofs of buildings encircling the compound, as close to the walls as possible. The crossbow, though its rate of fire is much slower than the Tuchuk bow, has a much greater range. With the crossbow in our hands, the business of bringing tarns in and out of the compound became proportionately more hazardous, which, of course, was what I intended. In fact, to my elation, some of my fledgling crossbowmen, on the first day, brought down four tarns attempting to enter the compound, though, to be sure, several escaped them. If we could get the crossbows into the compound itself, perhaps even to the outside walls, we could for most practical purposes close the compound to entrance and escape by air. I feared, of course, that this addition to our armament might hasten Saphrar's departure, but, as it turned out, it did not, perhaps because the first word Saphrar had of our intentions was the tumbling of dying tarns behind the walls of the compound.

Harold and I chewed on some bosk meat roasted over a fire built on the marble floor of the palace of Phanius Turmus. Nearby our tethered kaiila crouched, their paws on the bodies of slain verrs, devouring them.

"Most of the people," Harold was saying, "are out of the city now."

"That's good," I said.

"Kamchak will close the gates soon," said Harold, "and then we shall get to work on Saphrar's house and that tarn roost of Ha-Keel's."

I nodded. The city now largely clear of defenders, and

closed to the outside, Kamchak could bring his forces to bear on Saphrar's house, that fort within a fort, and on the tower of Ha-Keel, taking them, if necessary, by storm. Ha-Keel had, we estimated, most of a thousand tarnsmen still with him, plus many Turian guardsmen. Saphrar probably had, behind his walls, more than three thousand defenders, plus a comparable number of servants and slaves, who might be of some service to him, particularly in such matters as reinforcing gates, raising the height of walls, loading crossbows, gathering arrows from within the compound, cooking and distributing food and, in the case of the women, or some of them, pleasing his warriors.

After I had finished the bosk meat I lay back on the floor, a cushion beneath my head, and stared at the ceiling. I could see stains from our cooking fire on the vaulted dome.

"Are you going to spend the night here?" asked Harold.

"I suppose so," I said.

"But some thousand bosk came today from the wagons," he said.

I turned to look at him. I knew Kamchak had brought, over the past few days, several hundred bosk to graze near Turia, to use in feeding his troops.

"What has that to do with where I sleep?" I asked. "You are perhaps going to sleep on the back of a bosk—because you are a Tuchuk or something?" I thought that a rather good one, at any rate for me.

But Harold did not seem particularly shattered, and I sighed.

"A Tuchuk," he informed me loftily, "may—if he wishes—rest comfortably on even the horns of a bosk, but only a Koroban is likely to recline on a marble floor when he might just as well sleep upon the pelt of a larl in the wagon of a commander."

"I don't understand," I said.

"I suppose not," said Harold.

"I'm sorry," I said.

"But you still do not understand?"

"No," I admitted.

"Poor Koroban," he muttered. Then he got up, wiped his quiva on his left sleeve, and thrust it in his belt.

"Where are you going?" I asked.

"To my wagon," he said. "It arrived with the bosk along with better than two hundred other wagons today—including yours."

I propped myself up on one elbow. "I do not have a wagon," I said.

"But of course you do," he said. "And so do I."

I merely looked at him, wondering if it were merely Harold the Tuchuk at work again.

"I am serious," he averred. "The night that you and I departed for Turia, Kamchak ordered a wagon prepared for each of us—to reward us."

I remembered that night—the long swim against the underground current, the well, our capture, the Yellow Pool of Turia, the Pleasure Gardens, the tarns—and escape.

"At that time, of course," said Harold, "our wagons were not painted red, nor filled with booty and rich things, for we were not then commanders."

"But to reward us for what?" I asked.

"For courage," said he.

"Just that?" I asked.

"But for what else?" asked Harold.

"For success," I said. "You were successful. You did what you set out to do. I did not. I failed. I did not obtain the golden sphere."

"But the golden sphere is worthless," said Harold. "Kamchak has said so."

"He does not know its value," I said.

Harold shrugged. "Perhaps," he said.

"So you see," I said, "I was not successful."

"But you were successful," insisted Harold.

"How is that?" I asked.

"To a Tuchuk," said Harold, "success is courage—that is the important thing—courage itself—even if all else fails—that is success."

"I see," I said.

"There is something here I think you do not realize," said Harold.

"What is that?" I asked.

He paused. "That in entering Turia—and escaping as we did—even bringing tarns to the camp—we—the two of us—won the Courage Scar."

I was silent. Then I looked at him. "But," I said, "you do not wear the scar."

"It would have been rather difficult to get near the gates of Turia for a fellow wearing the Courage Scar, would it not?"

"Indeed it would," I laughed.

"When I have time," said Harold, "I will call one from the clan of Scarers and have the scar affixed. It will make me look even more handsome."

I smiled.

"Perhaps you would like me to call him for you as well?" inquired Harold.

"No," I said.

"It might take attention away from your hair," he mentioned.

"No, thank you," I said.

"All right," said Harold, "it is well known you are only a Koroban, and not a Tuchuk." But then he added, soberly. "But you wear the Courage Scar for what you did—not all men who wear the Courage Scar do so visibly."

I did not speak.

"Well," said Harold, "I am tired—and I am going to my wagon—I have a little slave there I am anxious to put to work."

"I did not know of my wagon," I said.

"I gathered not," said Harold, "seeing that you apparently spent the night after the battle comfortably resting on the floor of Kamchak's wagon—I looked around for you that night—but didn't find you." He added, "Your own wagon, you will be pleased to hear, was among the wagons, untouched by the Paravaci—as was mine."

I laughed. "It is strange," I said, "I did not even know of the wagon."

"You would have found out long ago," said Harold, "had you not rushed off to Turia again immediately after our return—when the wagons were moving toward Ta-Thassa. You did not even stop by Kamchak's wagon that day. Had you done so Aphris, or someone, might have told you."

"From the sleen cage?" I asked.

"She was not in the sleen cage the morning of our return from Turia with the tarns," said Harold.

"Oh," I said, "I am glad to hear it."

"Nor was the little barbarian," said Harold.

"What became of her?" I asked.

"Kamchak gave her to a warrior," he said.

"Oh," I said. I was not glad to hear it. "Why didn't you tell me of my wagon?" I asked.

"It did not seem important," he said.

I frowned.

"I suppose, however," he said, "Korobans are impressed with such things—having wagons and such."

I smiled. "Harold the Tuchuk," I said, "I am tired."

"Are you not going to your wagon tonight?" he asked.

"I think not," I said.

"As you wish," said he, "but I have had it well stocked—with Paga and Ka-la-na wines from Ar and such."

In Turia, even though we had much of the riches of the city at our disposal, there had not been much Paga or Ka-la-na wine. As I may have mentioned the Turians, on the whole, favor thick, sweet wines. I had taken, as a share of battle loot, a hundred and ten bottles of Paga and forty bottles of Ka-la-na wine from Tyros, Cos and Ar, but these I had distributed to my crossbowmen, with the exception of one bottle of Paga which Harold and I had split some two nights ago. I decided I might spend the night in my wagon. Two nights ago it had been a night for Paga. Tonight, I felt, was a night for Ka-la-na. I was pleased to learn there would be some in the wagon.

I looked at Harold and grinned. "I am grateful," I said.

"Properly so," remarked Harold and leaped to his kaiila, untethering the beast and springing to its saddle. "Without me," he said, "you will never find your wagon—and I for one will dawdle here no longer!"

"Wait!" I cried.

His kaiila sprang from the room, bounding across the carpet in the next hall, and then thudding down a corridor toward the main entrance.

Muttering I jerked loose the reins of my kaiila from the column to which I had tethered it, leaped to the saddle and raced after Harold, not wishing to be left behind somewhere in the streets of Turia or among the dark wagons beyond the gate, pounding on wagon after wagon to find which one might be mine. I bounded down the stairs of the palace of Phanius Turmus, and sped through the inner and outer courtyard and out into the street, leaving the startled guards trying to salute me as a commander.

A few yards beyond the gate I hauled my kaiila up short, rearing and pawing the air. Harold was sitting there calmly on the back of his kaiila, a reproachful look on his face.

"Such haste," he said, "is not seemly in the commander of a Thousand."

"Very well," I said, and we walked our kaiila at a stately pace toward Turia's main gate.

"I was afraid," I said, "that without you I would not be able to find my wagon."

"But it is the wagon of a commander," said Harold, as though puzzled, "so anyone could tell you where it is."

"I did not think of that," I said.

"I am not surprised," said Harold. "You are only a Koroban."

"But long ago," I said, "we turned you back."

"I was not there at the time," said Harold.

"That is true," I admitted.

We rode on a while.

"If it were not for your dignity," I remarked, "I would settle these matters by racing you to the main gate."

"Look out!" cried Harold. "Behind you!"

I spun the kaiila and whipped my sword from its sheath. I looked about wildly, at doorways, at roof tops, at windows.

"What?" I cried.

"There!" cried Harold. "To the right!"

I looked to the right but could see nothing but the side of a brick building.

"What is it?" I cried.

"It is," cried Harold decisively, "the side of a brick building!"

I turned to look at him.

"I accept your wager," he cried, kicking his kaiila toward the main gate.

By the time I had turned my animal and was racing after him he was almost a quarter of a pasang down the street, bounding over beams and rubbish, and litter, some of it still smoking. At the main gate I overtook him and together we sped through it, slowing our mounts on the other side to a decorous pace suitable to our rank.

We rode a bit into the wagons and then he pointed. "There is your wagon," he said. "Mine is nearby."

It was a large wagon, drawn by eight black bosk. There were two Tuchuk guards outside. Beside it, fixed in the earth, on a pole, there was a standard of four bosk horns. The pole had been painted red, which is the color of commanders. Inside the wagon, under the door, I could see light.

"I wish you well," said Harold.

"I wish you well," I said.

The two Tuchuk guards saluted us, striking their lances three times on their shields.

We acknowledged the salute, lifting our right hands, palm inward.

"You certainly have a fast kaiila," remarked Harold.

"The race," I said, "is all in the rider."

"As it was," said Harold, "I scarcely beat you."

"I thought I beat you," I said.

"Oh?" asked Harold.

"Yes," I said. "How do you know I didn't beat you?"

"Well," said Harold, "I don't know—but that would certainly seem unlikely, would it not?"

"Yes," I said, "I suppose so."

"Actually," said Harold, "I am uncertain who won."

"So am I," I admitted. "Perhaps it was a tie," I suggested.

"Perhaps," he said, "incredible though that might seem." He looked at me. "Would you care to guess seeds in a tospit?" he inquired. "Odd or even?"

"No," I said.

"Very well," said he, grinning, and lifted his right hand in Gorean salute. "Until morning."

I returned the salute. "Until morning," I said.

I watched Harold ride towards his wagon, whistling a Tuchuk tune. I supposed the little wench Hereena would be waiting for him, probably collared and chained to the slave ring.

Tomorrow I knew the assault would begin on the House of Saphrar and the tower of Ha-Keel. Tomorrow one or both of us, I supposed, might be dead.

I noted that the bosk seemed well cared for, and that their coats were groomed, and the horns and hoofs polished.

Wearily I gave the kaiila to one of the guards and mounted the steps of the wagon.

25

I am Served Wine

I entered the wagon and stopped, startled.

Within, a girl, across the wagon, beyond the tiny fire bowl in the center of its floor, standing on the thick rug, near a hanging tharlarion oil lamp, turned suddenly to face me, clutching about herself as well as she could a richly wrought yellow cloth, a silken yellow sheet. The red band of the Koora bound back her hair. I could see a chain running across the rug from the slave ring to her right ankle.

"You!" she cried.

She held her hand before her face.

I did not speak, but stood dumbfounded, finding myself facing Elizabeth Cardwell.

"You're alive!" she said. And then she trembled. "You must flee!" she cried.

"Why?" I asked.

"He will discover you!" she wept. "Go!"

Still she would not remove her hand from before her face.

"Who is he?" I asked, startled.

"My master!" she cried. "Please go!"

"Who is he?" I inquired.

"He who owns this wagon!" she wept. "I have not yet seen him!"

Suddenly I felt like shaking, but did not move, nor betray emotion. Harold had said that Elizabeth Cardwell had been given by Kamchak to a warrior. He had not said which warrior. Now I knew.

"Has your master visited you often?" I asked.

"As yet, never," said she, "but he is in the city—and may this very night come to the wagon!"

"I do not fear him," I said.

She turned away, the chain moving with her. She pulled the yellow sheet more closely about her. She dropped her hand from before her face and stood facing the back of the wagon.

"Whose name is on your collar?" I asked.

"They showed me," she said, "but I do not know—I cannot read!"

What she said, of course, was true. She could speak Gorean but she could not read it. For that matter many Tuchuks could not, and the engraving on the collars of their slaves was often no more than a sign which was known to be theirs. Even those who could read, or pretended to be able to, would affix their sign on the collar as well as their name, so that others who could not read could know to whom the slave belonged. Kamchak's sign was the four bosk horns and two quivas.

I walked about the fire bowl to approach the girl.

"Don't look at me," she cried, bending down, holding her face from the light, then covering it with her hands.

I reached over and turned the collar somewhat. It was attached to a chain. I gathered the girl was in Sirik, the chain on the floor attached to the slave ring running to the twin ankle rings. She would not face me but stood covering her face, looking away. The engraving on the Turian collar consisted of the sign of the four bosk horns and the sign of the city of Ko-ro-ba, which I took it, Kamchak had used for my sign. There was also an inscription in Gorean on the collar, a simple one: I am Tarl Cabot's girl. I restraightened the collar and walked away, going to the other side of the wagon, leaning my hands against it, wanting to think.

I could hear the chain move as she turned to face me. "What does it say?" she begged.

I said nothing.

"Whose wagon is this?" she pleaded.

I turned to face her and she put one hand before her face, the other holding the yellow sheet about her. I could see now that her wrists were encircled with slave bracelets, linked to the collar chain, which then continued to the ankle rings. A second chain, that which I had first seen, fastened the Sirik itself to the slave ring. Over the hand that shielded the lower part of her face I could see her eyes, and they seemed filled with fear. "Whose wagon is it?" she pleaded.

"It is my wagon," I said.

She looked at me, thunderstruck. "No," she said, "it is the wagon of a commander—he who could command a Thousand."

"I am such," I said. "I am a commander."

She shook her head.

"The collar?" she asked.

"It says," I said, "that you are the girl of Tarl Cabot."

"Your girl?" she asked.

"Yes," I said.

"Your slave?" she asked.

"Yes," I said.

She did not speak but stood looking at me, in the yellow sheet, with one hand covering her face.

"I own you," I said.

Tears shone in her eyes and she sank to her knees, trembling, unable to stand, weeping.

I knelt beside her. "It is over now, Elizabeth," I said. "It is finished. You will no longer be hurt. You are no longer a slave. You are free, Elizabeth."

I gently took her braceleted wrists in my hands and removed them from her face.

She tried to twist her head away. "Please don't look at me, Tarl," she said.

In her nose, as I had suspected, there glinted the tiny, fine golden ring of the Tuchuk woman.

"Don't look at me, please," she said.

I held her lovely head with its soft dark hair in my hands, gazing on her face, her forehead, her dark, soft eyes, with tears, the marvelous, trembling mouth, and set in her fine nose, delicate and lovely, the tiny golden ring.

"It is actually very beautiful," I said.

She sobbed and pressed her head to my shoulder. "They bound me on a wheel," she said.

With my right hand I pressed her head more closely against me, holding it.

"I am branded," she said. "I am branded."

"It is finished now," I said. "You are free, Elizabeth."

She lifted her face, stained with tears, to mine.

"I love you, Tarl Cabot," she said.

"No," I said softly, "you do not."

She leaned against me yet again. "But you do not want me," she said. "You never wanted me."

I said nothing.

"And now," she said, bitterly, "Kamchak has given me to you. He is cruel, cruel, cruel."

"I think Kamchak thought well of you," I said, "that he would give you to his friend."

She withdrew from me a bit, puzzled. "Can that be?" she asked. "He whipped me—he—touched me," she shuddered, "with the leather." She looked down, not wanting to look into my eyes.

"You were beaten," I said, "because you ran away. Normally a girl who does what you did is maimed or thrown to sleen or kaiila, and that he touched you with the whip, the Slaver's Caress, that was only to show me, and perhaps you, that you were female."

She looked down. "He shamed me," she said. "I cannot help it that I moved as I did—I cannot help that I am a woman."

"It is over now," I told her.

She still did not raise her eyes, but stared down at the rug.

"Tuchuks," I remarked, "regard the piercing of ears as a barbarous custom—inflicted on their slave girls by Turians."

Elizabeth looked up, the tiny ring glinting in the light of the fire bowl.

"Are your ears pierced?" I asked.

"No," she said, "but many of my friends—on Earth—who owned fine earrings, had their ears pierced."

"Did that seem so dreadful to you?" I asked.

"No," she said, smiling.

"It would to Tuchuks," I said. "They do not even inflict that on their Turian slaves." I added, "And it is one of the great fears of a Tuchuk girl that, should she fall into Turian hands, it will be done to her."

Elizabeth laughed, through her tears.

"The ring may be removed," I said. "With instruments it can be opened and then slid free—leaving behind no mark that one would ever see."

"You are very kind, Tarl Cabot," she said.

"I do not suppose it would do to tell you," I remarked, "but actually the ring is rather attractive."

She lifted her head and smiled pertly. "Oh?" she asked.

"Yes," I said, "quite."

She leaned back on her heels, drawing the yellow silken

sheet more closely about her shoulders, and looked at me, smiling.

"Am I slave or free?" she asked.

"Free," I said.

She laughed. "I do not think you want to free me," she said. "You keep me chained up—like a slave girl!"

I laughed. "I am sorry!" I cried. To be sure, Elizabeth Cardwell was still in Sirik.

"Where is the key?" I asked.

"Above the door," she said, adding, rather pointedly, "just beyond my reach."

I leaped up to fetch the key.

"I am happy," she said.

I picked the key from the small hook.

"Don't turn around!" she said.

I did not turn. "Why not?" I asked. I heard a slight rustle of chain.

I heard her voice from behind me, husky. "Do you dare free this girl?" she asked.

I spun about and to my astonishment saw that Elizabeth Cardwell had arisen and stood proudly, defiantly, angrily before me, as though she might have been a freshly collared slave girl, brought in but an Ahn before, bound over the saddle of a kaiila, the fruit of a slave raid.

I gasped.

"Yes," she said, "I will reveal myself, but know that I will fight you to the death."

Gracefully, insolently, the silken yellow sheet moved about and across her body and fell from her. She stood facing me, in pretended anger, graceful and beautiful. She wore the Sirik and was, of course, clad Kajir, clad in the Curla and Chatka, the red cord and the narrow strip of black leather; in the Kalmak, the brief vest, open and sleeveless, of black leather; and in the Koora, the strip of red cloth that bound back her brown hair. About her throat was the Turian collar with its chain, attached to slave bracelets and ankle rings, one of the latter attached to the chain running to the slave ring. I saw that her left thigh, small and deep, bore the brand of the four bosk horns.

I could scarcely believe that the proud creature who stood chained before me was she whom Kamchak and I had referred to as the Little Barbarian; whom I had been able to think of only as a timid, simple girl of Earth, a young, pretty little secretary, one of nameless, unimportant thousands of

such in the large offices of Earth's major cities; but what I
now saw before me did not speak to me of the glass and
rectangles and pollutions of Earth, of her pressing crowds
and angry, rushing, degraded throngs, slaves running to the
whips of their clocks, slaves leaping and yelping and licking
for the caress of silver, for their positions and titles and
street addresses, for the adulation and envy of frustrated
mobs for whose regard a true Gorean would have had but
contempt; what I saw before me now spoke rather, in its
way, of the bellowing of bosk and the smell of trampled
earth; of the sound of the moving wagons and the whistle of
wind about them; of the cries of the girls with the bosk stick
and the odor of the open cooking fire; of Kamchak on his
kaiila as I remembered him from before; as Kutaituchik
must once have been; of the throbbing, earthy rhythms of
grass and snow, and the herding of beasts; and here before
me now there stood a girl, seemingly a captive, who might
have been of Turia, or Ar, or Cos, or Thentis; who proudly
wore her chains and stood as though defiant in the wagon of
her enemy, as if clad for his pleasure, all identity and meaning swept from her save the incontrovertible fact of what she
now seemed to be, and that alone, a Tuchuk slave girl.

"Well," said Miss Cardwell, breaking the spell she had
cast, "I thought you were going to unchain me."

"Yes, yes," I said, and stumbled as I went toward her.
Lock by lock, fumbling a bit, I removed her chains, and
threw the Sirik and ankle chain to the side of the wagon,
under the slave ring.

"Why did you do that?" I asked.

"I don't know," she responded lightly, "I must be a Tuchuk
slave girl."

"You are free," I said firmly.

"I shall try to keep it in mind," she said.

"Do so," I said.

"Do I make you nervous?" she asked.

"Yes," I said.

She had now picked up the yellow sheet and, with a pin or
two, booty from Turia probably, fastened it gracefully about
her.

I considered raping her.

It would not do, of course.

"Have you eaten?" she asked.

"Yes," I said.

"There is some roast bosk left," she said. "It is cold. It

would be a bother to warm it up, so I will not do so. I am not a slave girl, you know."

I began to regret my decision in freeing her.

She looked at me, her eyes bright. "It certainly took you a long time to come by the wagon."

"I was busy," I said.

"Fighting and such, I suppose," she said.

"I suppose," I said.

"Why did you come to the wagon tonight?" she asked. I didn't care precisely for the tone of voice with which she asked the question.

"For wine," I said.

"Oh," she said.

I went to the chest by the side of the wagon and pulled out a small bottle, one of several, of Ka-la-na wine which reposed there.

"Let us celebrate your freedom," I said, pouring her a small bowl of wine.

She took the bowl of wine and smiled, waiting for me to fill one for myself.

When I had done so, I faced her and said, "To a free woman, one who has been strong, one who has been brave, to Elizabeth Cardwell, to a woman who is both beautiful and free."

We touched the bowls and drank.

"Thank you, Tarl Cabot," she said.

I drained my bowl.

"We shall, of course," Elizabeth was saying, "have to make some different arrangements about the wagon." She was glancing about, her lips pursed. "We shall have to divide it somehow. I do not know if it would be proper to share a wagon with a man who is not my master."

I was puzzled. "I am sure," I muttered, "we can figure out something." I refilled my wine bowl. Elizabeth did not wish more. I noted she had scarcely sipped what she had been given. I tossed down a swallow of Ka-la-na, thinking perhaps that it was a night for Paga after all.

"A wall of some sort," she was saying.

"Drink your wine," I said, pushing the bowl in her hands toward her.

She took a sip, absently. "It is not really bad wine," she said.

"It is superb!" I said.

"A wall of heavy planks would be best, I think," she mused.

"You could always wear Robes of Concealment," I ventured, "and carry about your person an unsheathed quiva."

"That is true," she said.

Her eyes were looking at me over the rim of her bowl as she drank. "It is said," she remarked, her eyes mischievous, "that any man who frees a slave girl is a fool."

"It is probably true," I said.

"You are nice, Tarl Cabot," she said.

She seemed to me very beautiful. Again I considered raping her, but now that she was free, no longer a simple slave, I supposed that it would be improper. I did, however, measure the distance between us, an experiment in speculation, and decided I could reach her in one bound and in one motion, with luck, land her on the rug.

"What are you thinking?" she asked.

"Nothing that I care to inform you of," I said.

"Oh," she said, looking down into her bowl of wine, smiling.

"Drink more wine," I prompted.

"Really!" she said.

"It's quite good," I said. "Superb."

"You are trying to get me drunk," she said.

"The thought did cross my mind," I admitted.

She laughed. "After I am drunk," she asked, "what are you going to do with me?"

"I think I will stuff you in the dung sack," I said.

"Unimaginative," she remarked.

"What do you suggest?" I asked.

"I am in your wagon," she sniffed. "I am alone, quite defenseless, completely at your mercy."

"Please," I said.

"If you wished," she pointed out, "I could in an instant be returned to slave steel—simply be reenslaved—and would then again be yours to do with precisely as you pleased."

"That does not sound to me like a bad idea," I said.

"Can it be," she asked, "that the commander of a Tuchuk Thousand does not know what to do with a girl such as I?"

I reached toward her, to take her into my arms, but I found the bowl of wine in my way, deftly so.

"Please, Mr. Cabot," she said.

I stepped back, angry.

"By the Priest-Kings," I cried, "you are one woman who is looking for trouble!"

Elizabeth laughed over the wine. Her eyes sparkled. "I am free," she said.

"I am well aware of that," I snapped.

She laughed.

"You spoke of arrangements," I said. "There are some. Free or not, you are the woman in my wagon. I expect to have food, I expect the wagon to be clean, the axles to be greased, the bosk to be groomed."

"Do not fear," she said, "when I prepare my meals I will make enough for two."

"I am pleased to hear it," I muttered.

"Moreover," she said, "I myself would not wish to stay in a wagon that was not clean, nor one whose axles were not greased nor whose bosk were not properly groomed."

"No," I said, "I suppose not."

"But it does seem to me," she said, "that you might share in such chores."

"I am the commander of a Thousand," I said.

"What difference does that make?" she asked.

"It makes a great deal of difference!" I shouted.

"You needn't shout," she said.

My eye glanced at the slave chains under the slave ring.

"Of course," said Elizabeth, "we could regard it as a division of labor of sorts."

"Good," I said.

"On the other hand," she mused, "you might rent a slave for such work."

"All right," I said, looking at her. "I will rent a slave."

"But you can't trust slaves," said Elizabeth.

With a cry of rage I nearly spilled my wine.

"You nearly spilled your wine," said Elizabeth.

The institution of freedom for women, I decided, as many Goreans believed, was a mistake.

Elizabeth winked at me, conspiratorially. "I will take care of the wagon," she said.

"Good," I said. "Good!"

I sat down beside the fire bowl, and stared at the floor. Elizabeth knelt down a few feet from me, and took another sip of the wine.

"I heard," said the girl, seriously, "from a slave—whose name was Hereena—that tomorrow there will be great fighting."

I looked up. "Yes," I said. "I think it is true."

"If there is to be fighting tomorrow," she asked, "will you take part in it?"

"Yes," I said, "I suppose so."

"Why did you come to the wagon tonight?" she asked.

"For wine," I said, "as I told you."

She looked down.

Neither of us said anything for a time. Then she spoke. "I am happy," she said, "that this is your wagon."

I looked at her and smiled, then looked down again, lost in thought.

I wondered what would become of Miss Cardwell. She was, I forcibly reminded myself, not a Gorean girl, but one of Earth. She was not natively Turian nor Tuchuk. She could not even read the language. To almost anyone who would come upon her she might seem but a beautiful barbarian, fit presumably by birth and blood only for the collar of a master. She would be vulnerable. She, without a defender, would be helpless. Indeed, even the Gorean woman, outside her city, without a defender, should she escape the dangers of the wild, is not likely long to elude the iron, the chain and collar. Even peasants pick up such women, using them in the fields, until they can be sold to the first passing slaver. Miss Cardwell would need a protector, a defender. And yet on the very morrow it seemed I might die on the walls of Saphrar's compound. What then would be her fate? Moreover, I reminded myself of my work, and that a warrior cannot well encumber himself with a woman, particularly not a free woman. His companion, as it is said, is peril and steel. I was sad. It would have been better, I told myself, if Kamchak had not given me the girl.

My reflections were interrupted by the girl's voice. "I'm surprised," she said, "that Kamchak did not sell me."

"Perhaps he should have," I said.

She smiled. "Perhaps," she admitted. She took another sip of wine. "Tarl Cabot," she said.

"Yes," I said.

"Why did Kamchak not sell me?"

"I do not know," I said.

"Why did he give me to you?" she asked.

"I am not truly sure," I said.

I wondered indeed that Kamchak had given the girl to me. There were many things that seemed to me puzzling, and I thought of Gor, and of Kamchak, and the ways of the

Tuchuks, so different from those native to Miss Cardwell and myself.

I wondered why it was that Kamchak had put the ring on this girl, had had her branded and collared and clad Kajir—was it truly because she had angered him, running from the wagon that one time—or for another reason—and why had he subjected her, cruelly perhaps, in my presence to the Slaver's Caress? I had thought he cared for the girl. And then he had given her to me, when there might have been other commanders. He had said he was fond of her. And I knew him to be my friend. Why had he done this, truly? For me? Or for her, as well? If so, why? For what reason?

Elizabeth had now finished her wine. She had arisen and rinsed out the bowl and replaced it. She was now kneeling at the back of the wagon and had untied the Koora and shaken her hair loose. She was looking at herself in the mirror, holding her head this way and that. I was amused. She was seeing how the nose ring might be displayed to most advantage. Then she began to comb her long dark hair, kneeling very straight as would a Gorean girl. Kamchak had never permitted her to cut her hair. Now that she was free I supposed she would soon shorten it. I would regret that. I have always found long hair beautiful on a woman.

I watched her combing her hair. Then she had put the comb aside and had retied the Koora, binding back her hair. Now she was again studying her image in the bronze mirror, moving her head slightly.

Suddenly I thought I understood Kamchak! He had indeed been fond of the girl!

"Elizabeth," I said.

"Yes," she said, putting the mirror down.

"I think I know why Kamchak gave you to me—aside from the fact that I suppose he thought I could use a pretty wench about the wagon."

She smiled.

"I am glad he did," she said.

"Oh?" I asked.

She smiled. She looked into the mirror. "Of course," she said, "who else would have been fool enough to free me?"

"Of course," I admitted.

I said nothing for a time.

The girl put down the mirror. "Why do you think he did?" she asked, facing me, curious.

"On Gor," I said, "the myths have it that only the woman who has been an utter slave can be truly free."

"I am not sure," she said, "that I understand the meaning of that."

"It has nothing to do, I think," I said, "with what woman is actually slave or free, has little to do with the simplicity of chains or the collar, or the brand."

"Then what?" she asked.

"It means, I think," I said, "that only the woman who has utterly surrendered—and can utterly surrender—losing herself in a man's touch—can be truly a woman, and being what she is, is then free."

Elizabeth smiled. "I do not accept that theory," she remarked. "I am free now."

"I am not talking about chains and collars," I said.

"It is a silly theory," she said.

I looked down. "I suppose so," I said.

"I would have little respect for the woman," said Elizabeth Cardwell, "who could utterly surrender to a man."

"I thought not," I said.

"Women," said Elizabeth, "are persons—surely as much as men—and their equals."

"I think we are talking about different things," I said.

"Perhaps," she said.

"On our world," I said, "there is much talk of persons—and little of men and women—and the men are taught that they must not be men and the women are taught that they must not be women."

"Nonsense," said Elizabeth. "That is nonsense!"

"I do not speak of the words that are used, or how men of Earth would speak of these things," I said, "but of what is not spoken—of what is implicit perhaps in what is said and taught.

"But what," I asked, "if the laws of nature and of human blood were more basic, more primitive and essential than the conventions and teachings of society—what if these old secrets and truths, if truths they be, had been concealed or forgotten, or subverted to the requirements of a society conceived in terms of interchangeable labor units, each assigned its functional, technical sexless skills?"

"Really!" said Elizabeth.

"What do you think would be the result?" I asked.

"I'm sure I don't know," she said.

"Our Earth," I suggested.

"Women," said Miss Cardwell, "do not wish to submit to men, to be dominated, to be brutalized."

"We are speaking of different things," I said.

"Perhaps," she admitted.

"There is no freer nor higher nor more beautiful woman," I said, "than the Gorean Free Companion. Compare her with your average wife of Earth."

"The Tuchuk women," said Elizabeth, "have a miserable lot."

"Few of them," I said, "would be regarded in the cities as a Free Companion."

"I have never known a woman who was a Free Companion," said Elizabeth.

I was silent, and sad, for I had known one such.

"You are perhaps right," I said, "but throughout the mammals it seems that there is one whose nature it is to possess and one whose nature it is to be possessed."

"I am not accustomed to thinking of myself," smiled Elizabeth, "as a mammal."

"What do you think of yourself as," I asked, "—biologically?"

"Well," she smiled, "if you wish to put it that way."

I pounded the floor of the wagon and Elizabeth jumped. "That," I said, "is the way it is!"

"Nonsense," said she.

"The Goreans recognize," I said, "that this truth is hard for women to understand, that they will reject it, that they will fear it and fight it."

"Because," said Elizabeth, "it is not true."

"You think," I said, "that I am saying that a woman is nothing—that is not it—I am saying she is marvelous, but that she becomes truly herself and magnificent only after the surrenders of love."

"Silly!" said Elizabeth.

"That is why," I remarked, "that upon this barbaric world the woman who cannot surrender herself is upon occasion simply conquered."

Elizabeth threw back her head and laughed merrily.

"Yes," I smiled, "her surrender is won—often by a master who will be satisfied with no less."

"And what happens to these women afterwards?" asked Elizabeth.

"They may wear chains or they may not," I said, "but they are whole—they are female."

"No man," said Elizabeth, "including you, my dear Tarl Cabot, could bring me to such a pass."

"The Gorean myths have it," I said, "that the woman longs for this identity—to be herself in being his—if only for the moment of paradox in which she is slave and thus freed."

"It is all very silly," said Elizabeth.

"It is further said that the woman longs for this to happen to her, but does not know it."

"That is the silliest of all!" laughed Elizabeth.

"Why," I asked, "did you earlier stand before me as a slave girl—if you did not, for the moment, wish to be a slave?"

"It was a joke!" she laughed. "A joke!"

"Perhaps," I said.

She looked down, confused.

"And so," I said, "that is why I think Kamchak gave you to me."

She looked up, startled. "Why?" she asked.

"That in my arms you would learn the meaning of a slave collar, that you would learn the meaning of being a woman."

She looked at me, astonished, her eyes wide with disbelief.

"You see," I said, "he thought well of you. He was truly fond of his Little Barbarian."

I stood up and threw the wine bowl to the side of the room. It shattered against the wine chest.

I turned away.

She leaped to her feet. "Where are you going?" she asked.

"I am going to the public slave wagon," I said.

"But why?" she asked.

I looked at her frankly. "I want a woman," I said.

She looked at me. "I am a woman, Tarl Cabot," she said.

I said nothing.

"Am I not as beautiful as the girls in the public slave wagon?" she asked.

"Yes," I said, "you are."

"Then why do you not remain with me?"

"Tomorrow," I said, "I think there will be heavy fighting."

"I can please you as well as any girl in the slave wagon," she said.

"You are free," I told her.

"I will give you more," she said.

"Please, do not speak so, Elizabeth," I said.

She straightened herself. "I suppose," she said, "you have

seen girls in slave markets, betrayed as I was by the touch of the whip."

I did not speak. It was true that I had seen this.

"You saw how I moved," she challenged. "Would it not have added a dozen gold pieces to my price?"

"Yes," I said, "it would have."

I approached her and gently held her by the waist, and looked down into her eyes.

"I love you, Tarl Cabot," she whispered. "Do not leave me."

"Do not love me," I said. "You know little of my life and what I must do."

"I do not care," she said, putting her head to my shoulder.

"I must leave," I said, "if only because you care for me. It would be cruel for me to remain."

"Have me, Tarl Cabot," she said, "if not as a free woman—as a slave."

"Beautiful Elizabeth," I said, "I can have you as neither."

"You will have me," she cried, "as one or the other!"

"No," I said gently. "No."

Suddenly she drew back in fury and struck me with the flat of her hand, a vicious slap, and then again and again, and again.

"No," I said.

Again she slapped me. My face burned. "I hate you," she said. "I hate you!"

"No," I said.

"You know your codes, do you not?" she challenged. "The codes of the warrior of Gor?"

"Do not," I said.

Again she slapped me and my head leaped to the side, burning. "I hate you," she hissed.

And then, as I knew she would, she suddenly knelt before me, in fury, head down, arms extended, wrists crossed, submitting as a Gorean female.

"Now," she said, looking up, her eyes blazing with anger, "You must either slay me or enslave me."

"You are free," I said sternly.

"Then slay me," she demanded.

"I could not do that," I said.

"Collar me," she said.

"I have no wish to do so," I said.

"Then acknowledge your codes betrayed," she said.

"Fetch the collar," I said.

She leaped up to fetch the collar and handed it to me, again kneeling before me.

I encircled her lovely throat with the steel and she looked up at me, angrily.

I snapped it shut.

She began to rise to her feet.

But my hand on her shoulder prevented her from rising. "I did not give you permission to rise, slave," I said.

Her shoulders shook with anger. Then she said, "Of course, I am sorry, master," and dropped her head.

I removed the two pins from the yellow silken sheet, and it fell from her, revealing her clad Kajir.

She stiffened in anger.

"I would see my slave girl," I said.

"Perhaps," she said, acidly, "you wish your girl to remove her remaining garments?"

"No," I said.

She tossed her head.

"I shall do it," I told her.

She gasped.

As she knelt on the rug, head down, in the position of the Pleasure Slave, I took from her the Koora, loosening her hair, and then the leather Kalmak, and then I drew from her the Curla and Chatka.

"If you would be a slave," I said, "be a slave."

She did not raise her head but glared savagely down at the rug, her small fists clenched.

I went across the rug and sat down cross-legged near the fire bowl, and looked at the girl.

"Approach me, slave girl," I said, "and kneel."

She lifted her head and looked at me, angrily, proudly, for a moment, but then she said, "Yes, master," and did as she was commanded.

I looked at Miss Elizabeth Cardwell, kneeling before me, head down, clad only in the collar of a slave.

"What are you?" I asked.

"A slave," she said bitterly, not raising her head.

"Serve me wine," I said.

She did so, kneeling before me, head down, handing me the black, red-trimmed wine crater, that of the master, as had Aphris to Kamchak. I drank.

When I had finished I set the wine crater aside and looked on the girl.

"Why have you done this, Elizabeth?" I asked.

She looked down sullenly. "I am Vella," she said, "a Gorean slave."

"Elizabeth—" I said.

"Vella," she said angrily.

"Vella," I agreed, and she looked up. Our eyes met and we looked at one another for a long time. Then, she smiled, and looked down.

I laughed. "It seems," I said, "that I will not make it to the public slave wagon tonight."

Elizabeth looked up, shyly. "It seems not, master."

"You are a vixen, Vella," said I.

She shrugged. Then, kneeling before me in the position of the Pleasure Slave, she stretched indolently, with feline grace, lifting her hands behind the back of her neck and throwing her dark hair forward. She knelt so for a languorous moment, her hands over her head holding her hair, looking at me.

"Do you think," she asked, "that the girls in the public slave wagon are as beautiful as Vella?"

"No," I said, "they are not."

"Or as desirable?" she asked.

"No," I said, "none is as desirable as Vella."

Then, her back still arched, with a half-smile, she stretched even more, and, as though weary, she slowly turned her head to one side, with her eyes closed, and then opened them and with a small, lazy motion of her hands threw her hair back over her head, and with a tiny motion of her head shook it into place.

"It seems Vella wishes to please her master," I said.

"No," said the girl, "Vella hates her master." She looked at me with feigned hatred. "He has humiliated Vella. He has stripped her and put her in the collar of a slave!"

"Of course," I said.

"But," said the girl, "perhaps she might be forced to please him. After all she is only a slave."

I laughed.

"It is said," remarked the girl, "that Vella, whether she knows it or not, longs to be a slave—the utter slave of a man—if but for an hour."

I slapped my knee with amusement. "That sounds to me," I said, "like a silly theory."

The girl shrugged in her collar. "Perhaps," she said, "Vella does not know."

"Perhaps," I said, "Vella will find out."

"Perhaps," said the girl, smiling.

"Are you ready, Slave Girl," I asked, "to give pleasure to a master?"

"Have I any choice?" she asked.

"None," I said.

"Then," she said, with resignation, "I suppose I am ready."

I laughed.

Elizabeth was looking at me, smiling. Then, suddenly, playfully, she put her head to the rug before me. I heard her whisper, "Vella asks only to tremble and obey."

I stood up and, laughing, lifted her to her feet.

She, too, laughed, standing close to me, her eyes bright. I could feel her breath on my face.

"I think now I will do something with you," I said.

She looked resigned, dropping her head. "What is to be the fate of your beautiful, civilized slave?" she asked.

"The dung sack," I replied.

"No!" she cried, suddenly frightened. "No!"

I laughed.

"I will do anything rather than that," she said. "Anything."

"Anything?" I asked.

She looked up at me and smiled. "Yes," she said, "anything."

"Very well, Vella," said I, "I will give you but one chance—if you well please me the aforementioned miserable fate will not be yours—at least for tonight."

"Vella will well please you," she said earnestly.

"Very well," I said, "please me."

I recalled keenly how she had sported with me earlier and I thought there might be some point in giving the young American a taste of her own medicine.

She looked at me startled.

Then she smiled. "I will teach you that I well know the meaning of my collar, master," she said.

Suddenly she kissed me, a deep kiss, moist, rich, too soon ended.

"There!" she laughed. "The kiss of a Tuchuk slave girl!" Then she laughed and turned away, looking over her shoulder. "You see," she said, "I can do it quite well."

I did not speak.

She was facing the other way. "But," she said, teasingly, "I think one will be enough for master."

I was a bit angry, and not a little aroused. "The girls in the public slave wagon," I said, "know how to kiss."

"Oh?" she said, turning about.

"They are not little secretaries," I said, "pretending to be slave girls."

Her eyes flashed. "Try this!" she said, approaching me, and this time, my head in her small hands, she lingered with her lips upon my mouth, warm, wet, breaths meeting and mingling in the savoring touch.

My hands held her slender waist.

When she had finished, I remarked, "Not bad."

"Not bad!" she cried.

Then fully and for much time, she kissed me, with increasing determination, yet attempted subtlety, then anxiety, then woodenly, and then she dropped her head.

I lifted her chin with my finger. She looked at me angrily. "I should have told you, I suppose," I remarked, "that a woman kisses well only when fully aroused, after at least half an Ahn, after she is helpless and yielding."

She looked at me angrily and turned away.

Then she spun about laughing. "You are a beast, Tarl Cabot," she cried.

"And you, too," I laughed, "are a beast—a beautiful little collared beast."

"I love you," she said, "Tarl Cabot."

"Array yourself in Pleasure Silk, Little Beast," I said, "and enter my arms."

The blaze of a challenge flared suddenly in her eyes. She seemed transfused with excitement. "Though I am of Earth," she said, "try to use me as slave."

I smiled. "If you wish," I said.

"I will prove to you," she said, "that your theories are false."

I shrugged.

"I will prove to you," she said, "that a woman cannot be conquered."

"You tempt me," I said.

"I love you," she said, "but even so, you will not be able to conquer me, for I shall not permit myself to be conquered— not even though I love you!"

"If you love me," I said, "perhaps I would not wish to conquer you."

"But Kamchak, generous fellow, gave me to you, did he not," she asked, "that you should teach me as slave to be female?"

"I think so," I admitted.

"And in his opinion, and perhaps yours, would that not be in my best interests?"

"Perhaps," I said. "I do not really know. These are complicated matters."

"Well," said she, laughing, "I shall prove you both wrong!"

"All right," I said, "we shall see."

"But you must promise to try to make me truly a slave—if only for a moment."

"All right," I said.

"The stakes," she pronounced, "will be my freedom against—"

"Yes?" I asked.

"Against yours!" she laughed.

"I do not understand," I said.

"For one week," she said, "in the secrecy of the wagon—where no one can see—you will be my slave—you will wear a collar and serve me and do whatever I wish."

"I do not care much for your terms," I said.

"You seem to find little fault in men owning female slaves," she said. "Why should you object to being a slave owned by a female?"

"I see," I said.

She smiled slyly. "I think it might be rather pleasant to have a male slave." She laughed. "I will teach you the meaning of a collar, Tarl Cabot," she said.

"Do not count your slaves until you have won them," I cautioned.

"Is it a wager?" she asked.

I gazed on her. How every bit of her seemed alive with challenge! Her eyes, her stance, the sound of her voice! I saw the tiny nose ring, barbaric, glinting in the light of the fire bowl. I saw the place on her thigh where not many days before the fiery iron had been so cruelly pressed, leaving behind it, smoking for the instant, deep and clean, the tiny mark of the four bosk horns. I saw on her lovely throat the harsh ring of Turian steel, gleaming and locked, so contrasting with, so barbarically accentuating the incredible softness of her beauty, the tormenting vulnerability of it. The collar, I knew, bore my name, proclaiming her, should I wish, my slave. And yet this beautiful, soft, proud thing stood there, though ringed and branded, though collared, bold and brazen flinging at me, eyes bright, her challenge, the eternal challenge of the unconquered female, that of the untamed woman, daring the male to touch her, to try, she resisting, to reduce her to yielding prize, to force from her the unconditional surrender, the total and utter submission of the woman who has no choice but to acknowledge herself his, the helpless, capitulated slave of him in whose arms she finds herself prisoner.

As the Goreans have it, there is in this a war in which the woman can respect only that man who can reduce her to utter defeat.

But it seemed to me there was little in the eyes or stance of Miss Cardwell which suggested the plausibility of the Gorean interpretation. She seemed to me clearly out to win, to enjoy herself perhaps, but to win, and then exact from me something in the way of vengeance for all the months and days in which she, proud, independent wench, had been only slave. I recalled she had told me that she would teach me well the meaning of a collar. If she were successful, I had little doubt that she would carry out her threat.

"Well," she challenged, "Master?"

I gazed at her, the tormenting vixen. I had no wish to be her slave. I resolved, if one of us must be slave, it would be she, the lovely Miss Cardwell, who would wear the collar.

"Well," she again challenged, "Master?"

I smiled. "It is a wager," said I, "Slave Girl."

She laughed happily and turned, and standing on her tiptoes, lowered the tharlarion oil lamps. Then she bent to find for herself among the riches of the wagon yellow Pleasure Silks.

At last she stood before me, and was beautiful.

"Are you prepared to be a slave?" she asked.

"Until you have won," I said, "it is you who wear the collar."

She dropped her head in mock humility. "Yes, Master," she said. Then she looked up at me, her eyes mischievous.

I motioned for her to approach, and she did so.

I indicated that she should enter my arms, and she did so. In my arms she looked up at me.

"You're sure you're quite ready to be a slave?" she asked.

"Be quiet," I said gently.

"I shall be pleased to own you," she said. "I have always wanted a handsome male slave."

"Be quiet," I whispered.

"Yes, Master," she said, obediently.

My hands parted the Pleasure Silk and cast it aside.

"Really, Master!" she said.

"Now," I said, "I will taste the kiss of my slave girl."

"Yes, Master," she said.

"Now," I instructed her, "with more passion."

"Yes, Master," she said obediently, and kissed me with feigned passion.

I, hand in her collar, turned her about and put her on her back on the rug, her shoulders pressed against the thick pile.

She looked at me, a sly smile on her face.

I took the nose ring between my thumb and forefinger and gave it a little pull.

"Oh!" she cried, eyes smarting. Then she looked up. "That is no way to treat a lady," she remarked.

"You are only a slave girl," I reminded her.

"True," she said forlornly, turning her head to one side.

I was a bit irritated.

She looked up at me and laughed with amusement.

I began to kiss her throat and body and my hands were behind her back, lifting her and arching her, so that her head was back and down.

"I know what you're trying to do," she said.

"What is that?" I mumbled.

"You are trying to make me feel owned," she said.

"Oh," I said.

"You will not succeed," she informed me.

I myself was beginning to grow skeptical.

She wiggled about on her side, looking at me. My hands were still clasped behind the small of her back.

"It is said by Goreans," remarked the girl, very seriously, "that every woman, whether she knows it or not, longs to be a slave—the utter slave of a man—if but for an hour."

"Please be quiet," I said.

"Every woman," she said emphatically. "Every woman."

I looked at her. "You are a woman," I observed.

She laughed. "I find myself naked in the arms of a man and wearing the collar of a slave. I think there is little doubt that I am a woman!"

"And at the moment." I suggested, "little more."

She looked at me irritably for a moment. Then she smiled. "It is said by Goreans," she remarked, with very great seriousness, with mock bitterness, "that in a collar a woman can be only a woman."

"The theory you mention," I said, grumbling, "about women longing to be slaves, if only for an hour, is doubtless false."

She shrugged in her collar and put her head to one side, her hair falling to the rug. "Perhaps," she said, much as she had before, "Vella does not know."

"Perhaps Vella will find out," I said.

"Perhaps," she said, laughing.

Then, perhaps not pleasantly, my hand closed on her ankle.

"Oh!" she said.

She tried to move her leg, but could not.

I then bent her leg, that I might, as I wished, display for my pleasure, she willing or not, the marvelous curves of her calf.

She tried to pull her leg away, but she could not. It would move only as I pleased.

"Please, Tarl," she said.

"You are going to be mine," I said.

"Please," she said, "let me go." My grip on her ankle was not cruel but in all her womanness she knew herself held.

"Please," she said again, "let me go."

I smiled to myself. "Be silent, Slave," said I.

Elizabeth Cardwell gasped.

I smiled.

"So you are stronger than I," she scoffed. "It means nothing!"

I then began to kiss her foot, and the inside of her ankle, beneath the bone, and she trembled momentarily.

"Let me go!" she cried.

But I only kissed her, holding her, my lips moving to the back of her leg, low where it joins the foot, where an ankle ring would be locked.

"A true man," she cried out suddenly, "would not behave so! No! A true man is gentle, kind, tender, respectful, at all times, sweet and solicitous! That is a true man!"

I smiled at her defenses, so classical, so typical of, the modern, unhappy, civilized female, desperately frightened of being truly a woman in a man's arms, trying to decide and determine manhood not by the nature of man and his desire, and her nature as the object of that desire, but by her own fears, trying to make man what she could find acceptable, trying to remake him in her own image.

"You are a female," I said casually. "I do not accept your definition of man."

She made an angry noise.

"Argue," I suggested, "explain—speak names."

She moaned.

"It is strange," I said, "that when the full blood of a man is upon him, and he sees his female, and will have her, that it should be then that he is not a true man."

She cried out in misery.

Then, as I had expected, she suddenly wept, and doubtless with great sincerity. I supposed at this time many men of Earth, properly conditioned, would have been shaken, and would have fallen promptly to this keen weapon, shamed, retreating stricken with guilt, with misgivings, as the female wished. But, smiling to myself, I knew that on this night her weeping, the little vixen, would gain her no respite.

I smiled at her.

She looked at me, horrified, frightened, tears in her eyes.

"You are a pretty little slave," I said.

She struggled furiously, but could not escape.

When her struggles had subsided I began, half biting, half kissing, to move up her calf to the delights of the sensitive areas behind her knees.

"Please!" she wept.

"Be quiet, pretty little Slave Girl," I mumbled.

Then, kissing, but letting her feel the teeth which could, if I chose, tear at her flesh, I moved to the interior of her thigh. Slowly, with my mouth, by inches, I began to claim her.

"Please," she said.

"What is wrong?" I asked.

"I find I want to yield to you," she whispered.

"Do not be frightened," I told her.

"No," she said. "You do not understand."

I was puzzled.

"I want to yield to you," she whispered, "—as a slave girl!"

"You will so yield to me," I told her.

"No!" she cried. "No!"

"You will yield to me," I told her, "as a slave girl to her master."

"No!" she cried. "No! No!"

I continued to kiss her, to touch her.

"Please stop," she wept.

"Why?" I asked.

"You are making me a slave," she whispered.

"I will not stop," I told her.

"Please," she wept. "Please!"

"Perhaps," I said to her, "the Goreans were right?"

"No!" she cried. "No!"

"Perhaps that is what you desire," I said, "to yield with the utterness of a female slave."

"Never!" she cried, weeping in fury. "Leave me!"

"Not until you have become a slave," I told her.

She cried out in misery. "I do not want to be a slave!"

But when I had touched the most intimate beauties of her she became uncontrollable, writhing, and in my arms I knew the feeling of a slave girl and such, for the moment, was the beautiful Elizabeth Cardwell, helpless and mine, female and slave.

Now her lips and arms and body, now those only of an enamoured wench in bondage, sought mine, acknowledging utterly and unreservedly, shamelessly and hopelessly, with helpless abandon, their master.

I was astonished at her for even the touch of the whip, her involuntary response to the Slaver's Caress, had not seemed to promise so much.

She cried out suddenly as she found herself fully mine.

Then she scarcely dared to move.

"You are claimed, Slave Girl," I whispered to her.

"I am not a slave girl," she whispered intensely. "I am not a slave girl."

I could feel her nails in my arm. In her kiss I tasted blood, suddenly realizing that she had bitten me. Her head was back, her eyes closed, her lips open.

"I am not a slave girl," she said.

I whispered in her ear, "Pretty little slave girl."

"I am not a slave girl!" she cried.

"You will be soon," I told her.

"Please, Tarl," she said, "do not make me a slave."

"You sense that it can be done?" I asked.

"Please," she said, "do not make me a slave."

"Do we not have a wager?" I asked.

She tried to laugh. "Let us forget the wager," said she. "Please, Tarl, it was foolishness. Let us forget the wager?"

"Do you acknowledge yourself my slave?" I inquired.

"Never!" she hissed.

"Then," said I, "lovely wench, the wager is not yet done."

She struggled to escape me, but could not. Then, suddenly, as though startled, she would not move.

She looked at me.

"It soon begins," I told her.

"I sense it," she said, "I sense it."

She did not move but I felt the cut of her nails in my arms.

"Can there be more?" she wept.

"It soon begins," I told her.

"I'm frightened," she wept.

"Do not be frightened," I told her.

"I feel owned," she whispered.

"You are," I said.

"No," she said. "No."

"Do not be frightened," I told her.

"You must let me go," she said.

"It soon begins," I told her.

"Please let me go," she whispered. "Please!"

"On Gor," I said, "it is said that a woman who wears a collar can be only a woman."

She looked at me angrily.

"And you, lovely Elizabeth," said I, "wear a collar."

She turned her head to one side, helpless, angry, tears in her eyes.

She did not move, and then suddenly I felt the cut of her nails deep in my arms, and though her lips were open, her teeth were clenched, her head was back, the eyes closed, her hair tangled under her and over her body, and then her eyes seemed surprised, startled, and her shoulders lifted a bit from the rug, and she looked at me, and I could feel the beginning in her, the breathing of it and the blood of it, hers, in my own flesh swift and like fire in her beauty, mine, and knowing it was then the time, meeting her eyes fiercely, I said to her, with sudden contempt and savagery, following the common Gorean Rites of Submission, "Slave!" and she looked at me with horror and cried out "No!" and half reared from the rug, wild, helpless, fierce as I intended, wanting to fight me, as I knew she would, wanting to slay me if it lay within her power, as I knew she would, and I permitted her to struggle and to bite and scratch and cry out and then I silenced her with the kiss of the master, and accepted the exquisite surrender which she had no choice but to give. "Slave," she wept, "slave, slave, slave—I am a slave!"

It was more than an Ahn later that she lay in my arms on the rug and looked up at me, tears in her eyes. "I know now," she said, "what it is to be the slave girl of a Master."

I said nothing.

"Though I am slave," she said, "yet for the first time in my life I am free."

"For the first time in your life," I said, "you are a woman."

"I love being a woman," she said. "I am happy I am a woman, Tarl Cabot, I am happy."

"Do not forget," I said, "you are only a slave."

She smiled and fingered her collar. "I am Tarl Cabot's girl," she said.

"My slave," I said.

"Yes," she said, "your slave."

I smiled.

"You will not beat me too often will you, Master?" she asked.

"We will see," I said.

"I will strive to please you," she said.

"I am pleased to hear it," I said.

She lay on her back, her eyes open, looking at the top of the wagon, at the hangings, the shadows thrown on the scarlet hides by the light of the fire bowl.

"I am free," she said.

I looked at her.

She rolled over on her elbows. "It is strange," she said. "I am a slave girl. But I am free. I am free."

"I must sleep," I said, rolling over.

She kissed me on the shoulder. "Thank you," she said, "Tarl Cabot, for freeing me."

I rolled over and seized her by the shoulders and pressed her back to the rug and she looked up laughing.

"Enough of this nonsense about freedom," I said. "Do not forget that you are a slave." I took her nose ring between my thumb and forefinger.

"Oh!" she said.

I lifted her head from the rug by the ring and her eyes smarted.

"This is scarcely the way to show respect for a lady," said the girl.

I tweaked the nose ring, and tears sprang into her eyes. "But then," she said, "I am only a slave girl."

"And do not forget it," I admonished her.

"No, no, Master," she said, smiling.

"You do not sound to me sufficiently sincere," I said.

"But I am!" she laughed.

"I think in the morning," I said, "I will throw you to kaiila."

"But where then will you find another slave as delectable as I?" she laughed.

"Insolent wench!" I cried.

"Oh!" she cried, as I gave the ring a playful tug. "Please!"

With my left hand I jerked the collar against the back of her neck.

"Do not forget," I said, "that on your throat you wear a collar of steel."

"Your collar!" she said promptly.

I slapped her thigh. "And," I said, "on your thigh you wear the brand of the four bosk horns!"

"I'm yours," she said, "like a bosk!"

"Oh," she cried, as I dropped her back to the rug.

She looked up at me, her eyes mischievous. "I'm free," she said.

"Apparently," I said, "you have not learned the lesson of the collar."

She laughed merrily. Then she lifted her arms and put them about my neck, and lifted her lips to mine, tenderly, delicately. "This slave girl," she said, "has well learned the lesson of her collar."

I laughed.

She kissed me again. "Vella of Gor," said she, "loves master."

"And what of Miss Elizabeth Cardwell?" I inquired.

"That pretty little slave!" said Elizabeth, scornfully.

"Yes," I said, "the secretary."

"She is not a secretary," said Elizabeth, "she is only a little Gorean slave."

"Well," said I, "what of her?"

"As you may have heard," whispered the girl, "Miss Elizabeth Cardwell, the nasty little wench, was forced to yield herself as a slave girl to a master."

"I had heard as much," I said.

"What a cruel beast he was," said the girl.

"What of her now?" I asked.

"The little slave girl," said the girl scornfully, "is now madly in love with the beast."

"What is his name?" I asked.

"The same who won the surrender of proud Vella of Gor," said she.

"And his name?" I asked.

."Tarl Cabot," she said.

"He is a fortunate fellow," I remarked, "to have two such women."

"They are jealous of one another," confided the girl.

"Oh?" I asked.

"Yes," she said, "each will try to please her master more than the other, that she will be his favorite."

I kissed her.

"I wonder who will be his favorite?" she asked.

"Let them both try to please him," I suggested, "each more than the other."

She looked at me reproachfully. "He is a cruel, cruel master," she said.

"Doubtless," I admitted.

For a long time we kissed and touched. And from time to time, during the night, each of the girls, Vella of Gor and the little barbarian, Miss Elizabeth Cardwell, begged, and were permitted, to serve the pleasure of their master. Yet he, unprecipitate and weighing matters carefully, still could not decide between them.

It was well toward morning, and he was nearly asleep, when he felt them against him, their cheek pressed against his thigh. "Girls," mumbled he, "do not forget you wear my steel."

"We will not forget," they said.

And he felt their kiss.

"We love you," said they, "—Master."

He decided, falling asleep, that he would keep them both slave for a few days, if only to teach them a lesson. Also, he reminded himself, it is only a fool who frees a slave girl.

26

The Egg of Priest-Kings

In the dampness and darkness long before dawn the forces of Kamchak, crowding the streets of Turia in the vicinity of Saphrar's compound, waited silently, like dark shapes on the stones; here and there the glint of a weapon or accouterment could be made out in the fading light of one of the flying moons; someone coughed; there was a rustle of leather; I heard to one side the honing of a quiva, the tiny sound of a short bow being strung.

Kamchak, Harold and I stood with several others on the roof of a building across from the compound.

Behind the walls we could hear, now and then, a sentry calling his post, answering another.

Kamchak stood in the half darkness, his palms on the wall running about the edge of the roof of the building on which we stood.

More than an hour ago I had left the commander's wagon, being roused by one of the guards outside. As I had left Elizabeth Cardwell had awakened. We had said nothing, but I had gathered her into my arms and kissed her, then left the wagon.

On the way to the compound I had met Harold and together we had eaten some dried bosk meat and drank water, from one of the commissary wagons attached to one of Hundreds in the city. As commanders we could eat where we chose.

The tarns that Harold and I had stolen from Saphrar's keep several days ago had both been brought into the city and were nearby, for it was thought that such might be needed, if only to convey reports from one point to another. There were also, in the city, of course, hundreds of kaiila, though the main body of such mounts was outside the city, where game could be driven to them with greater ease.

I heard someone chewing nearby and noted that Harold, who had thrust some strips of bosk meat from the commissary wagon in his belt, was busily engaged, quiva in hand, with cutting and eating the meat.

"It's nearly morning," he mumbled, the observation somewhat blurred by the meat packed in his mouth.

I nodded.

I saw Kamchak leaning forward, his palms on the wall about the roof, staring at the compound. He seemed humped in the half darkness, short of neck, broad of shoulder. He hadn't moved in a quarter of an Ahn. He was waiting for the dawn.

When I had left the wagon Elizabeth Cardwell, though she had said nothing, had been frightened. I remembered her eyes, and her lips, as they had trembled on mine. I had taken her arms from about my neck and turned away. I wondered if I would see her again.

"My own recommendation," Harold was saying, "would be first to fly my tarn cavalry over the walls, clearing them with thousands of arrows, and then, in a second wave, to fly dozens of ropes of warriors to the roofs of the main buildings, to seize them and burn the others.

"But we have no tarn cavalry," I noted.

"That is what is wrong with my recommendation," granted Harold, chewing.

I closed my eyes briefly, and then looked back at the dim compound across the way.

"No recommendation is perfect," said Harold.

I turned to a commander of a Hundred, he who was in charge of the men I had trained with the crossbow. "Did tarns enter or leave the compound last night?" I asked.

"No," said the man.

"Are you sure?" I asked.

"There was moonlight," he said. "We saw nothing." He looked at me. "But," he added, "there are, by my count some three or four tarns from before within the compound."

"Do not permit them to escape," I said.

"We shall try not to do so," he said.

Now, in the east, as on Earth, we could see a lightness in the sky. I seemed to be breathing very deeply.

Kamchak still had not moved.

I heard the rustling of men below in the streets, the checking of arms.

"There is a tarn!" cried one of the men on the roof.

Very high in the sky, no more than a small speck, speeding toward the compound of Saphrar from the direction of the tower I believed held by Ha-Keel, we saw a tarn.

"Prepare to fire!" I cried.

"No," said Kamchak, "let it enter."

The men held their fire, and the tarn, almost at the center of the compound, as far from our encircling positions as possible, suddenly plummeted downward, its wings high, opening them only at the last minute to land on the top of the keep, beyond accurate crossbow range.

"Saphrar may escape," I pointed out.

"No," said Kamchak, "there is no escape for Saphrar."

I said nothing.

"His blood is mine," said Kamchak.

"Who is the rider?" I queried.

"Ha-Keel, the mercenary," said Kamchak. "He is coming to bargain with Saphrar, but I can better whatever terms he is offered—for I have all the gold and women of Turia, and by nightfall I will have the private hordes of Saphrar himself."

"Beware," I warned, "the tarnsmen of Ha-Keel—they might yet turn the brunt of battle against you."

Kamchak did not respond.

"The thousand tarnsmen of Ha-Keel," said Harold, "left before dawn for Port Kar. Their tower is abandoned."

"But why?" I demanded.

"They were well paid," said Harold, "with Turian gold—of which substance we have a great deal."

"Then Saphrar is alone," I said.

"More alone than he knows," remarked Harold.

"What do you mean?" I asked.

"You will see," he said.

It was now clearly light in the east, and I could see the faces of men below me, some of them carrying rope ladders with metal hooks at the ends, others scaling ladders.

It seemed to me that a full storming of the compound would take place within the Ahn.

The House of Saphrar was encircled literally by thousands of warriors.

We would outnumber the desperate defenders of his walls perhaps by twenty to one. The fighting would be fierce, but it did not seem that the outcome would be in doubt, even from the beginning—particularly now that the tarnsmen of Ha-Keel had left the city, the saddle packs of their tarns bulging with Turian gold.

Then Kamchak spoke again. "I have waited long for the blood of Saphrar of Turia," he said. He lifted his hand and one who stood near him climbed to the wall of the roof and blew a long blast on a bosk horn.

I thought this might signal the beginning of the storming of the compound, but none of the men below moved.

Rather, to my astonishment, a gate of the compound itself opened and wary men-at-arms, their weapons ready, each carrying a cloth sack, emerged. They filed before us in the street below, each under the contemptuous eyes of the warriors of the Wagon Peoples, each in turn going to a long table whereon were placed many pairs of scales, and each at that table was weighed out four Gorean stone of gold, about six Earth pounds, which he put in his cloth sack and scurried away, through an avenue opened for him between the warriors. They would be escorted beyond the city. Four Gorean stone of gold is a fortune.

I was utterly startled, overcome. I was shaking. Hundreds upon hundreds of men must have passed thus before us.

"I—I do not understand," I stammered to Kamchak.

He did not turn to face me, but continued to stare at the compound. "Let Saphrar of Turia die by gold," he said.

Only then did I understand with horror the depth of Kamchak's hatred of Saphrar of Turia.

Man by man, stone by stone of gold. Saphrar was dying, his walls and defenses being taken grain by grain from him, slipping away. His gold could not buy him the hearts of men. Kamchak, in his Tuchuk cruelty, would stand quietly to one side and, coin by coin, bit by bit, buy Saphrar of Turia.

Once or twice I heard swords ringing from within the walls, as perhaps some men, loyal to Saphrar, or to their codes, attempted to prevent their fellows from leaving the compound, but I gather, judging from the continued exodus from the walls, that those who were this loyal were scattered and few in number. Indeed, some who might have fought for Saphrar, seeing their fellows deserting in such numbers, undoubtedly realized their own imminent danger, now increased a hundred fold, and hastened to join the deserters. I even saw some slaves leaving the compound, and these, though they were slave, were given the four stone of gold as well, perhaps the more to insult those free men who had accepted the bribes of Tuchuks. I gathered that Saphrar, in the years he had built his power in Turia, had for his own purposes gathered such men about him, and now he would pay the price—with his own life.

Kamchak's face was impassive.

At last, perhaps an Ahn after daylight, no more men came from the compound and the gates were left open.

Kamchak then descended from the roof and mounted his kaiila. Slowly, at a walk, he rode toward the main gate of the compound. Harold and I, on foot, accompanied him. Behind us came several warriors. On Kamchak's right there walked a master of sleen, who held two of the vicious, sinuous beasts in check by chain leashes.

About the pommel of Kamchak's saddle were tied several bags of gold, each weighed out to four stone. And following him, among the warriors, were several Turian slaves, clad in chains and the Kes, among them Kamras, Champion of Turia, and Phanius Turmus, the Turian Ubar, all of whom carried large pans filled with sacks of gold.

Inside the gate of the compound I saw that it seemed deserted, the walls emptied of defenders. The clear ground between the walls and the first buildings was similarly empty, though here and there I saw some litter, pieces of boxes, broken arrows, patches of cloth.

Kamchak stopped inside the compound and looked about, his dark, fierce eyes looking from building to building, examining with great care the roof tops and windows.

Then he gently moved his kaiila toward the main portal. I caught sight of two warriors standing before it, ready to defend it. Behind them I was startled to see suddenly a scurrying figure in white and gold, Saphrar of Turia. Then he stood back from the door, holding something large in his arms, wrapped in purple cloth.

The two men prepared to defend the portal.

Kamchak stopped the kaiila.

Behind me I heard hundreds of ladders and grappling hooks strike against the wall, and, turning, I saw, climbing over the walls, as well as entering through the open gates, hundreds and hundreds of men, until the walls were swarming with Tuchuks, and others of the Wagon Peoples. Then, on the walls and within the compound, they stood, not moving.

Astride his kaiila Kamchak announced himself. "Kamchak of the Tuchuks, whose father Kutaituchik was slain by Saphrar of Turia, calls upon Saphrar of Turia."

"Strike him with your spears," screamed Saphrar from within the doorway.

The two defenders hesitated.

"Give greetings to Saphrar of Turia from Kamchak of the Tuchuks," said Kamchak calmly.

One of the guards turned woodenly. "Kamchak of the Tuchuks," he said, "gives greetings to Saphrar of Turia."

"Kill him!" screamed Saphrar. "Kill him!"

Silently a dozen Tuchuk bowmen, with the short horn bow, stood afoot before Kamchak's kaiila, their arrows trained on the hearts of the two guards.

Kamchak untied two of the sacks of gold from the pommel of his saddle. He threw one to one side for one guard, and the other to the other side for the other guard.

"Fight!" cried Saphrar.

The two guards broke from before the door, each picking up his sack of gold and fled through the Tuchuks.

"Sleen!" cried Saphrar, and turned and ran deeper within the house.

Not hurrying Kamchak walked his kaiila up the stairs of the house and, on kaiilaback, entered the main hall of the House of Saphrar.

In the main hall he looked about and then, Harold and I following, and the man with the two sleen, and the slaves with gold, and his archers and other men, he began to walk his kaiila up the broad marble stairs, following the terrified Saphrar of Turia.

Again and again we encountered guards within the House but each time, when Saphrar took refuge behind them, Kamchak would throw gold to them and they would dissipate and Saphrar, panting, puffing, still clutching the large, purple-wrapped object in his arms, would on his short legs hurry off again. He would lock doors behind himself but they were forced open. He would throw furniture down stairs towards us, but we would step around it. Our pursuit carried us from room to room, through hall after hall, in the great house of Saphrar of Turia. We passed through the banquet hall, where long before we had been entertained by the fleeing merchant.

We passed through kitchens and galleries, even through the private compartments of Saphrar himself, where we saw the multitudinous robes and sandals of the merchant, each worked predominantly in white and gold, though often mixed with hundreds of other colors. In his own compartments the pursuit had seemed to end, for it seemed Saphrar had disappeared, but Kamchak did not show the least irritation or annoyance.

He dismounted and picked up a lounging garment from the vast sleeping platform in the room, holding it to the noses of the two sleen. "Hunt," said Kamchak.

The two sleen seemed to drink in the scent of the robe and then they began to tremble, and the claws on their wide, soft feet emerged and retracted, and their heads lifted and began to sway from side to side. As one animal they turned and pulled their keeper by the chain leashes to what appeared to be a solid wall, where they rose on their back two legs and set their other four legs against it, snarling, whimpering, hissing.

"Break through the wall," said Kamchak. He would not bother to search for the button or lever that might open the panel.

In a few moments the wall had been shattered, revealing the dark passage beyond.

"Bring lamps and torches," said Kamchak.

Kamchak now gave his kaiila to a subordinate and, on foot, carrying torch and quiva, began to prowl down the passage, beside him the two snarling sleen, behind him Harold and I, and the rest of his men, several with torches, even the slaves with gold. Guided by the sleen we had no difficulty in following the track of Saphrar through the passage, though often it branched variously. The passage was, on the whole dark, but where it branched there was often set a small, burning tharlarion oil lamp. I supposed Saphrar of Turia must have carried lamp or torch, or perhaps that he knew the passage by heart.

At one point Kamchak stopped and called for planks. The floor of the passage had been dropped, by the release of a bolt, for an area of its width and for a length of about twelve feet. Harold tossed a pebble into the opening and it took about ten Ihn before we heard it strike water far below.

Kamchak did not seem disturbed at the wait, but sat like a rock, cross-legged before the opening, looking across it, until planks were brought, and then he, and the sleen, were the first to cross.

Another time he warned us back and called for a lance, with which he tripped a wire in the passage. Four spears, with bronze heads, suddenly burst across the passage, emerging from circular openings, their tips striking into other small openings across the passage. Kamchak, with his boot, broke the spear shafts and we moved between them.

At last we emerged into a large audience room, with a domed ceiling, heavily carpeted and hung with tapestries. I recognized it immediately, for it was the room in which Harold and I had been brought prisoner before Saphrar of Turia.

In the room there were four persons.

Sitting in the place of honor, cross-legged, calm, on the merchant's cushions, on his personal dais, applying a bit of oil to the blade of his sword, sat the lean, scarred Ha-Keel, once of Ar, now a mercenary tarnsman of squalid, malignant Port Kar.

On the floor below the dais were Saphrar of Turia, frantic, clutching the purple-wrapped object, and the Paravaci, he who still wore the hood of the Clan of Torturers, he who would have been my assassin, he who had been with Saphrar of Turia when I had entered the Yellow Pool of Turia.

I heard Harold cry out with delight at the sight of the fellow, and the man turned to face us, a quiva in his hand. Beneath his black mask I wager he turned white at the sight of Harold of the Tuchuks. I could sense him tremble.

The other man with them was a young man, dark-haired and eyed, a simple man-at-arms, perhaps not more than twenty. He wore the scarlet of a warrior. He carried a short sword and stood between us and the others.

Kamchak regarded him, and I thought with the merest trace of amusement.

"Do not interfere, Lad," said he, quietly. "There is the business of men afoot in this place."

"Stand back, Tuchuk," cried the young man. He held his sword ready.

Kamchak signaled for a bag of gold, and Phanius Turmus was kicked forward, and from a large, bronze pan which he carried, Kamchak removed a sack of gold and threw it to one side.

The young man did not move from his place, but set himself to take the charge of the Tuchuks.

Kamchak threw another sack of gold to his feet, and then another.

"I am a warrior," said the young man proudly.

Kamchak signaled his archers and they came forward, their arrows trained on the young man.

He then threw, one after another, a dozen bags of gold to the floor.

"Save your gold, Tuchuk sleen," said the young man. "I am a warrior and I know my codes."

"As you wish," said Kamchak and raised his hand to signal the archers.

"Do not!" I cried.

In that moment, uttering the Turian war cry, the young man rushed forward with his sword on Kamchak and the dozen arrows flew simultaneously, striking him a dozen times, turning him twice. Yet did he try still to stagger forward and then another arrow and another pierced his body until he fell at Kamchak's feet.

To my astonishment I saw that not one of the arrows had penetrated his torso or head or abdomen, but that each had struck only an arm or leg.

It had been no accident.

Kamchak turned the young man over with his boot. "Be a Tuchuk," he said.

"Never," wept the young man in pain, between clenched teeth. "Never, Tuchuk sleen, never!"

Kamchak turned to certain of the warriors with him. "Bind his wounds," he said. "See that he lives. When he can ride teach him the saddle of the kaiila, the quiva, the bow and lance. Put him in the leather of a Tuchuk. We have need of such men among the wagons."

I saw the astonished eyes of the young man regarding Kamchak, and then he was carried away.

"In time," said Kamchak, "that boy will command a Thousand."

Then Kamchak lifted his head and regarded the other three men, seated Ha-Keel, calm with his sword, and the frantic Saphrar of Turia, and the tall Paravaci, with the quiva.

"Mine is the Paravaci!" cried Harold.

The man turned angrily to face him, but he did not advance, nor hurl his quiva.

Harold leaped forward. "Let us fight!" he cried.

At a gesture from Kamchak Harold stepped back, angry, a quiva in his hand.

The two sleen were snarling and pulling at their collars. The tawny hair hanging from their jaws was flecked with the foam of their agitation. Their eyes blazed. The claws when they emerged and retracted and emerged again tore at the rug.

"Do not approach!" cried Saphrar, "or I shall destroy the golden sphere!" He tore away the purple cloth that had enfolded the golden sphere and then lifted it high over his head. My heart stopped for the instant. I put out my hand, to touch Kamchak's leather sleeve.

"He must not," I said, "he must not."

"Why not?" asked Kamchak. "It is worthless."

"Stand back!" screamed Saphrar.

"You do not understand!" I cried to Kamchak.

I saw Saphrar's eyes gleam. "Listen to the Koroban!" he said. "He knows! He knows!"

"Does it truly make a difference," asked Kamchak of me, "whether or not he shatters the sphere?"

"Yes," I said, "there is nothing more valuable on all Gor—it is perhaps worth the planet itself."

"Listen to him!" screamed Saphrar. "If you approach I shall destroy this!"

"No harm must come to it," I begged Kamchak.

"Why?" asked Kamchak.

I was silent, not knowing how to say what had to be said.

Kamchak regarded Saphrar. "What is it that you hold?" he asked.

"The golden sphere!" cried Saphrar.

"But what is the golden sphere?" queried Kamchak.

"I do not know," said Saphrar, "but I know that there are men who will pay half the wealth of Gor for this—"

"I," said Kamchak, "would not give a copper tarn disk for it."

"Listen to the Koroban!" cried Saphrar.

"It must not be destroyed," I said.

"Why?" asked Kamchak.

"Because," I said, "—it is the last seed of Priest-Kings—an egg—a child—the hope of Priest-Kings, to them all— everything, the world, the universe."

The men murmured with surprise about me. Saphrar's eyes seemed to pop. Ha-Keel looked up, suddenly, seeming to forget his sword and its oiling. The Paravaci regarded Saphrar.

"I think not," said Kamchak. "I think rather it is worthless."

"No, Kamchak," I said, "please."

"It was for the golden sphere, was it not," asked Kamchak, "that you came to the Wagon Peoples?"

"Yes," I said, "it was." I recalled our conversation in the wagon of Kutaituchik.

The men about us shifted, some of them angrily.

"You would have stolen it?" asked Kamchak.

"Yes," I said. "I would have."

"As Saphrar did?" asked Kamchak.

"I would not have slain Kutaituchik," I said.

"Why would you steal it?" asked Kamchak.

"To return it to the Sardar," I said.

"Not to keep it for yourself, nor for riches?"

"No," I said, "not for that."

"I believe you," said Kamchak. He looked at me. "We knew that in time someone would come from the Sardar. We did not know that you would be the one."

"Nor did I," I said.

Kamchak regarded the merchant. "Is it your intention to buy your life with the golden sphere?"

"If necessary," said Saphrar, "yes!"

"But I do not want it," said Kamchak. "It is you I want."

Saphrar blanched and held the sphere again over his head.

I was relieved to see that Kamchak signaled his bowmen not to fire. He then waved them, and the others, with the exception of Harold and myself, and the sleen keeper and his animals, back several yards.

"That is better," wheezed Saphrar.

"Sheath your weapons," ordered the Paravaci.

We did so.

"Go back with your men!" cried Saphrar, backing away from us a step. "I will shatter the golden sphere!"

Slowly Kamchak, and Harold and I, and the sleen keeper, dragging the two sleen, walked backwards. The animals raged against the chain leashes, maddened as they were drawn farther from Saphrar, their prey.

The Paravaci turned to Ha-Keel, who had now resheathed his sword and stood up. Ha-Keel stretched and blinked once. "You have a tarn," the Paravaci said. "Take me with you. I

can give you half the riches of the Paravaci! Bosk and gold
and women and wagons!"

"I would suppose," said Ha-Keel, "that all that you have is
not worth so much as the golden sphere—and that is Saphrar
of Turia's."

"You cannot leave me here!" cried the Paravaci.

"You are outbid for my services," yawned Ha-Keel.

The Paravaci's eyes were white in the black hood and his
head turned wildly to regard the Tuchuks clustered in the far
end of the room.

"Then it will be mine!" he cried and raced to Saphrar,
trying to seize the sphere.

"Mine! Mine!" screamed Saphrar, trying to retain the
sphere.

Ha-Keel looked on, with interest.

I would have rushed forward, but Kamchak's hand
reached out and touched my arm, restraining me.

"No harm must come to the golden sphere!" I cried.

The Paravaci was much stronger than the fat, tiny merchant and he soon had his hands well on the sphere and was
tearing it out of the smaller man's clutching hands. Saphrar
was screaming insanely and then, to my astonishment, he bit
the Paravaci's forearm, sinking the two golden upper canine
teeth into the hooded man's flesh. The Paravaci suddenly
cried out in uncanny fear and shuddered and, to my horror,
the golden sphere, which he had succeeded in wresting from
Saphrar, was thrown a dozen feet across the room, and
shattered on the floor.

A cry of horror escaped my lips and I rushed forward.
Tears burst from my eyes. I could not restrain a moan as I
fell to my knees beside the shattered fragments of the egg. It
was done, gone, ended! My mission had failed! The Priest-
Kings would die! This world, and perhaps my other, dear
Earth, would now fall to the mysterious Others, whoever or
whatever they might be. It was done, gone, ended, dead,
dead, hopeless, gone, dead.

I was scarcely aware of the brief whimpering of the
Paravaci as, twisting and turning on the rug, biting at it,
holding his arm, his flesh turning orange from ost venom, he
writhed and died.

Kamchak walked to him and tore away the mask. I saw
the contorted, now-orange, twisted, agonized face. Already it
was like colored paper and peeling, as though lit and burned
from the inside. There were drops of blood and sweat on it.

I heard Harold say, "It is Tolnus."

"Of course," said Kamchak. "It had to have been the Ubar of the Paravaci—for who else could have sent their riders against the Tuchuk wagons, who else could have promised a mercenary tarnsman half the bosk and gold and women and wagons of the Paravaci?"

I was only dimly aware of their conversation. I recalled Tolnus, for he had been one of the four Ubars of the Wagon Peoples, whom I, unknowing, had met when first I came to the Plains of Turia, to the Land of the Wagon Peoples.

Kamchak bent to the figure and, opening his garments, tore from his neck the almost priceless collar of jewels which the man had worn.

He threw this to one of his men. "Give this to the Paravaci," he said, "that they may buy back some of their bosk and women from the Kataii and the Kassars."

I was only partly cognizant of these things, for I was overcome with grief, kneeling in Saphrar's audience hall before the shards of the shattered golden sphere.

I was conscious of Kamchak now standing near to me, and behind him Harold.

Unabashed I wept.

It was not only that I had failed, that what I had fought for had now vanished, become ashes—not only that the war of Priest-Kings, in which I had played a prominent part, fought long before over such matters, had now become fruitless, meaningless—that my friend Misk's life and its purpose would now be shattered—even that this world and perhaps Earth itself might now, undefended, fall in time to the mysterious Others—but that what lay in the egg itself, the innocent victim of intrigues which had lasted centuries and might perhaps being worlds into conflict, was dead—it had done nothing to warrant such a fate; the child, so to speak, of Priest-Kings, what could have become the Mother, was now dead.

I shook with sobs, not caring.

I heard, vaguely, someone say, "Saphrar and Ha-Keel have fled."

Near me Kamchak said, quietly, "Release the sleen. Let them hunt."

I heard the chains loosened and the two sleen bounded from the room, eyes blazing.

I would not have cared to have been Saphrar of Turia.

"Be strong, Warrior of Ko-ro-ba," said Kamchak, kindly.

"You do not understand, my friend," I wept, "you do not understand."

The Tuchuks stood about, in their black leather. The sleen keeper stood nearby, the chain leashes loose in his hands. In the background there stood the slaves with their pans of gold.

I became aware of a strong odor, of rottenness, exuding from the shattered thing which lay before me.

"It smells," Harold was saying. He knelt down near the fragments, disgust on his face, fingering the stiff, leathery ruptured egg, some of the golden pieces broken from it. He was rubbing one of them between his thumb and forefinger.

My head down, I cared for nothing.

"Have you examined the golden sphere carefully?" Kamchak was asking.

"I never had the opportunity," I said.

"You might do so now," said Kamchak.

I shook my head negatively.

"Look," said Harold, thrusting his hand under my face. I saw that his thumb and forefinger were marked with a golden stain.

I gazed at his hand, not comprehending.

"It is dye," he said.

"Dye?" I asked.

Harold got up and went to the shattered, stiff shards of the egg. From it, wet, wrinkled. rotted, dead for perhaps months or years, he drew forth the body of an unborn tharlarion.

"I told you," said Kamchak, kindly, "the egg was worthless."

I staggered to my feet, standing now and looking down at the shattered fragments of the egg. I stooped down and picked up one of the stiff shards and rubbed it, seeing the golden stain now left on my fingertips.

"It is not the egg of Priest-Kings," said Kamchak. "Do you truly think we would permit enemies to know the whereabouts of such a thing?"

I looked at Kamchak, tears in my eyes.

Suddenly, far off, we heard a weird scream, high, wavering, and the shrill howls of frustrated sleen.

"It is ended," said Kamchak. "It is ended."

He turned in the direction from which the scream had come. Slowly, not hurrying, in his boots he tramped across the rug, toward the sound. He stopped once beside the twisted, hideous body of Tolnus of the Paravaci. "It is too bad," he said, "I would have preferred to stake him out in the path of the bosk." Then, saying no more, Kamchak, the rest of us following, left the room, guiding ourselves by the distant, frustrated howls of disappointed sleen.

We came together to the brink of the Yellow Pool of Turia. At its marbled edge, hissing and quivering with rage, throwing their heads now and again upward and howling in frustrated fury were the two, tawny hunting sleen, their maddened round eyes blazing on the pathetic figure of Saphrar of Turia, blubbering and whimpering, sobbing, reaching out, his fingers scratching the air as though he would climb it, for the graceful, decorative vines that hung above the pool, more than twenty feet above his head.

He struggled to move in the glistening, respiring, sparkling substance of the Yellow Pool, but could not change his place. The fat hands with the scarlet fingernails seemed suddenly to be drawn and thin, clutching. The merchant was covered with sweat. He was surrounded by the luminous, white spheres that floated under the surface about him, perhaps watching, perhaps somehow recording his position in virtue of pressure waves in the medium. The golden droplets which Saphrar wore in place of eyebrows fell unnoticed into the fluid that humped itself thickening itself about him. Beneath the surface we could see places where his robes had been eaten away and the skin was turning white beneath the surface, the juices of the pool etching their way into his body, taking its protein and nutriment into its own, digesting it.

Saphrar took a step deeper into the pool and the pool permitted this, and he now stood with the fluids level with his chest.

"Lower the vines!" begged Saphrar.

No one moved.

Saphrar threw back his head like a dog and howled in pain. He began to scratch and tear at his body, as if mad. Then, tears bursting from his eyes, he held out his hands to Kamchak of the Tuchuks.

"Please!" he cried.

"Remember Kutaituchik," said Kamchak.

Saphrar screamed in agony and moving beneath the yellow glistening surface of the pool I saw several of the filamentous fibers encircle his legs and begin to draw him deeper into the pool and beneath the surface.

Then Saphrar, merchant of Turia, struggled, pounding against the caked material near to him, to prevent his being drawn under. The eyes were bulging perhaps a quarter of an inch from the little round head and the mouth, with its two golden teeth, now emptied of ost venom, seemed to be screaming but there was no sound.

"The egg," Kamchak informed him, "was the egg of a tharlarion—it was worthless."

The fluid now had reached Saphrar's chin and his head was back to try and keep his nose and mouth over the surface. His head shook with horror.

"Please!" he cried once more, the syllable lost in the bubbling yellow mass that reached into his mouth.

"Remember Kutaituchik," said Kamchak, and the filamentous fibers about the merchant's legs and ankles drew him slowly downward. Some bubbles broke the surface. Then the merchant's hands, still extended as though to grasp the vines overhead, with their scarlet fingernails, the robes eaten away from the flesh, disappeared beneath the sparkling, glistening surface.

We stood silently there for a time, until Kamchak saw small, white bones, like bleached driftwood, rocking on the sparkling, now watery surface, being moved bit by bit, almost as if by tides, to the edge of the pool, where I gathered attendants would normally collect and discard them.

"Bring a torch," said Kamchak.

He looked down into the sparkling, glistening living fluid of the Yellow Pool of Turia.

"It was Saphrar of Turia," said Kamchak to me, "who first introduced Kutaituchik to the strings of kanda." He added, "It was twice he killed my father."

The torch was brought, and the pool seemed to discharge its vapor more rapidly, and the fluids began to churn, and draw away from our edge of the pool. The yellows of the pool began to flicker and the filamentous fibers began to writhe, and the spheres of different colors beneath the surface began to turn and oscillate, and dart in one direction and then the other.

Kamchak took the torch and with his right hand, in a long arc, flung it to the center of the pool.

Suddenly like an explosion and conflagration the pool erupted into flames and Kamchak and I and Harold and the others shielded our faces and eyes and withdrew before the fury of the fire. The pool began to roar and hiss and bubble and scatter parts of itself, flaming, into the air and again to the walls. Even the vines caught fire. The pool then at-

tempted to dessicate itself and retreat into its hardened
shell-like condition but the fire within the closing shell burst it
apart and open and then it was again like a lake of burning
oil, with portions of the shell tossed like flaming chips upon
it.

For better than an hour it burned and then the basin of
the pool, now black, in places the marble fused and melted,
was empty, save for smears of carbon and grease, and some
cracked, blackened bones, and some drops of melted gold,
what had been left perhaps of the golden drops which
Saphrar of Turia had worn over his eyes, and the two golden
teeth, which had once held the venom of an ost.

"Kutaituchik is avenged," said Kamchak, and turned from
the room.

Harold and I, and the others followed him.

Outside the compound of Saphrar, which was now burning, we mounted kaiila to return to the wagons outside the
walls.

A man approached Kamchak. "The tarnsman," he said,
"escaped." He added, "As you said, we did not fire on him
for he did not have with him the merchant, Saphrar of
Turia."

Kamchak nodded. "I have no quarrel with Ha-Keel, the
mercenary," he said. Then Kamchak looked at me. "You,
however," he said, "now that he knows of the stakes in these
games, may meet him again. He draws his sword only in the
name of gold, but I expect that now, Saphrar dead, those
who employed the merchant may need new agents for their
work—and that they will pay the price of a sword such as
that of Ha-Keel." Kamchak grinned at me, the first time
since the death of Kutaituchik. "It is said," remarked
Kamchak, "that the sword of Ha-Keel is scarcely less swift
and cunning than that of Pa-Kur, the Master of Assassins."

"Pa-Kur is dead," I said. "He died in the siege of Ar."

"Was the body recovered?" asked Kamchak.

"No," I said.

Kamchak smiled. "I think, Tarl Cabot," he said. "you
would never make a Tuchuk."

"Why is that?" I asked.

"You are too innocent," he said, "too trusting."

"Long ago," said Harold, nearby, "I gave up expecting
more of a Koroban."

I smiled. "Pa-Kur," I said, "defeated in personal combat

on the high roof of the Cylinder of Justice in Ar, turned and to avoid capture threw himself over the ledge. I do not think he could fly."

"Was the body recovered?" Kamchak asked again.

"No," I said. "But what does it matter?"

"It would matter to a Tuchuk," said Kamchak.

"You Tuchuks are indeed a suspicious lot," I remarked.

"What would have happened to the body?" asked Harold, and it seemed he was serious.

"I suppose," I said, "it was torn to pieces by the crowds below—or lost with the other dead. Many things could have happened to it."

"It seems then," said Kamchak, "that he is dead."

"Surely," I said.

"Let us hope so," said Kamchak, "—for your sake."

We turned the kaiila from the courtyard of the burning House of Saphrar and, abreast, rode from that place. We rode without speaking but Kamchak, for the first time in weeks, whistled a tune. Once he turned to Harold. "I think in a few days we might hunt tumits," he remarked.

"I would enjoy that," remarked Harold.

"Perhaps you will join us?" inquired Kamchak.

"I think," I said, "I shall leave the Wagons soon—for I have failed in my mission on behalf of Priest-Kings."

"What mission is that?" inquired Kamchak innocently.

"To find the last egg of Priest-Kings," I said, perhaps irritably, "and to return it to the Sardar."

"Why do Priest-Kings not do their own errands?" asked Harold.

"They cannot stand the sun," I said. "They are not as men—and if men saw them they might fear and try to kill them—the egg might be destroyed."

"Someday," said Harold, "you must speak to me of Priest-Kings."

"Very well," I agreed.

"I thought you might be the one," said Kamchak.

"What one?" I asked.

"The one that the two men who brought the sphere told me might come one day to claim it."

"The two men," I said, "are dead—their cities warred upon one another and in battle they slew one another."

"They seemed to me fine warriors," said Kamchak. "I am sorry to hear it."

"When did they come to the wagons?" I asked.

"As recently as two years ago," he said.

"They gave you the egg?" I asked.

"Yes," he said, "to keep for Priest-Kings." He added, "It was wise of them, for the Wagon Peoples are among the farthest and most fierce of the Goreans, living free hundreds of pasangs from all cities, save Turia."

"Do you know where the egg is now?" I asked.

"Of course," he said.

I began to shake in the saddle of the kaiila, trembling. The reins moved in my hands and the beast shifted nervously.

I reined in the kaiila.

"Do not tell me where it is," I said, "or I should feel bound to attempt to seize it and take it to the Sardar."

"But are you not he who is to come from Priest-Kings to claim the egg?" inquired Kamchak.

"I am he," I said.

"Then why would you wish to seize it and carry it away?" he asked.

"I have no way to prove that I come from Priest-Kings," I said. "Why would you believe me?"

"Because," said Kamchak, "I have come to know you."

I said nothing.

"I have watched you carefully, Tarl Cabot of the City of Ko-ro-ba," said he, Kamchak of the Tuchuks. "Once you spared my life, and we held grass and earth together, and from that time, even had you been outlaw and knave, I would have died for you, but still, of course, I could not give you the egg. Then you went with Harold to the city, and so I knew that to seize the egg against such overwhelming odds you were ready to give your life. Such a venture would not in all likelihood have been attempted by one who labored only for gold. That taught me that it was indeed probable that you were he chosen by Priest-Kings to come for the egg."

"That is why," I asked, "you let me go to Turia—though you knew the Golden Sphere was worthless?"

"Yes," said Kamchak, "that is why."

"And why, after that," I asked, "did you not give me the egg?"

Kamchak smiled. "I needed only one last thing," said he, "Tarl Cabot."

"And what was that?" I asked.

"To know that you wanted the egg for Priest-Kings alone, and not for yourself." Kamchak put out his hand and touched my arm. "That is why," he said, "I wanted the golden sphere shattered. I would have done it myself had it not been broken, to see what you would have done, to see if you would have been enraged at your loss, or if you would have been overcome with grief, on behalf of Priest-Kings." Kamchak smiled gently. "When you wept," he said, "I knew then that you cared for it, and for Priest-Kings—that you had truly come for the egg and that you wanted it for them—and not for yourself."

I looked at him, dumbfounded.

"Forgive me," he said, "if I am cruel—for I am a Tuchuk—but though I care much for you I had to know the truth of these matters."

"No forgiveness is necessary," I said. "In your place, I think I might well have done the same thing."

Kamchak's hand closed on mine and we clasped hands.

"Where is the egg?" I asked.

"Where would you think to find it?" he asked.

"I don't know," I said. "If I did not know better—I would expect to have found it in the wagon of Kutaituchik—the wagon of the Ubar of the Tuchuks."

"I approve of your conjecture," he said, "but Kutaituchik, as you know, was not the Ubar of the Tuchuks."

I gazed at him.

"I am Ubar of the Tuchuks," he said.

"You mean—" I said.

"Yes," said Kamchak, "the egg has been in my wagon for two years."

"But I lived in your wagon for months!" I cried.

"Did you not see the egg?" he asked.

"No," I said. "It must have been marvelously concealed."

"What does the egg look like?" he asked.

I sat still on the back of the kaiila. "I—I don't know," I said.

"You thought, perhaps," he asked, "it would be golden and spherical?"

"Yes," I said, "I did."

"It was for such a reason," he said, "that we Tuchuks dyed the egg of a tharlarion and placed it in the wagon of Kutaituchik, letting its position be known."

I was speechless, and could not respond to the Tuchuk.

"I think," said he, "you have often seen the egg of Priest-Kings, for it lies about in my wagon. Indeed, the Paravaci who raided my wagon did not regard it as of sufficient interest to carry away."

"That!" I cried.

"Yes," said he, "the curiosity—the gray, leathery object—that."

I shook my head in disbelief.

I recalled Kamchak sitting on the gray, rather squarish, grained thing with the rounded corners. I recalled he had moved it about with his foot, that once he had kicked it across the wagon for me to examine.

"Sometimes," said Kamchak, "the way to conceal something is not to conceal it—it is thought that what is of value will be hidden, and so it is natural to suppose that what is not hidden will not be of value."

"But," I said, my voice trembling, "you rolled it about—you would throw it to the side of the wagon—once you even kicked it across the rug to me that I might examine it." I looked at him, incredulously. "Even," I said, "did you dare to sit upon it!"

"I shall hope," chuckled Kamchak, "that the Priest-Kings will take no offense, but understand that such little bits of acting—rather well carried off, I think—were important parts of my deception."

I smiled, thinking of Misk's joy at receiving the egg. "They will take little offense," I said.

"Do not fear the egg was injured," said Kamchak, "for to injure the egg of Priest-Kings I would have had to use a quiva or ax."

"Wily Tuchuk," I said.

Kamchak and Harold laughed.

"I hope," I said, "that after this time the egg is still viable."

Kamchak shrugged. "We have watched it," he said, "we have done what we could."

"And I and Priest-Kings are grateful to you," I said.

Kamchak smiled. "We are pleased to be of service to Priest-Kings," he said, "but remember that we reverence only the sky."

"And courage," added Harold, "and such things."

Kamchak and I laughed.

"I think it is because—at least in part," I said, "that you reverence the sky—and courage—and such things—that the egg was brought to you."

"Perhaps," said Kamchak, "but I shall be glad to be rid of it, and besides it is nearly the best time for hunting tumits with the bola."

"By the way, Ubar," asked Harold, winking at me, "what was it you paid for Aphris of Turia?"

Kamchak threw him a look that might have been a quiva in the heart.

"You have found Aphris!" I cried.

"Albrecht of the Kassars," remarked Harold, casually, "picked her up while raiding the Paravaci camp."

"Wonderful!" I cried.

"She is only a slave, and unimportant," growled Kamchak.

"What did you pay for her return?" inquired Harold, with great innocence.

"Almost nothing," muttered Kamchak, "for she is nearly worthless."

"I am very pleased," I said, "that she is alive and well— and I gather that you were able to purchase her from Albrecht of the Kassars without difficulty."

Harold put his hand over his mouth and turned away, sniggering, and Kamchak's head seemed to sink angrily into his shoulders.

"What did you pay?" I asked.

"It is hard to outwit a Tuchuk in a bargain," remarked Harold, turning back, rather confidently.

"It will soon be time to hunt tumits," growled Kamchak, looking off across the grass toward the wagons beyond the walls.

Well did I recall how Kamchak had made Albrecht of the Kassars pay dearly for the return of his little darling Tenchika, and how he had roared with laughter because the Kassar had paid such a price, obviously having allowed himself to care for a mere slave girl, and she a Turian at that!

"I would guess," said Harold, "that so shrewd a Tuchuk as Kamchak, the very Ubar of our wagons, would have paid no more than a handful of copper tarn disks for a wench of such sorts."

"The tumits run best this time of year rather toward the Cartius," observed Kamchak.

"I'm very happy," I said, "to hear that you have Aphris back. She cared for you, you know."

Kamchak shrugged.

"I have heard," said Harold, "that she does nothing but sing around the bosk and in the wagon all day—I myself would probably beat a girl who insisted on making all that noise."

"I think," said Kamchak, "I will have a new bola made—for the hunting."

"He is, of course," observed Harold, "quite handsome."

Kamchak growled menacingly.

"At any rate," continued Harold, "I know that he would have upheld the honor of the Tuchuks in such matters—and driven a hard bargain with the unwary Kassar."

"The important thing," I said, "is that Aphris is back and safe." We rode on for a while more. Then I asked, "By the way, as a matter of fact, what did you pay for her?"

Kamchak's face was black with rage. He looked at Harold, who smiled innocently and questioningly, and then at me, who was only honestly curious. Kamchak's hands were like white clubs knotted on the reins of the kaiila. "Ten thousand bars of gold," he said.

I stopped the kaiila and regarded him, astounded. Harold began to pound his saddle and howl with laughter.

Kamchak's eyes, had they been jets of fire, would have frizzled the young, blond Tuchuk in his saddle.

"Well, well," I said, a certain regrettable malicious elation perhaps unfortunately detectable in my voice.

Now Kamchak's eyes would have frizzled me as well.

Then a wry glint of amusement sparkled in the Tuchuk's eyes and the furrowed face wrinkled into a sheepish grin. "Yes," he said, "Tarl Cabot, I did not know until then that I was a fool."

"Nonetheless, Cabot," remarked Harold, "do you not think, all things considered, he is on the whole—albeit unwise in certain matters—an excellent Ubar?"

"On the whole," I agreed, "albeit perhaps unwise in certain matters—an excellent Ubar."

Kamchak glared at Harold, and then at me, and then he looked down, scratching his ear; then he looked at us again, and all three of us suddenly burst together into laughter, and tears even streamed down Kamchak's face, running here and there among the scarred furrows on his cheeks.

"You might have pointed out," said Harold to Kamchak, "that the gold was Turian gold."

"Yes," cried Kamchak, "that is true—it was Turian gold!" He cracked his fist on his thigh. "Turian gold!"

"One might claim," said Harold, "that that makes quite a difference."

"Yes!" cried Kamchak.

"On the other hand," said Harold, "I for one would not claim that."

Kamchak straightened in the saddle and thought about it. Then he chuckled and said, "Nor would I."

Again we laughed and, suddenly, we urged the kaiila forward in great bounding strides, eager to reach the wagons, each of us, for waiting in these wagons were three girls, desirable, marvelous, ours, Hereena, she who had been of the First Wagon, the slave of Harold, her master; Aphris of Turia, almond-eyed and exquisite, once the richest and perhaps the most beautiful woman of her city, now the simple slave of the Ubar of Tuchuks, he Kamchak; and the slender, lovely, dark-haired, dark-eyed Elizabeth Cardwell, once a proud girl of Earth, now only the helpless and beautiful slave of a warrior of Ko-ro-ba; a girl in whose nose had been fixed the delicate, provocative golden ring of Tuchuk women, a girl whose thigh bore unmistakably the brand of the four bosk horns, whose lovely throat was encircled by a collar of steel, bearing my name; a girl whose rapturous and uncontrollable submission had, in its utterness, astounded both herself and me, both he who commanded and she who served, he who took and she who was given no choice but to yield unreservedly. When she had left my arms she had lain upon the rug and wept. "I have nothing more to give," she cried. "Nothing more!"

"It is enough," I had told her.

And she had wept with joy, pressing her head with its loose, wild hair to my side.

"Is my master pleased with me?" she had asked.

"Yes," I had told her. "Yes, Vella, Kajira mira. I am pleased. I am pleased indeed."

I leaped from the back of the kaiila and ran toward the wagon and the girl waiting there cried out with joy and ran to me and I swept her into my arms and our lips met and she wept, "You are safe! You are safe!"

"Yes," I said, "I am safe—and you are safe—and the world is safe!"

At the time I believed that what I had said was true.

27

The Sparing of the Home Stone of Turia

I gathered that the best season for hunting tumits, the large, flightless carnivorous birds of the southern plains, was at hand, for Kamchak, Harold and others seemed to be looking forward to it with great eagerness. Kutaituchik avenged, Kamchak was no longer interested in Turia, though he wished the city to be restored, perhaps in order that the Wagon Peoples might have a valuable trade outlet whereby they could manage, if the caravan raids turned out poorly, to barter hides and horn for the goods of civilization.

On the last day before the withdrawal of the Wagon Peoples from nine-gated, high-walled Turia, Kamchak held court in the palace of Phanius Turmus. The Turian Ubar himself, with Kamras, former Champion of Turia, both clad in the Kes, were chained at the door, to wash the feet of those who would enter.

Turia had been a rich city, and though much gold had been given to the tarnsmen of Ha-Keel and the defenders of the House of Saphrar, it was a tiny amount when compared with the whole, not even counting that lost by being carried by civilians through the gates Kamchak had designated as escapes from the burning city. Indeed, Saphrar's secret hordes alone, kept in dozens of vast underground storehouses, would have been enough to have made each and every Tuchuk, and perhaps each Kataii and Kassar as well, a rich man—a very rich man—in any of the cities of Gor. I recalled that never before had Turia fallen, not since the founding of the city, perhaps thousands of years ago.

Yet a large portion of this wealth—perhaps a third—Kamchak designated should be left behind in the city, to aid in its rebuilding.

Kamchak, as a Tuchuk, could not bring himself to be quite as generous with the city's women, and the five thousand most beautiful girls of Turia were branded and given to the commanders of Hundreds, that they might be distributed to the bravest and fiercest of their warriors; the others were permitted to remain in the city or flee through the gates to seek their fellow citizens beyond the walls. Additionally, of course, beyond the free women, numerous slaves had fallen into the hands of the warriors, and these, too, were sent to the commanders of Hundreds. The most marvelous set of the latter were the beauties from the Pleasure Gardens of Saphrar of Turia. The girls of the Wagon Peoples, of course, who had been enslaved, were freed; the others, however, save for some of Ko-ro-ba on whose behalf I spoke, would change their perfumed silks and their warmed, scented baths for the hardships of the trek, the care of bosk, and the arms of warrior masters. Few it seemed to me, surprisingly perhaps, much objected to leaving the luxurious delights of the gardens of Saphrar for the freedom of the winds and prairies, the dust, the smell of bosk, the collar of a man who would master them utterly but before whom they would stand as human shes, individual, each different, each alone and marvelous and prized in the secret world of her master's wagon.

In the palace of Phanius Turmus, on his throne, sat Kamchak, the purple of the Ubar's robes thrown casually over one shoulder, over his Tuchuk leather. He did not now sit dourly as before, stern and lost in thought, but attended to the details of his business with good humor, stopping only now and then to throw scraps of meat to his kaiila, which was tethered behind the throne. As a matter of course various goods and riches were heaped about his throne, and among them, as part of the booty, there knelt some of the most beautiful of Turia's maidens, clad only in the Sirik, but at his right knee, unchained and clad Kajir, there knelt Aphris of Turia.

About his throne as well there stood his commanders, and some leaders of Hundreds, many with their women. Beside me, clad not Kajir but in the brief leather of one of the Wagon Girls, though collared, stood Elizabeth Cardwell; similarly attired and collared, I noted, standing a bit behind Harold of the Tuchuks, I saw the fiery Hereena; she was perhaps the only one of all the girls of the Wagon Peoples that day in Turia who was not free; she alone remained slave, and would so remain until or unless it might please Harold, her master, that it should be otherwise; "I rather like the look of a collar on her throat," he once remarked in his wagon, before ordering her to prepare food for Kamchak and Aphris, and myself and Elizabeth, or Vella, as I would sometimes call her. I gathered that the proud Hereena might long be the slave of Harold of the Tuchuks.

As fellow after fellow, men of importance in Turia, were dragged before his throne, in the Kes and chained, Kamchak would say to them, "Your goods and your women are mine. Who is the Master of Turia?"

"Kamchak of the Tuchuks," they would say, and be dragged away.

To some he would ask, "Has Turia fallen?"

And they would bow their heads and say, "She has fallen."

At last Phanius Turmus and Kamras were pulled before the throne and thrust to their knees.

Kamchak gestured to the riches piled about him. "Whose is the wealth of Turia?" he asked.

"Kamchak of the Tuchuks'," said they.

Kamchak thrust his fist affectionately into the hair of Aphris of Turia and twisted her head to him.

"Whose are the women of Turia?" he asked.

"—Master," said Aphris.

"Kamchak of the Tuchuks'," said the two men.

"Who," laughed Kamchak, "is Ubar of Turia?"

"Kamchak of the Tuchuks," said the two.

"Bring the Home Stone of the city," commanded Kamchak, and the stone, oval and aged, carved with the initial letter of the city, was brought to him.

He lifted the stone over his head and read fear in the eyes of the two men chained before him.

But he did not dash the stone to the floor. Rather he arose from his throne and placed the stone in the chained hands of Phanius Turmus. "Turia lives," said he, "Ubar."

Tears formed in the eyes of Phanius Turmus and he held the Home Stone of the city to his heart.

"In the morning," called Kamchak, "we return to the wagons."

"You will spare Turia, Master?" asked Aphris, wondering, knowing the hatred he had borne the city.

"Yes," said he, "Turia will live."

Aphris looked at him, not understanding.

I myself was startled, but would not speak. I had thought that Kamchak might destroy the stone, thus breaking the heart of the city, leaving it in ruins in the minds of men. It was only at that time, as he held court in the palace of Phanius Turmus that I realized he would permit the city its freedom, and its soul. I had hitherto only understood that Turians might perhaps return to the city, and that its walls would be left standing. I had not understood that it would be permitted to retain a Home Stone.

It seemed to me a strange act for a conqueror, for a Tuchuk.

Was it only because Kamchak believed, as he had once said, that the Wagon Peoples must have an enemy? —or was there some other reason, beyond that?

Suddenly there was commotion at the door and three men, followed by some others, burst into the hall.

The first was Conrad of the Kassars, and with him were Hakimba of the Kataii and a third man I did not know, but who was Paravaci. Behind them were some others, among whom I saw Albrecht of the Kassars, and behind him, to my astonishment, clad in brief leather, not collared, was Tenchika, who held a small bundle tied in cloth in her right hand.

Conrad, Hakimba and the Paravaci strode to the throne of Kamchak, but none of them, as befitted Ubars of their peoples, knelt.

Conrad spoke. "The Omens have been taken," he said.

"They have been read well," said Hakimba.

"For the first time in more than a hundred years," said the Paravaci, "there is a Ubar San, a One Ubar, Master of the Wagons!"

Kamchak stood up and threw from his shoulders the purple of the Turian Ubar and stood in the black leather of a Tuchuk.

As one man the three Ubars raised their arms to him.

"Kamchak," they cried, "Ubar San!"

The cry was taken up by all in the room, even myself. "Kamchak, Ubar San!"

Kamchak held forth his hands and the room was quiet. "Each of you," he said, "the Kassars—the Kataii—the Paravaci—have your own bosk and your own wagons—live so— but in time of war—when there are those who would divide us—when there are those who would fight us and threaten

our wagons and our bosk and women—our plains, our land—
then let us war together—and none will stand against the
Wagon Peoples—we may live alone but we are each of us of
the Wagons and that which divides us is less than that which
unites us—we each of us know that it is wrong to slay bosk
and that it is right to be proud and to have courage and to
defend our wagons and our women—we know that it is right
to be strong and to be free—and so it is together that we will
be strong and we will be free. Let this be pledged."

The three men came to Kamchak and he and they placed
their hands together.

"It is pledged," they said. "It is pledged."

Then they stood back. "All hail Kamchak," they cried,
"Ubar San!"

"All hail Kamchak," rang throughout the hall, "Kamchak!
Ubar San!"

It was late in the afternoon before the business of the day
had subsided and the great hall emptied.

At last only a few remained in that place, some commanders and some leaders of Hundreds, and Kamchak and Aphris.
Harold and I were there, too, and Hereena and Elizabeth.

Shortly before Albrecht and Tenchika had been there, and
Dina of Turia with her two Tuchuk guards, who had kept
her safe from harm during the fall of the city.

Tenchika had approached Dina of Turia.

"You wear no collar now," Dina had said.

Tenchika had dropped her head shyly. "I am free," she
said.

"Will you now return to Turia?" asked Dina.

"No," said Tenchika, smiling. "I will remain with Albrecht
—with the wagons."

Albrecht himself was busy elsewhere, talking with Conrad,
Ubar of the Kassars.

"Here," said Tenchika, thrusting the small cloth sack she
held into Dina's hands. "These are yours—you should have
them—you won them."

Dina, wondering, opened the package and within it she
saw the cups and rings, and pieces of gold, which Albrecht
had given her for her victories in the runnings from the bola.

"Take them," insisted Tenchika.

"Does he know?" asked Dina.

"Of course," said Tenchika.

"He is kind," said Dina.

"I love him," said Tenchika, kissing Dina and hurrying away.

I approached Dina of Turia. I looked at the objects she held. "You must have run well indeed," I remarked.

She laughed. "There is more than enough here to hire help," she said. "I shall reopen the shop of my father and brothers."

"If you like," I said, "I will give you a hundred times that."

"No," she said, smiling, "for this is my own."

Then she lowered her veil briefly and kissed me. "Good-bye, Tarl Cabot," she said. "I wish you well."

"And I," I said, "wish you well—noble Dina of Turia."

She laughed. "Foolish warrior," she chided, "I am only the daughter of a baker."

"He was a noble and valiant man," I said.

"Thank you," said she.

"And his daughter, too," I said, "is a noble and valiant woman—and beautiful."

I did not permit her to replace her veil until I had kissed her, softly, one last time.

She refastened her veil and touched her fingertips to her lips beneath it and then pressed them to my lips and turned and hurried away.

Elizabeth had watched but she had shown no sign of anger or irritation.

"She is beautiful," said Elizabeth.

"Yes," I said, "she is." And then I looked at Elizabeth. "You, too," I told her, "are beautiful."

She looked up at me, smiling. "I know," she said.

"Vain wench," I said.

"A Gorean girl," she said, "need not pretend to be plain when she knows that she is beautiful."

"That is true," I admitted. "But where," I asked, "did you come by the notion that you are beautiful?"

"My master told me," she sniffed, "and my master does not lie—does he?"

"Not often," I said, "and particularly not about matters of such importance."

"And I have seen men look at me," she said, "and I know that I would bring a good price."

I must have appeared scandalized.

"I would," said Elizabeth firmly, "I am worth many tarn disks."

"You are," I admitted.

"So I am beautiful," she concluded.

"It is true," I said.

"But," said she, "you will not sell me—will you?"

"Not immediately," I said. "We shall see if you continue to please me."

"Oh, Tarl!" she said.

"Master," I prompted.

"Master," she said.

"Well?" I asked.

"I shall," she said, smiling, "strive to continue to please you."

"See that you do," I said.

"I love you," she said suddenly, "I love you—Tarl Cabot, Master." She put her arms about my neck and kissed me.

I kept her long in my arms, savoring the warmth of her lips, the delicacy of her tongue on mine.

"Your slave," she whispered, "Master—forever your slave."

It was hard for me to believe that this marvelous, collared beauty in my arms was once a simple girl of Earth, that this astounding wench, Tuchuk and Gorean, was the same as Miss Elizabeth Cardwell, the young secretary who so long before had found herself inexplicably thrust into intrigues and circumstances beyond her comprehension on the plains of Gor. Whatever she might have been before, a clock number, a set of records in a personnel file, an unimportant employee, with her salary and benefits, under the obligation to please and impress other employees, scarcely more important than herself, she was now alive, and free in her emotions though her flesh might be subject to chains; she was now vital, passionate, loving, mine; I wondered if there were other girls of Earth in whom such a transformation might be wrought, others who might, not fully understanding, long for a man and a world—a world in which they must find and be themselves, for no other choice would be theirs—a world in which they might run and breathe and laugh and be swift and loving and prized and in their hearts at last open and free— though paradoxically perhaps, for a time, or until the man should choose otherwise, wearing the collar of a slave girl. But I dismissed such thoughts as foolish.

None remained now in the court of the Ubar other than Kamchak and Aphris, Harold and Hereena, and myself and Elizabeth Cardwell.

Kamchak looked across the room to me. "Well," said he, "the wager turned out well."

I recalled he had spoken of this. "You gambled," I said, "when you did not surrender Turia—to return to defend the bosk and wagons of the Tuchuks—that the others, the Kataii and Kassars, would come to your aid." I shook my head. "It was a dangerous gamble," I said.

"Perhaps not so dangerous," said he, "for I know the Kataii and the Kassars—better than they knew themselves."

"You said there was more to the wager though," I remarked, "that it was not yet done."

"It is now done," said he.

"What was the latter part of the wager?" I asked.

"That," said he, "the Kataii and the Kassars—and, too, in time the Paravaci—would see how we might be divided against ourselves and singly destroyed—and would thus recognize the need for uniting the standards, bringing together the Thousands under one command—"

"That they would," I said, "recognize the need for the Ubar San?"

"Yes," said Kamchak, "that was the wager—that I could teach them the Ubar San."

"Hail," said I, "Kamchak, Ubar San!"

"Hail," cried Harold, "Kamchak, Ubar San!"

Kamchak smiled and looked down. "It will soon be time for hunting tumits," he said.

As he turned to leave the throne room of Phanius Turmus, to return to the wagons, Aphris lightly rose to her feet to accompany him.

But Kamchak turned and faced her. She looked up at him, questioningly. It was hard to read his face. She stood quite close to him.

Gently, ever so gently, Kamchak put his hands on her arms and drew her to him and then, very softly, kissed her.

"Master?" she asked.

Kamchak's hands were at the small, heavy lock at the back of the steel, Turian collar she wore. He turned the key and opened the collar, discarding it.

Aphris said nothing, but she trembled and shook her head slightly. She touched her throat disbelievingly.

"You are free," said the Tuchuk.

The girl looked at him, incredulously, bewildered.

"Do not fear," he said. "You will be given riches." He

smiled. "You will once again be the richest woman in all of Turia."

She could not answer him.

The girl, and the rest of us present, stood stunned. All of us knew the peril, the hardship and danger the Tuchuk had sustained in her acquisition; all of us knew the price he had been willing to pay only recently that she, fallen into the hands of another, might be returned to him.

We could not understand what he had done.

Kamchak turned abruptly from her striding to his kaiila, which had been tethered behind the throne. He put one foot in the stirrup and mounted easily. Then, not pressing the animal, he took his way from the throne room. The rest of us followed him, with the exception of Aphris who remained, stricken, standing beside the throne of the Ubar, clad perhaps Kajir, but now uncollared, now free. Her fingertips were before her mouth. She seemed numb. She shook her head.

I walked behind Kamchak, on his kaiila. Harold walked beside me. Hereena and Elizabeth followed us, each, as was proper, some two paces behind.

"Why is it," I asked Harold, "that he so spared Turia?"

"His mother was Turian," said Harold.

I stopped.

"Did you not know?" asked Harold.

I shook my head. "No," I said. "I did not know."

"It was after her death," said Harold, "that Kutaituchik first tasted the rolled strings of kanda."

"I did not know," I said.

Kamchak was now well in advance of us.

Harold looked at me. "Yes," he said, "she had been a Turian girl—taken as slave by Kutaituchik—but he cared for her and freed her. She remained with him in the wagons until her death—the Ubara of the Tuchuks."

Outside the main gate of the palace of Phanius Turmus, Kamchak, on his kaiila, waited for us. Our beasts were tethered there, and we mounted. Hereena and Elizabeth would run at our stirrups.

We turned from the gate, to ride down the long avenue leading toward the main gate of Turia.

Kamchak's face was inscrutable.

"Wait!" we heard.

We turned our mounts and saw Aphris of Turia, barefoot, clad Kajir, running after us.

She stopped beside Kamchak's stirrup, standing there, her head down.

"What means this?" demanded Kamchak sternly.

The girl did not respond, nor did she raise her head.

Kamchak turned his kaiila and began to ride toward the main gate, the rest of us following. Aphris, as Hereena and Elizabeth, ran by the stirrup.

Kamchak reined in, and we all stopped. Aphris stood there, her head down.

"You are free," said Kamchak.

Without raising her head, she shook it negatively. "No," she said, "I am Kamchak of the Tuchuks'."

She put her head timidly to Kamchak's fur boot in the stirrup.

"I do not understand," said Kamchak.

She lifted her head and there were tears in her eyes. "Please," she said, "Master."

"Why?" asked Kamchak.

She smiled. "I have grown fond of the smell of bosk," said she.

Kamchak smiled. He held his hand to the girl. "Ride with me, Aphris of Turia," said Kamchak of the Tuchuks.

She took his hand and he drew her to the saddle before him, where she turned, sitting across the saddle, and placed her head against his right shoulder, weeping.

"This woman," said Kamchak of the Tuchuks, brusquely, his voice stern but almost breaking, "is called Aphris—know her—she is Ubara of the Tuchuks, she is Ubara Sana, of my heart Ubara Sana!"

We let Kamchak and Aphris ride ahead, and followed them, by some hundred yards, toward the main gate of Turia, now leaving the city, and its Home Stone and its people, returning to the wagons and to the open, windswept land beyond the high walls of the city, once-conquered, nine-gated Turia of the southern plains of Gor.

28

Elizabeth and I Depart from the Wagon Peoples

Tuka, the slave girl, did not fare well at the hands of Elizabeth Cardwell.

In the camp of the Tuchuks Elizabeth had begged that I not free her for but another hour.

"Why?" I had asked.

"Because," she had said, "masters do not much care to interfere in the squabbles of slaves."

I shrugged. It would be at least another hour before I was ready to take wing for the Sardar, with the egg of Priest-Kings safe in the saddle pack of my tarn.

There were several people gathered about, near the wagon of Kamchak, among them Tuka's master, and the girl herself. I recalled how cruel she had been to Elizabeth in the long months she had been with the Tuchuks, and how she had tormented her even when she was helpless in the cage of a sleen, mocking her and poking at her with the bosk stick.

Perhaps Tuka gathered what might have been on Elizabeth's mind, for no sooner had the American girl turned toward her than she turned and fled from the wagon.

Within something like fifty yards we heard a frightened squawk and saw Tuka thrown to the ground with a tackle that might have done credit to a qualified professional player of the American form of football. There shortly thereafter followed a vigorous and dusty broil among the wagons, involving much rolling about, biting, slapping, scratching and, from time to time, the easily identified sound of a small fist, apparently moving with considerable momentum, meeting with various partially resistant, protoplasmic curvatures. There was only so much of this and we soon heard Tuka shrieking for mercy. At that juncture, as I recall, Elizabeth was kneeling on top of the Turian maiden with her hands in her hair pounding her head up and down in the dirt. Elizabeth's Tuchuk leather had been half torn from her but Tuka, who had been clothed only Kajir, had fared not even this well. Indeed, when Elizabeth finished, Tuka wore only the Curla, the red band that ties back the hair, and this band now knotted her wrists behind her back. Elizabeth then tied a thong in Tuka's nose ring and dragged her to the creek, where she might find a switch. When she found a suitable implement, of proper length and flexibility, of appropriate diameter and suppleness, she then secured Tuka by nose ring and thong to the exposed root of a small but sturdy bush, and thrashed her soundly. Following this, she untied the thong from the root and permitted the girl, thong still streaming from her nose ring, wrists still bound behind her, to run for her master's wagon, but pursued her each foot of the way like a hunting sleen, administering innumerable stinging incitements to greater and ever greater speed.

At last, panting, bleeding here and there, discolored in places, half-naked, triumphant, Elizabeth Cardwell returned to my side, where she knelt as a humble, obedient slave girl.

When she had somewhat caught her breath I removed the collar from her throat and freed her.

I set her on the saddle of the tarn, telling her to hold to the pommel of the saddle. When I myself mounted I would tie her to the pommel with binding fiber. I would fasten about myself the broad safety strap, usually purple, which is an invariable portion of the tarn saddle.

Elizabeth did not seem affrighted to be astride the tarn. I was pleased that there were some changes of clothing for her in the pack. I observed that she needed them, or at least one of them.

Kamchak was there, and his Aphris, and Harold and his Hereena, still his slave. She knelt beside him, and once when she dared to touch her cheek to his right thigh he good-naturedly cuffed the slave girl away.

"How are the bosk doing?" I asked Kamchak.

"As well as might be expected," he responded.

I turned to Harold. "Are the quivas sharp?" I inquired.

"One tries to keep them that way," said Harold.

I turned back to Kamchak. "It is important," I reminded him, "to keep the axles of the wagons greased."

"Yes," he said, "I think that is true."

I clasped the hands of the two men.

"I wish you well, Tarl Cabot," said Kamchak.

"I wish you well, Kamchak of the Tuchuks," I said.

"You are not really a bad fellow," said Harold, "for a Koroban."

"You are not bad yourself," I granted, "—for a Tuchuk."

"I wish you well," said Harold.

"I wish you well," I said.

Swiftly I climbed the short ladder to the tarn saddle, and tied it against the saddle. I then took binding fiber and looped it several times about Miss Cardwell's waist and then several times about the pommel of the saddle, then tieing it.

Harold and Kamchak looked up at me. There were tears in the eyes of both men. Now, diagonally, like a scarlet chevron coursing the flight of the cheek bones, there blazed on the face of Harold the Tuchuk the Courage Scar.

"Never forget," said Kamchak, "that you and I have together held grass and earth."

"I will never forget," I said.

"And while you are remembering things," remarked Harold, "you might recollect that we two together won the Courage Scar in Turia."

"No," I said, "I will not forget that either."

"Your coming and going with the Wagon Peoples," said Kamchak, "has spanned parts of two of our years."

I looked at him, not really understanding. What he said, of course, was true.

"The years," said Harold, smiling, "were two—the Year in which Tarl Cabot Came to the Wagon Peoples and the Year in which Tarl Cabot Commanded a Thousand."

Inwardly I gasped. These were year names—which would be remembered by the Year Keepers, whose memories knew the names of thousands of consecutive years.

"But," I protested, "there have been many things of much greater importance than those in these years—the Siege of Turia, the Taking of the City, the Election of the Ubar San!"

"We choose most to remember Tarl Cabot," said Kamchak.

I said nothing.

"If you should ever need the Tuchuks, Tarl Cabot," said Kamchak, "or the Kataii or the Kassars—or the Paravaci—

you have only to speak—and we will ride. We will ride to
your side, be it even to the cities of Earth."

"You know of Earth?" I asked. I recalled what I took to
be the skepticism of Kamchak and Kutaituchik long ago
when they had questioned myself and Elizabeth Cardwell of
such matters.

Kamchak smiled. "We Tuchuks know of many things," he
said, "—of more than we tell." He grinned. "Good fortune
attend you, Tarl Cabot, Commander of a Thousand Tuchuks,
Warrior of Ko-ro-ba!"

I lifted my hand to them and then drew on the one-strap
and the wings of the great tarn began to strike the resistant
air and the Tuchuks on all sides fell back stumbling in the
dust and the driven wind smote from beneath the mighty
wings of the bird and in that instant we saw the wagons fall
away beneath us, extending in their squares for pasangs, and
we could see the ribbon of the creek and then the Omen
Valley and then the spires of distant Turia, far off.

Elizabeth Cardwell was weeping, and I put my arms about
her, to comfort her, and to protect her from the blasts of the
swift air. I noted with irritation that the sting of the air had
made my own eyes moist as well.